GRAY FOR YOU

8 MILLION HEARTS - BOOK 2

SPENCER SPEARS

INTRODUCTION

Free Bonus Epilogue

Join my mailing list and instantly get access to *Mr. Right*, a free, explicit epilogue for *Gray For You*. You can't get *Mr. Right* anywhere else! You'll also be notified of my new releases and when I have more free stuff, you'll be the first to know.

Sign up at: http://eepurl.com/deH83X

Thanks for downloading this book. I appreciate your support. Visit my website or my Author Central page on Amazon to see the rest of my catalog and keep up with my new releases.

www.spencerspears.com

For A, B, C, and S

Egészségetekre!

here is the deepest secret nobody knows

(here is the root of the root and the bud of the bud

and the sky of the sky of a tree called life; which grows

higher than soul can hope or mind can hide

and this is the wonder that's keeping the stars apart

i carry your heart (i carry it in my heart)

— E. E. Cummings

1

GRAY

*Y*ou know that scene in the beginning of *The Little Mermaid* where Ariel sings about how you probably think she's the girl who has everything?

Basically, that's me. Except replace *'girl'* with *'grown man'* and replace gadgets and gizmos with dildos and strawberry flavored lube. Other than that, though, the parallels are pretty on point.

Let me see if I can explain.

I wasn't supposed to end up like this.

I was supposed to end up hooked on meth and still deeply closeted, back home in Fairmont, West Virginia. Or, perhaps, hooked on meth, less closeted, but ultimately homeless and jobless in New York City, where I'd moved when I was 16. You're not supposed to live the life I'd lived, make the choices I'd made, and turn out okay.

Granted, *okay* is a relative term. In the past three months, I'd lost my aunt and my boyfriend of eight years—and I had no idea what I was doing with my life, since I'd quit the only job I'd ever been good at. Which was porn, for the record.

Frankly, I was kind of a mess.

Only now, I was a rich mess. Like, owning an entire building in lower Manhattan rich. Owning a house in Montauk rich. Owning a bar and a pile of investments I didn't know what to do with rich. So rich it didn't matter that I wasn't fucking people on camera for a living anymore, so rich that it didn't matter that I actually kind of sucked at running the bar.

But I wasn't happy.

I know, I know. Cry me a fucking river. My aunt leaves me everything when she dies and here I am, complaining. Trust me, I'm at least as disgusted with myself as you are. But I couldn't help feeling like despite everything that looked right on the surface, somewhere along the line, I fucked up deeply.

When I was a kid, I was obsessed with movies. Old ones, new ones, didn't matter. I'd check them out from our town's podunk library and watch them over and over, like maybe if I watched and wished hard enough, I could magically end up in one of the stories I saw on the screen of my mom's shitty little rabbit-eared TV in the corner of our trailer.

We were poor, and not the pretty kind where you live in a rambling farmhouse in the country and your grandma cans tomatoes. We were the ugly kind, living in a rented double-wide right next to the highway and my mom hadn't spoken to anyone in her family in years. All I wanted was to be... *not there* anymore. Whether it was wartime Casablanca or wherever the hell *Space Jam* was set, I wasn't picky.

But as I grew up, I realized a few hard truths. Number one: NBA players and cartoon characters do not actually play basketball games together. Number two: movies, even ones without cartoons, weren't real. And number three: nothing in my life was getting better.

In fact, it was getting worse. My mom's boyfriends had always changed with the seasons—or with whoever was willing to put us up when she was late on rent. But when I was in fourth grade, she started dating Lonny and by fifth grade, she was barely coming home.

Plus, that was the year when I realized that I was at least as interested in guys as I was in girls—and that that wasn't the case for everyone else in my class. And right when I needed to escape somewhere, to forget about the hunger from missed meals and the fact that our utilities kept getting shut off—the movies I'd always turned to couldn't give that to me.

But fifth grade was also the year that I had a realization. The characters, the stories themselves, weren't real—but the actors in the movie were. And what was more, actors got to live in places like Los Angeles or New York, which might as well have been the moon to me, and lead perfect lives. They got paid to pretend to be other people—paid to enact these stories that we were supposed to lose ourselves in.

And if I thought escaping into movies for an hour or two was good—what would it be like to get to live inside them all the time? To get to make the stories that some other poor kid in the middle of nowhere would turn to as lifelines—the stories that told that kid that someday, somewhere, he might find a place he belonged?

I left for New York when I was 16. I hadn't seen my mom in years—she'd taken off with some new boyfriend and I'd bounced around the foster care system since she left. There was nothing keeping me in Fairmont—other than common sense. But what 16 year old has much of that?

It was a stupid decision, and it shouldn't have worked. I didn't know anyone there, didn't even have a high school diploma. And I certainly had no idea how to go about finding work as an actor. All I knew was that I'd die if I stayed in West Virginia another day.

So with the vaguest notions of getting a restaurant job while working my way into acting, I bought a bus ticket to New York—and promptly realized how fucking dumb I was. I had nowhere to live, very little money saved, and no one wanted to hire a 16 year old to do anything other than wash dishes, much less act.

Would it shock you to hear that within a month of arriving, I was homeless and still jobless? It shouldn't—but it did shock me, because, again, I was an idiot. All 16 year olds sort of are, but I was really striving to take the gold medal there. I should have given up, gone home, but in addition to being dumb, I was stubborn as hell.

And then I met Maggie. Or rather, I met a middle-aged woman holding out a cup of coffee and a donut to me as she hovered over the park bench I was curled up on one morning. If she hadn't seen me sleeping there for four nights in a row and decided to take matters into her own hands, I don't know what would have happened to me.

I didn't know what to make of this strange woman with her curly, fly-away hair and her insistence that I couldn't live like that. My own mother had never taken an interest in me. The best of my foster families could barely be bothered, and that was only because they got paid to do so. The worst had actively made my life hell. And here was someone offering me a place to sleep, telling me she'd help me find a job, insisting I get my GED—all because, as she put it, she couldn't bear to see someone as young as me sleeping on the streets.

But I didn't really have any other options. And so, improbably, I'd gotten taken in and found the closest thing to a family I'd ever had. It wasn't all rainbows and puppies, either, but Maggie's affection for me—love, I eventually allowed myself to understand that it was—never wavered. Even when I put her through hell.

Ethan, for instance. I met Ethan the year I turned 22, the same way all 22 year olds meet: out at a club, shitfaced. I was infatuated from the start. Ethan was everything I wasn't— educated, articulate, from a family that rubbed shoulders with Rockefellers and Kennedys.

Ethan wasn't out, because of his family. They had expectations for him—the kind of school he'd go to, the kind of job he'd get, the kind of woman he'd marry. Not just kind, actually. There was a specific woman—Christie—a girl who'd been a family friend since he was a kid.

Ethan explained to me that there was nothing between them. That he only wanted to be with me. That he just had to keep up appearances with Christie for a little while, just until his parents released his trust fund to him. That he was going to talk to them—that he was definitely coming out—soon.

I didn't know then that sometimes, '*soon*' means '*never*'.

Maggie never liked him, but she put up with him for me. Was gentle with me whenever Ethan did something that broke my heart and glad for me when he put it back together. She didn't like him, but she loved me, and I guess that meant she was willing to deal with him if he made me happy.

And he did—mostly—for a while. Or at least, I convinced myself he did. I'd never really had a boyfriend before, never known what it felt like for someone to actually care about me, to put me first. Ethan gave me the feeling of being *desired* and that was close enough.

So I was willing to overlook things, like how Ethan swore we had a future together, but always needed just a little more time before he came out. Like how he said he supported me becoming an actor, but always seemed pleased when I didn't get the parts I went out for.

Maybe it's just not meant to be, babe. You're too sweet, too sensitive for those assholes anyway. They don't deserve you.

Ethan always told me how great I was, but I wondered about the satisfied glint in his eyes whenever I got rejected for something. And then, of course, there was the one time I actually got cast, got a part in a big-budget action movie that was filming in Vancouver.

I'd have to be gone for three months. But Ethan didn't think he could do long distance. And Ethan really was going to talk to his parents. Because Ethan really did love me, and he didn't think he could be without me for that long.

So I turned the part down. And stayed in New York. And

Ethan never talked to his parents. All because I'm a fucking idiot. Are you noticing a theme here?

I should have broken up with him then. Told him I was done, I'd put up with years of this from him and if he wasn't serious, he needed to let me go.

But I was still in love with him. And the part in that movie was gone, not coming back. So like a gambler with nothing left to lose, I doubled-down.

I told myself it was okay I'd said no to the movie. Maybe Ethan was right, maybe I wasn't cut out to be an actor. He'd always told me I was too gentle, too good to deal with the bullshit that came with it.

So fine, then, I wouldn't be an actor. I'd find something else to do that kept me in New York. And when Ethan was finally ready, I'd be there.

Admittedly, neither of us expected that thing to be porn. But we were at a party one night about five years ago and I met someone who knew someone who knew someone who was looking for models—you know how it goes—and next thing you know, I'm standing in a room full of strangers, stripping naked and showing them my cock.

I'd asked Ethan if it would bother him, of course. I wouldn't have done it if he'd been uncomfortable at the thought of me sleeping with other people, even if it meant nothing. He said it didn't.

But that didn't stop him from making snide remarks about it.

'Can't wait to bring my pornstar boyfriend home for Thanksgiving.' Or *'Grandmother will be just thrilled to meet you now.'*

I pointed out that he'd never brought me home for Thanksgiving, or let me meet his family at all, before this, so it wasn't exactly like that changed anything. And I told him again that I'd stop if he wanted me to.

'What? Of course not. It's your life. You should do what you want.'

Just aggressive enough to hurt, just passive enough to maintain the fiction that he wasn't pissed at me. And that became our weird detente. Ethan didn't like me doing porn, but denied that it bothered him, so I did it anyway. I didn't like that we still weren't public, but I didn't want to end things, so he kept me a secret anyway. That's how things went for... way longer than they should have.

Until about 12 months ago, actually, when Maggie got sick. Well, sick*er*. She'd been fighting cancer on and off for a while, but it was a year ago that we realized, shit, this time might be different.

As she got weaker, and spent more time in and out of the hospital, it got harder for her to run her bar—conveniently named 'Maggie's'. And I wanted to spend the time I had left with her. Plus, to the extent that one's heart can ever be in porn—well, mine no longer was. So I quit.

I was 30 anyway, which is like 70 in porn years, and I was starting to get cast in 'daddy' roles. And not that I'm judging anyone's preference for a little daddy kink, but it *was* a wake-up call.

I was 'old' now. It was time to start thinking about what I wanted out of life. And dumb as it sounds, the thing that I wanted, deep down, especially now that I'd given up on acting but maybe even beneath that all along, was to feel

like I belonged somewhere. Like I was a part of something—
a family.

A total cliche, I know. The porn star who just wants to settle
down with a nice boy and have 2.5 kids and a golden
retriever. But even after I met Maggie, after she more or less
adopted me, I still just wanted someone I could call
my own.

I thought I'd found that with Ethan. Thought he meant it
when he'd laugh and tell me he loved me after I shared
some daydream I'd had about our future together. Thought
he wanted the same things I did. Thought he was telling
the truth.

Only, as time went on, I found myself wanting that stupid
fantasy more and more—but Ethan's answers weren't
changing.

*Of course I want that—but what's the rush? That sounds
amazing—but let's enjoy this while we have it. I want that too—
but we're only young once, right?*

When Maggie got sick, things with Ethan got worse. When I
needed him most, he started slipping away. Coming home
later, cancelling date nights at the last minute, promising to
make it to the hospital or to cook dinner with me and
Maggie and then never showing up.

He said he didn't deal well with illness. But I'd never
expected to feel like I was losing my boyfriend, my best
friend, at the same time that I was losing Maggie.

At least I had time with Maggie. At least we got to spend
those last months together. I worked a lot at the bar that last
year, and we made the time we had together count. And, as

Maggie put it, I was giving myself space to *find my passion*. Figure out my next step.

Unfortunately, my genius self decided that my passion was Ethan, and that my next step was proposing to him.

It... didn't go well.

He didn't believe in marriage, Ethan said. He'd been thinking about it, and he didn't think it made people happy. He loved me, but if this was something I really wanted, he wasn't going to be able to give it to me.

And in case you've never had the joy of being in this situation first hand, let me tell you—once someone's turned down your marriage proposal, it's pretty awkward to keep dating them. Ethan and I made it a whole six days past the lazy-Saturday-morning, breakfast-in-bed, ring-hidden-inside-a-croissant debacle before he broke up with me.

Maggie died three weeks later.

It was after the funeral that I found out Maggie had made me her sole beneficiary. I just wish I felt like I was doing more to justify Maggie's faith in me. She'd always said I was special—but what the fuck made me special other than having a larger than average cock?

My boyfriend had dumped me, I'd quit my job, and no matter how hard I looked for my next step, I couldn't seem to find it. And after a few months, I'd begun to wonder if it was even out there. Maybe this was it for me.

After all, you can take the boy out of Appalachia, but you can't take the crippling failure and pervasive sense that you don't deserve happiness out of the boy.

So, if you'd told me a week ago I'd be stripping naked and inviting a group of relative strangers to stare at my cock, I would have asked you what you were smoking—and, quite possibly, if I could have some.

Oddly enough, it goes back to Ethan. And yes, before you ask, Ethan and I were still talking. Mostly because I'm an idiot, but also because he'd been my best friend for as long as he'd been my boyfriend, and I wasn't ready to give that up.

And fine, okay, so a little part of me couldn't help thinking that maybe if we kept talking, if I stayed in his life, he'd realize what he was missing one of these days.

Call me pathetic. Really, do. It's no worse than what I called myself every time I saw I'd gotten a new message on my phone and hoped it was from him. I *knew* it was pathetic. And I did it anyway.

ETHAN: You will never guess who I ran into today

GRAY: ??

ETHAN: Funniest fucking thing

ETHAN: Your friend Violet was at this arts benefit my parents were hosting—did you know she's famous now?

I did know that, actually. Violet's last movie played at Sundance last year and I was thrilled she was starting to make a name for herself.

I'd met Violet when she was 18 and in film school. She'd been thrilled to get a paying job on any production crew, even if it was working as a runner and assistant—in porn. Incurably cheerful and determined, she was the first to arrive on set, the last to leave, and would not stop peppering everyone around her with questions about how everything worked.

Violet drove Scott, the director for most of my shoots, up a wall, but I'd always liked her. Hard not to like someone who can look at you with a straight face while you've got some guy's cum drying on your chest and ask you if you want a Caesar or Waldorf salad for lunch, honestly. Violet was unflappable.

Ethan had met her a couple of times, though he'd always tried to put so much distance between himself and my job that I was surprised he actually remembered Violet.

GRAY: Yeah—haven't talked to her in a while though. How is she?

ETHAN: Idk, but she told me she's working on a new movie and she wants YOU to be in it

What?

GRAY: What?

ETHAN: I mean I told her you wouldn't be interested, obviously. You gave up acting years ago. But isn't that funny?

I wasn't prepared for the weird cocktail of emotions that was exploding in my chest. Anger, sadness—and loss. Loss of something that had never been mine in the first place.

Ethan was right. I *had* given up acting what felt like ages ago. So why the hell did I feel disappointed?

GRAY: Yeah, weird

I didn't know what else to say. But I couldn't stop thinking about it for the rest of the day. I hadn't considered acting seriously in years. And I was too old to start now, wasn't I?

Besides why should I think I'd actually be any good at it. In all my years of auditioning, I'd gotten cast in one major role —the one I'd turned down to stay with Ethan. If I were actually any good, wouldn't I have gotten cast more?

Violet probably hadn't even been serious when she'd talked to Ethan. It was probably just one of those things you say when you're making small talk. Hell, for all I knew, she'd been joking.

There was no reason to be hung up on this. It wasn't real, it wasn't a possibility. I needed to let it go, and by the time the evening rolled around, I'd convinced myself that was exactly what I would do.

And then Violet walked into the bar.

"Gray?" she said, her face breaking into a broad grin as she walked up. "I thought that was you. God, it's been ages. How are you?"

I couldn't help smiling right back, walking around from the back of the bar to pull her into a hug.

"I'm good," I said. "Good enough, anyway." When people ask that, they never actually want the full explanation. "Better now that you're here. It's been too long."

"Sorry," Violet said, making a sheepish face. "I know I've been shitty at keeping in touch."

"Whatever," I said, waving her apology away. "You actually *are* too busy and important to keep up with people like me now. You're fucking killing it—you have a good excuse to be too busy."

"Still, I should have been better about it. But I'm hoping," she said, giving me a sidelong glance, "that that won't be a problem anymore, if I can convince you to say yes to me."

I cocked my head to the side. "Is this about—I mean, um —Ethan told me he ran into you yesterday," I finished lamely.

Violet frowned. "How much did he tell you?"

"Not much," I shrugged. "Just that you were working on a new project."

Violet rolled her eyes. "Well, that's true as far as it goes. Did he tell you I want you to be in it?"

"He uh—he kind of mentioned—I wasn't sure if—"

God, I sounded like a complete idiot. Why was I stammering? This was Violet, for Christ's sake. She'd seen me getting spitroasted and now I couldn't even get out a complete sentence?

Violet shook her head. "Fucking Ethan." She frowned up at me. "You have a few minutes to talk?"

Feeling weirdly anxious, I nodded and motioned for her to come back to my office. Micah, my friend and one of my bartenders, could take over in front for a while. A minute later, I was cracking open a beer and passing it to Violet, then opening one for myself as we settled into two old, threadbare armchairs.

"So how much do you actually know about this project?" Violet asked after taking a sip of her beer. She kicked her shoes off and pulled her legs up into a criss-cross position on the chair, resting the can on her knee.

I winced apologetically. "Not really anything."

She took a long drink from her can and gave me a level look. "Okay, so. I know maybe you haven't been thinking about acting in a while. And that you've hung up your porn spurs and retired to humble domesticity and all that. But basically, I'm doing a new movie, it's this kind of crowd-funded, very indie sort of project, and I think you'd be perfect for it."

I laughed. "Is that another way of saying you think I'll work for cheap?"

"I mean, not gonna lie," Violet said with a snort, "that might be part of it. But no, not really. That's not the main thing."

"So…"

"Have you ever heard of a book called *Foresight*?"

I blinked. "Can't say that I have. Though I'm not exactly keeping up with Oprah's book club these days."

"It's not exactly the kind of book you'd *find* in Oprah's book club," Violet laughed. "Though honestly, there are a lot of people out there who'd argue that it should be. Myself included. But for starters, it's a romance novel—"

I barked a laugh. "Vi, I don't think I've read a romance novel in my life—"

"And it's self-published," Violet went on. "And it's gay."

I blinked.

"And not in the derogatory, 'that's so gay' sense of the word," Violet added, picking up speed as she talked, her tone growing more excited. "Obviously not that anyone should ever say that in the first place. But it's a story about two guys who fall in love. And it's amazing, and the author who wrote it is a friend of a friend and basically, long story short, they published it a year and a half ago and have been getting requests since day one to turn it into a movie. And one thing led to another and between crowd-funding and some very generous patrons—well, producers, now—they've hired me and we're actually gonna make it."

I squinted at the onslaught of words, sorting through them. Whatever I'd been expecting her to say, this was... not it.

"And you want me? To be..."

"To be one of the leads. Yep." Violet nodded. "Wyatt Day. Taciturn but kind-hearted calculus teacher. Lover of the natural world. Possessor of a giant dick."

"Possessor of what?" I yelped. "Vi, I thought this was an actual movie."

"It is! I swear. It's just also... " she chuckled. "A movie of whatever the gay equivalent of a bodice-ripper is. A boner-ripper."

"That is a singularly terrifying phrase. Please promise me you'll never say it again."

"Promise me you'll be in this movie and you'll get your wish."

That shut me up. I knew I should just say no. I wasn't an actor. I might have wanted to be, once. But this... if Violet was right, and it actually *was* a good project, I'd probably just make a fool of myself. And ruin her movie, too.

The only skill I had was making guys come really fast. Not exactly the sort of thing you bragged about at a dinner party, much less put on your resume.

If it had been anyone else but Violet, I would have just said no. But she deserved better from me than that. I sighed, and picked the easiest objection first.

"So it's porn, basically. Like, porn dressed up in fancy clothes," I said. "I quit, Vi. I'm not doing that anymore."

"I'd argue it's a life-changing, heart-wrenching romance dressed up in slutty clothes," Violet countered. "Gray, the book is insanely good. I think you'd like it if you read it. And Danny, the author, adapted their own book for the screenplay, and it's fucking amazing. But I mean, yeah. There's definitely fucking. That's kinda the selling point. You have no idea what the fans are like. People are clamoring for this kind of thing, but we're the first ones to actually find a viable funding model to do it and people are so excited and supportive."

"What's your distribution plan?" I asked, interested in spite of myself.

"Online. I mean, we'll do a premiere somewhere, and if we can get a limited run in some independent cinemas, I'm sure Dave and Andrew—they're the guys underwriting this— will want to do that. But yeah, basically online."

"Crowdfunded, you said? Can you even afford to pay industry rates?"

"Yeah, nooo. Definitely not." Violet snorted. "Honestly, it's like, a pittance. This is *not* a studio film and we don't have anything like a studio budget. But we're doing a royalty share, and the two leads will continue to get a cut of any future profits."

"Vi, I don't—I mean, even assuming I were willing to do this, I'm not an actor. I'm pretty sure I'd be terrible, and I don't want to sink your movie."

"Maybe you haven't been putting yourself out there recently," Violet said. "But you're comfortable in front of a camera. And Gray, don't forget that I watched you on set for years. You know how to connect with people. You're empathetic and responsive. In a regular movie, that's like, 70% of the job right there. And when it comes to shooting sex scenes that actually turn people on, that's 100% of the job. I've seen the way you can put guys at ease, get them to come apart in your hands. You'd be... fuck, Gray, you'd be amazing in this. Please? Please just consider it?"

And okay, I'm not made of stone. You can't listen to someone say shit like that to you and not feel a little bit flattered, at least, and by the time Violet was done speaking, I was fighting a blush. Which was ridiculous. I could suck a guy's cock in front of her without a trace of discomfort but God forbid she give me a compliment. Still, though...

"Vi, I'm just not sure—I mean, I appreciate the thought, but I'm not sure this is the right thing for me right now."

Violet gave me a sympathetic look. "Gray, I know we haven't talked a whole lot this year..."

"Pssh, don't start with that." I waved away the rest of her apology. "You think I'm mad at you because you've been out there kicking ass and taking names?"

Violet rolled her eyes. "What I was *going* to say was that I know it's been a hard year, losing Maggie. And from what I can tell, things are, um, *different* between you and Ethan."

"If by different, you mean he told me he doesn't believe in marriage and thought all the times that we talked about getting married were just metaphorical and then dumped me while Maggie was dying, then yeah. Different."

"I was trying to be delicate."

"Vi, you're trying to get me to fuck somebody for money and film it. We're past the point of delicacy."

"In between scenes of poignant beauty and affecting dialog," Violet said, frowning at me. "Fuck somebody for money in between scenes of poignant beauty and dialog. There's a difference."

"Maybe there is, but I still don't think—"

"Oh Jesus Christ, just shut up and say yes already," called a voice from the hallway.

Two seconds later the door to my office burst open and Micah walked in, carrying a crate of new glassware, still shrink-wrapped, in his arms. He shifted his stance, balancing the crate on his right hip, and glared at me.

"You have to do this."

"Fuck, Micah, how long have you been standing out there listening?"

"Long enough for my arms to be tired," Micah said with a huff.

"I don't suppose telling you not to eavesdrop would help you out?"

"I don't know, would telling you to get your head out of your ass help *you* out? You have to do this movie," Micah shot back. He turned and flashed Violet a bright smile. "You must be Violet. Gray's told me a lot about you. I'm Micah, Gray's incorrigible friend and favorite employee."

"Soon to be favorite ex-employee," I grumbled. I looked between the two of them. "Look, I'm... flattered that you think I'd be a good fit for this, Vi. But the reality is, I can't take time out of my life right now to do this. I've got a bar to run—"

"I can run the bar," Micah interjected. "And you need to get out of your rut."

"Who says I'm in a rut?"

"The whole world, dumbass," Micah said with a hard look. "You've told me yourself, for heaven's sake. Gray, I've known you for a very long time and a rut is exactly what you're in."

I huffed. "Even if that *were* true—"

"Which it is—"

"That doesn't mean that me trying and failing to be an actor and ruining Vi's movie for her is the way to fix it." I turned to Vi. "If it's as important a book as you say it is, why would you want to take a chance on me? I could fuck it all up."

"Gray, you won't. You're talented."

"Saying, *'fuck, you're so tight,'* doesn't exactly take much acting talent," I said drily. "And that's pretty much all the experience I have. You sure you wanna take this risk?"

Violet smiled widely. "If it makes you feel any better, I can't actually just *give* you the part. If you agree, you're still gonna need to come by and meet the producers, do a screen test, read with the guys who come in to audition as Dylan—the other male lead," she added when she saw my confused look. "So if you really suck, I'm sure they'll say no."

"Great. That makes me feel so much better."

"Oh, stop whining," Micah said. "You're doing this. You have every right to be upset about Maggie, obviously, but I'm *sick* of watching you mope over Ethan and how you'll be alone forever. The guy's a douche. If this movie does nothing else other than remind you that there are other fuckable fish in the sea—even if only in the context of make-believe—it'll have done its duty."

"I'm not *moping*."

"Fine, not *moping*. But sulking, for sure." Micah sighed, set the crate of glasses down on the side of my desk, and gave me a long look. "Listen, I know I make it a policy to make fun of you at all times—"

"Really? I hadn't noticed."

"But in all seriousness, Gray, I think this would be good for you. And if it's any help, I've, uh, read the book it's based on. And it *is* good. Like, really good."

"You read?" I said, but it didn't have much bite.

"Shocking, I know," Micah said with a snort. "I can count to twenty and tie my shoes, too. But seriously. You always said Maggie was like, the person who made you feel like it was okay to be yourself. This is the kind of book—the kind of movie, I assume—that could make that difference for someone else. The kind of thing that could make people feel braver being in their own skin. Don't you wanna help people, if you can?"

"Low blow, Micah."

"Hey, I never claimed to be above a little emotional manipulation."

"I've got the sides for the auditions that I can give you now," Violet offered. "But if you're willing to wait, I can check with Danny and see if they're willing to let me send you the whole screenplay. You could read it and see what you think?"

"I'll do you one better," Micah grinned. "I've got the book on my kindle. Read it tonight. If you hate it, fine, you don't have to do the movie. But if you like it…"

"Micah, I have to work tonight. For that matter, so do you. Who's watching the bar right now?"

"Kellie's got it, don't worry. Besides, it's a Monday night. You know that's our slowest shift. Plenty of time to read between customers."

Violet smiled at Micah. "I like you. You promise you'll make him actually read it? Not just skim?"

"Cross my heart," Micah said with a laugh.

"Good." Violet nodded and unfolded her legs, slipping her shoes back on before she stood up. "Then I'm gonna go let Danny, Dave, and Andrew know that you're a strong maybe."

I looked at her.

"Okay, a *medium* maybe," she said with a grin. "That better?"

"Vi, I love you but... I don't wanna disappoint you," I said as I stood up and pulled her in for a quick hug. "Just don't get your hopes up, okay?"

"Don't worry," Micah said, shaking his head and rolling his eyes at Violet as I pulled away. "Get your hopes up as high as they can go. He's gonna love it."

I didn't want Micah to be right.

I didn't.

But God. I wasn't ready. I sat down on a stool at the corner of the bar that night, idly twisting a straw between my fingers, as I pulled up *Foresight* by Danny Wilson on Micah's kindle, and sighed, reading the epigraph.

trust your heart

if the seas catch fire

(and live by love

though the stars walk backward)

— E.E. Cummings

Oh God. This was going to be some high-brow, overwrought opus by a self-important ex-English major, wasn't it?

Except... then... it wasn't. Instead, it was just... perfect.

I read the entire thing in one sitting. Micah banished me back to my office halfway through, grinning and telling me that he knew I'd be useless until I finished it. And when I finally did?

I was wrecked. A puddle on the floor. I wasn't even sure I wanted to pick myself back up—maybe it was just enough to lie there and be grateful for the capacity to feel. I couldn't tell you the last time a book had made me feel so many things. I wasn't ready for it.

It was a simple story. Set at a boys boarding school in Halewech, Maine over the course of a fall semester. Part of me stuttered a bit at the fact that it was a teacher/student romance, but hell, the kid was 18 and the book was too good for me to care.

The author made the characters, their hopes and fears and their love, so real, exploring what it meant for them to live their lives fully. And by the end of it, I was convinced that somehow, I could be living mine more fully as well.

I wandered out of my office in a daze and stared at Micah blankly until he noticed me. He turned from closing out the cash register for the night and laughed.

"Your face," he said, not even bothering to hide his grin.

"I just…" I trailed off. "I'm not—I wasn't—it was just so…"

"Yeah." Micah nodded. "Trust me. I know."

"How did—I can't—Jesus Christ, Micah, I feel like I died and came back to life five times while I was reading that."

"Told ya."

"You did *not* tell me," I grumbled. "You didn't come anywhere close to warning me. Christ, what day is it even?"

"Still Monday," Micah laughed as I wobbled over and took a seat at the bar. "You gonna be okay there, buddy?"

I grabbed a bottle of Bulleit Rye and poured out a finger for myself and a finger for Micah into two glasses. I pushed the second glass along the bar towards him.

"I honestly have no fucking clue," I said, picking up the glass and staring at it. "I'm not used to getting fucked up over... art."

"Well you're fucked up alright, if you're pouring us the good stuff." Micah glanced at me over the top of his glass. "So."

"So..."

"What's the verdict then. You telling Violet yes?"

I puffed out my cheeks and blew a long breath of air out. If you'd asked me a few hours ago, I would have said no. For sure.

But now?

It felt like a thousand doors had just opened before me. Suddenly, I wasn't just willing to admit I was in a rut—I felt like I might actually be able to do something to fix that. That the world was too big and wide and full of possibility for me to want to sit around moping—don't you dare tell Micah I used that word—over Ethan.

"I think I might be." I grimaced. "I mean, I'm still sure I'll be terrible. But what's the worst that could happen? I don't get the part? Or I do, but then the movie bombs and what, I miss a month of work here but then everything goes back to normal. No big deal, right?"

"Cheers to that," Micah said, raising his glass.

I tossed the whiskey back. It burned and it felt like the start of something.

~

So *that's* how I ended up standing in the corner of a converted commercial garage out in Red Hook on Wednesday evening, pulling my shirt off over my head.

They'd finished with auditions for the role of Dylan 45 minutes ago. I'd caught the tail end of the last kid's performance as I slipped in through a side door. Violet had nodded at me and motioned for me to wait, then called the names of the guys she wanted to stay and read with me.

The screen tests went fine, I thought. Well, as fine as they could, given that I had no idea what the fuck I was doing *and* the fact that Danny fucking Wilson, author of *Foresight*, was there in the flesh and I was having a hard time not hyperventilating.

Danny sat in the back of the room watching next to Dave and Andrew, the two producers, watching me read. When was the last time I'd gotten so nervous in front of someone? I just prayed I didn't mangle the lines too much.

I didn't know who Violet and company liked the best of the actors who read with me, but she thanked all the guys and sent them home, promising to call soon. Then she shepherded me, Danny, Dave, and Andrew into a little office in the back. It wasn't even a separate room, just a corner of the garage that had been blocked off with bookshelves and a folding screen.

"See, Gray, I told you," Violet said with a warm smile. "You were great. How'd that feel?"

In all honesty, it hadn't felt that great. I'd been tongue-tied and stiff in ways I'd never felt before in front of a camera.

Sure, some porn had plots—but that wasn't really the point of it, you know? Then, I'd always concentrated most on connecting with the guy in front of me, making sure he was feeling safe and feeling good. Any characters we were playing were incidental.

Today, for the first time, I actually cared about getting it right.

"I feel like I'm supposed to say *awesome*, but to be honest, I still feel like I don't know what the hell I'm doing."

"Well, it didn't show," Violet said with a grin. She glanced over at the other three. "Right, guys?"

Danny nodded and smiled, and Andrew and Dave did too—but then Dave leaned over and whispered something in Andrew's ear that made him blush.

"What?" I asked, uncertain. That couldn't be a good sign. "Really, if you don't think I was good, I won't be offended. *I* don't think I was good, so it's not like—"

"No, no, it's not that," Andrew said quickly. "It's just—forget it, it's not important."

"It *is* important," Dave objected.

"Yeah, but it's not, you know, *polite*," Andrew shot back.

Violet looked at the two of them in confusion and I shook my head.

"Really, it's fine. I'd rather know, if there's a note, or something you think I could—"

"We were wondering if you could strip," Dave said, flushing and tripping over his words. "You know, just so we know what we're working with. Since it's been a while since you've—"

"Ohh." I laughed. God, I'd been so worried they were going to tell me I'd sucked that this paled in comparison. "Yeah, sure. No worries."

I began pulling my shirt off over my head when Violet put her hand on my arm.

"No, Gray, stop. Leave your clothes on." Violet shot daggers at Dave and Andrew. "Just because they're the producers doesn't give them license to be creepy. You don't have to do that. We know your dick didn't fall off since you stopped doing porn."

I laughed and shrugged. "It's fine. I don't mind. Really."

Honestly, if I'd been the type to get uncomfortable every time someone suggested I lose some clothing, I definitely would have wound up in a different business. Dave and Andrew were far from the pushiest producers I'd ever worked with.

I pulled my shirt all the way off and tossed it on the back of a chair, then kicked off my shoes, undid my belt and fly, and let my jeans fall softly to the floor.

Dave whistled.

"Damn," he said with a grin. "You sure you quit? You're in good enough shape to have stepped off a set two hours ago."

"Don't objectify him, David," Andrew said, poking Dave gently in the gut. "Some people take their health and physical fitness seriously. Something to think about, if you ever—"

He stopped, open-mouthed, and left his sentence unfinished as I hooked my fingers into the waistband of my boxer-briefs and slid them to the ground, freeing my cock. I wasn't hard—standing around in an over-air-conditioned garage with nothing but my socks on wasn't exactly a ticket to boner-city—but I knew I was impressive nonetheless.

You don't exactly get voted 'New York's Favorite Power Top' four years running without the equipment to back it up.

"Shit," Andrew finished, lamely.

"Now who's objectifying him?" Dave said with a grin.

"It's fine," I said again, making my voice warm and reassuring. I wondered if I was going to have to do a lot of that. Dave and Andrew might be huge—and deep-pocketed—fans of the book. But if they ended up offering me the part, Violet and I might be the only two people who'd worked in porn before. "Really, it's flattering."

"Besides, like, how could we not? I'm sorry, but is there anyone here who's capable of *not* objectifying him?" Andrew protested. He glanced around and snorted when he saw Danny looking down at their laptop screen. "I don't know how she's managing to look at anything else. Superhuman strength, must be."

"What? Oh. Me." Danny glanced up in confusion, then laughed when they realized Andrew was talking about them. "I use they/them pronouns."

"Oh, sorry," Andrew said quickly.

"No worries." Danny smiled, pushing their hair back behind their ear. "And it's not superhuman strength at all. I've just seen a lot of dicks in my day."

"See," Dave said, taking the opportunity to poke Andrew back. "You're just being rude."

"Really, it's not a big deal," I said, bending down to tug my jeans up. "It's not like you guys aren't going to see a lot more when—"

"Uh, hello? Is anyone here?"

We all stopped talking at the sound of a new voice cutting across the empty garage, followed by footsteps crossing the concrete towards us. I knew I should have been pulling my clothes back on, but surprise and confusion froze my hands, my jeans only halfway back up my thighs. Hadn't we sent everyone home?

All I could do was watch as a hand appeared at the edge of the folding screen, followed by a head of shaggy, light-brown hair and inquisitive, hazel eyes.

"Hi!" the guy said, his voice warm and cheerful. "Are you guys still holding auditions for *Foresight*?

Even in my stupor, I was able to register that whoever this was, he was gorgeous—if about a decade too young for me. And I was just standing there, naked.

For the first time that day, I felt uncomfortable.

"Sorry, I didn't mean to interrupt," the guy continued, "but I knew I was running late and I—"

"Tyler Lang?" Violet's voice was baffled as she interrupted him. "What the hell are you doing here?"

2

TYLER

*B*efore you ask, I really, truly do not remember buying that cocaine.

Everyone always asks that—like literally everyone, from people on the street to random baristas at coffee shops, who ask like we're best friends gossipping at a sleepover instead of total strangers exchanging money for a non-fat, extra-whip caramel latte—so I'll just save you the trouble and tell you upfront that I really don't remember.

I know that sounds impossible and I don't expect you to believe me. No one does. Hell, if I didn't know for a fact that I was as surprised as the cops were to find bags of the stuff shoved inside a cookie jar shaped like a hedgehog, rolling around in the trunk of my car, I wouldn't believe me either.

My lawyer wanted me to say it wasn't mine, that someone else must have put it there. But who the hell else could have done that? And it wasn't like I'd never bought drugs before —so the only thing that made sense was that I had bought it, or agreed to transport it, or something, and I was so high at the time that I couldn't remember. That or I was just losing my goddamn mind.

It was just so weird. I always bought my drugs in small quantities, specifically *because* I didn't ever want to get busted with more than a tiny amount on me. Plus, I never kept them in my car—I kept them in a collector's edition lunch box with my face on it from my time on *Criss-Cross Applesauce*, like any other self-respecting, narcissistic former child-star.

Hell, I never even drove the car they were found in. Why the hell would I drive a minivan, a fucking Honda Odyssey that my dad made me buy for tax purposes four years ago, when I had an actual Lamborghini at my disposal?

Well, at my disposal most of the time. The day before everything went to shit, I'd driven up to a friend's place in Malibu and gotten drunk enough that even I knew better than to drive home. What can I say? I'll do dumb shit from sunup to sundown, but I won't get behind the wheel when I'm drunk or high. I know it sounds trite, but we did one of those 'very special episodes' about drunk driving on *Shoestring Miracles* when I was 14 and it actually made an impression. Go figure.

So anyway, I'd taken an Uber home, woken up after noon with a massive hangover, and was just about to chase it with a bottle of Sambucca and a handful of pills I hadn't looked at too closely when Gil showed up.

And yeah, I should have known better than to listen to Gil. After all, my two most recent arrests had come after nights spent out with him. I might not be the brightest crayon in the box but it doesn't take a genius to figure out that Gil plus me plus mind-altering substances usually leads to terrible decisions.

But I'd had another fight with my dad the day before—the whole reason I'd gotten wasted in Malibu—and I was still nursing that anger in addition to my hangover. So when Gil announced that we were going to a 'golf pros and tennis hoes' party out in the Valley, I honestly couldn't think of any good reason to say no, other than a principled objection to the misogyny in the party's theme, and let's be honest, I'd been in Hollywood since I was six, so it's not like I was about to start developing principles *now*.

And since neither of us had anything that would work as a costume, Gil decided we'd stop at the mall on the way. Only, he'd taken a cab to my place and the only car I was currently in possession of was the shitty old minivan my dad had me buy five years ago, back when I still lived with him and we weren't quiiite as deep into the delightful *'Tyler fucks up and Dad gets furious'* cycle.

I mean, don't get me wrong, I was still fucking up back then and he was still pissed about dealing with my bullshit all the time—but things didn't kick into high gear til I turned 18 and he moved into his own apartment. But he'd left the fucking Odyssey at my place and that afternoon, it seemed like a godsend.

Actually though—back up. Maybe I was speaking too quickly earlier. Because now that I think about it, I can probably blame the whole fiasco (which, yeah yeah, I know I'm supposed to be accepting responsibility for my actions but just go with me here for a sec) on the fact that I actually *had* developed principles. Or was trying to, anyway.

Because yeah—the whole *Suspender-gate* thing that you heard about in the papers? That was actually supposed to be my stab at the patriarchy. Why were we limiting the 'ho' part of the equation to women, I figured? I could be just as much of a ho as anyone else, couldn't I?

Which, yes, I realize is kind of ironic, if you actually knew anything about me and how embarrassingly inexperienced I was at ho-ery of any kind, but honestly, no one *did* know that—that was kind of the point. You make yourself desirable by seeming to always be hooking up with people. You keep yourself desirable by never actually doing it.

So anyway, my genius brain had decided that I was going to buck tradition by being a golf ho, because fuck toxic masculinity, or something like that. Which is how I ended up wearing a pair of herringbone trousers and polka dotted suspenders over no shirt in the dressing room of a Men's Dress For Less in a shitty mall in Panorama City, and how Gil dared me to just walk out of there without paying.

And because I'm the fucking worst, I didn't even have the excuse of being drunk or high at the time. I just did it because I'm an idiot. Because it would make a good story. Because I was sick of feeling shitty about myself and doing something that stupid and pointless just seemed fun.

Right up until the sensors started beeping as I walked out the door and Gil bolted and the mall cops showed up. That's when the fun feeling stopped.

So I'm standing there, shirtless in suspenders at the front of the fucking store, people walking by and taking my picture —which honestly, you'd think they'd have gotten tired of by now; it's not like pictures of me doing something asinine in public are exactly hard to come by—when they radio for the actual cops to come in.

And that's when it hits me. My dad's going to fucking kill me. My dad, who's spent the past 10 years of my life reminding me how irresponsible I am, dealing with my shortcomings, cleaning up after my messes, is going to fucking murder me for getting my name in the tabloids for something un-acting-related. Again.

So I ran.

I honestly think the only reason I even made it to the parking lot was because no one was expecting me to do that. *I* wasn't even expecting me to do it, but some kind of panic monster took over my brain and I just bolted. Made it to the car, hopped in, and peeled out of there like I was in some kind of action movie—except one where I was doing my own stunts instead of letting a trained professional do them for me like I had in *Konterra Rising* two years ago.

I didn't have a plan. I wasn't even thinking past the next step. Get away from the cops. Get in the car. Get on the highway. At every point, I half-expected to be stopped. I never even thought I'd make it out of the parking lot.

But I did, and suddenly I'm driving down the fucking 405 in a goddamn Honda Odyssey like I'm in the world's worst reenactment of the OJ Simpson chase. Only, turns out, I'm not built for car chases at all. Even on a normal day, I'm a terrible driver. Something about being around all these large, metal semi-autonomous death machines makes me nervous, which in turn makes me stupid, and all my reflexes go on high-alert, which somehow makes me clumsier rather than smoother.

All I could see was the traffic, and trying to weave through it made me feel like my heart was going to explode. I didn't want to hurt anybody. It wasn't their fault they were on the highway at the same time that I was having a fucking break-down of epic proportions.

And, because it's LA and when is there ever *not* traffic, someone braked hard in front of me. And I swerved to avoid hitting them. And promptly crashed into the barrier on the far side of the shoulder, got punched in the face by the airbag, and passed out.

The EMTs told me later that I was lucky I'd been wearing my seatbelt. I didn't even remember putting it on, but I wished I hadn't. Because at that moment, dying horrifically in a car crash seemed preferable to what was happening— the cops arresting me for the fucking stolen suspenders I was still wearing, for resisting arrest, for public endanger-ment, and, after they searched the vehicle, for possession and intent to sell a truly baffling amount of cocaine.

Like, I'd seen coke before. Duh. For better or for worse (okay, mostly for worse) I'd done more than just *see* it. Many times. But I'd never seen a fucking half kilo of the stuff, all portioned out into individually sized baggies and stuffed inside a ceramic porcupine.

And I had no idea how it got there. Which I told them. But of course the cops didn't believe me. And I couldn't really blame them.

But unlike the other times I'd been arrested, this wasn't the kind of thing that could get swept under the rug. Public drunkenness, starting fights, even simple possession. I'd been through all of that before. But no one wanted to go easy on me this time. Not when I'd done something so terminally stupid—stealing fucking $14.99 suspenders— and reckless, driving onto the freeway like that.

I honestly think they were shocked when the tests showed I wasn't actually intoxicated at the time, but it didn't matter. They were still determined to make an example out of me. Which would have been fine, except that apparently, this time, my dad agreed with them.

All of the other times I'd been arrested, my dad had hired one of those expensive, can't-put-your-finger-on-it-but-you-know-they're-sleazy lawyers who represent mob bosses or kitten murderers or whatever and somehow manage to get them off scot free. And so I'd pay a fine, or rather, my dad would pay it for me out of my accounts because he didn't trust me with my money and honestly, that was fair. And he'd yell at me and tell me what a fuck-up I was and it's not like I could really disagree with him, so I'd promise to be better and for like a month or two I would be and then— well, there's that cycle I mentioned.

Except this time it was different. My dad refused to hire one of those lawyers. Said I'd gone too far. That I needed to learn a lesson. I remember the conversation like it was yesterday, instead of a year and 14 days ago, before my court-ordered sentencing, or *The Dark Ages*, as I liked to call it.

We were standing at the doorway of his one-bedroom apartment in Santa Monica. He'd stopped returning my calls, so I'd had to drive over there to find him and now he wasn't even letting me inside.

"I'm tired of following after you, fixing the damage you leave in your wake," he'd spit, his harsh tone so at odds with the warm light spilling out from his living room, the bougainvillea flowers curling around the stucco walls of his porch.

"But Dad, I didn't even—I don't remember buying it," I'd protested.

"Really, Tyler? You expect me to believe that?" He shook his head. "You'll never learn to be responsible if you never face the consequences of your actions. That's always been your problem. You're weak, and I've enabled it. But I'm not doing it anymore."

That had stung. Because sure, even though I knew I pretty much had the market cornered on 'selfish spoiled brat makes dumb-ass decisions and is shocked when he has to reckon with the consequences,' it's one thing to have that sneaking suspicion about yourself and quite another to have someone confirm it, to your face.

My dad had never been one to sugar coat things. And I didn't blame him. You don't grow up with an asshole like me for a kid and not end up having to bluntly tell them—me, I mean—exactly how and when they're fucking things up.

But still—it hurt and it pissed me off and so I'd told him I'd just hire the damn lawyer myself. Which just made him laugh.

"With what money, Tyler?"

"What do you mean? With *my money*. Or have you forgotten who it is who's bringing in all the cash that you live off of?"

"Bringing in cash? Is that what you think you're doing?" My dad laughed in my face. "Tyler, you've been spending money faster than you've earned it since you were 16. And when, exactly, have you earned a single dollar since your last movie flopped two years ago? Unless you've been taking on projects I haven't heard about."

"That's not—"

"But who am I kidding, we both know that would never happen," he sneered. "I've gotten you every job you've ever had. You're too lazy to do it yourself—that's why you haven't had a project in over a year."

"I'm taking a break," I said, hating how defensive my tone was, how pathetic I sounded, but unable to prevent it. My dad knew me too well and he knew just what to say to make me see what a fraud I was. My break was ostensibly to take some time out and consider what projects I really wanted to pursue. But it had kind of turned into one long, drug-fueled haze.

"Bullshit. You can say whatever you want, kid, but you're not fooling anyone. Not even 21 and you're already washed up."

"But—"

"And I'm sick of covering for you. Sick of working for a kid who's so ungrateful. A kid who can't even say thank you for everything I do for him. You never wanted my help when I was offering it, only when you needed it. And trust me, you need it now. You've spent all your damn money and you've burned through all the goodwill you'd stored up. Good luck finding someone who wants to help you now—because it's sure as hell not gonna be me."

And the thing was—he was right.

I didn't know how I'd done it—and when I say *'didn't know'* I mean that literally, because I'd never bothered to learn how stuff like money actually worked—but I'd somehow managed to spend most of the money I'd ever made in the two years since my dad had stopped actively managing my finances.

So I couldn't afford a fancy, mob-boss lawyer. I could barely even afford the shitty kind of lawyer that advertises on daytime TV. And by the time it was all over, the sentence handed down, fines paid and my other debts settled, I was left with a total of fourteen hundred dollars in a checking account I was still afraid to log into for fear of losing even more money.

And thus began *The Dark Ages*, AKA 12 months of court-ordered community service, ankle-bracelet-wearing, group-home-living asceticism. I went into it convinced I'd just do whatever highway-side trash pickup they wanted me to do and ignore the rest of it.

Sure, I'd abused my fair share of substances, but I wasn't an *addict*. I didn't need some 12 step program to help me find God and enlightenment or whatever. And I certainly didn't need to find my inner child and give them a hug, telling them how cosmically valid and loved they were.

Except a funny thing happened. But not funny haha, more like funny this really sucks and is not, in fact, funny at all. And it was more than one thing, it was a series of things and by the end of it—well, by the end of it suddenly I was glad I was living in a fucking group home with strangers with their own goddamn problems because I didn't have to pretend I was okay around anyone there.

It started with the fact that no one would talk to me. No one from my old life, that is. I guess you could say I should have known better, that *no shit*, most friendships in Hollywood aren't based on real affection but rather on real desire to use each other for maximum career mileage and nothing else.

But suddenly no one was returning my calls or texts, not even people I'd known for years, people I'd thought actually liked me and not the fact that I could get them into parties or introduce them to directors looking for new and unique but still completely same-y looking faces.

And it wasn't just my friends. Those directors wouldn't take my calls either. Or any producers. Or even my dad. He hadn't been bluffing, apparently. He really was done with me.

There was nothing that said I couldn't work during that year, but I'd been blacklisted so hard, it might as well have been inscribed in stone or scribbled in fine-tipped black Sharpie across a red letter A plastered to my chest at all times—A for Asshole, for Arrogant, for All My Life I've Tried Really Hard Not To Think About This Crushing Emptiness I Feel And Now There's No Avoiding It, So Thanks For That.

That's when I realized that maybe I did have more of a problem than I wanted to admit. Because suddenly, I couldn't get drunk or high or do something phenomenally stupid to take my mind off how worthless I felt. It used to be that on days when I found myself wondering if there was something wrong with me, if I was just a shitty person who deserved to feel so unloved, I could do something to push those feelings away.

Only now, they weren't just feelings, I wasn't just wondering if there were something wrong with me. I knew it. I'd never wanted to get high as badly as I did those first two months. And I couldn't. So make that A stand for Addict, as well.

One of the big tenets at the group home was the importance of taking responsibility for your choices. In my case that meant, among other things, taking responsibility for the fact that I was so messed up, so drugged out that I could buy a bank-breaking amount of cocaine and then forget about it so thoroughly that I was surprised it was mine when it resurfaced. That, or some part of me did remember, but was in such denial about what that said about me that I was lying to myself about what I knew.

I couldn't decide which option sucked less—so deep in my well of addiction that I'd legitimately forgotten it was there, or such a hypocrite that I couldn't admit to myself that it was mine. Both options made me feel like I should forfeit my right to take up oxygen on the planet.

And I guess that was supposed to be a good thing or something. My rock bottom, my realization that I was broken and needed help. Only it turns out I'm really fucking bad at doing everything that comes next. So by the end of the past year, I hadn't really moved past the rock bottom stage.

And suddenly, I was out. With nowhere to live, no one willing to hire me, and no one even willing to talk to me. So I did the only thing I could think of.

I moved home. And not home back-in-with-my-dad-home. But home home, to Garden City, Long Island. To the house I'd lived in with my mom and brother and father until I turned six and auditioned for that stupid children's show and fucked everything up thereafter.

My parents had gotten divorced when I was 12, but my mom

still lived there, and Luke, my older brother, lived in Manhattan. So with nine hundred dollars left in my checking account now—because cross country flights aren't cheap, as I'd just learned—I'd flown into JFK, let Luke pick me up, and deposit me in my childhood bedroom. It still had the same creepy-eyed lion painting on the wall above my bed.

Only—there's only so long you can go living with your mom as a grown-up without going slowly insane. And yes, I realize that maybe it's stretching it a bit to call someone like me a grown-up. But listen, I turned 21 a week after I moved back to New York and I'd celebrated by melting shredded cheese onto some Tostitos on the microwave, drinking my mom's Diet Dr. Pepper, and watching old episodes of *Midsomer Murders*, and for me, that counted as pretty fucking mature.

Maybe it wouldn't have been so bad if I were just able to sink down into ignoble obscurity, left to walk my mom's dog and contemplate my failures in peace. But you don't spend 14 years as one of the most recognizable young faces in Hollywood and then get to disappear, apparently.

Back in LA, back when we were getting started, my dad used to call the paparazzi and tell them where I was going to be. The whole thing was orchestrated to get me as much publicity as possible. And now, when the last thing I wanted in the world was to be in anyone's magazine or website or tabloid, I couldn't even go to the grocery store for my mom without someone snapping a picture and asking me how I felt about how hard I'd flamed out.

All I wanted was to work again. Which, yes, I knew was a bit ironic, given that I'd been on a never ending, self-imposed break from acting before I got arrested. I'd started it because I'd been burned out—that part had been legitimate. But I'd definitely prolonged it because I was a fucking asshole and getting high and buying a yacht was more fun than actually showing up to a set on time.

And now, here I was, desperate to work, and no one would have me. So I basically just sat in my mom's house and hid from photographers. My mom worked all day but she'd started out giving me projects to do—clear out the attic, organize the basement shelves, wash our goddamn walls, which apparently get dirty and need washing, if you can believe that.

But eventually, there was nothing left to clean and since my few attempts at learning to cook had come disastrously close to burning the house down, I'd taken to watching The Price Is Right, checking to see if it was safe to go out and get the mail, and reading about new movies and TV shows and other jobs I'd never get again online.

This was my brain off drugs—clear, lucid, and able to map out in excruciating detail how all of the choices I'd made in my life had led me to where I was: completely and utterly fucked.

∼

Fucked, it turned out, was a word that was going to come up a lot in the next 24 hours—most currently, while I sat at the world's most crowded gas station.

How was every single pump at this random Kum 'n' Go occupied? Had the entire population of Long Island suddenly decided they needed to fill their tanks today? It was a Wednesday afternoon, for Christ's sake, it's not like they were all gassing up to go out to the Hamptons or something.

I drummed my fingers on the steering wheel with nervous energy and glanced at the time on the clock. 2 p.m. I was supposed to be at Luke's by 2:45. The package was scheduled for delivery at 3 but Luke being Luke, he'd made me promise to be there early just in case.

I couldn't think of a single instance where a delivery person had been on time, but then again, that wasn't exactly the kind of thing I usually paid attention to, so maybe I was wrong and all parcel delivery services on the island of Manhattan ran with the precision of the German train system.

Still, since Luke was one of the few people who was still talking to me these days, and he was letting me stay at his place for a few days while he was out of town, being on time to accept a package for my big brother was the least I could do. I'd been about to atrophy of boredom out in the suburbs at our mom's house, so I'd practically begged him to let me sign for the package.

Except in typical Tyler fashion, I was about to fuck that up, too.

I heaved a sigh of relief when a car pulled away from one of the pumps. I wasn't facing the right way for it—the gas tank was on the wrong side—but that was nothing a little K-turn couldn't fix. Unfortunately, a lime-green Mazda idling on the other side of the gas station seemed to have the same idea.

"Oh hell no," I muttered. "You're not getting my spot."

I threw the car into reverse, pressing down on the gas to make my move quickly before the Mazda could steal my pump—and promptly backed up over the high curb running around the edge of the gas station's lot.

Luke's car made a sickening crunch.

Fuck.

That hadn't sounded good. At least two drivers currently pumping their gas looked up and winced when they'd heard it. Twin, hot rivers of shame and frustration coursed through me. I had *not* just fucked up Luke's car. I would not allow that to have happened.

Gritting my teeth, I put the car in drive and stepped on the gas. Something scraped along the underside as I came down off the curb. Worse, I could hear a loud rumbling as the car accelerated.

Double fuck. This was not good. And that Mazda had totally taken my spot.

I put the car in park once I was off the curb, turned off the engine, and got out to inspect the damage. The outside of the Corolla looked fine—dull gray with some nicks that had *definitely* been there before Luke started letting me drive it. But the underside? Yikes.

Ugh, why had I decided to drive to his apartment? I could have been on the subway instead of making an ass out of myself for the 79% of Long Island who seemed to be staring at me right now.

Except, of course I hadn't taken the subway. Because normally, that would have a much higher likelihood of people taking your picture and putting it online and asking you in a voice pitched just loud enough for the entire train car to hear whether you were proud of the decisions you made. Like, no I'm not proud of my decisions, I'm riding the goddamn E train, sweating balls and regretting my life choices just like everyone else here.

So, yeah, I'd decided to avoid that near certain eventuality and drive Luke's car instead. He kept it at our mom's place and I figured it'd be an easy enough way to get into the city unnoticed, even if I did have to stop to fill it with gas first. Except I forgot to factor in the part where I suck at everything and now had at least five people staring at me as I surveyed the damage I'd done to Luke's car. With my luck, there'd be pictures of this online by tomorrow.

I could see a dent in the—what did you call that thing, a tail pipe? Plus some scrapes on the underside of... some other car part I couldn't have named. I'd bought more cars than I could count, usually whenever my dad said something to remind me of how I wasn't living up to expectations, but I didn't actually know a damn thing about them.

Was a dented tailpipe enough to make the noises I was hearing? Or had I done something even worse that I couldn't see? Fuck, this was not good.

With a sinking feeling in my stomach, I got back into the car and pulled slowly forward to an empty pump—finally—and cursed myself mercilessly. What the hell was the point of me spending a fucking year in a group home working on mindfulness and not making rash decisions when I couldn't even manage not to do something stupid while I was completely sober?

If I'd just slowed down for a second and waited, this never

would have happened. If I could just learn to be *a little more patient*, like all the counselors had said. Stop letting my fears rule me or whatever. But even after a year of trying to get my life together, I was as messed up as ever.

God, at least Luke was out of town. Maybe I could get it fixed without him ever finding out. I tried to squelch the little voice in the back of my head that told me I should own up to what I'd done—like, *lol, not now, conscience*—just like I tried to squelch the question of what money I was going to use to pay to fix the damage. Figures I'd learn how a checking account actually worked and how to check my daily balance right when that daily balance got real depressing.

I finished pumping my gas and ducked back in the car quickly. The woman at the pump next to mine had been frowning at me and I knew that look too well. The look said *I'm not sure where I know you from, but I'm pretty sure I don't like you.* Better to get out of there before she figured it out.

Miraculously, I found a parking spot on the street only a few blocks from Luke's building in Midtown—because *of course* Luke lives in Midtown—and pulled the car to a rattling, rumbling stop. Even with the traffic I'd hit, I was going to make it. Barely. If I sprinted.

And I'm not ashamed to admit it—I did sprint. Because goddammit, I needed some good karma to balance out fucking up my brother's car. And yeah, I know that believing in karma is the most hippie-dippie LA stereotype in the book but whatever, I'd take what I could get.

But when I burst into his apartment at 2:44 p.m., practically throwing myself through the door, I was not at all prepared to see Luke himself, lying on his couch in the living room, looking hungover as fuck. Because A), he was supposed to be in Montana right now or something. And B) Luke barely drank. It was one of the few things we had in common, now. So none of this made sense.

"What are you doing here?" I asked, realizing too late that I sounded like I was accusing my brother of the capital offense of lying on his own sofa in his own apartment.

"I have the flu," Luke said, sounding like he was announcing his own death. "I couldn't get on the plane this morning."

"I thought you didn't get sick," I said, arching an eyebrow.

"I don't." Luke's voice was morose. "I don't understand what's happening to me. You're supposed to get the flu in the winter, aren't you?"

It wasn't like I was taking pleasure in the fact that my brother was sick, but I couldn't help feeling a *tiny* bit vindicated. Ever since I'd come home, our mom had instituted family dinners and Luke had been on me about eating healthier, like I was inviting heart disease and diabetes and all the other 'Western-world' afflictions if I ate a single cheese fry.

The first time he'd said that, I'd retorted that he was probably going to die from sitting at his corporate job all day. That's when I found out he had a treadmill desk.

The honest truth was, eating normally was something I was still trying to get used to. From age six to age eighteen, my dad had controlled my diet, and somehow seemed to know if I'd eaten so much as a quarter of a brownie from catering on set. Then, once he moved out, my diet consisted mostly of alcohol, pharmaceuticals, and bad decisions. And then this past year, it was back to careful monitoring at the group home.

So yeah, maybe I was a little lacking in life skills, but at least I wasn't taking half my dinners with a side of cocaine anymore. That had to count as improvement, right?

"Sorry, man," I said, wincing and moving around in front of the couch. "Do you want me to go get you something? Chicken soup, or—"

"No. I'm okay." Luke sighed. "Ben and Adam came by earlier and brought me some stuff."

He gestured to the coffee table and I realized for the first time it was covered in bottles of apple cider vinegar and green juices. A jar of echinacea was spilling its contents out and the little capsules were lying next to a few cloves of raw garlic. God, Luke had some weird ideas about getting—

"Wait a second." I frowned. "If you've been sick since this morning, why didn't you call me and tell me I didn't have to rush out here to meet your package?"

"I forgot," Luke said, looking away from me.

"Really?"

"Really." He flushed and looked back at me, his expression sheepish. "And fine, when I remembered, I wanted to see if you'd actually get here on time."

"Jesus, you have that little faith in me?" I said, letting a hint of hurt creep into my tone. "I know you probably think I'm just some irresponsible jackass, but I've really been making an effort." I bit my lip and willed tears into my eyes. Maybe I was laying it on a little thick, but it was hard to stop now. "It meant a lot to me that you asked me to sign for your package, like you were finally trusting me, and I thought maybe this would bring us closer, maybe you would—"

"Shit, Tyler, I'm sorry," Luke said. "Really, that wasn't cool of me. I should have—wait—" he frowned when he realized for the first time that I was trying to hide a smile. "Why are you laughing?"

"I couldn't help it!" I protested. "You're so earnest and perfect all the time. It makes it too easy to mess with you."

"You're a dick, you know that?"

"I do," I said, nodding. "I do know that. In fact, I think it's part of LA county court record that I'm a dick."

"A good actor though," Luke said with a snort. "I'll give you that."

"Tell that to casting directors," I said with a sigh. "Tell that to literally *any* director. Remind people that there's one thing in life I don't actually suck at, and that I'm willing to work for *really cheap* to do it."

Luke gave me a sympathetic look. "I'm sure you'll get something soon. Maybe people just need a little more time to… adjust."

"Maybe," I said, looking down at the floor with a dour glance. "Who knows, maybe they'll even do it before I'm 80 and too old to play King Lear."

Luke laughed. "Since when do you do Shakespeare?"

"Burn, dude." I snorted. "I do actually recognize good parts when I see them. Can I help it if no one wants to hire a catch-phrase spouting former child star to play Hamlet or Julius Caesar?"

"Yeah, but now you're on a redemption arc, right?" Luke said, turning onto his side slightly and giving me what he clearly thought was an animating smile. Oh God, he was going to give me an encouraging pep talk, wasn't he? "Totally different story. Just watch. I give you a month, two tops, before you've found something. You'll be back to driving Ferraris and burning hundred dollar bills for fun in no time."

Shit. Driving Ferraris reminded me of driving Toyotas which reminded me of the very specific Toyota I needed to get fixed, ASAP. How much did that kind of thing cost? Again, not something I'd actually ever bothered to learn, but I remembered people complaining about that type of thing.

My phone buzzed, helping me push those uncomfortable thoughts out of my mind, and also saving me from having to agree that Luke was right, that the world would soon bend to my will, that everything would be coming up Tyler. Because if there was one thing I'd learned from the past year, it was that the world didn't give a shit about your problems.

I pulled my phone out and looked at the screen in surprise.

"It's Tiana," I said, glancing back at Luke with a silent question.

"Take it, take it," he said, waving me away. "Don't worry, I have enough tissues here to stuff a mattress, I'll be fine."

Snorting, I stood up and hit answer, walking into the kitchen. Tiana was my agent and pretty much the only person in LA who was still speaking to me—the only person who'd picked up when I'd called, who'd accepted my apologies, who'd reminded me that we all fucked up, who'd told me that no one was perfect.

As if that didn't make her enough of a saint, she was also keeping her eyes out for roles for me, no matter how hopeless my situation seemed.

"Hey T," I said, doing my best to sound positive and upbeat and not like I'd been reliving all the ways I'd failed and disappointed everyone I knew. "What's up?"

"Maybe something, maybe nothing," Tiana said briskly. "I might have found a role for you."

"T, that's amazing. Seriously, anything, I'm willing to take it—"

"Listen to me before you agree," she cut in.

Dammit. There I went again, jumping the gun.

"Right. Sorry. Listening." I took a deep breath and squared my shoulders. Whatever it was, no matter how small the part, I wasn't going to refuse. "What is it. Is it tiny? It really doesn't matter, I'll still—"

"It's not *tiny*," she said slowly. "It's actually a leading role."

"Holy shit, really?"

"An indie movie. So we're not talking big money here."

"Doesn't matter, I'll do it."

"I mean, you still have to audition. But they're having

trouble finding the right fit, so they might be willing to cast a wider net and look at you. Also, the director's Violet Lynch, if that makes a difference."

"Oh, shit."

Violet Lynch wasn't a big name director in terms of studios and franchises and multi-movie deals, but she'd been making her name on the indie scene and I liked her work. Her last movie, *Semafore* had gotten some critical attention —and deserved it, if you wanted my opinion. Which, granted, no one really did.

"I'll do it, T," I said. "Seriously, this actually sounds really awesome."

"Okay, so, one thing you should know—the character's gay."

"Okay."

"Okay?"

"Yeah. Okay."

I mean, I'm not gonna lie and say my stomach hadn't fallen to the floor when Tiana had said that, but I wasn't going to tell *her* that. Because telling her would involve explaining things I didn't even like to think about myself.

Tiana didn't need to know that I'd been wondering if I were gay or bi or some kind of 'into guys' for a long time. Tiana didn't need to know that I'd been too terrified to ever do more than just wonder, to explore, because I was convinced someone would talk and then rumors would spread and— worst of all—my dad would find out. I wasn't sure what my dad thought about gay rights in the abstract sense, but I knew for a fact that he considered any actor who came out to be an idiot who'd never get work again.

But me taking a role that was gay wasn't the same thing as me coming out, right? There was still plausible deniability there. Hell, it could even be considered edgy or prestigious —the fucking Academy went nuts for an actor playing against type like that.

So yeah—it's not like I didn't have some feelings about the role, but they weren't going to stop me from gunning for the part.

"When's the audition?" I asked.

"So, the audition's today," Tiana began, "but I think maybe you should—"

"Jesus, today? Shit, what time?"

"Well, like, nowish. Says it wraps up at 5 p.m."

"Okay. Okay, I can still make that, I think."

If I rushed, at least. But I was willing to. Not just because I'd take any job, literally anything, just to be working again, but because if I got this, I might actually have the money to get Luke's car fixed. And if Violet Lynch were directing, it might actually be good, on top of all that. I mean, I wasn't above taking something shitty, but—

"Tiana, thank you so much. Really, you're a life-saver."

"Yeah, yeah, I know," Tiana said with a laugh. "But Tyler?"

"Yeah?"

"Um... you need to read this casting call over carefully, okay?

Like... it's kind of an... unconventional movie. And I know you really want something, but there just aren't a lot of—"

"I get it, T." I sighed. I did get it. I might be kind of dumb, but I wasn't *that* dumb. "I'm toxic. No one wants to hire the poor little rich boy who would be in prison if he weren't famous and white. But I just want to work. If this is a chance to do that, I'll take it."

"Okay," Tiana said, her voice still sounding a little doubtful. "You might change your mind when you read it. I don't know. Up to you. I totally get it if it's not your thing but you told me to literally send you anything and, well..."

"You're amazing and I love you more than anyone on this earth."

"Sure, sure. Alright. I'm sending you the email now. Talk soon hun, okay?"

Tiana was as good as her word and the email was in my inbox by the time I'd hung up the phone. I swiped it open quickly.

Casting call for *Foresight*, indie movie, directed by Violet Lynch. Set in a boys boarding school, coming of age story, seeking actors ages 18 through 25 to play an 18 year old student. Those interested should reply to the email with headshot and resume to receive the sides and information for the audition.

Well the boarding school setting explained the gay part, I figured. Who knew, maybe I'd even have to kiss another guy. No one had to know that that'd be the most action I'd gotten in—well, a long time. When you realize you're maybe not that into women but you're definitely too scared to go for guys, that doesn't leave you with a lot of options for, um, physical encounters.

The rest of the email seemed to just be information about the funding situation and standard legal disclaimers. I didn't bother reading it—Tiana had already said it was an indie movie so I knew there wouldn't be much money in it.

But something had to be better than nothing, right? And I didn't care how much it paid, as long as it was a chance to work again. To show people that I'd changed.

Or, if 'changed' was too strong a word, to show people I'd at least sloughed off a few layers of bullshit. I might be the same crappy person underneath, but I was at least trying not to inflict that on other people now.

And if people didn't want to believe that, I could at least remind them that I was a good actor, couldn't I? Honestly, that was really the only thing I'd ever been good at.

The address for the audition was at the top of the email. Some place in Red Hook. I glanced at the time and grimaced. I really was going to have to run to make it. I stuck my head around the corner of the living room wall.

"Hey, do you still have your prep school uniform by any chance?"

"Uh, yeah, I think I do," Luke said, giving me a funny look. "I wore it as a Halloween costume a while back."

"I thought I remembered pictures of that," I called out as I walked back to his bedroom. It took me a minute to find it, rifling through Luke's disturbingly neat and organized closet, but eventually I located it folded up in the back of a drawer along with his ski pants and his old rowing uni.

I could hear Luke saying something as I stripped and pulled the uniform on but his voice was too weak to carry. He gave me a very suspicious look when I walked back out to the living room and bent to pick up my messenger bag from where I'd left it next to the coffee table.

"Am I hallucinating right now? Are you really wearing that?" he asked. "I thought my fever broke but maybe I'm wrong."

"Cute," I said, making a face at him. "I need this for an audition. That's what Tiana was calling about. Some movie called *Foresight*. It's out in Brooklyn, so I gotta run but I can stop by the store and get you something on the way back?"

"Wait, what? An audition?" Luke tried to push himself upright and then gave up, settling for folding his arms across his chest and staring at me as I moved towards the door. "That's awesome, but why do you need my—"

"Movie's set at a boarding school, apparently." I shrugged. "Figured I might as well look the part." I did a little twirl and then headed for the door. "Whaddya think, can I pass for 18?"

"Eighteen. Jesus, I thought you were trying to play Hamlet, not—wait. Did you say the movie was called *Foresight*?"

"Yeah." I stopped at the door and glanced down at my watch. "Shit, Luke, I really gotta go."

"Wait!" Luke called, and I paused, my hand on the knob. "Do you know if it's based on the book?"

"No idea," I said, looking over my shoulder. "Tiana didn't say. Maybe I'll find out more at the audition. I'll let you know when I'm back."

I opened the door and stepped outside, calling, "Feel better!" over my shoulder.

I had just enough time to hear Luke say something—it sounded maybe like *'Tyler, wait, it's'*—before the door closed behind me. Whatever Luke wanted to say, it would have to wait. I was not going to miss my first real shot at redemption.

Of course, the audition was in fucking Red Hook, so I still had to hike when I got off at the Smith Street station. The pleasant surprise that no one recognized me while I was wearing an 18 year old's prep school uniform was offset by the amount I was sweating by the time I got to the dubious-looking warehouse where the audition was, just minutes before 5 p.m.

The building looked like it used to be a garage for some kind of wholesale shipment company. It had a massive, metal door rolled down tight facing the street and it took me a little bit to even *find* the small, human-sized door on the side.

I poked my head inside the door and frowned. There was nobody there. I took a step inside and looked around. It was a smallish room with eight black, metal folding chairs in two rows along the wall. A trash can and a water cooler stood in the corner but other than that it was empty.

Dammit. I knew I was running late but I'd thought auditions would still be going. Tiana had said five, hadn't she? Maybe they'd finished early—but that was never the case, not in my experience with auditions. Granted, I hadn't actually had to audition for anything in years—I was one of those obnoxious kids who just started getting handed roles by the time I turned 16—but still, I could remember what it was like.

There were usually 60 guys for every three-line speaking role available. Why hadn't more people showed up? Sure, Violet Lynch wasn't a *huge* name yet, but if you paid attention to film at all, you should know she was someone you wanted to work with.

There was another door on the far wall. Crossing the room, I opened it to find a giant, well, garage, I guessed, with paint spatters all over the floor. There was a long table against one wall, more folding chairs, and a video camera on a tripod next to the table. But no people. What the hell?

"Uh, hello? Is anyone here?" I called out as I walked into the center of the room.

No response, but I heard something—or rather, the lack of something. A dull murmur I'd almost missed under the hum of a generator somewhere had stopped suddenly, and I realized it was the sound of a conversation that had just paused. And that's when I noticed that one corner of the garage wasn't just lined with bookshelves—they were blocking off a small alcove.

I crossed the rest of the room quickly. Somebody had to still be here—they wouldn't leave that camera just lying around —and the quickest way to figure out if auditions were still running was to pop my head in and ask. Preparing my most self-deprecating smile and hoping I wasn't about to interrupt Russian mobsters torturing someone, I peeked around the folding screen blocking off the little alcove.

"Hi! Are you guys still holding auditions for *Foresight*?" I asked, speaking before I'd even registered who I was talking to.

My eyes swept the group of people clustered in front of me. Violet Lynch was there—I recognized her from some interviews I'd seen—plus three guys I didn't know, one of them shirtless, with dark brown hair and blue eyes, really working the ruggedly handsome thing, and a third person in the corner with some really impressive cat-eye eyeliner.

"Sorry, I didn't mean to interrupt," I went on, keeping my voice cheerful and light. "But I knew I was running late and I—"

I stopped, my brain finally catching up with my mouth, and swiveled my head back to Shirtless Guy. Because he wasn't just shirtless. He was also pantsless. And his massive cock was just hanging out there for all to see.

Jesus, what the hell had I just walked in on?

3

GRAY

"Tyler Lang? What the hell are you doing here?"

It was like Violet's voice made time start moving again and as the kid peeking around the screen frowned, I got my arms working again and pulled my jeans the rest of the way up.

The kid was clearly trying not to stare but was just as clearly failing. Not that I could blame him. You try talking to a room full of people wearing clothes and one naked guy and see where your eyes are drawn.

"Uh, sorry." The kid smiled, a little lopsided this time, and his cheeks flushed. "Sorry, I, uh—I replied to the email with my headshot and stuff on the train on the way over here but I know it was kind of late. Are you uh—are you guys still seeing people?"

Violet blinked and cocked her head to the side, clearly confused. After a moment, she seemed to make her mind up about something and nodded.

"We can be. Don't worry about the email—I haven't checked my phone in a while and honestly, I'm not sure I would have believed you even if I had seen it."

"Oh." The kid looked crestfallen. "Um, okay. I mean, if you don't want to—"

"No, no," she interrupted. "I didn't mean it like that." She snorted. "I just meant, you know. Tyler fucking Lang? Auditioning for *Foresight*? It's not something I would have predicted."

"Right," Tyler said slowly. "Yeah, I know it's not—well, I just thought—"

"Really, Tyler, it's great that you're here," Violet said firmly. "Why don't you come out with me and I can get you the sides—you won't have seen them yet—and then when you're ready, we can get started."

She ushered him out of the office and into the main room. I turned to stare at the others in confusion. Danny's eyes were wide and Andrew had a hand clapped over his mouth. Dave was trying, and failing, to suppress giggles, biting down on his own wrist.

"Jesus," Andrew said. "I definitely didn't expect *that* to happen."

"Tyler motherfucking Lang," Dave said softly. "Auditioning for our movie? Am I dead? Seriously, somebody tell me. In what universe does this fucking happen?"

"Should I... know who he is?" I asked.

"You don't know who Tyler Lang is?" Dave said, his jaw dropping.

"Um. No. From your reaction, I'm gathering I'm in the minority. He's famous?"

"Yeah." Dave laughed. "That's putting it mildly."

"Tyler Lang," Andrew said patiently, "is *very* famous. First for being in, what was it called, like *Criss-Cross Applesauce* or something. This *Mickey Mouse Club* knock-off whose production values were as low as its popularity was high. Which is to say, *incredibly*. In both instances."

"Yeah, and then he was on *Shoestring Miracles*?" Dave said, frowning at my blank look. "Really? Nothing? God, that show was on forever. I mean, it was terrible, but Tyler Lang was like, the wet dream of every teenage girl—and boy—in America for a while. God, never knew he was into guys though. Always got the impression he was straight. Just goes to show, I guess. But still, I never thought he'd—I mean, you knew things had to be rough for him, but I didn't think—"

But Violet popped her head back in before Dave could finish.

"Gray, can I borrow you for a minute?" she asked. "If you don't mind, I'd love for you to read with Tyler once he's ready, instead of making him do it on his own first. Might as well kill two birds with one stone."

"Yeah, sure," I said, following her out into the main room. I tapped her wrist and stopped her, though, before we crossed over to where Tyler was sitting, pouring over the lines she'd handed him. "Quick question."

"What's up?"

"Just—I kind of got the impression that all the other guys

who read today were all kind of new? Like this would be their first major role?"

"Yeah, more or less," Violet said, looking up like she was flipping through a mental roster. "A couple of them have a little film experience, but for the most part it's playing corpses on cop shows and a lot of off-off-Broadway theater."

"Right. So. I mean." I swallowed. "Dave and Andrew made it sound like this guy, Tyler, actually knows what he's doing. Like, he's really experienced and stuff?"

Violet nodded. "Yeah, you could say that."

"So what's he doing here, then?"

Violet pursed her lips. "You really have no idea who he is?"

"None. I'm apparently the only person in the world who doesn't, though?"

"To be fair, you've had other things on your mind. Recently, at least." She sighed. "Well, I'll let him tell you the details if he wants, but suffice it to say, Tyler took some time off for a while." She shrugged. "Frankly, I have no idea why he'd want to do this movie, but I'm not dumb enough to tell him we're not interested without even seeing what he can do."

"Is he good?" I winced at the sharp look Violet gave me and hastened to explain. "Not that I'm judging. I meant it more like, am I about to look like a complete idiot acting against someone who actually makes a successful living at this?"

Violet smiled. "To be honest, I'm not really sure how good he is. The two shows he was on didn't really ask for a lot beyond charm and cute factor, which he had in spades, and the movies he did after required even less. But I've got a hunch he can do more than what he was ever able to show."

"Dammit." I sighed. "Well, pretending I didn't suck at this was nice while it lasted. Though I guess I already accidentally sexually harassed him, so it's not like it can really get worse."

"Gray, you're worrying too much." Violet put her hand on my shoulder and gave it a squeeze. "I promise, you're a natural. Besides, like you said. We're making fancy porn. If Tyler's here, he knows what he's getting into. And if he gets the part, he'd better get used to seeing your dick."

With a reassuring pat on the back, she walked over to the camera. I looked at Tyler with misgiving. Regardless of what Violet had said, I felt like a complete ass. Maybe I could at least apologize before I had to read with him?

I walked over to Tyler and stood a couple of feet from him, waiting for him to look up. His eyes darted back and forth across the page in front of him and his lips moved silently as he read. Eventually I realized he was so engrossed he wasn't going to notice me on his own, so I cleared my throat.

Tyler looked up with a smile. "Oh, hey. Sorry, I didn't see you." He glanced down at the script and then back up at me. "This is *really good* writing."

I smiled back, trying to sort through both a flush of pleasure that he recognized the strength of Danny's screenplay and fear that that indicated he knew what he was doing.

"Yeah, it is," I said with a smile, finally. "The screenwriter, Danny, was the one in the office with the laptop and I've been trying to stop myself from fawning all afternoon."

"No shit." Tyler's eyes widened. "Well, she's got another fanboy in me."

"They," I said quickly. "They use they/them pronouns."

"Oh, sweet," Tyler said. "Well, they've got another fanboy then. God, it's been a while since I've read anything this good."

"Listen," I said slowly, still not quite sure how to phrase my apology. *Sorry for assaulting your eyes with my penis?* "I, uh, wanted to apologize for, well, back there—"

"What? Oh." Tyler waved a hand dismissively. "Don't even worry about it. Honestly, I've seen weirder things."

"I mean, I know that maybe it's like, kind of expected, in a way," I said, still feeling like I hadn't quite conveyed how awkward I felt for putting him in that position. "Like, given —all of this." I waved my hand around the garage like an idiot, as though that gesture conveyed *'the fact that you're reading for a role where I fuck you.'* "But I didn't want to make you uncomfortable."

"What, because it's gay?" Tyler said, his brow furrowing in confusion. "I mean, I guess. Really though, don't stress about it. A movie's a movie. Art's art. Telling a good story— that's all that matters, in the end. Reaching people you know?"

"Right," I said slowly, nodding along like I had any idea what he was talking about. I wasn't even sure I could parse it. But at least he didn't seem upset by it. I stuck out my hand. "I'm Gray, by the way. I guess I'm, um, gonna be Wyatt in this. Assuming they don't change their minds after they see you act and realize how terrible I am in comparison."

"I'm sure you're better than you think," he said with a grin. "And I'm Tyler."

He reached out and took my hand, and if I hadn't known better, I'd have said a shiver went through me when we touched. But that was ridiculous. I was probably still just embarrassed about the way we'd met.

So sue me—the kid was cute. Even if our relationship was strictly professional—even if it he didn't get the part and I never saw him again—I'd have to be dead to not at least be a little aware of how attractive he was.

"You feeling ready, Tyler?" Violet called out, and both Tyler and I looked over our shoulders to see her standing at the camera. Danny, Andrew, and Dave had joined her by the back table and they were all looking at us expectantly.

"Yeah, sure," Tyler said, standing up.

"Any questions before we get started?" Violet flashed him a grin. "I know it's not exactly your typical film, especially compared to the work you've done but—"

"Nah, I'm good," Tyler said, frowning like he didn't understand what she meant. He tossed the script down on the chair and started walking to the center of the room.

"You can hold onto that," Violet said. "You just got it five minutes ago, we don't expect you to have it memorized."

"Yeah," I put in, grabbing my own packet of papers from the table. "I've been reading this all afternoon and I still don't have it down."

"It's okay. I got it," Tyler said.

I wondered if he was trying to show off. Violet said he hadn't worked in a while. Maybe he felt like he had something to prove?

In fact, the more I looked at his stance, the surer I grew that Tyler was nervous, underneath the confidence he was trying to project. You can't spend years in porn without developing a sense for when someone was trying to cover up their nerves. Not if you were any good at your job, anyway.

I had the strangest urge to reach out and tell Tyler it was okay, he didn't need to prove anything. But I had no idea where that was coming from. Maybe it was just misplaced guilt of accidentally exposing myself 15 minutes ago.

Whatever. If the kid wanted to risk fucking up his audition, that wasn't really any of my business.

Tyler walked to the center of the room and I followed him, expecting him to turn around when he stopped moving. But he didn't, he just sort of stood there, facing away from me and looking down at his shoes. I frowned, and looked over my shoulder back at Violet.

She was standing by the camera, Dave and Andrew by her side. Danny was sitting down a little ways off, but actually looking up from their laptop for once. Violet smiled at my confusion.

"You good to go, Tyler?" she called out.

"Yep!"

Tyler didn't turn around and Violet just shrugged.

"Alright. Action."

I glanced back at Tyler, waiting for him to move or do something for a few seconds before remembering that actually, I was the one who started this scene. Or rather, Wyatt was. I glanced down at the script in my hands and cleared my throat.

"Dylan? Dylan, what's wrong? Will you at least talk to me?"

Tyler turned, finally, and all the brash confidence, the jangly, pushed down nerves I'd sensed just moments ago, was gone. In its place was anger.

"What's wrong? What's *wrong*?"

Tyler took a step towards me and before I knew what I was doing, I took one back. None of the other guys who'd read this scene with me had done that. None of them had looked like they couldn't decide if they wanted to kiss me or punch me.

"What's wrong is everything. What's wrong is that you're just standing there, looking at me, looking so goddamned perfect and gorgeous and fucking *concerned*, and you have no clue, do you? You don't even see it, what you do to me. The way you're ripping me apart. The way I can't stop thinking about you and I can't even do anything about it, because you won't let me. It's not fair. It's not fucking fair."

He took another step towards me, then another, but I couldn't move back this time. His eyes were holding me in place, the rings of brown and green and gold burning like agates.

"I love you, and that's not fair, and you don't want me to tell you, and that's not fair, and I know you're probably disgusted right now, wishing you could just get out of this room, wishing you'd never asked, and you're never gonna talk to me again because I put you in this position after you asked me not to, and that's not fucking fair for either of us. Everything's so fucking fucked up."

Tyler was only inches away from me when he finished speaking, so close I could feel his breath on my neck as he glared up at me. Despite the fact that I was taller and probably had 25 pounds on him, my heart was pounding in my chest as I looked down into his eyes.

I wanted to turn, to break eye contact, to tear myself away. And at the same time, I wanted to wrap my arms around him, to comfort him, to tell him that somehow, I'd make it all okay again.

"Cut!" Violet yelled.

Tyler took a step back, rolling his shoulders out and smiling as he looked over at Violet. I exhaled, and it was only then that I realized I'd been holding my breath.

Jesus, what the hell had just happened? I could feel sweat breaking out on my brow, the kind of cold sweat of relief that comes right after a danger has passed. I didn't know quite what I'd expected from Tyler, but it hadn't been... that.

So much for thinking he was just trying to impress you.

The kid hadn't just memorized the script, he'd become Dylan so much that I'd forgotten who he really was, forgotten who *I* really was for a minute. Maybe that hadn't been nervous energy I'd detected before. Or maybe *that* had been part of the performance too.

None of the other guys I'd seen do that scene had taken the monolog in that direction. None of them had found the anger underlying the words, an emotion that was clear as day now, but that I hadn't seen earlier. And none of them had had that magnetism, that way of casting some kind of spell on me with their eyes.

Christ. Tyler was rolling his neck in a slow circle like he was stretching out his muscles and I took advantage of the fact that he *wasn't* looking at me for once to glance over at Violet and the others. Vi was smiling widely, Dave and Andrew were whispering to each other, and Danny's eyes were wide as they rested their chin in their hand, a small smile playing at the corners of their lips.

I caught Danny's eyes briefly, shaking my head in wondering disbelief, and Danny looked right back at me with the same expression. At least I wasn't the only one who was flabbergasted.

"Ready for scene two?" Violet asked when she was done repositioning the camera.

I glanced over at Tyler and he gave me a broad grin.

"I am if you are," he said with an easy smile that I couldn't help returning. God, this kid was giving me whiplash. How could he flip back and forth through emotional ranges so quickly?

"Yeah," I said, hoping I seemed anywhere near as confident as he did. "Yeah, sure."

"We're good, Violet," Tyler called out, and then turned away from me again.

I frowned, trying to make sense of things. This scene was supposed to be set in the library of the school, with Dylan and Wyatt looking out a window. So why was he—

"Why do they bother doing that?" Tyler asked, gesturing out

at the air in front of him. "More leaves are just going to fall tomorrow."

I blinked. The other guys I'd read this scene with had all looked at me when they'd said that line. But if Tyler could look out an imaginary window, I damn well could too. I took a step forward, bringing myself even with him, and I swear I saw him shiver.

"What would Lawrence Pennington Prep be without its pristine lawns?" I said, glancing out the 'window' and then down at the script.

"Why do we need a fucking lawn anyway? It's a losing battle with nature," Tyler said, looking up at me this time.

I swallowed. He was doing that thing with his eyes again, and suddenly it was all I could do to remember to breathe. I'd always had a good sense of smell—which wasn't necessarily a good thing when your job involved as much body odor as mine had—but all I picked up from Tyler was something lemony, clean and bright, and underneath that, just skin.

Tyler looked up at me and I realized I still hadn't responded. God, I couldn't remember my lines and I'd just looked down at them. What the fuck was happening to my brain?

"Gives them a sense of control in a universe inclined to entropy." I cleared my throat after I forced the words out, hoping I'd gotten them right. "Masters of their fate, captains of their soul and all that."

"You teaching English now, in addition to Calc?" Tyler asked with a wry smile. "You're a little out of date, if so. We read *Invictus* last year."

I risked a glance down at the script. "Right, they switched that, didn't they?" I tried for a nonchalant grin. "I think we did it senior year when I was here."

Tyler laughed and rolled his eyes, then turned away. Glancing out the window again. His gaze was so focused I could almost see a window hanging in mid-air, sweeping lawns and broad trees with fall foliage on the other side. And I couldn't stop myself from heaving a sigh of relief once his eyes were off of me.

I took a step back, shaking my head slightly to clear it. I hadn't had this much trouble with any of the other guys, pausing and freezing and panicking about my lines. But something about Tyler made me forget this was a scene, made me forget that we were reading lines, that I could look down any moment if I needed to check. It was unsettling.

"I always forget you went here, too," Tyler said quietly. Still not looking at me, still staring out the window, and yet I froze.

"I can't believe you came back," he continued, and his voice dropped so low it was almost like he wasn't talking to me anymore. Maybe he wasn't. "I fucking hate it here. Can't wait to get out." Tyler's fists tightened around the window frame —and how he got me to see that so clearly, I couldn't have explained. "I hate everything, sometimes."

His shoulders slumped, and suddenly, the man I was looking at changed. This wasn't Tyler, the confident actor, or even Tyler the nervous actor. Suddenly, I was looking at a scared kid—a boy who'd been trying so hard to act like he didn't care, he'd forgotten what it felt like to let himself be vulnerable.

"Ty-Dylan," I said, correcting myself at the last minute.

Jesus. He was acting. He didn't need me to wrap my arms around him, to tell him everything would be okay. So why the hell did I want to?

Tyler spun and looked at me, his eyes burning with intensity. "What? Dylan *what?*"

"It's not—" I paused, cleared my throat again. Dammit, I knew this line and I still couldn't get it out without stammering. "It's not always going to be like this."

Tyler rolled his eyes and God did it make him look young. It should have made him less attractive, somehow. But it didn't.

"Don't give me that *'it gets better'* crap," he said, his mouth twisting in disdain. "If it gets so much better, why the hell aren't you out?"

I remembered this scene from the book. Wyatt was filled with self-loathing, completely convinced he was a horrible person—and equally convinced he could never let Dylan know, never let Dylan really see him.

If I were a better actor, I probably could have gotten myself to feel that too, gotten myself into Wyatt's head. But Tyler had me so confused that it was all I could do to meet his gaze, to look back without flinching, before I realized that fuck, I was doing it again, I'd paused too long and I had to look down to remember my line.

"It's complicated, I said, snapping my gaze back up to him. "But that has more to do with me than anything else."

"What's that supposed to mean?"

"It means you shouldn't look at me as a role model."

"And yet I should listen to what you say?" Tyler snorted.

"You should listen because I—" I started, taking a step towards him before I froze.

That wasn't my line at all. What the hell was I thinking? In a flash, I saw myself in front of him, squaring my chest and grabbing him by the shoulders. Trying to get him to believe me.

'You should listen to me because I don't want you to make the same mistakes I did,' was what I'd been about to say. What the fuck?

I looked down, found my line, and forced out a nervous laugh. "Fair point," I said weakly. "Fair point."

Tyler frowned, and for a second I worried that my accidental improvisation had thrown him. But then his face cleared and he arched an eyebrow.

"You never talk about yourself, you know?" Tyler said. "Other teachers do. Something Principal Shelton encourages. Because we're all a family here, apparently. So how come I don't know anything about you?"

I glanced down. "Not much to say, really. I'm not that interesting a person."

"Are you from around here?"

"No." I waited for Tyler to speak again, before realizing that even while *staring at the fucking script,* I'd fucked up my line. "Mississippi," I added belatedly.

"Is your family still there?"

I nodded. "My dad and stepmom."

"Do you miss them?"

"We're... not close."

Tyler's brow furrowed in concentration, like I was an equation he was trying to solve. Fuck, I probably was. He was probably wondering how someone as fucking shitty at acting as I was had gotten this job.

"Anyone up here with you?" Tyler asked. He glanced down at my hands. "No wedding ring. Got a girlfriend?"

"Dylan—"

"Boyfriend?"

"Do other teachers share this kind of stuff with you guys?" I asked drily, proud of myself for actually getting that line right without looking. I quirked an eyebrow. "Really?"

Tyler shrugged and blushed. God, for an on-demand blush, it was disturbingly real looking. And fucking adorable, too. Which I should *not* have been noticing right then.

My job was to read my lines, not wonder what it would feel like to run the pad of my thumb along his cheekbone and what kinds of sounds he'd make if I worried the skin on his neck, right where it disappeared into the collar of his polo shirt.

Fuck, what was he doing to me?

"The married ones do," Tyler said with a lopsided grin. "We literally can't get Señora Gonzalez to stop talking about '*querido* Gregory' and his rose garden once she gets started."

I checked my lines and snorted. "You guys lead Cathy down that path on purpose and you know it."

"Do not."

"Do too. You think you're the first group of students to figure out that trick to get out of learning the subjunctive? It's a time honored tradition."

"So why are you here?" Tyler said suddenly, catching me off guard with the quick transition.

"What?" It came out automatically—and happened to actually be my line as well.

"Why'd you come back?" Tyler said. "I mean, you're a doctor, right, even if you don't make us call you that. Mr. Rupp says you got your PhD from fuckin' MIT. What the hell are you doing teaching at a place like this?"

"That's... more than I'm willing to share," I said, glancing down again.

"See," Tyler said, and I looked up in time to catch a sad smile. "Like I said. You're a mystery."

"You already know more about me than I'm comfortable with."

I said it quickly, too quickly. I should have paused longer, given it more of a beat, I was sure. God, even when I knew my lines, I messed them up. But Tyler didn't blink. He just smiled slowly, then took a step towards me.

Fuck, that wasn't in the script.

"Yeah? What do I know?"

"Dylan—"

"You keep saying that." The smile on his face broadened and my stomach turned a somersault. "I'm beginning to think you just like saying my name." He took another step and I swallowed, hard. "Do you?"

"Dylan—"

His name was nothing but a whisper when it left my lips that time. I had no idea if that was my line. I couldn't do anything except stare at him.

He took a final step, brought his hands up, laid them on either side of my chest. Jesus, could he feel my heart beating? Could he tell how fast it was racing? I wanted to pull away, to look down, to reorient myself to the script. But I didn't.

Tyler pushed up onto his tiptoes, bringing his face even with mine. I wrenched my eyes away from his. A herculean effort that came to nothing, because they landed on his lips instead of the script and oh God, his lips. They were pink, parted slightly, and his tongue darted out nervously to swipe at them.

Tyler leaned in. Oh fuck. Oh fucking fuck, I needed to—I had to—

At the last second, Tyler swerved, bringing his lips to my ear instead of my mouth. His voice was like silk sliding over sandstone, soft and breathy. I could feel the heat of his body as he whispered.

"It's okay, you know. If you do. You can like anything about me, if you want."

I shivered, and closed my eyes for a moment to steady myself.

"Cut!"

Tyler stepped back, his hands leaving behind patches of warmth where they'd pressed to my chest. I opened my eyes to see him rolling his shoulders again. My head swam.

I felt like I was surfacing from something—a dream, a fucking two-week stay in the depths of the Mariana Trench. I glanced around the room—Andrew and Dave were whispering again and Vi was beaming as she showed something to Danny on the camera. Playing back part of the scene, maybe.

They all looked happy, but none of them seemed to have noticed the tectonic upheaval I'd felt. I looked back at Tyler and he grinned up at me.

"That was really good," he said, his eyes bright and excited. "Fingers crossed they liked it."

It would have been impossible for them not to like it. Christ, but Tyler could act. I still felt a little wobbly, recovering from whatever the hell it was that he did to warp gravity and tilt the earth so you were sliding towards him.

It might have helped if he were hideous looking—but sadly, it was quite the opposite. Which only made me feel skeevy, in addition to off-balance. Just because the movie was about a teacher-student relationship didn't mean I needed to go and be a gross old man in real life.

I wondered how old Tyler actually was—and then mentally kicked myself for wondering. The guy might become my co-worker, he didn't need me leering at him. Besides, a kid that good looking had to have a boyfriend—that, or a revolving door of guys hopping into his bed each night.

"Tyler, can you hang out for a few minutes?" Violet asked, looking up from her conversation with Danny. "We just need to have a quick chat and then we can get back to you."

"Sure," Tyler said. He flashed me a wide-eyed grin as Violet shepherded the rest of us back into the office and I couldn't help returning it.

"So," Violet said once we were all huddled together. "Thoughts?"

"We'd be stupid *not* to hire him, right?" Dave said immediately. "He was *so good.*"

Andrew nodded vehemently. "Seriously. I have no idea why he *wants* to do the film, but he was like, a thousand times better than anyone else we saw. If he's willing to work for what we can give him, we'd better snatch him up while we can."

"Just think of the publicity," Dave said, his eyes going wide and a little bit dreamy. "Can you imagine how much buzz we'd get if we could announce that *Tyler Lang* was doing our movie?"

Violet looked at Danny and me. "What'd you two think?"

"He was amazing," Danny said simply.

"Gray? What about you?"

"I—yeah. I mean, it's your movie, whatever you guys decide. But he's—yeah." I shook my head and laughed weakly. "Literally the only reason I can think of to not hire him is that it's gonna be real apparent, real quick that he can act circles around me."

"No way." Violet shook her head. "You were great with him."

"Absolutely," Dave agreed. "And besides, we're gonna be shooting out in Bumblefuck, New Jersey, so how much trouble can he really get up to?"

"Don't say it like that, babe," Andrew said with a laugh. "Makes it sound like a challenge."

∾

Tyler pretty much lost his mind when Violet told him he'd gotten the part.

"Holy shit, really? You're serious?" He was grinning from ear to ear.

"Yeah," Violet said, smiling right back at him. "You were fantastic, Tyler. There's no question in our minds that you're right for this part."

"Jesus." Tyler shook his head, his eyes still round as saucers. "Thank you. Just... thank you, so much. This is—this means —I swear, you will not regret this."

I had to stifle a laugh. I'd never seen anyone so excited to be cast in something—though, to be fair, my experience was all with roles that were a *tad* lower on the respectability scale. But Tyler's enthusiasm was infectious. He was practically bouncing up and down as Violet began walking him through paperwork, explaining the shooting schedule and logistics.

"It's just standard stuff, really," Violet said. "Payment's a little different, but other than that, it's the usual non-disclosure agreements and terms. We're gonna ask you guys not to post on social media or share anything about this til we've had a chance to—"

My phone buzzed and I stopped listening when I pulled it out and saw a text from Ethan.

ETHAN: *Hey what are you up to?*

Still riding the fumes of Tyler's good mood, I decided I might as well tell him now.

GRAY: *Actually, just finished auditioning for Violet's movie*

ETHAN: *Wait, really? Why?*

GRAY: *I don't know, wanted to, I guess. What's the harm, right?*

ETHAN: *But I thought you'd stopped all that*

It was such an innocuous sentence, but I could practically feel the judgement rolling out through the phone. Because it wasn't just *I thought you'd stopped*. It was *I thought you'd finally realized that I was right all along, that you never should have done that in the first place.* Still, I didn't like the feeling of being at odds with Ethan.

GRAY: *It's just the one movie. It's not a huge deal*

ETHAN: *Maybe. Maybe not*

What the fuck did he mean by that? But before I could figure it out, he'd changed the subject.

ETHAN: *They cast the other lead yet? Is he cute?*

And just like that, I was laughing and everything seemed okay again. I knew I shouldn't care what Ethan thought about my life—especially now—but it was hard not to fall prey to those residual feelings.

GRAY: *Don't be gross. But yes*

ETHAN: *I knew it!*

GRAY: Actually... maybe don't tell anyone this until it's public knowledge but the guy playing the other lead is I guess someone kinda famous?

ETHAN: Omg who?

GRAY: Tyler Lang?

ETHAN: WHAT? THE? FUCK?

ETHAN: Are you fucking serious?

ETHAN: No way

GRAY: Way?

ETHAN: Jfc I can't believe it. Tell me everything

ETHAN: No, better yet, come tell me more about it in person

ETHAN: My parents' friends are hosting this dinner thing in one of their offices in Midtown and I'm going to die if I have to spend one more minute here by myself. Come keep me company

I paused. Fuck. Ethan kept doing this to me and it kept fucking with my head. He'd invite me to do things with him —sometimes things that he wouldn't even do when we were dating like meeting his parents' friends—and sometimes I swore he was even still flirting with me. I knew I should say no, I knew I was just setting myself up for disappointment— and I kept saying yes.

This time, I was going to be strong.

GRAY: I'd love to but I should probably go check in with Micah at the bar

ETHAN: Come on, it'll be fun. We can make fun of all the snobby old assholes. It'll be like old times

ETHAN: Besides I need to hear more about Tyler Lang

ETHAN: Come on dude, I miss you

Dammit. Like kryptonite. It worked every time.

GRAY: Fine, send me the address

Tyler had already left by the time I put my phone back in my pocket. I felt a flash of disappointment, which didn't make any sense. The guy barely knew me—there was no reason he needed to say goodbye before taking off. He probably had *famous-people* things to go do, not that I had any idea what that involved.

I said goodbye to the others and walked outside to flag down a taxi. Just in time, too—it started to rain lightly as I got in the car, and it only got steadier as we drove. I gave the driver the address and then looked out the window, trying to think about anything other than how dumb meeting Ethan probably was, and how shitty I'd probably feel at the end of the night.

"Stop!" I said suddenly, startling the taxi driver. "Sorry, just for a second, I—"

I rolled down my window and called out to the figure I saw walking along the street.

"Hey! Tyler! You want a ride?"

Tyler, whose shoulders were hunched against the rain, looked over at me in confusion for a moment until his face cleared.

"Oh. Gray. Um, thanks," he said hesitatingly. "I'm okay though. Gonna take the subway."

"Where are you headed?"

"Midtown," Tyler said with a rueful smile. "And before you make fun of me, *I know*."

"I'm actually going to Midtown too. Get in, we can just split the fare. It'll be way faster."

Tyler frowned. "Thanks, but, really, I don't mind."

"The subway's blocks away," I said, my voice doubtful. "And it's raining."

As if to punctuate my words, thunder cracked overhead and the rain intensified. Tyler's face was still clouded and he was biting at his lip worriedly. And suddenly, I got that strange sensation again, that desire to pull him close, to protect him.

From what? The rain?

It was ridiculous. The kid could have a million reasons for not wanting to share a cab with me—not the least of which was the fact that no matter how well our reading had gone, I was still the guy who'd accidentally flashed him earlier.

I knew I should let it go. Not be the creepy guy who forced the issue. But something about his body language, the look in his eyes, said that it wasn't sharing the cab with me that he was worried about, but something else. Something bigger. And I was overcome with the urge to put his fears at ease.

"Honestly, you'd be doing me a favor," I said with a smile. "I'm about to do something I shouldn't and I could use a conversation to distract me from my impending stupidity."

Tyler barked a laugh and—finally—smiled. "Well I am kind

of an expert at stupid decisions, so I guess I could help you out."

I pushed the door open as he walked towards the car and tried not to breathe in the scent of him too deeply as he slid into the backseat next to me. We rode in silence for a while, Tyler staring down at his hands. I was beginning to wonder if this was a mistake, if Tyler actually *was* uncomfortable around me, when he looked up and flashed me a smile.

"You were really good in there."

"Seriously?" I blinked. "I was lost that whole time."

"Yeah, seriously. You were amazing." Tyler nodded emphatically. "The way you kept looking down, that nervousness? It was so good, so easy to play off of. You were just inhabiting the Wyatt character so perfectly.

That wasn't me inhabiting Wyatt, that was just me reacting to the black magic you were working on my brain.

But that didn't seem like quite the right thing to say, so I just nodded and said, "Thanks."

"No. Really." Tyler was staring at me earnestly now, evidently bothered that I was unconvinced of my own competence. "I can see why they cast you."

"I think that might have more to do with my other, uh, assets and experiences," I said with a snort. "But that's nice of you to say."

Tyler gave me a weird look and I cursed myself inwardly. Was that a weird thing to say? Had I gone back to making him uncomfortable? I began to talk to fill the silence.

"Anyway, whatever skills I might have are *nothing* compared to you," I said. "You're fucking phenomenal. Honestly, I have no idea why you'd want to be doing this movie when you could be doing like, actual, serious projects but you're gonna raise the quality level of this thing exponentially."

"This isn't a serious project?" Tyler said, giving me that confused look again.

"No, I didn't mean—I just meant, you know, it's not like, the *traditional* kind of movie you'd like, tell your mom about."

"Oh, you mean the financing?" Tyler shrugged. "Honestly, I think we're going to see more and more of this kind of crowd-funding, online distribution model in the future. You can make a decent quality film with an iPhone camera these days, so it's really only a matter of time before this becomes like, the main way we make movies."

"Right. Yeah. Definitely." I nodded as though that were the answer I'd expected. Clearly I didn't fool Tyler, though.

"Sorry." Tyler flushed. "This kind of shit is like, all I really know about. Sometimes I talk about it too much."

My phone buzzed again and I apologized to Tyler as I pulled it out, then rolled my eyes when I read the message.

ETHAN: Where are you I'm literally dying of boredom

GRAY: In a cab, there soon

ETHAN: I might actually perish

ETHAN: Hurry

I snorted and shoved my phone back in my pocket, shaking my head.

Tyler smiled at me slyly. "Your bad decision?"

"You could say that."

My phone started ringing, the sharp sound shattering the quiet of the car.

"Jesus, Ethan," I grumbled, pulling my phone out. But it wasn't Ethan, it was Micah. My eyes widened when I realized I'd forgotten to tell him I'd be late coming back to Maggie's.

"Hey," I said, already wincing a bit as I picked up.

"Hey yourself, Mr. Moviestar," Micah said with a laugh. "Weren't you supposed to text me and tell me if I could expect you for your shift tonight? Or are you so cool and famous now that you forgot you own a bar?"

"Sorry, no, I didn't—I know I said I'd text you, I just got busy."

"You'd better apologize," Micah said, "or once you're famous I'm gonna make so much money selling stories about you to the tabloids."

"What stories?"

"Oh who even knows. I'll make something good up." Micah laughed. "So, how was it? You get to make out with any cute 18 year olds?"

"Jesus, Micah, try not to be disgusting for one day, would it kill you?"

Christ, had Tyler heard that?

"Yes, it probably would," Micah said brightly. "Anyway, point is, can I expect you tonight?"

"Uh, not til late."

"Interesting. Why?"

Should have known that Micah would pounce on that.

"Just going out for dinner. I'll come by after."

"Who with? Your new costar?"

"No."

"Dammit. I was hoping for gossip."

"I hate to disappoint you."

"So then who—"

"Ethan. Just Ethan."

Micah made a noise somewhere between a sigh and a growl in the back of his throat but for once in his life, didn't say anything.

"What? You making plans to come find me and murder me?" I asked. If he was going to yell at me, I wished he'd just do it already.

"Murder you?" Micah said, all innocence. "Why on earth would I want to do that? I mean, you're clearly determined to commit emotional suicide yourself, you don't need my help."

"Micah—"

"No, by all means, go ahead. You want to get your heart broken—*again*? Be my guest."

"It's not like that."

"It is like that and you know it," Micah said. "Or have you forgotten that this is the guy who told you for years he wanted to get married and then dumped you when you proposed, right before Maggie died? Have you forgotten how fucking awful that felt?"

"No—no—it's not—" I sighed. "You're right. About all of that. But I—I think we've turned a corner. I think we might actually be able to be friends again. That's what I'm hoping anyway. I know the relationship ended but I don't think the friendship has to, too."

That sounded pathetic enough—Micah didn't need to know that I was actually hoping Ethan and I might be something more than friends again at some point. In the back of my mind, I wondered how insane Tyler thought I was from the one-sided conversation he was overhearing.

"Gray, honestly, I—I don't know what to tell you. I think this is a terrible idea but I can't stop you so... I'll lock up tonight if you're not back by the time we close. Just... don't do anything stupid, okay?"

"Your confidence in me is touching."

"I speak as I find, Gray, I speak as I find."

I winced after hanging up with Micah and glancing over at Tyler, who was doing his best to appear unobtrusive. Not very easy, considering we were crammed together in the back of a cab.

"Sorry about that," I said. "Probably kind of weird for you to overhear."

"Eh," Tyler said with a shrug and a smile. "If we're gonna be working together, I'm sure it'd come up eventually. Besides, you've probably heard worse about me."

Not for the first time, I wondered just what it was that everyone seemed to know about Tyler. But it didn't feel right to ask him outright what he meant by that, so I just smiled and cast around in my mind for a new topic of conversation.

"So who was that?" Tyler asked abruptly. "Ex-boyfriend? Current boyfriend? Jealous friend?"

"None of the above," I said with a snort. "Current friend who thinks my plans for the evening are really dumb."

"Didn't you already know they were really dumb?"

"Well, yeah. But he likes to remind me." I laughed lightly, and then decided to indulge in at least one tiny bit of curiosity. It wasn't too creepy, I decided, given what we were talking about already. "So you know some of my drama now. What about you? Got a boyfriend waiting at home for you?"

Tyler blinked, like he was surprised by the question. "Uh, no."

Dammit, okay, that probably had been too forward. Crap, had I embarrassed him? I couldn't imagine what he had to be embarrassed about—it's not like he couldn't get any guy he wanted, at least from what I could see.

"That's probably good," I said, trying to put him at ease. "Relationships are hard enough, before you add this kind of a job into the mix."

"Yeah," Tyler said. "Acting's hard on relationships, I guess."

I laughed. "In my experience, the *acting* part is the least objectionable bit. But sure."

"Oh." Comprehension dawned on Tyler's face. "You mean the whole kissing other people part?"

Kissing other people was one of the more euphemistic ways I'd heard it put, but fair enough.

"Right," I said, continuing with my earlier point. "Honestly, though, what being single really simplifies is the whole testing awkwardness. I mean, we'll be using condoms, of course, but still, testing is important—and the whole thing can raise all sorts of weird questions and feelings among couples. And it's not that your partner wouldn't have a right to be nervous about it. It's just—well, it's simpler to be single, in this business, in a lot of ways.

"What?" Tyler was looking at me like I'd stopped speaking English and had started spouting gibberish instead.

"It's really nothing to worry about," I said quickly. "I mean, I don't know if you've ever gotten tested before but it's something you do before any shoot. And it's super safe, quick, non-invasive. Completely standard in the industry and completely not a big deal."

"The industry?" Tyler repeated, his eyes wide.

Fuck, I was trying to make him less nervous but everything I said seemed to make it worse. Maybe it would just be better to address it head on?

"Sorry," I said slowly. "I get the feeling I'm making you uncomfortable and that's not my intention at all. I completely understand if you don't wanna talk about it. But, well—I did this for a long time—God, too long—so if there's ever anything you want to ask about how this works, you absolutely can. I'm guessing this is your first time doing any work of the *adult* variety, right?"

"Adult," Tyler said slowly, like he was hearing the word for the first time and trying to decipher its meaning. His brow furrowed—and suddenly, it hit me.

Fuck. No wonder this conversation had been so awkward. A hundred little pieces fell into place in my mind. Oh God. This was *not good*. But impossible as it seemed, it was the only thing that made sense.

"Tyler," I said as gently as I could. "You do realize that *Foresight* is porn, right?"

4

TYLER

I blinked.

A million things clicked all at once, and suddenly everything was much less confusing... and also much more so. At the same time.

Motherfucking fucker.

"Uh yeah. Totally." I smiled brightly, hoping that Gray interpreted any confusion on my face as confusion over why he would even bother to ask me because *of course I knew*, because *who the fuck could manage to audition for a porn without even realizing it?*

Me, that's who. Goddammit, in the *Encyclopedia of Ridiculous Choices Made By Tyler Lang*, this deserved some kind of special entry, right up front. Or maybe at the very end, the *piece de resistance* of my stupidity. All the other dumb shit I'd done in my life was reduced to so many trays of passed appetizers, before *this*, the main course, my centerpiece of idiocy. The metaphorical pig with an apple in its mouth.

Except—*cock* in its mouth. Because let's not forget what we're talking about here.

That was why I'd walked in on Gray naked. That was what Gray was referring to when he'd mentioned his 'other assets.' That was why he wanted to know if I had a jealous boyfriend. Because I'd auditioned for a fucking porno.

Jesus, not just auditioned. *Gotten the part.*

Gray frowned slightly and then gave me a kind look. "It's okay, Tyler. You don't—you don't have to pretend."

"No, I mean, I got the email about the audition," I said, hating the defensiveness in my tone but unable to hide it. Christ, I could have used some of that 'fucking phenomenal' acting talent Gray thought I had right about now.

"Did you... read the email?" Gray asked, his tone gentle.

I glared at him—and then sighed. "I might have been a little distracted at the time. I just—I thought—I mean, with Violet attached to the project? And then, like, the script was so good?"

I sounded like an idiot. What kind of person could miss information like that in the email? It was because Gray was being so kind, I decided. It was throwing me off, making me admit to things I didn't even feel comfortable admitting to myself.

But of course, instead of saying something sarcastic or making fun of me, Gray just laughed lightly.

"Honestly, that's a fair point. I've never seen a script like that in porn and I've been doing that for, well, long enough to know how uncommon it is."

"It's fucking uncommon in regular projects too," I said force-fully. Dammit, it had to be some kind of cosmic joke the universe was playing on me, dangling a project with writing this good in front of me, only to make it impossible to do it.

I mean, right? Because it was impossible to do. Or insane, at least.

I couldn't—or well, I wouldn't do it. I thought. Maybe. Prob-ably? Definitely. Maybe. Okay, maybe *'wouldn't'* wasn't exactly as watertight as I thought, but *'shouldn't'*—*'shouldn't'* was for sure correct.

I shouldn't do it. I knew that. It was crazy to even be consid-ering it. Completely crazy. I wasn't even considering it, not really. I was just... thinking through how colossally bad an idea it would be. And it would be *very*, very bad. Right?

Could you imagine the headlines? After I'd been arrested, they called the whole incident 'Suspender-gate', but it'd be *Sexpender-gate* now. *Out of Work and Out of Options—Tyler Lang Sinks Even Lower (Down Onto Some Guy's Cock* being the obvious unspoken coda).

No one would take me seriously after this. No one would work with me, my prospects would dry up completely. And if I thought my dad was pissed at me now, I didn't even want to contemplate how livid he'd be if I did this.

It was a stupid idea.

So why couldn't I stop thinking about it?

"Please don't feel bad about it at all," Gray said after a moment, and I looked up in surprise, only then realizing how long I'd been silent. "Seriously, it's a mistake anyone could have made. Just call and tell Violet that you've reconsidered. Something else came up. Another offer or something."

"That'd be a lot easier to believe if my current situation weren't quite as completely pathetic as it is," I said with a sharp laugh. "Which Violet—hell, anyone who hasn't been living under a rock—knows all about. And if she doesn't, she's undoubtedly calling people tonight to check up on me and finding out." I gave Gray a bitter smile. "Hey, maybe we'll get lucky and she'll fire me herself, make the decision for me."

"I don't—I mean, why, um, why would she fire you?" Gray asked, tilting his head to the side. I must have looked confused because he winced and gestured with his hands. "Rock. Me. I've been living under it, I guess."

"Wait, you don't—" my brow furrowed and now I knew I looked confused. Not just confused. Flabbergasted. "You don't know about—wait, okay, so this is going to sound super horrible but do you like, know who I am?"

Gray laughed, warm and easy, like the sound of sundrenched waves crashing up on shore. "Tyler, until an hour ago, I had no idea you existed."

"Oh my God." My eyes widened. "Oh my God? I... holy shit. You have no idea who I am."

"None whatsoever."

"That's—that's *amazing*." My face split into a wide grin. I couldn't help it. Gray didn't know—God, he didn't know *anything*. Anything about my past, my childhood, the ass I'd made of myself over the past few years. And then my face fell. "But you—I mean, it's fine if you want to Google it or something. Whatever."

I trailed off, having completely lost my train of thought. Because just as quickly as I'd gotten excited about finally meeting someone who had no reason to think anything about me, positive or negative, except what I showed him from here on out, I realized how stupid that was. Gray could look me up in a second. And probably would.

Besides which, none of that would even matter if I wasn't going to see Gray ever again after I got out of this taxi. Which I probably wouldn't. Not unless I was going to do this stupid movie. Which I wasn't.

"Tyler." Gray's voice was soft but firm and it pulled my eyes up to him inexorably. "I won't look you up if you don't want me to."

"It's fine," I said quickly. "It's not a big deal, honestly. My point was just that—well, I don't even know what my point was. I guess it doesn't matter, if I'm not doing the film."

"I guess, yeah," Gray said slowly.

So why the hell couldn't I stop thinking about it? Not just the movie, but what Gray thought about me. Something about his eyes, the way they were focused on me, but open. Not judging, not assuming anything. They were the most honest eyes I'd ever seen. And I might never see them again.

Maybe I could do the movie. Was that completely insane? It was. It had to be. So why couldn't I stop picturing his eyes on me, trapping my gaze as he pulled me to him. There'd been this energy about him in the audition today, this kind of half nervous, half wild pulse, and I could almost feel an echo of it now.

It had to be my imagination. The same imagination that couldn't stop picturing Gray pushing me up against a wall and thrusting against me, pinning me down on a mattress and letting his hands roam across my body, his lips hot and wet on my skin. Jesus, I'd barely done anything with anyone —maybe that was the problem—and yet I couldn't stop wondering what Gray would look like when he was hard. I'd already seen how big he was. It hadn't been a long glance, but enough to know that hard, he'd be...

Fuck, I could not really be considering this, could I?

I realized I was blushing and I cleared my throat abruptly, casting around for something to say.

"Did I totally misunderstand what kind of movies Violet makes?" I asked. "Her last movie, *Semafore*—that wasn't anything like—"

"Yeah, no," Gray said with a smile. "Vi told me that she just knew Danny already and when they asked her if she'd be interested in the project, she loved the book so much that she said yes."

"And she was willing to take on—I mean, it's kind of different, right? Why would she be willing to take a risk on something like this?"

Gray shrugged. "You'd have to ask her. But I'd imagine it's because she really believes that this is going to be something good, something special." He laughed lightly. "And she's never made a secret out of the fact that she got her start working in porn. That's how she and I know each other, actually. She was an assistant at a studio I worked for years ago."

"Wow." I paused. "Is that why you're doing this, then? Because you know her? Or—"

"That," Gray said, nodding, "that, for sure. That's how I found out about it. But I wasn't going to say yes until Vi asked me to just read the book and, well, the rest is history. You saw the sides today—Danny's an amazing writer. So I guess I figured if I was going to come out of retirement for anything..."

"Out of retirement?"

"Well, I haven't done anything in—" he frowned and cocked his head at me. "Do you really not watch porn at all?"

I flushed. I didn't, actually. But explaining why only made me sound even weirder than I probably already seemed to Gray.

The thing was, my dawning realization that I was maybe kinda sorta probably attracted to guys happened in lockstep with the realization that my dad would *not* be pleased with that development. Add to that the fact that he basically controlled every minute of my life til I was 18 and I was too scared to even visit porn sites online. I wouldn't have put it past him to be monitoring that somehow.

And even after my dad moved out, he still kind of took care of everything. Every time I fucked up somehow, he was there to pick up the pieces. But that also meant that his potential disapproval cast a long shadow. It probably sounds nuts to say that I once flew to Bali for a month just to get away from him, but was still too scared to look at porn but, hey, since when have my decisions ever made any sense?

"Not much," I said, finally, in answer to Gray's question. "I guess I've never really been all that into it?" I winced when I heard my own words. Did that sound judgey? "I mean, not that there's anything wrong with it. I totally respect people's choices to watch it or make it or whatever, I just—"

"Tyler, Tyler, it's fine. Don't worry about it," Gray said, chuckling. He shook his head as he smiled. "Believe me, I've experienced *plenty* of people who *don't* respect my choices. I know what that looks like, and what it doesn't."

I wasn't sure what to say to that, so I just looked down at my lap. God, this was a weird conversation. To be having anywhere, but especially in the back of a taxi. The driver was talking away into his bluetooth headset and not paying the slightest bit of attention, but still.

"It's okay to change your mind, you know," Gray said after a moment. "You didn't know what you were saying yes to."

"Yeah but—" I bit my lip. Was I really arguing against him here? "I don't know, that seems kinda shitty. Filming starts in a week, right? Violet's probably already told all those other guys no. Backing out feels—"

"Tyler, you do know what this involves, right?" Gray broke in, frowning. "I mean, not to be crass, but there are going to be cameras zoomed in on your face, on your cock, your ass. And yeah, you get used to it after a while, but there's no way it's not going to feel invasive the first time you're being filmed while you're getting fucked."

"While I'm..." I couldn't finish the sentence—could barely even start it.

"Physically, sure, it's nothing you haven't done before," Gray said soothingly. "Well, unless you usually top. In the book, Dylan's definitely a bottom and I don't think they're changing that part. But it's one thing to have sex in the privacy of your own home and quite another to do it while a camera is filming every thrust."

My breath started to go funny, coming in shorter bursts as Gray spoke. He just assumed that I'd had sex with guys before—lots of it, from the sound of things—and he was tossing around those words the way someone else would talk about the price of a gallon of milk. It wasn't like I didn't know what he meant, but I'd somehow never thought about those words applying to me.

God, was I really thinking about doing this? Not just having sex with a guy for the first time *ever* but doing it on camera? Multiple times? And having tens of—maybe hundreds of thousands of people see it once the movie was distributed? Maybe more, if it did well? Was I really considering being *that guy* for the rest of my life? Having people always think that about me when they saw me?

I couldn't be considering that. Except—apparently I was.

"Can I ask you a question?" I said after a moment. The cab was getting closer to Luke's apartment and suddenly there were a million things I wanted to say, wanted to find out and ask all at once.

"Shoot."

"Do people... treat you differently? Because of what you've done?"

Gray gave me a sad smile. "I wish I could tell you they didn't. That this is the kind of thing that people are always respectful about, that people understand that it's just a job and it doesn't say anything about you as a person. That people won't judge you for it. But..."

"They do?" I finished, my chest constricting.

Gray's smile went lopsided. "I mean, not everyone. I guess you could even look at it as a good thing, in a way. You do something like this, you'll realize quickly who your real friends are. Who still cares about you, sees you as the same person. And who doesn't. And honestly, anyone who's going to treat you worse because of what you've done as a job... fuck 'em, right?"

"Right," I said slowly, his words still sinking in.

Gray gave me a concerned look and I flashed him a tight smile. I didn't want him to think he'd said something wrong. He hadn't. It was just...

He'd been talking about people potentially losing respect for me, judging me, for a project I'd done. For something work-related. But people were already judging me, had been for years, for shit that wasn't work-related at all. Just judging me for being me. And I couldn't blame them.

Gray said that something like this made you realize who your real friends were, but I'd already realized that—and discovered I didn't actually have many. He'd been trying to warn me, but all he'd really done was put a fine point on the fact that I'd already completely fucked up my life.

I didn't have friends. I didn't have anyone's respect. And it wasn't because of any jobs I'd taken. It was because of who I was, because of the choices I'd made. I deserved everything people thought about me.

At this point, the thought of people judging me for a project I was working on? That sounded like a fucking picnic. Like a breath of fresh air. Like a fun break from the constant stream of regular old judgment I was bathing in.

Tiana was the only person I knew from my life in LA who hadn't spurned me completely. Luke was the only person my age who I knew in New York at all, really, and he kind of had to talk to me, since I was his brother. If I weren't, I wasn't sure he'd want anything to do with me.

The only other person who treated me like a normal human being? Who hadn't already made up his mind about me? Who I felt like I could be myself in front of? Gray. And I'd only known him for an hour.

"I don't know what to tell you," Gray went on. "I know we don't really know each other, so I can't exactly give you advice. But this isn't a decision you should make lightly."

I snorted. "Trust me, it's not."

'Lightly' was not how I'd describe the thoughts swirling around my mind right now. But now Gray was giving me that concerned look again and I didn't know how to explain myself without telling him everything and then sounding really pathetic.

"I'm just not sure I'm really in a position to turn down a paycheck right now," I said with a grin, trying to lighten the mood.

Gray's expression went from gently concerned to downright worried. Fuck. So much for lightening the mood. *And* for not sounding pathetic.

"Sorry," I said, my grin slipping off my face. "That probably sounds really weird. And sad."

"Eh, I've been there," Gray said, his voice reassuring. "I just..." He shook his head. "God, I sound like such an old asshole right now, telling you not to make the same mistakes I did."

"Probably too late for that, honestly," I said with an abrupt laugh. "Pretty sure the mistakes I've made go way beyond what most people have done. But thanks. *Dad*."

Gray rolled his eyes. "You're welcome."

The taxi pulled to a stop and I looked up, realizing with surprise that we weren't just at a light, we were outside Luke's building. Shit, I'd thought I had more time. I started pulling out my wallet—even though I knew the only useful monetary items it contained were a Chipotle gift card and four dollars, cash—when I felt a hand on my arm.

"Don't worry about it," Gray said when I looked up on him. "I'll get it."

"But I—"

"Really," Gray said, giving my hand a squeeze before letting go. "I've got it."

I closed my eyes for a minute, letting a fresh wave of shame crash over me, before opening them and trying for a carefree laugh that really just sounded kind of sickly.

"I must seem really pathetic right now."

"Not pathetic." Gray shook his head. "Just—maybe a little lost."

"Yeah. Well. Can't really argue with that," I said flatly.

Gray pressed his lips together. "Tyler, I don't know what's happened in your life but I honestly can't imagine that this makes any sense as a next step. Unless—well, unless you want to do it."

I bit my lip and looked back at him.

"Do you?" Gray asked.

I didn't have a good answer for him. I didn't have *any* answer for him. I shouldn't do it. It was a crazy idea. A dumb one for lots of reasons. And yet.

"I'm not sure," I said, my voice barely above a whisper. "I—I need to think about it. Would you mind, um, not talking to Violet? Until I've had a chance to—well, I'm gonna sleep on it. And talk to her in the morning."

"My lips are sealed," Gray said.

"Thanks." I grabbed my bag and put my hand on the door handle. "Thanks for uh, talking to me about this all, too. I appreciate that."

"My pleasure." Gray flashed me a smile. "Just—whatever you decide—make sure you're honest with yourself. About what you want. I'm not saying you need to have like, pure and perfect reasons for the decisions you make. Just—make sure you know what your reasons are, you know?"

I knew he meant to be encouraging. So I smiled and thanked him and got out of the car, watched it drive off in the rain outside of Luke's building. And only after it turned the corner and was out of sight did I let go of the ragged breath I'd been holding inside me.

How the fuck did he do that? I'd known Gray for what, a millisecond, in the grand scheme of my life? He knew nothing about me. But it was like he could see inside me. And in the space of an hour, I'd gone from excited about getting a part to nervous about what that part actually entailed to feeling stripped bare by a complete stranger.

Being honest with myself about what I wanted, actually reflecting on why I made the choices I made—that had never been my strong suit. I'd never liked the things I found inside myself when I engaged in much introspection—the neediness, the gnawing certainty that I was alone, that I'd never be good enough.

At the group home, we'd had to do all sorts of therapy and self-work, and I'd realized that those fears, that low-grade sense of worthlessness, was the reason I'd acted out, the reason I'd fucked everything up so dramatically. But that didn't mean dwelling on that knowledge was pleasant.

Gray was right—I needed to be honest with myself, whatever I decided about *Foresight*. I grimaced. If I were being honest, I still thought doing the movie would be crazy. But I also couldn't help wondering what it would be like to get people to talk about my work for once, instead of about me. Couldn't help thinking about how nice it would be to lose myself in a character again, after the past year of being very much stuck in myself.

And I couldn't help thinking, as I watched the taillights of cars gleaming red as they passed in the rain, that if I said no, I'd never see Gray again—the first person I'd met in years who saw me. Not my history, not my baggage, but me.

It was stupid to think that meant anything. Stupid to believe he wasn't going to look me up the second he got home, stupid to think that even if I said yes to the movie, he'd ever actually want to get to know me. Just because he'd been kind in a cab ride didn't mean he wanted to be my friend.

But for a guy I'd only met a couple hours ago, I definitely didn't like the idea of giving him up.

When I got back into the apartment, Luke had pushed himself up into a sitting position, his back resting against the arm of the couch. He was watching C-SPAN, because of course he was, but he muted it as I walked into the living room.

"Hey," he said, quirking an eyebrow. "How'd the audition go?"

"It was—" I stopped, shaking my head, not even sure where to start. I dropped my bag on the floor and sank into the armchair opposite the sofa. "There were some complications. But I—wait, why are you laughing?"

"I'm not—I just—oh God, I can't—" Luke gave up trying to talk, gave up even pretending to suppress his laugh, and just let it out. I watched, completely confused, as his laugh grew from a stifled giggle into something full-blown, until he was wheezing, clutching at his sides.

"You finished?" I said acidly as he finally sat back against the couch and wiped tears from the corners of his eyes.

"God, I'm sorry," he said, his voice rich with mirth. "I just... the complications didn't involve them asking you to take off your pants, did they?"

"No they—wait." My eyes narrowed. "How did you..."

Suddenly, I remembered that as I'd been leaving the apartment earlier that day—which felt like a lifetime ago, to be honest—Luke had been trying to ask me something about the movie.

"Holy shit, did you know? You knew this was a fucking porno and you didn't *tell me*?"

"Okay, technically I didn't *know* it was porn," Luke said, still clearly on the edge of laughter.

"Well if you'd read the book—"

"I *haven't* read the book," Luke cut in. "I've just heard about it. This movie's like, a massive deal in the gayer parts of the internet. It's basically impossible to be on any kind of social media and *not* know about it. Besides, I tried to say something, but *somebody* was too busy running out the door like his hair was on fire to listen."

Well that was both embarrassing and accurate.

"Did you really not know?" Luke asked. "Tiana didn't tell you?"

"Tiana... Tiana sort of implied I should read the email she was forwarding to me carefully," I said slowly, remembering our conversation from earlier with a sigh. God, multiple people had tried to tell me but I hadn't listened. "And, of course, I didn't."

"Eh, don't worry too much about it," Luke said with a smile.

"Everyone needs a horrible audition story, right? Now you've got a perfect one for when you're hobnobbing at your fancy celebrity cocktail parties, or whatever it is famous people do. *'By the way, Leonardo, have I ever told you about the time I almost auditioned for porn?'* It'll be perfect."

"I didn't *almost* audition for it," I said quietly. "I actually auditioned. And it was totally normal."

Well, aside from the fact that it began with me walking in on my costar naked. But Luke didn't need to know that part.

"Shit, really?" Luke asked, leaning forward slightly.

"Yeah. And the writing is amazing and so's the director and the guy who's playing Wyatt was really great and they, um, they offered me the part."

"What?"

"Yeah. I didn't actually even realize it was porn until the cab ride home. When I was talking to Gray. He's the guy playing Wyatt."

"Jesus. But you—you're not doing it, right?"

"I—" I stopped, and took a deep breath, thinking about what Gray had said. "Yeah, so, um, actually, I realized some other things on the cab ride too. Some things I need to tell you. If that's okay?"

"Okay," Luke said cautiously.

"I, um." I stopped again and looked up at the ceiling. "Ugh, okay, so I kind of fucked up your car earlier today. At a gas station. I was totally sober, it was just a stupid accident, I backed up over a curb, but now it's making a weird noise and I wanted to fix it for you without telling you so that you wouldn't worry, but I don't really have enough money—well, any money—right now to do that? So when Tiana told me about the audition, I was thinking maybe if I got the part, I'd be able to fix the car without ever having to tell you. But I've been thinking about, like, honesty and stuff, and I guess I realized I shouldn't lie to you about it, so anyway, I wanted to tell you. I'm totally still going to fix it and I'm going to find the money to pay for it, I promise, I just—well, I didn't want to lie about it to you."

The words came out in a rush and I exhaled deeply after I finished. When I finally looked down from the ceiling, Luke's eyes were wide and glued to me.

"Yeah. So um, that's... a thing... I wanted to say. That, and that I'm sorry for messing up your car. I know you trusted me with it and I feel shitty about letting you down," I finished lamely.

"Tyler you—you don't have to—" Luke shook his head. "I appreciate you telling me about the car, and I also appreciate the offer to cover it yourself, but honestly, I can just pay for it."

"No, but I—"

"You cannot seriously be considering doing gay porn just to pay for fixing my car," Luke broke in. "Or if you are, stop. I'll get it. Hell, you can pay me back once you have money, if you really want to. But that's not a good enough reason to do porn. Fuck, you're not even into guys."

"That's um—" I closed my eyes and paused, wishing passionately for the floor to open up and swallow me so that I didn't have to keep talking. "That's another thing I wanted to tell you. God, I'm sorry, this is probably a really weird way to be finding all this shit out, it's just that Gray like, got me thinking about why I'm making the decisions I make and it made me realize I needed to be more honest even though I'm fucking terrible at it and now I'm just word vomiting at you but anyway, I think I might actually um... kind of... like... guys? Or whatever. And I'm sorry I didn't tell you, I know that's a shitty thing to do, but I just knew Dad would be mad if he knew, because it would affect the roles I got offered. But now I have literally no job prospects except for this one thing and it's just like, what's even the point of hiding it anymore? Besides, it's not like I even like, have to come out, right? It's just a role. So, anyway, yeah. There's that."

I buried my face in my hands when I was done, feeling vulnerable and hating it. It was just Luke I was coming out to. *He* was gay, for God's sake. If there were anyone in the world who wasn't going to judge me, it would be him.

"Tyler," Luke said gently. When I opened my eyes and peered out from between my fingers, I saw that he'd gotten off the couch and was kneeling next to my chair. He laid a hand on my arm. "Tyler, it's okay. It's nothing to be embarrassed about. And you don't have to apologize for not telling me, or anyone. It's completely your business."

"Yeah," I said, peeling my fingers away from my face, "but like, isn't it kind of crappy to have known for years but not told anyone just because I was scared?"

"No. No, it's not. Tons of people are scared to come out. And you don't owe anybody anything. The only person you owe is yourself, and you have to do what's right for you."

"Right," I snorted. "Sure."

"Tyler, I'm serious." Luke squeezed my arm, drawing my eyes down to look at him. "If you don't feel safe—"

"Ugh, it's not that dramatic," I said, flushing at Luke's tone. "It's not like I was some kid who was in like, physical danger if he came out. Like, poor me, I was famous and rich and I just didn't wanna do it because I didn't wanna deal with Dad being pissed at me."

"Honestly, Tyler, given how controlling he is, that actually does sound sorta unsafe to me. But Dad's also an asshole, so fuck him and what he thinks. You're better off without him. We all are."

"He was just trying to take care of me," I said, frowning. "He was looking out for my career."

"Are you seriously defending him?" Luke asked, his eyebrows climbing up to his scalp. "The guy who wouldn't talk to you after you got arrested, the guy who never visited you once last year, the guy who still isn't taking your calls, like you're some kind of *client* instead of his son."

I shook my head. "You don't understand. I know he seems— it's just—that's just how he is. I haven't made it easy for him. But he's done so much for me, and if he hadn't managed me and my career, there's no way I'd—"

"Be where you are right now? Unable to get a job that isn't in porn? Excommunicated by Dad and everyone else after succumbing to pressures they put on you?" Luke's tone grew angrier. "You're damn right you wouldn't be there, if he'd actually ever been a father to you and not just an asshole manager."

"No. No, that's on me. Luke, everything I've done, those are my actions, my consequences. I made shitty decisions because I felt insecure and scared, not because of anything anyone else made me do."

"I'm just saying that maybe you wouldn't have felt so shitty if—"

"Listen, you don't *know him*," I said, shaking off Luke's grip on my arm. "I know you don't like him, but Dad's put up with a lot from me. I wasn't an easy kid. You weren't there to see it, but I was selfish, I was lazy, I was ungrateful—and if Dad hadn't been there, I don't know what I'd—I mean, I'd just—I just owe him a lot, is what I'm trying to say, okay?"

Luke looked at me for a long moment before speaking. "You're right. I don't really know him. And I wasn't there. Because he left with you when you were six, and he never really came back. And maybe I'm wrong, but when I look at him? I see the guy who never let us visit you when you were little. The guy who never came home, the guy who made Mom's life a living hell during the divorce."

"It's not—he's not—fuck, Luke, I'm sorry. God, okay, I'm sorry. But it's not Dad's fault, it's mine. I'm the one who wanted to be on that stupid show, I'm the one who messed everything up. I'm sorry and I wish I hadn't, okay? I didn't want to ruin everything. I never meant to make your lives harder."

Luke's eyes widened. "You think *you* ruined it? Tyler, I don't blame you at all. None of this is your fa—"

"Will you stop trying to tell me things aren't my fault?" I exploded. "Will you just fucking stop? That was the whole point of this past year, learning to take responsibility for my actions. Will you just fucking let me do that?"

Luke's eyes narrowed in surprise, then hurt, and then, if I wasn't mistaken, sadness. Dammit, I'd fucked this up again, hadn't I. I shouldn't have yelled. I shouldn't have—

"Okay, okay, I'm sorry," Luke said softly. "I didn't mean to do that, and I'll stop. Please just—no, Tyler, please it's—"

But he didn't finish his sentence, because like an idiot, I'd started crying, and suddenly Luke was pulling me into a hug. It was awkward, Luke still on his knees on the floor, me leaning over in the chair, but it was still kind of nice, and I realized I couldn't remember the last time someone had hugged me—which only made me want to cry even more.

"Jesus, sorry," I said, pulling away brusquely. "I didn't mean to yell. I'm such a fucking mess."

"You're not."

"I am," I snorted, "and that's not really arguable."

"Fine—but you're also my brother, and you don't have to apologize for it, okay? That's what family's for."

"Thanks," I said, looking down. "God, I probably got snot all over your uniform."

"Don't worry about it," Luke said, waving my apology away with a grin. "It's not like I was planning on wearing it this weekend or anything." He paused, looking pensive for a moment.

"Are you seriously thinking about doing this movie, Tyler? Pretend the car thing isn't an issue for a second. In fact, pretend the whole last year never happened. No arrest, no group home. You can still get any part you want. Would you still be thinking about doing this?"

Gray's face, and those startling blue eyes of his, popped into my mind and I flushed. For the chance to get to know him?

"Maybe."

"Really?"

"It's hard to explain," I said, sighing. "But it doesn't matter. Pretending that I'm not in the situation I'm in is just wishful thinking. I am in it, and that's the reality I have to deal with."

"A reality where you're going to let some random guy fuck you on camera."

I blushed and bit my tongue at my urge to defend Gray as not being just *'some random guy'*. Because he was, wasn't he? I didn't really know him.

"I don't know." I shrugged. "It could be nice to change the narrative for a while, you know? Get people talking about me for literally *any* other reason than what a fuck-up I am? Maybe remind them that I actually can act?"

"And then have this movie follow you around for the rest of your life?"

I bit my lip, not sure how to explain everything I was feeling, not sure I could even identify it all. Fear, nerves, and worry, yes. But also curiosity. And excitement. And a perverse streak of stubbornness.

Because maybe it wasn't even about changing the narrative. Maybe it was about just doing something for myself for once. Which yes, sounded bizarre, I know. Making a movie that, in order to be a success, would need to be seen by thousands upon thousands of people. A movie in which people watched me get fucked. Probably repeatedly.

But Gray had told me to be honest with myself. And if I were being honest, there was something about this movie that I couldn't stop thinking about. Something about it that wouldn't quite let me just walk away. Something pulling me in.

And I know it sounds dumb, but I couldn't help thinking that maybe this part had fallen in my lap for some kind of reason. Maybe the universe was trying to tell me something.

Or maybe I was just really desperate. Six of one, half a dozen of the other, really.

"It's a good script," I said, finally. "And Violet's great, and you said it's already gotten a ton of buzz. This could be a really important project. And fuck, it's not like anyone can think worse of me than they already do. So fuck 'em," I finished, smiling slightly as I remembered Gray saying that in the car.

Luke's mouth twisted in doubt but finally he nodded. "Well, if you're really sure, then I'm happy for you."

"Oh God, I'm not sure about anything," I said with a laugh. "Sorry, did I give you that impression somehow? I'm completely lost."

"But you're gonna do this?"

"Yeah," I said, my stomach flipping a somersault. "Yeah, I think I am."

GRAY

*V*IOLET: *Hey—Emergency meeting 4pm today at Bailey Park. We'll meet in the library*

I blinked at my phone in confusion. I'd just pulled it out to confirm the directions for driving out to Bailey Park, where we'd be filming for the next month, when I saw Violet's message. Emergency meeting? That didn't sound good.

"What's up?" Micah said from the other side of the bar, and I glanced over to see him frowning at me.

"Just got a weird text from Vi. There's an emergency meeting today once we're all out on site

"What's it about?" Micah asked.

"Dunno." I tapped out a response.

GRAY: Got it. Something wrong?

Her reply came immediately.

VIOLET: We'll talk about it once everyone's here

"Shit," I said, making a face as I passed my phone to Micah so he could read it. "That's not good."

Micah looked down at the screen, nodded, and then snorted.

"Neither is you showing me that, apparently," he said as he passed my phone back.

I looked down at the screen again in confusion to see a final text from Violet.

VIOLET: *Just try not to talk to anyone else about this in the meantime*

I winced. "Yikes."

"Eh, I'm sure I don't count," Micah said with a reassuring smile. "I wonder what it's about though."

"Maybe she's replacing me with a real actor," I said with a sigh. "Maybe they found someone last minute who's going to suck less than I do."

Micah rolled his eyes. "I'm sure she wouldn't make you drive all the way out to Jersey just to tell you that."

"Maybe," I said darkly. "Maybe they're just trying to let me down gently."

Ridiculous as it sounded, I'd been having nightmares for the past week, ever since the night I'd auditioned. Every day was a blur of activity—meetings with Violet and the producers, meetings with Micah and the staff at *Maggie's* to prepare them for my month-long absence, calls to my suppliers and service-people—and every night, without fail, I'd wake up in a cold sweat from a series of increasingly bizarre dreams.

I dreamt that I'd forgotten my lines and every time we had to cut and restart, my voice would get fainter and fainter until no one could hear me. I dreamt I'd memorized my lines flawlessly but suddenly we were doing the shoot in Spanish and I had to learn the entire language in one day. Just last night, I'd dreamt that we were shooting on the deck of a cruise boat that had started sinking, and each time I flubbed a line, we sank a little deeper into the ocean. That one had ended with me begging Violet for one more chance as I treaded water, pineapples and butt plugs floating past me in the warm, Caribbean sea.

The thing was, even amid the rush of the week, I had memorized my lines. Most of them, anyway. Violet had sent the full script over and each night, when I came upstairs to my apartment above the bar, I ran through sections of it in front of my mirror. But I felt awkward, spouting words at myself stiffly like a middle-school student practicing a stump speech for class president.

Had I really once thought I wanted to act? Had I really thought I was any good at it? If possible, I felt less confident now than I had when the week began—probably because I was way more familiar with the scope of my talents. That scope was not, if you asked me, very broad.

"Oh, you're *fine*," Micah said, giving me a stern look. "I know it's fun to think about how much you suck all the time, but you're probably way better than you think. You'll feel better once you're on set. And you can always run lines with your costar, right?"

Could I? I still wasn't sure if Tyler were doing the movie or not. I hadn't heard from him in the week since our cab ride, though that honestly wasn't surprising at all, since we hadn't exchanged numbers. I hadn't heard from Violet either, though, and I assumed I would have if Tyler had pulled out.

Oh God, what if *that* were what the emergency meeting was about?

"What now?" Micah said. "You look like someone just tasered your butthole."

"Tasteful. It's just—nevermind. It's not important."

It *was* important—important enough that production might be shutting down if Tyler were only pulling out now —but Violet had just asked me not to talk to anyone about it and I hadn't even told Micah who my costar was, because I knew Micah'd probably demand selfies and delight in telling me every piece of gossip he knew about Tyler.

It's not like Tyler needed me to protect him at all, but some-how, I'd decided that as long as I was working with him, I wasn't going to look up anything about him or whatever past he'd seemed so pleased I didn't know about. It was the least I could do, right?

"Are you panicking about leaving the bar again?" Micah asked. "Because I promise you, Gray, it's not going to burn down. And you're going to New Jersey, not the moon. You can get back here if you need to, and last I checked, cell phones work on both sides of the Hudson."

I hadn't been worrying about that—but now I was again. Bailey Park was an old mansion out in Montclair that Andrew's grandmother had bought, partially renovated, and lived in for six months before she moved to Palm Springs. Apparently it had actually *been* a private school at one point, so there was more than enough space for us to shoot there and all stay there as well.

Violet had explained that the idea was to shoot the whole movie in under a month for financial reasons. She'd make use of as many hours in the day as possible by having us all sleep in the same place we were filming. Micah was right—Bailey Park wasn't that far away from Manhattan. And it wasn't like he hadn't managed the bar before. He knew what to do.

But still—I'd never been gone for this long. I tried to console myself with the idea that I could swing by any nights and weekends that I wasn't needed. Just a half hour drive, an hour with traffic. It should be fine. Right?

"You're right," I said forcefully, more to convince myself than out of actual enthusiasm. "And you'll—"

"Call you if absolutely anything happens," Micah said with a smile. "Yes, Mom, I promise. Now get out of here. If you're supposed to be there by four, you don't want to be late."

"Now who's the mom," I grumbled, bending down to pick my duffel up off the floor.

Micah laughed. "Gotta start practicing. Caro just told me she wants me to be The Bean's godfather. I need to brush up on my admonishment skills."

"Really? That's awesome, Micah."

Caro was Micah's best friend. She and her husband had been trying to get pregnant for a while now and were thrilled when they'd finally announced the pregnancy. I hadn't known they were going to do the godparent thing, but it didn't surprise me they'd picked Micah.

"I figure I need at least some 'real adult' skills to pass on," Micah said with a grin, "to balance out all the bad influencing I'll also be doing. But seriously, dude. Go."

"I'm going, I'm going," I said, shouldering my bag. "I'll see you—"

And then my phone buzzed again and it's not like I could stop myself from looking at it immediately, even though I could hear Micah laughing behind me. What if it was Violet? What if it was, somehow, Tyler? Because my stupid brain couldn't stop thinking that that was some kind of a possibility, even though I knew it wasn't.

But it wasn't either of them.

ETHAN: *Hey! What's up?*

"Well?" Micah said expectantly.

"It's..." I glanced over my shoulder and sighed. "You're not gonna like the answer."

Micah's eyes narrowed. "Seriously? After he ditched you last week?"

Micah had a point. Last week, after my cab ride with Tyler, I'd been two blocks away from the office where that dinner thing was happening when Ethan called me to ask me not to come. Apparently Christie had shown up and he had to spend the night pretending they were a couple—a couple who didn't need Ethan's secret ex-boyfriend showing up.

I'd said it was fine.

Because what else could I say? It's not like I could blame him, exactly. It wasn't a real date he'd invited me on, and I knew things were complicated with Christie. Both of their parents had expectations for them.

I'd just—well, I shouldn't have gotten excited about it, shouldn't have thought it meant anything, the two of us getting dinner again. Like we used to.

But I'm a fucking idiot, so of course I did, so of course by the time I got back to the bar, I looked like a depressed, drowned turd-on-legs and it hadn't taken Micah long to drag the story out of me—and add it to his list of Ethan's sins.

"I know," I said heavily. "I know. I'm not going to respond to him."

"Really?" Micah folded his arms across his chest and arched an eyebrow.

"Really."

"Gray."

"Okay, fine, I probably will," I said, feeling my cheeks burn. "But I'll wait at least an hour."

"That'll show him," Micah said with a laugh.

"I know, right? I've got at least 60 minutes worth of self-respect." I slid the phone back into my pocket. "I really should go, though."

"Alright. You know you can call if you need anything," Micah said. "Not just to check on the bar. You can call if *he*"—Micah glared at the phone in my hand—"won't stop harassing you."

"What are you, my sponsor? I'm supposed to call you in moments of weakness?"

"Hey, if it works..."

Bailey Park turned out to be an old, gray stone manor house set way back from the road amid lush trees and sweeping lawns. The building was massive—the size of a city block, four stories tall, with a number of chimneys that boggled the mind. The whole place had the feel of somewhere that should be inhabited by at least 12 ghosts and possibly a wailing woman in a white dress, threatening to fling herself off the roof.

I drove up the smooth, sloping drive to the front of the house, where the driveway curved and encircled a weathered bronze statue of what I was pretty sure was a woman weeping. So that was encouraging.

Maybe she was just hiding her eyes from the impending acts of sin and lust that were about to be filmed at her back for the next month.

Creepier still, there wasn't another car in sight. I did have the right address, didn't I? I was just about to hop out and check when a young woman in a black t-shirt and jeans raced out of the front door with a clipboard and a headset.

"Mr. Evans?" she asked breathlessly, skidding to a stop next to my car.

"Uh, yeah."

I couldn't remember the last time anyone had addressed me

that way—maybe the executor of Maggie's will, actually. I'd never particularly liked my last name. Reminded me too much of the family—well, my mom, anyway—who'd left me behind back in West Virginia all those years ago.

"Yeah, that's me," I said, making myself smile. No reason to make this poor production assistant's life harder just because this house made me feel like I was in a brooding Gothic novel. I checked the name tag stuck to the front of her shirt and stuck out my hand. "Hannah, is it? Nice to meet you."

Hannah stared at my hand like she wasn't sure what to do with it and I had to bite back a smile. Violet had mentioned that a lot of the assistants on this shoot were student or former-student volunteers from a class she taught occasionally at NYU. Hannah was probably as nervous as I was. Eventually, Hannah reached out and shook my hand, but her eyes still registered her shock and she blushed as she glanced down at her clipboard.

"You're going to be staying on the second floor of the east wing," Hannah said. "Your door will have your name on it. But we're asking everyone to park over by the old stables. Violet wants to keep the front clear for some exterior shots at dusk tonight and the back's going to be a mess with equipment."

"Got it," I said, trying to set her at ease with a smile. "I'll head over there now."

I drove down another curling swoop of driveway that struck off at an angle from the house and crested a small hill before descending to a shaded, low-slung building of wooden beams and stone with a green roof. It seemed to be mostly garages and offices now, but you could still see vestiges of its past in the wide, barn-style doors and the horseshoe nailed to the roof.

I parked next to a van where two sound techs were unloading boom mics and followed a gaggle of people ferrying cameras and lights on carts back to the main house. While the front of the house had seemed solemn and dismal, the back was a cheerful hive of activity.

A small army of people ran around, shouting directions at each other. There was the buzz of happy chaos that always accompanied the beginning of a shoot, when no one's hungry or tired or grumpy after shooting their fifth 16 hour day in a row. Though to be honest, none of the 'films' I'd ever been in had been this large-scale.

I dodged around someone pushing a rack of what looked liked school uniforms across the driveway and slipped through a door that led into the house. It only took me three tries to find a staircase that went up—I found two separate ones that descended into some kind of dim cellar that I had no intention of setting foot in—hidden behind some kind of old fashioned larder.

But of course, when I got to the second floor, I realized that wherever I was, it wasn't the east wing. All the rooms I peered into looked like the kind of thing you'd see in a BBC drama—huge galleries hung with portraits of haughty-looking dead people, instruments that probably hadn't been played in decades, if not centuries, and giant chandeliers that seemed like they might crash down and kill me, kicking off a drawing room mystery.

Feeling completely out of place, I set off down a long

hallway that seemed to run along the spine of the house. I walked along the worn, blue silk carpet that covered the warm, wooden floorboards, trying not to panic. Even if I managed to *find* my room before the 4 p.m. meeting, there was still a 250% chance of me getting lost and at least a 75% chance of me getting murdered on my way to the library, wherever the hell that was.

I was walking so quickly that I barely had time to throw a hand up in front of my face when one of the doors off the hallway to the left opened suddenly, smacking my open palm.

"Oh Jesus, sorry, I didn't mean to—" Tyler's head popped out from behind the door, following his voice, and he stopped in surprise. "Oh God, now I really *am* sorry. I didn't realize it was you."

I laughed as I dropped my hand and shook it out, trying to get rid of the sting.

"What, you wouldn't have cared as much if you'd hit someone else?"

Tyler gave a rueful grin. "No, I just *extra* don't want you to hate me. You're like, the one person I'm not extremely uncomfortable around here."

"Seriously?"

"Seriously." Tyler smiled sheepishly. "I've been here for two hours and I've just been hiding in my room. I'm, um, really great at being an adult. Obviously."

I couldn't help but laugh.

"Besides," Tyler went on. "Giving the lead a black eye with

my bedroom door the day before we start shooting would be pretty shitty."

"Co-lead. And it wouldn't be the worst black eye I've ever gotten," I said. Tyler cocked and eyebrow and I grinned. "Once, I slipped on a patch of lube on the floor and skidded into the guy I was filming with. Took us both down, and he ended up sitting on my face. And not in the fun way."

Tyler's cheeks turned bright pink and I cringed inside, realizing I'd done it again. That night in the cab, after he'd left, I'd replayed our whole conversation and realized just how truly creepy I must have come off. I'd told myself that if he ended up doing the film—something I hadn't considered very likely—I'd do my best to put him at ease. And here I was, acting like a disgusting old lech within the first minute of talking to him.

"I'm um—" I started, then paused, wondering if this was only going to sound grosser, then started again because now I just looked like an idiot, my mouth hanging open as I stared at him, "It's good to see you. I thought—well, I wasn't sure if you—I mean—I'm glad you're here?"

I finished my awkward speech with a lame laugh, but Tyler laughed too and it felt warm and kind and not like it was laughing at my inability to string together an actual sentence.

"Yeah," Tyler smiled. "Me too. I decided, in the end, fuck 'em. Like you said."

"I like that attitude." I winced again. God, suddenly everything seemed like some kind of double-entendre. Since when did I have the brain of a 14 year old boy, wanting to add 'that's what she said' to the end of everything. Or what *he* said, in this case, I supposed. "I really am glad you're here though. I was worried, when I got Violet's text, that maybe—"

"I was quitting?" Tyler asked. "I kind of thought the same thing, actually—that they'd decided they didn't want me on the project anymore."

"Oh please. If anyone's getting fired, it's me."

Tyler frowned. "You're really not as bad as you think."

"Well tell that to my subconscious, because it's already cooking up another nightmare about how bad I suck again tonight. Given the surroundings, it's definitely gonna involve ghosts."

"Ghosts? Seriously?"

I flushed. "Nothing's creepier than rich, old, dead people. Anyway, I should probably go find my—"

"Oh, it's just down the hall. Second door on your left." Tyler shrugged and smiled. "I did a tiny bit of exploring before I heard footsteps and ran back to my room to hide."

"You know you are actually going to have to interact with people during this shoot, right?" I said as I walked down the hall. Tyler followed me. "We're not going to shoot the whole thing from your room."

"Wait, are you suggesting that I use healthy coping mechanisms and actually face my fears?" Tyler snickered. "I see you and I have some work to do in lowering your opinion of me. That or the *'Career Interruptions and Arrests'* section of my Wikipedia page was redacted when you were stalking me online."

"I didn't, um—I didn't... actually... do... that?" I said, my footsteps slowing as I came to a stop in front of my room.

Tyler looked surprised. "Really?"

"I told you I wouldn't."

"People say a lot of things," Tyler shrugged. "Doesn't mean they do them."

"Well I do," I said, feeling slightly awkward. Tyler looked uncomfortable and even though I didn't know what I'd done, I was pretty sure it was my fault. "After I drop my stuff off, you wanna go find the library together? That way you'll have company if we hear any more footsteps."

"Unless they turn out to belong to ghosts." Tyler arched an eyebrow. "Then I guess I'm on my own, huh?"

"Don't be cute," I said, throwing him a withering glance as I opened the door to my room. "Besides, ghosts don't have footsteps. They float."

The room was tiny: a single, dormitory-style bed in one corner, a battered old wooden desk in the other, a mirror on the far wall. There was a closet on the righthand wall and, next to the door, a massive chest of drawers with roses carved into its front. That was about it.

Tyler peered his head in as I tossed my bag on the bed.

"Looks about the same as mine. Your dresser's nicer though. Mine's got clowns on it and clearly comes from a cursed children's bedroom set." He grinned up at me. "Probably chock full of ghosts. You'd love it."

I rolled my eyes. "No bathroom?"

"Other end of the hall."

"Communal?" I blinked.

"Yeah." Tyler shrugged. "We did a whole season on *Criss-Cross Applesauce* where we all went to 'Australia.' It was really just a crappy ranch in Stockton, and the only bathroom was an outhouse and the shower was basically a hose thrown over a tree branch. Trust me, the bathroom situation could be worse."

"Shit, I think you've got even me beat," I said, "and I usually win for hell shoot stories. My worst was this 'motorcycle club' one that we shot in a gas station on Staten Island. The bathroom smelled awful but at least it had running water. And we didn't have to stay overnight."

"Are you serious?" Tyler asked, his eyes delighted. "What was the movie called?"

I gave him a hard look. "No judgment."

"What, from me?" Tyler protested, his eyes way too innocent. "I would never."

I sighed. "*Cranking His Hog*. Do you wanna—"

Tyler didn't even try to stifle the giggles that erupted from him. I folded my arms and waited for him to finish.

"I'm sorry, I'm sorry," he gasped finally. "It's just—it's so good. Sorry. You were saying?"

"I was *saying*," I said, glaring at him, "that maybe we should go find the library now."

"Yes." Tyler nodded and tried to pull himself together.

"Absolutely. Let's go do that. Can't stand around here yapping our traps and cranking our hogs all day, after all."

"You'd better hope there aren't any ghosts," I said as I followed him out the door. "I'm definitely telling them to take you first."

~

Violet looked up from the table in the center of the library —an old room literally lined with shelves of books, dust-motes dancing in the sunlight that streamed through the windows—and smiled tightly when she saw me and Tyler enter.

"Good," she said. "You're both here. We can get started."

It was just the three of us, plus Andrew, Dave, and Danny. Danny, as usual, was sitting in a corner, deeply engrossed in something on their laptop. Andrew and Dave looked sort of nervous.

I realized, then, that I'd started feeling a little more at ease with being here after talking to Tyler. Unfortunately, I was only realizing that now because seeing everyone else look tense drained that easy feeling out of my body.

"Sit," Violet said, gesturing to the other chairs at the table.

Tyler gave me a confused look. I answered with a silent shrug, and we both sat, looking at Violet expectantly. I had the strangest flashback at that moment—getting called in to the principal's office in sixth grade, terrified I was going to get in trouble for fighting with Casey Ashland on the playground.

Instead, Mrs. Miller had told me that my mom and her boyfriend at the time—Wayne—had left town that morning. The school nurse had seen them packing up Wayne's Pontiac, tying a mattress to the top, on her lunch break. Our town was small enough that everyone knew everyone, but when the nurse had asked where they were going, my mom and Wayne hadn't answered—just got in the car and drove away.

Mrs. Miller asked me if I knew anything about this. I didn't. I hadn't even seen my mom in a month. Mrs. Miller said they were probably just running errands. Or going on a trip. Or maybe my mom and Wayne and I were moving, that they'd come pick me up after school that day. She said that everything was going to be fine.

I already knew it wouldn't be. It had never been fine—I'd just been good at covering that fact up. But now that the school knew my mom had left me, things were going to get worse. They wouldn't let me keep living on my own, now.

I wasn't the first kid in my school, or even in my grade, to have family problems. I knew what came next. The search for relatives to take me in. And then, when they couldn't find any, foster care. Indifference at best, cruelty at worst. And as I sat there in Mrs. Miller's office, sun streaming through the windows as shrieks of other children at recess filtered up from the playground, I knew my life was about to change, and there was nothing I could do to stop it.

I shook my head, trying to clear it of those cobwebby memories, and focused on Violet's face. That had all happened so long ago, and I hadn't thought about it in years—for good reason. Thinking about my mom could put me in a black mood that lasted for weeks. Better to focus on the present.

"So," Violet said. "I'm not gonna beat around the bush. We have an issue. You guys have heard of *Celebreality*?"

I had, but only because I knew one of Ethan's friends from college, Troy, had started it. *Celebreality* was a celebrity gossip website, Troy's brainchild after he got fired from his job at the *New York Times*. Back when I was still trying to act, Ethan loved reading me snippets from Celebreality to prove that I was somehow 'better' than the people getting written up in there.

"They just ran a story about how you two are the leads in *Foresight*," Violet continued.

"Is that... bad?" I asked, after a moment's silence.

Violet was looking at the two of us like she'd just pronounced someone's death sentence, and Tyler's eyes were wide, so he clearly understood the significance of what Violet had said, but I was lost.

"I mean, we are the leads, aren't we?" I continued. "Unless— I mean, if you've decided that you don't want—"

"You are," Violet said, cutting me off. "But it is bad. Not catastrophically so, but we'd planned an announcement for the end of the week, a quick little press release with some photos and a chance to talk about how excited we all are about this project. This undercuts that. And, you guys both signed NDAs about this. Any press you do for the project runs through us—and we'd specifically told you to keep quiet about casting for the time being."

My stomach went all hot and twisty.

"Shit," Tyler said, his voice sounding broken. "Shit, Violet, I'm really sorry. I only told my brother, and I thought he knew how this stuff went, so I didn't think I needed to remind him. But he must have—oh God, I'm so sorry. I really didn't want to fuck anything up on this project and I'm already—shit, I understand if you want to—"

"No."

Violet and I spoke at the same time and looked at each other in surprise. I rushed to keep talking. I wasn't sure what she was going to say, but I knew I needed to speak first.

"No, it—it was me," I said, my heart sinking as I spoke. "I'm sure of it. I told someone who—well, someone I shouldn't have."

I replayed my text conversation with Ethan in my head. I knew, without even having to ask, without needing to meet Tyler's brother, that it was Ethan who'd leaked the casting details to *Celebreality* and not him. Even though *Foresight* had nothing to do with Ethan, he still would have called Troy about it.

Because he wouldn't have been able to help himself. Ethan loved gossip, whether it was about people he knew or complete strangers. He probably hadn't even thought about what kind of effect his actions would have on me.

"It's completely my fault," I went on. "I told him it wasn't common knowledge but I left enough wiggle room that he probably felt like he could say something. Hell, he'd probably have said something even if I swore him to secrecy. I'm sorry, I really wasn't smart, telling him. I apologize."

Violet gave me a long look and then sighed. "Ethan?"

I nodded. "Yeah. Really, Vi, I'm so sorry, I just didn't think—well, that's it. I didn't think. I understand if you—"

"Alright, alright," she said, holding up a hand. "No need to go falling on your sword. I wanted to make sure that we're all taking this seriously—just because this isn't a big studio project doesn't mean we're not all professionals—but nobody's getting fired or anything like that."

I heaved a sigh of relief and then frowned at myself. I was *relieved* at not being fired? Really? If Violet had fired me five hours ago, I would've rejoiced. Or at least, it had felt that way.

"Now," Violet went on, "we just need to talk about strategy."

"Strategy? What strategy?" I asked.

"Clean-up," Dave put in. "We're getting backlash already."

"Is it me?" Tyler asked. His voice was soft and he asked the question like he already knew the answer. "I'm sorry, I know you're taking a big risk working with me, with my past and everything. I'm not the most popular guy."

"It's not you," Andrew put in quickly. "Or, well, it is, but it's not *that*. It's just..." he screwed his face up uncomfortably. "Well, there's..."

"Some people are complaining about your casting," Dave broke in, "saying that because you're not officially *out*, you might not even be gay or bisexual or whatever, and that we just cast you because you're famous."

"Which is completely unfair," Andrew added, taking over from Dave, "since you were obviously the best person who auditioned, but we're getting some flack for not casting an out-and-proud actor in this part—"

"And obviously, we think you're amazing and it's not our job to give everyone who auditions an 'are you gay enough for this role' quiz—"

"But, well, since we're playing catch-up," Andrew finished, "and we want to take back control of the story, would you mind maybe doing a statement this week where you, well, come out?"

"Oh." Tyler's voice was quiet, surprised. And uncomfortable. "Um. Uh, right. Yeah, I mean, I guess, um, it's just—"

"Wait."

All of our heads swung around to look at Danny, who'd just spoken for the first time since we'd entered the room and was finally looking up from their computer.

"Sorry," they continued. "I wasn't really paying attention before, but are you asking him to come out? I don't really feel comfortable with that."

"Well nobody's doubting you, of course," Dave put in quickly, glancing towards Tyler. "Obviously, you wouldn't be doing this movie if you were straight. But still, it might help optics if you were willing to—"

"Fuck optics," Danny cut in. "I don't like it. One of the themes of *Foresight* itself is learning to be comfortable in your own skin. I don't want to be a part of anything that forces someone to come out before they're ready."

"But it—" Dave began, but Violet cut him off.

"It's Tyler's choice," she said firmly. "I agree that we want to get control of the story back, but there's no need to force this decision now. Tyler, why don't you take some more time and think about what you're comfortable with. We'll put out a short statement this afternoon about how pleased we all are to be working together and we can do something more in depth by the end of the week. Sound good?"

She looked around the table and made eye contact with everyone. Danny nodded firmly, Andrew and Dave eventually agreed, and Tyler smiled weakly.

"Thanks," Tyler said. For a second, he looked like he was going to say something more, but he didn't. He just looked down at the table, quiet and pensive.

Again, I was struck by that strange urge to reach out and squeeze his hand or something. He just looked so young and lost.

But that was ridiculous. The guy'd been in the spotlight for years. He knew more about dealing with the press than any of us did, probably. He didn't need my protection.

"Alright, I think that covers everything," Violet said. "One of the volunteers is bringing schedules by later tonight, but we'll be starting with the morning run scene tomorrow. And Gray?"

"Yeah," I said, pausing as I pushed my chair back and stood up from the table.

"Let's try to keep Ethan *out* of the loop from now on, okay?"

"Can do," I said with a rueful laugh. I turned, figuring I'd catch Tyler on his way out, walk back upstairs with him. But he was already gone.

I felt unsettled as I walked back to my room after the meeting. Even though Violet hadn't reamed me out, I knew I'd fucked up, talking to Ethan. Which made me mad at him, but also mad at myself.

I thought about texting him, asking him why he'd done that, but I decided not to in the end. I wasn't sure I'd get a satisfying answer and I *really* wasn't sure I trusted myself to be around him or interact with him at all, even over the phone. It clearly made me act like an idiot.

Hannah came by with the schedule and I tried reading my lines over again for the scenes we were shooting tomorrow, but I couldn't concentrate. I felt antsy somehow, for some reason I couldn't define.

I'm nervous about tomorrow, I realized. Even though I already had the lines memorized, even though I was as prepared as I could be. It was almost like having too much time to think was making it worse. I found myself wishing I could go back to the city and lose myself in the rhythms of work at Maggie's. Anything to stop the slow growing feeling of panic in my stomach.

What if I was completely terrible tomorrow? What if I froze, or I flubbed every line, or I fucked up the shoot so badly that we got irreparably delayed? What if Violet finally decided I really was shitty, that I was bringing the movie down? My stomach flipped uncomfortably at the thought.

I realized then that I hadn't eaten anything since breakfast. I wasn't sure food would actually help me feel better, but finding some dinner might at least give me something to do other than sit in this cell-like bedroom, contemplating my inevitable failure.

Dave and Andrew had hired a local catering company to

provide food once the shoot started, but for tonight, at least, we were on our own. I left my room and headed down the hall, reaching the top of the stairs before I paused.

Maybe I should...

I turned and walked back in the direction I'd come from, stopping and knocking on a door a couple down from mine.

A muffled "Coming!" floated out from behind the door, followed by feet walking across the creaking floorboards before the door opened and Tyler's head popped out. He blinked at me in surprise.

"Hey!" he said, smiling uncertainly. "Do you—does Violet need something?"

He looked nervous.

"What? Oh, no, nothing like that." I smiled, trying to put him at ease. "I was just going out to find some dinner and I wondered if you'd already eaten, or if maybe you wanted to come with."

"Why?" Tyler asked, his voice a mix of confusion and suspicion.

"Because I'm hungry? And because I thought company might be nice?" I wasn't sure what to make of Tyler's reaction. Sure, maybe there was still a part of me that felt... something... tugging inside my chest when I looked at him sometimes. But *he* didn't know that, and I didn't think asking someone to come get dinner with me was that strange. "Aren't those the usual reasons someone suggests eating dinner with someone else?"

"Yeah, but you don't have to—" Tyler started and then

stopped. When he spoke again, his voice sounded less defensive. "I just meant like, are you sure?"

"Sure that I want to get dinner? Yeah, my stomach's gnawing at my spine."

"No, like... are you sure you want to get dinner with *me*," Tyler said. "You don't—you don't have to. I mean, like, if you're just asking because you feel bad for me. I have dinner." He jerked his thumb behind him, gesturing towards the saddest looking sandwich I'd ever seen, sitting half eaten on top of a crumpled paper towel. The bread looked shrunken and wrinkled and as far as I could see, the only filling was a single slice of American cheese, hanging limply out one side.

"What *is* that?" I asked before I could stop myself, my voice doing a poor job of covering up my revulsion.

"Okay, it's not *that* bad," Tyler said, that defensive tone back again. "I know it's not gonna win a Michelin star any time soon, but—"

"Come to dinner with me," I insisted, and before Tyler could protest again, I added, "I'm buying."

Tyler bit his lip. "I'm not sure that's a great idea."

Jesus, I was trying to get the kid to eat dinner with me, not face a firing squad. What the hell was so hard about this?

"I mean, you don't have to," I said with a shrug. "It was just an offer. Don't worry about it."

I started to turn around.

"No, Gray—wait," Tyler said suddenly. I stopped and looked back. He was looking down at his shoes and he took a visible breath before he looked up and forced a smile onto his face. "I'll go," Tyler continued. "I'm going to have to leave this room at some point anyway. Let's do this. And thanks for asking."

So on that enthusiastic note, we started walking down the hall.

"What were you thinking of?" Tyler asked as we descended the stairs. "For dinner, I mean."

"I dunno," I said. "Figured I'd just walk into town and see what looked good. I got caught in traffic on my way out here, so I'd rather not get back in my car if I don't have to." I glanced at him. "If you wanna drive, though, we could take your—"

"I don't have a car," Tyler said quickly, his face flushing. "I'm not, uh, the greatest driver."

"Really?" I looked at him, confused. "How'd you get out here, then?"

"Took the train."

"Jesus." I blinked. "I didn't know you could do that."

Tyler snorted. "You can do a lot of things when you don't have any other options."

We were quiet as we left the mansion, but Tyler seemed to perk up a bit once we got outdoors. The sun was setting and even though it was September, it was still pleasantly warm. As we walked, Tyler pointed out all the different houses that looked like they might have ghosts living inside them, asking how much money I'd need to be paid to spend a night in one of them alone.

It was hard not to laugh. When Tyler wasn't watching me suspiciously, or uncomfortably, or with misgiving, he was actually pretty fun to be around. He had a playful side that came out when he wasn't embarrassed or ashamed and it was helping keep me from focusing on my own spiraling panic.

Tyler grinned at me mischievously as we crossed underneath a large maple tree shading the sidewalk.

"If you dragged me out tonight as a way to butter me up to keep the ghosts away from you as we sleep, that's gonna take more than just one dinner, by the way. My services aren't cheap."

I rolled my eyes. "That's cute that you think I'm sleeping at all. I'm gonna be wide awake all night."

"That might stop the like, low-level ghosts," Tyler said. "The apprentices of the ghost world. But the hardcore ghosts don't care if you're awake."

"Good," I said emphatically. "Have them come in and murder me, then I won't have to actually go through with filming tomorrow."

Tyler glanced up at me in bewilderment. "Are you seriously that worried? You're gonna be fine."

"Easy for you to say. You're a professional."

"So are you," Tyler countered.

"Yeah, but not for what I do with my mouth. Well, not the talking part, anyway."

Tyler's cheeks flushed and I had to fight the urge to notice how it highlighted his cheekbones, the light splash of freckles scattered across his face. It was bad enough that I kept saying shit like that—I didn't need to leer at him besides.

"Well," Tyler said eventually. "I'm not exactly an expert on the other things. So maybe that makes us even."

"Hardly," I said. "You've at least hooked up with people before. Doing it on camera isn't all that different. I, on the other hand, have never actually had to make people believe me when I say things—never had to actually act convincingly. Every time I try to practice my lines, I just feel so stiff and awkward."

Tyler flushed again and just smiled at me, not responding that time.

"Oh, this looks decent," I said, stopping to peer at the menu in the window of a restaurant we were passing. "You like Thai food?"

"Whatever sounds good to you," Tyler said with a shrug.

"I don't want to eat somewhere you don't like," I said. "Really."

Tyler looked up at me, his brow furrowing as he gave me a puzzled look.

"What?" I asked.

"Nothing. You're just... nice, is all."

"And that's weird?"

"Maybe," Tyler said. He glanced back at the menu. "Anyway, I'd drown myself in a swimming pool of Panang curry if I could, so Thai food sounds great."

Warm, spicy aromas from the kitchen wafted out of the door to the restaurant as soon as I opened it. I tried to usher Tyler in ahead of me, but he hung back instead, waiting for me to pass. Confused, I stepped forward into the dimly lit interior.

The walls of the restaurant were painted a deep jade green and a giant, gold-painted Buddha fountain tinkled softly in the corner. It was a Monday night and the restaurant was mostly empty. As I stepped forward to ask the host for a table for two, Tyler lingered back by the door, apparently engrossed in examining the leaves of a potted bamboo plant.

"Right this way," the host said, grabbing two menus and heading towards a table by the front windows.

Tyler snagged my sleeve as I started to walk forward and I turned to him in confusion.

"Could you ask him if we could take that booth in the back instead?" he asked, his eyes pleading.

I frowned. "I mean, yeah but—"

Before I could finish pointing out that Tyler could just ask the host himself, the host realized we weren't following him anymore and turned around. His face flashed from confusion to surprise to disbelief in the space of a second.

"Oh my God," the host said. "You're Tyler Lang."

"Uh, hi," Tyler said, pulling a grin across his face.

"Tyler Lang. Holy shit," the host continued. "Oh my God. Tyler Lang."

That was why Tyler had been so weird, I realized. Just because *I* hadn't known who Tyler was doesn't mean no one else did. This must happen to him all the time. And judging by the way his smile was tight around the edges, I was pretty sure Tyler didn't like it.

"Aren't you like, supposed to be in rehab or something?" the host blurted out and Tyler's face fell.

"Could we get that booth back in the corner?" I said, snapping to action. "Would you mind?"

"Oh." The host blinked, then seemed to realize what he'd said was more than a little inappropriate. *Rehab*. Was that what Tyler hadn't wanted me to know about him? "Oh, of course. Yeah, just follow me."

He led us to the booth in the back corner and Tyler slid gratefully into the side with his back to the door. I settled in on the other side, then looked up at the host expectantly. He was still clutching our menus to his chest and staring like he couldn't believe Tyler was in his restaurant, or possibly even real.

"Could we start with two waters, please?" I asked gently, trying to prod him into action.

"Oh. Oh, yeah, of course," the host said. He put the menus down on the table and then shook his head. "Prija will be your server tonight. I'll send her over with the waters. Um. Right. Yeah."

He walked away, still shaking his head in disbelief.

"Thanks," Tyler said quietly as the host's back retreated.

"God, I'm sorry," I said. "I never thought—I mean, I'd totally forgotten that you're like... that people know you." My eyes widened, a thought occurring to me. "Is that what you meant, when you said you weren't sure this was a good idea?"

Tyler shrugged helplessly. "It can be kinda weird sometimes, especially if you don't know what you're getting into."

"That must get annoying."

"Honestly, this wasn't that bad," Tyler said with a rueful smile. "I was more worried it would be annoying for you. Sometimes things can get kind of weird with photographers and paparazzi and stuff."

"Jesus. That sounds really stressful." I glanced down at the menu. "Wanna drink in response?"

Tyler blanched. "I um—I don't actually drink, really?"

Shit. Right. *Rehab.*

"Oh, ok," I said, nodding and trying to cover up how much of an idiot I felt like. "Cool."

Tyler gave me another inscrutable look.

"What?" I asked. "Am I being weird again?"

"Not weird," Tyler said with a small smile. "Just... nice."

"Which is weird, apparently."

"A little," Tyler said with a shrug. "If you're not used to it."

I wasn't sure how to respond to that. Was Tyler really not used to common courtesy from people? Just what *had* his life been like, before he started this movie? I found myself half-wishing that I had Googled him, because my curiosity was killing me.

Prija, our server, came with our waters and after she'd taken our orders, gathered the menus and walked away. When I looked back at Tyler, he was chewing on his lower lip and studying my face.

"Okay, how was I weird *that* time?" I asked. "All I did was order Pad Thai."

"You weren't weird," Tyler said slowly. "I was just thinking. About what you said earlier, about feeling stiff and awkward when you were reading your lines."

"I wasn't saying that to try to guilt you into running lines with me or anything," I said quickly.

"Guilt me?" Tyler said. "For the record, I wouldn't mind. But that wasn't what I meant." He paused, like he was trying to choose exactly the right words to use. "What I was getting at more was that... I think a lot of people think of acting as being all about your lines—remembering them, saying them convincingly, projecting this character. But I think that kind of misses the point."

"How do you mean?"

"Just like—it's like, if you spend all your time trying to remember to say your lines *this* way or *that* way, you're kind of in your own head, right? You're not really listening to the other person, you know?" Tyler started talking more quickly, his tone excited and his hands moving around to emphasize his points. "So like, no matter how much you're 'in character' or whatever, it's still not going to feel real in the scene, so it's not going to translate and feel real to anyone who's watching. Because you're not really behaving the way you would in an ordinary conversation, where you don't know what the person you're talking to is going to say. A lot of acting is really just listening."

He stopped and looked at me, screwing up his face like he wasn't sure how I'd react. "Does that make any sense?" he asked. "Sorry, sometimes I just get really into this stuff. I know it's kind of pretentious."

"What? No, no." I shook my head. "It's not pretentious at all. It makes a lot of sense, actually. I just..." I paused. "Well, how do I know if I'm listening right?"

"You just listen," Tyler said with a laugh. "There's no right way to do it."

"Yeah, but—"

"Like, weren't you listening right now?" Tyler asked. "You weren't thinking about what you were going to say next."

"Right, but that's because I didn't have lines I had to get right."

"Yeah, but for tomorrow, you already have your lines memorized. They'll come out when you need them, trust me. Worrying too much about that part is what trips people up, is what I'm saying. I mean—" he stopped and looked uncomfortable, "not that you're like, doing this wrong or not good or anything. I just—you said you felt kind of awkward so I just—"

"Tyler, Tyler," I said, reaching out and laying my hand on his for a moment. He flinched, but he didn't move his hand away. "You don't have to apologize. I appreciate it. This is really helpful. It's just... I dunno, I can't help feeling like I'm going to make a mess of things anyway."

Prija came over with our food at that point, and when I looked up from the massive plate of Pad Thai she'd set in front of me, Tyler was staring at me again.

"I'll show you," he said, his eyes fixed on me.

"Show me what?"

"How to listen," he said, picking up his fork.

"Okay," I said hesitantly.

"Are you from New York originally?"

"What?"

"Are you from New York originally?" Tyler repeated.

"How does that have anything to do with—"

"We'll get to that," Tyler said with a smile. "This is important though."

I didn't see how where I was from was relevant but I shrugged, took a bite of my Pad Thai, and spoke after I swallowed.

"No, I grew up in West Virginia."

"Wow, West Virginia," Tyler said, his eyes widening slightly. "That's cool."

"Eh, not exactly the word I'd use to describe it," I said. But Tyler didn't need to know the details. He hadn't asked, and I wasn't going to tell him anyway. I didn't talk about my past for a reason. "But sure."

"So when did you move here, then?" Tyler asked. "To New York, I mean."

I had to think about it for a minute. "God, 14 years ago. Fuck, that makes me sound old."

"No it doesn't," Tyler snorted. "What did you move here for?"

I paused. I didn't usually tell people why. No one really wanted to know the real reason—that I'd been kicked out by my latest foster family, that I'd been outed in high school and everyone there made my life hell, that running away to New York had been a desperate move that had almost led to disaster.

But something about the way Tyler's eyes, warm and golden, focused on mine made me feel all warm and shivery at the same time, like the feeling you get sinking down into a hot tub.

"Do you want the real answer or the one I tell people?" I asked.

"The real one," Tyler said, not missing a beat.

And here I was. Not a minute ago, I was convinced Tyler didn't want the details and sure I wouldn't tell him if he did. And now I was thinking about telling him the truth. What the hell was it about him that fucked with my head so much?

"Well, I usually say it was for work," I began. I looked down —it was easier to talk about it as I studied the angle of my fork, resting on the edge of my plate. "But the truth is, it's because I didn't have anywhere else to go. My family situation wasn't the best," I said, flicking my gaze up to see Tyler still watching me with those compassionate eyes. "Foster care," I added. "None of the families I was placed with wanted me, and once the last one found out I was bi—well, it wasn't great. So I left. When I was 16."

"That sounds really hard. What was it like, moving here?"

"Big?" I said with a laugh. "Scary? I didn't have any idea what I was doing, but I was convinced, if you can believe this, that I wanted to be an actor. Then I got here and realized pretty much every job requires you to at least have a high school diploma, which I didn't have, and wants you to be 18, which I wasn't."

"Shit," Tyler said, nodding slowly.

"I was lucky," I felt compelled to add. "Really lucky. If I hadn't met Maggie..." I trailed off, feeling a sudden rush of warmth and happiness and sadness all at once as I remembered meeting her for the first time.

"Who's Maggie?" Tyler asked. "I can tell from your expression that she's important to you."

"My aunt," I said with a smile. "I mean, not really, but close enough. She more or less adopted me after she saw me sleeping on a park bench a few too many times for her liking and invited me inside."

"Jesus," Tyler said. "That sounds really scary. You didn't have an apartment?"

I shook my head. "I didn't have a job, barely had any money saved. Moving to the city really was a pretty dumb idea."

It was strange. I'd expected it to feel harder, telling Tyler all of this. It felt personal, sort of like undressing in front of someone and not knowing how they'd react to your unclothed body. But under Tyler's gaze, I just felt sort of warm and tingly. Almost like I was buzzed, except I wasn't. And while we'd gotten completely off topic about 'listening,'

I found I actually enjoyed talking about Maggie with someone.

"Anyway," I said after a moment, "I don't want to think about what would have happened to me if I hadn't met Maggie. But she took me in, helped me get my GED, find a job... basically became the parent I'd never had. She even put up with Ethan—my ex," I added in response to the silent question in Tyler's eyes. "He's the uh—the one who talked to that website."

"And your stupid decision," Tyler said. "From that night in the cab last week," he said quickly when I'd looked at him in confusion.

"Ohhh. Yeah." I smiled ruefully. "Yeah, turns out I'm pretty stupid when it comes to him. Maggie never liked him but— well, she put up with him for me."

Tyler's eyes crinkled and he gave me a gentle look. "You're talking about her in the past tense. Did something—"

"She died," I said. I tried to smile but it just turned out wobbly and wouldn't stay in place. "God, sorry, this just got really depressing, didn't it?"

"It's fine. Maggie sounds like a really wonderful person."

"She was." I sighed. "God, she really was. I miss her so much."

"What happened? I mean, if you don't mind me asking."

"It's fine," I said. "It's kind of nice to talk about her actually? I don't know if that's weird but... anyway, it was cancer. Lung cancer. She was never a smoker, but she'd fought it on and off for years. This last time—it just wore her out, I guess."

"I'm so sorry, Gray," Tyler said, and his voice was soft and soothing, sorta like laying down on cool sheets on a hot summer night.

"It was three months ago," I said, not really sure why I was offering that up.

"God, that's like, no time at all." Tyler stared at me. "I can't believe you're doing this movie. I'd be a wreck if I were you."

"Don't let the pulled-together facade fool you," I said, laughing a little. "I definitely still am." I shook my head, thinking back on the past few months. "I was so freaked out, during the last few weeks with Maggie, that I was losing everyone and everything, that I actually proposed to Ethan —even though he'd always told me he needed more time, even though he still wasn't out to his family. Anyone with half a brain could have predicted how poorly that would turn out."

"Holy shit. What happened?"

"Exactly what you'd imagine," I said with a snort. "He said no, I said *'ok sure, totally, that's fine, nevermind.'* And then a week later he broke up with me."

"God, Gray. That's awful."

"I mean, it's not really his fault," I said, feeling suddenly defensive. "He told me he didn't believe in marriage. That he'd seen how unhappy it had made his parents. That he'd tried to want it, for my sake, but he just couldn't do it. And you can't really get mad at someone for something like that, you know?"

"But still, couldn't he have told you that earlier?" Tyler said. "It sounds like you guys were together for a while..."

"Yeah," I said. "It's... complicated. Or maybe it's not. Maybe I'm just a dumbass. But if we just wanted things that were incompatible, that's not really anyone's fault, right?"

"Maybe," Tyler said frowning. "But still. The timing of it... It really isn't my place to say this, but I hope you went out and immediately hooked up with like, 20 hot guys or something."

I burst out laughing. "Try *'wallowed for three months and completely failed to get over him, even though I knew I should'* instead."

"Or that," Tyler said, joining in with a giggle. "Or that."

"Wait, though—it gets worse," I said, holding a hand up. "You wanna hear the real, depressing reason I'm doing this movie? Basically, it's because my friend Micah thinks it'll get me out of the sad, depressing rut I'm in."

"That's not a terrible reason. Besides," Tyler said with a grin, "that means you'll have Ethan to thank when you *do* get out of your rut *and* become a famous movie star and move to Hollywood and meet someone who makes you forget all about him."

I couldn't help grinning back. There was no way any of that was going to happen, but I couldn't help noticing that I felt more relaxed than I had in a long time. Maybe talking about this all had helped, somehow.

"I mean it," Tyler went on. "And then someday you'll write your memoir and you'll have a whole scathing section just devoted to how awful he is."

"Yeah, right." I rolled my eyes. "Because I'm going to become famous enough that anyone would care. Maybe I should concentrate on just getting through this movie first." I frowned. "Aren't you supposed to be showing me how to listen right or something, anyway?"

Tyler smiled impishly. "I just did."

"What?"

"That—this whole conversation—was me listening to you."

"Yeah but you didn't do anything special."

"Exactly. But I'll bet you fifty dollars that I don't actually have that you weren't planning on telling me all of this stuff when I first asked you how long you'd lived in New York," Tyler said, his smile taking on a touch of self-satisfaction.

"I wasn't," I said slowly. "But I was just answering your questions."

"Would you have answered that way to anyone who asked you?"

"Maybe," I said, thinking about it. "If they'd asked—Oh. Ohhh." I stopped and looked at Tyler. "If they'd asked me the way you did."

Tyler grinned again. "Told ya."

I arched an eyebrow. "Why do I feel like I got conned here somehow?"

"You didn't!" Tyler protested. "It's not sorcery or anything. I was just asking, and *listening* to your responses, instead of just waiting for my turn to speak and trade lines."

He was right, I realized. Tyler hadn't forced me to talk or anything. I'd just felt... comfortable, doing it. In a way I didn't usually.

I'd attributed that to Tyler himself. Something about the way his hazel eyes gleamed in the dim light of the restaurant, the way his lips pursed in thought, the way his whole face registered shock, anger, sadness, even joy as he'd listened to me talk.

But I guessed it was just a technique. Something actors—or anyone really—could do. Tyler didn't necessarily find me fascinating—and for good reason. What was special about me? But still...

"You make it sound so easy," I grumbled.

"It *is* easy," Tyler countered. "It's just that most of the time, people don't bother to do it. Most of the time, people don't actually care."

"That's a depressing thought."

Tyler rolled his eyes. "Tell me about it. Fifteen years in LA and I can count on one hand the number of people I met who ever did that—with fingers left over. But it's not actually that hard."

"So I'm supposed to just be able to do it? Like you did?" I asked, narrowing my eyes.

"Yeah," Tyler said encouragingly. "I promise."

"Alright," I said with a grin. "Let's try it then."

"What do you mean?"

"What I mean is that it's my turn."

"Your turn?"

"Yeah," I said with a grin. "My turn to find out all about the mysterious Tyler Lang that our host and waitress can't stop staring at."

"Oh, I don't know if—"

"Fair's fair," I said, my smile widening. "You know all my pathetic secrets now. So lay it on me, so I can learn how to listen. Tell me, Tyler Lang—what's your story?"

TYLER

*W*hat was my story?

Just a degenerate malcontent who makes the lives of those around him harder and more stressful with his mere presence.

I probably owed Gray my story, at this point. He'd let me pry into his life with my little 'active listening' demonstration—which had been real, by the way, I wasn't just spouting off bullshit as an excuse to grill him. Finding out every detail of his life was just a... side-benefit, if you will.

He was going to find out eventually anyway, I supposed. Hell, the host had basically given me away when we'd walked in. Wouldn't it be best to be the one to explain everything to him? Wouldn't that give the highest probability of him leaving this table not completely disgusted with me?

Though that probability had never been that high. There was no way to explain the person I'd been—the person I still was, really—without destroying any chance that Gray would want to be my friend after this. Which I'd known from the beginning. It was a ridiculous thing to hope for. It was just—it had been a nice week, knowing there was someone out there who'd met me and didn't hate me.

I flushed. "My story... is probably not all that interesting, in the end."

"Really?" Gray cocked an eyebrow. "Says the guy who was shocked I didn't know who he was."

"Maybe I'm trying to turn over a new leaf," I said with a grin that I hoped seemed playful. "Maybe I don't want to burden you with the knowledge of my awesomeness. I'm very humble, you see."

"Clearly."

"I don't know," I said, looking down and twisting the paper wrapper from my straw around my fingers. I hated how on the spot I felt, hated the way I could still feel Gray's blue eyes on me, even though I wasn't looking. "I mean, it's really *not* all that interesting. Like, I'm kind of an asshole, but I'm not even original about it. I'm just following in the footsteps of lots of assholes before me, not blazing a new trail or anything."

"You really think that little of yourself?"

A hot rush of shame flicked up inside me and I forced it back down, shifting in my seat. I looked up at Gray and shrugged. "You might reevaluate that question in a little bit."

"Well for someone who's trying to demonstrate the power of listening, you're making it kinda hard for me to do any of that," Gray said. He laughed, and I knew he was trying to keep things light, but his words struck home. It was time to stop avoiding this. If he was going to find out, might as well rip the band-aid off quickly.

"You're right." I nodded and met his eyes. "I'm sorry. Ask away."

Gray's lips pursed in thought. "Where are you from?"

"Long Island," I said automatically. It was the answer I was used to giving in interviews, designed to make me seem average and approachable. But it wasn't entirely true. "Well, kinda. I've lived in LA since I was six."

Gray's eyes widened in surprise. "California. That's a big move."

"Yeah, well, I was six and the prospect of living 'close to Disneyland' was pretty exciting."

"Still, must have been hard to leave all your friends and stuff. Even if you still have your family, getting torn away from everything you know can't be easy."

"Uh... yeah," I said slowly. "Well, it was just me and my dad who moved. Luke—my brother—and my mom stayed in New York."

"Wow."

"It sounds more fucked up than it is," I said quickly. "At first, we weren't sure how long the acting thing was going to last. I'd been picked to be on this TV show but we weren't even sure it was going to get a full season order. So it didn't make sense for the whole family to up and move, for my mom to quit her job. And then—" I balled the straw wrapper up and rolled it between my fingers. "Then I guess once we knew I'd be there for a while, it was harder for them to move. Didn't make a lot of sense. Luke was in school, he had friends. Their whole lives were there."

"Yeah, but them leaving wouldn't have been any worse than what you went through."

"I guess." I shrugged. "To be honest, I can't even remember any of my childhood friends. Like, I'm sure I had them, but it's just—it's been so long." I snorted. "God, that makes sense of some stuff."

Gray frowned. "What?"

"Nothing, it's just—" I paused.

It had just occurred to me that I'd never actually *had* friends. I couldn't remember a single name or face of someone I knew before my dad and I moved out to LA. And once we were there, sure, there were other actors my age on the show, but we were never really friends. More like co-workers in miniature, 10 year olds whose relationships were no deeper than those you'd find in any corporate office.

I knew what friendship was *supposed* to be like. Hell, I'd starred on a fucking TV show where we solved mysteries with the power of friendship. Love, trust, intimacy, loyalty. Other people must have had that in their friendships— otherwise why the hell had I sung cutesy songs about it each week? But I'd never actually felt that myself.

God, what did that say about me? Even as a child, no one had wanted to be my friend.

"Tyler, are you—are you okay?" Gray asked and I looked up at him in surprise, realizing too late how quiet I'd been and how long the silence had dragged out.

"Yeah, sorry, fine," I said, with a shake of my head and a grin. "I was just thinking about—well, nothing important."

"Are you sure?" Gray's eyes filled with concern. Goddammit, why did he have to go around being so nice to me right before he was about to start hating me? Way to pour salt in the fucking wound. "You don't have to—I mean, I was just joking about you telling me your story. You don't—"

"Nah, I want to," I said brusquely. "After all, fair's fair."

"Okay but—"

"Let me see," I said, barrelling on. Maybe the best thing to do was just to get it all out at once. "So we moved when I was six. I was cast on *Criss-Cross Applesauce*, which I don't recommend looking up on Youtube unless you want to lose hours of your life and have *The Good Ship Friendship* stuck in your head forever."

"*The Good Ship*—"

"A sea shanty sung by eight year olds about the power of friendship to calm the stormy seas of life. It's incredibly dumb and incredibly catchy, so seriously, avoid at all costs," I said, my lips twisting. "Anyway, that lasted til I was 12, but then the show shut down because of budget cuts from the network and some legal trouble with our mascot Sammy the Seahorse—well, the guy who played him, obviously, not the mascot himself—and we were almost going to move back to Long Island but then my dad got me an audition on this other sitcom so we ended up staying."

"Jesus—that's... a lot."

I laughed. "That's not even that bad. When I was on *Shoe-string Miracles*—that was the sitcom—the network's lawyers were constantly bailing people out of shit. One season, we had one actor using heroin, another with a gambling problem, another who got a DUI, and three people arrested for underage drinking, one of them being me."

"Shit," Gray laughed. "I guess the lawyers were really earning their paychecks then."

"You know, maybe I should have tried that line on my dad when he had to bail me out of jail," I said thoughtfully. "It couldn't have worked any worse than, *'But everyone else was doing it'*."

"Oh God, did he take it badly?"

"Oh, you know, not really. Just threatened to disown me and reminded me that no one else was going to put up with my bullshit if he ever stopped."

"Jesus, that's harsh."

"I mean, he wasn't serious," I said, a little annoyed at Gray's tone. "Or honestly, maybe he was, but I deserved it. I wasn't that great a kid. Like, he did so much for me, finding me roles, getting me tutors so I didn't have to be in school, negotiating what I got paid and making sure I didn't get taken advantage of. And how did I repay that? By getting drunk and throwing up in public and ruining my reputation —and his."

"That's—"

"So yeah, it was all kind of downhill from there," I said quickly, cutting Gray off. I didn't want to hear whatever he was going to say, especially not if it was sympathy. I didn't deserve sympathy, frankly. "When I was 17, I punched a photographer who called my friend fat, but I was drunk at the time, so that's what the story became—that and the assault charges that resulted. They were dropped later, but still enough to make the network nervous and cause my insurance rates to spike. So that went over real well with my dad. And then when I was 18, a bunch of us were out on a boat that got detained and searched and I was arrested for possession of cocaine—nothing like what went down later but... enough so that my dad got disgusted with me and moved out."

"Holy shit."

"Yeah. Like I said—not the greatest kid. I mean, he was still my manager, but things definitely got worse from then on, because, if you can believe this, taking a shitty, irresponsible teenager and suddenly giving him a ton of freedom is *not* actually a recipe for success."

"Yeah, but that's not—"

"No, Gray, please," I interrupted. "I know you're trying to be nice because you don't know me very well and don't want to judge someone you're gonna be working with, but you don't have to. In fact, you really shouldn't. I basically spent the next two years of my life drunk, high, or hungover and trying to become drunk or high. My dad got me a bunch of movies but they mostly flopped. So I stopped working and just bought stupid shit or invested my money in things that literally made no sense."

"Really?"

"Yeah. Vegan dog food? Turns out that's actually like, really bad for them? Gold-leaf, diamond-encrusted, designer water bottles? JetKicks?" I laughed at Gray's blank look.

"Those are actual shoes with jetpacks in them, like if you crossed hoverboards with ski boots."

"That doesn't even—"

"Make any sense? I know. Tell that to 19 year old me before he invests two million dollars in shoes that explode if you actually try to wear them. One of the guys in the JetKicks lab apparently lost a few toes before they shut the project down."

"Jesus."

"Yeah. Apparently teenagers with an obsession with rocket fuel don't make the greatest start-up CEOs. Or investors. My dad had a fucking field day with that one. By that point, though, I think he kind of enjoyed getting to point out all the ways I was fucking up. Like, the whole time I was a kid, all I'd do was complain about how hard he made me work, how I wanted my freedom. And now I finally had it and I was basically proving his point back to him—I wasn't good enough, or hard-working enough, or fucking smart enough to know what to do with it."

I could feel my lips curling bitterly and I flicked the little straw wrapper ball away from me in annoyance. It bounced against the side wall and rolled backwards, coming to rest in the puddle of condensation my cup had left on the wooden tabletop.

"Anyway, my last movie, *Sojourn to Darkness*, did terribly and I made the mistake of getting high at the premiere and then thought I was having a heart attack, so I started undressing in the middle of an interview at the after party—don't ask me why I thought that would stop the heart attack because I don't fucking know—and was down to my underwear before someone hustled me away."

"That's—"

I snorted. "Come to think of it, maybe that willingness to undress in public was just a sign of things to come. My agent, Tiana, talked me into taking a break after that, which could have been a good idea, except I just used it as an excuse to get loaded constantly. Needless to say, things with my dad were not great by that point. And then um—"

This was the part I'd been dreading, and I had to take a deep breath before continuing.

"Then about a year ago, I shoplifted a pair of fucking polka-dotted suspenders, ran away from the mall cops who apprehended me, and then led the actual police on the world's most depressing car chase that lasted for literally like a mile and a half before I crashed my car into the barrier."

"Oh my God." Gray's eyes widened. "That sounds terrifying."

"Honestly, not even the worst car accident I've been in," I said, unable to keep my disgust with myself out of my voice. "I ran my car into a tree once because my cell phone rang really loudly and surprised me. That one left me with a broken arm that delayed filming on one of my movies for a month."

"Jesus."

"Anyway, the cops caught up with me, obviously, and when they searched the car they found like, a fuckton of cocaine in a hedgehog cookie jar."

"Holy shit."

"Yeah. So, I don't... blame anyone for what happened next. I'd exhausted pretty much everyone's patience with me. I got sentenced to a year of rehab and community-service, which was honestly better than I deserved, but everyone was pretty pissed off about that, because, if I weren't, like, famous and shit, it probably would have been way worse. And yeah, turns out I'm an addict. And no one will work with me now. And I have no money left, because I blew it all on stupid shit. And now I'm living back home with my mom because my dad won't talk to me and I literally can't afford to live on my own."

I wanted to keep my eyes down. I mean, wouldn't you? It's not the sort of thing it's easy to be proud of. *Oh me? Just broke, unemployable, and unliked by 99% of the people who know me.*

But some perverse strand of stubbornness made me look up and meet Gray's eyes. I wanted to see his judgement. Wanted to see the moment when he lost respect for me.

But when I caught Gray's gaze, that wasn't what I saw. As I watched, I saw those clear blue eyes of his go from surprised to concerned to... Jesus Christ, was that amusement?

"What the fuck, are you laughing?" I asked, glaring at him. "Don't laugh about it. It's pathetic, not funny."

"It's not pathetic," Gray said. "God, it's not even funny either, I'm sorry, I don't know why I'm laughing." He shook his head and squeezed his eyes shut like that might help. It didn't. When he opened them, they were just as filled with mirth. "It's just—you're so like, defiant about it? Is that the word? Like you're daring me to still like you?"

"You *shouldn't* still like me. I'm a fucking mess. And an asshole. All I've done is ruin things for myself and everyone around me."

"Okay, well, maybe," Gray said, holding up his hand. "But maybe, you're just... I don't know, a kid. Sorry, God, that's a shitty thing to say—and makes me feel about a hundred years old—but you were just a kid when a lot of that happened anyway."

"Most kids haven't been arrested multiple times before they're 18."

"Yeah, but most kids also don't grow up in the kind of environment you did. It can't have been easy, having to be on camera all the time. Be on, be perfect. You acted out—most teenagers do. You just... had a little more disposable income when you did, so it made it a bit splashier."

"I don't think you're grasping the situation here. I was selfish. And thoughtless. And lazy. And blamed other people for my problems. I was not the kind of person you should want to spend time with."

"Sure, but that's all past tense, right? In the time that I've known you, all I've seen is you being talented, dedicated, thoughtful—" Gray stabbed the air with his fork to punctuate each word, "so pretty much the opposite of all of that other stuff. I mean, sure, it's not *great* to have a trunkful of coke, but hey, that's entrepreneurial spirit, right?"

"I don't even—" I stopped. There was no point in going into that. "Nevermind."

"You don't even what?"

"It's not a big deal."

"Tyler, what were you going to say?" Gray tilted his face down to catch my eyes, but his tone was playful. "Come on, tell me why that wasn't entrepreneurial spirit and was just pride and avarice instead."

"It's not entrepreneurial spirit if I don't even remember buying it," I snapped back.

I regretted it immediately. There was no reason to be a dick to Gray, but of course, I couldn't help acting like one anyway.

"Whatever, it's stupid," I said with a sigh, steepling my fingers and resting my face against them. I was suddenly incredibly tired."It's just—I don't remember buying it and I have no idea how it got into the car. I'd sure as hell never seen that cookie jar before. So before you go absolving me of all my sins, maybe ask yourself what kind of a person can either be so high that he doesn't remember buying a shit-load of cocaine, or is so fucking in denial that he's not only lying to himself, he actually believes his lie that he didn't buy it. Not that it even fucking makes a difference. It was my car, they were my drugs."

"Christ, it makes a lot of difference," Gray said. "If you don't remember buying it—"

"Then maybe it wasn't really mine?" I finished for him. I knew I sounded pissy but it wasn't like I hadn't already had this conversation with myself a hundred times. "Then how the hell did it get in my car? None of my friends had keys. I don't think there was some giant, Illuminati-backed plot to assassinate my character. The simplest explanation is usually the right one: I bought it, I put it there."

That was the knowledge I'd had to live with for the past

year. That I'd been so messed up, I couldn't even remember buying all of that. Shit, no wonder I'd lost all my money, if I couldn't even keep track of a fucking half kilo of coke.

I'd wanted so badly to believe it hadn't been mine. I'd tried telling myself that at first. But pretty much the entire focus of our lives at the group home was taking responsibility for our choices. And the longer I thought about it, the clearer it became. I was lying to myself, trying to get out of owning up to my own actions. The coke was mine, and I needed to accept that.

"Maybe," Gray said, giving me a level look. "I don't know. But that's not actually what I was going to say. What I meant was that it makes a difference because it must feel really awful, having the whole world judge you for something that you can't even remember. It must have made you doubt yourself, and that couldn't have felt good."

"Oh," I said softly.

"Yeah. Oh." Gray smiled. "Anyway, my point was, much as you're trying to get me to believe you're a terrible person, I'd like to reserve my judgement on that for a while, if that's okay with you."

"If I say it's not okay, will that annoy you enough to start disliking me?" I asked with a wry grin.

"Well at this point I'm just going to like you on principle," Gray said, grinning right back. "So you might as well get used to it."

"God, this shoot's gonna be torture, isn't it?" I said, rolling my eyes.

"Yup," Gray agreed, spearing his last noodle. "You definitely should have backed out when you had the chance."

The rest of the meal was uneventful. Prija, our waitress, told me she thought I was cute, but remarkably, no one asked for a picture. It was night by the time we began walking back to Bailey Park, the darkness drawn down over the housetops like a blanket.

I liked the feeling of walking back through unfamiliar streets in a place I didn't know. It made *me* feel less known, less noticeable. Made me feel more like no one, which I relished. Like maybe I could blend in here. But it was a little chilly now so I was happy to get into the warmth of the mansion.

We walked up to the second floor together and I stopped outside my door in the hallway and looked up at Gray, biting my lip at what I knew I needed to say.

"Um—thanks. For, well, everything," I said, wincing at how stupid I sounded. "I'll, uh, pay you back for dinner—and that cab ride last week—once we get our first paychecks."

"Really, it doesn't matter at all," Gray said, leaning against the doorframe.

"I'm, uh, sorry I snapped at you, too," I continued. "I'm just not very good at like—people stuff."

"That's obviously not true," Gray said. "You couldn't be as good an actor as you are if you were really that bad at it."

"Well, not good at being myself, then," I said. "At like, talking about myself, normally."

"Tyler." Gray's voice was warm and firm and sent a shiver through me. "You were fine. But if you really want to apologize, okay, apology accepted."

"Thanks. That, uh—it means a lot. I'm not—I'm just not used to people like, *not* judging me? If that makes sense?"

"Please," Gray laughed. "Who am I to judge? There's honestly probably just as much of me online as you—and far more naked, even including your post-heart-attack stripping debacle."

"Yeah, but at least you were getting paid for your incidents," I said, looking down as my cheeks flushed.

"Some people would say that makes me even worse."

"Well fuck those people," I said, surprised by the ferocity in my voice. Gray just smiled.

"I agree." He paused, like he was considering saying something else, but when he spoke next, all he said was, "Goodnight, Tyler. Try not to invest in any socks with lasers on them in your sleep."

I smiled. "Try not to get murdered by any vengeful ghosts."

I stepped into my room and closed the door quickly after Gray turned to walk down the hall. I was *not* going to watch him walk away. I checked my phone where I'd left it sitting on the dresser, more out of habit than because I expected anything. There weren't too many people trying to talk to me these days.

But it turned out I had a text waiting for me from Luke.

LUKE: How was the first day? Everything ok?

I snorted and texted back.

TYLER: Good. Got your note in my lunchbag and had people to play with at recess and everything

TYLER: Thanks Mom

LUKE: Fuck you

LUKE: Dick

TYLER: So is now a good time to ask you for a favor?

LUKE: Depends, what's in it for me?

TYLER: I mean, I can't promise to stop being a dick, but I can promise to try...

TYLER: Kinda broke still. Only other thing I can offer is tickets for whenever the movie premieres

LUKE: So I can see my brother have sex with someone?

LUKE: Hard pass

LUKE: What's up tho?

I tried to shove down the twisty feeling of guilt that serpentined through my stomach as I typed out my text.

TYLER: So there's this paperwork I have to fill out for getting paid

TYLER: Like direct deposit stuff? And I'm just completely lost

TYLER: They want my routing number and account number and stuff and I like don't even know what those are?

God, I was a fucking embarrassment. But I'd never learned

how to do this sort of shit—my dad had always done it for me. And Luke worked in finance—didn't that mean he liked doing money stuff?

LUKE: You can find those when you log into your bank account. There should be a place where they're listed. If you log on, I can talk you through it

TYLER: Can't you just do it for me?

LUKE: No

LUKE: Wait, are you serious?

TYLER: YES. I'm gonna fuck it up if I do it

LUKE: There's literally nothing to fuck up. It's just logging in and clicking a few buttons

TYLER: Pleeeeeeease?

TYLER: I just feel like I'm gonna mess it up. I don't get it and I'm not good with money and I just...

TYLER: PLEASE???

TYLER: I can send you my log-in info and all the forms

LUKE: Dude you're not sending me your forms. You have to learn how to do this yourself

TYLER: You're the worst

TYLER: I thought you were my brother

TYLER: I thought our bond meant something to you

TYLER: I guess I was wrong

TYLER: My mistake. I won't make it again

TYLER: *It's been nice knowing you*

LUKE: *OMG*

LUKE: *Just send me the stupid info*

TYLER: *You're the best*

LUKE: *THIS IS ME ROLLING MY EYES AT YOU*

TYLER: *ILU big brother*

I shot him a quick email with my log-in for my bank account, then plugged my phone in, stripped, and collapsed onto my weird clown bed. I was fucking exhausted, even though nothing had really happened tonight.

It was strange—I was so used to everyone knowing how and when and where I'd fucked up, I hadn't been prepared for how draining it felt to have to actually explain everything from the beginning. I was just sick of feeling like I was some kind of carnival attraction, like everyone was pointing and gawking at me.

I groaned, thinking about what Dave and Andrew wanted me to do. Coming out shouldn't be that hard, right? What they'd said was right—I was essentially outing myself anyway by doing this movie. Having sex with another guy on camera. So what the fuck was the big deal about making a little statement?

And yet the thought made me squirm uncomfortably on my twin bed. How could I come out when I'd never even done anything with a guy? What if I was wrong and it turned out I wasn't into them? I mean, sure, if that were the case, I might have bigger problems than a press release—like the fact that Gray was supposed to fuck me by the end of the month.

But being in the movie didn't *have* to mean I was gay, right? Like, couldn't I just spin it as some kind of avant garde, 'I did it for Art with a capital A' kind of thing? And why the fuck did people need me to make some kind of a statement anyway? Why wasn't my work enough on its own?

I just wanted to do this movie and figure everything out on my own. In private. In front of thousands of people. Right. I groaned at the contradictions in my thinking and turned onto my side.

I thought I liked guys. I was pretty sure. The only time I'd even kissed a guy was at a party two years ago and it was in exchange for getting a hit of some girl's coke. It was just some random dude and I'd been drunk enough to be able to laugh it off the next day as a funny story.

But I still remembered the scent of that guy's aftershave. The way his shoulders had felt under my hands as I steadied myself. The rasp of his stubble against my cheek.

Other than that, though, it was just stolen glances. Tight feelings in my gut when I saw certain guys. Recurrent sex dreams and panic attacks that I'd get an accidental boner at the wrong time.

And with women—I didn't even know. I'd had sex a couple times, but it was never anything special. I'd gotten off, and tried to make sure they did too, but it felt like just going through the motions. My mind was always a million miles away—usually thinking about whatever guy I had a crush on at the time.

I stared at my phone, resting on the nightstand where I'd plugged it in, and bit my lip. There was something I'd wanted to do all week but had been too nervous to actually try. But it wouldn't be wrong, exactly, right? Gray had never asked me not to. He'd even mentioned it again, just now, which he wouldn't have done if he cared, would he?

It took me all of 30 seconds to find a porn site with dozens of videos of Gray. Gray bending some guy over a desk, Gray pressing some guy up against a tree trunk, Gray—*Jesus*—Gray eating some guy out at the edge of a pool. My heart was pounding all of a sudden, like I was at the very top of a rollercoaster, but I clicked the first video before I chickened out.

My eyes widened as I watched. Because it was *Gray*. The same guy who'd sat across from me at dinner tonight, who was sweet and funny and warm and kind, and now he was standing at the edge of a massive desk, holding some guy's legs up in the air in a V shape, thrusting his cock—which, Jesus, yes, was big—into the other guy's ass.

And holy shit was it hot.

And before I knew what I was doing, I'd snaked a hand down into my pants and begun to stroke myself. I couldn't help it—I'd gotten hard from like, 10 seconds of watching that, hearing Gray's deep, strong voice asking that guy if he liked Gray's cock, hearing that guy whimper and moan that he did, and all I could think of was that I wanted Gray to ask me the same thing.

Except not even that. The most embarrassing thing was that what my brain couldn't stop conjuring up was Gray saying *sweet* things to me. Just like he'd done at dinner, only, you know, sexier.

Yes, Tyler, that's so good, you're so good.

Kill me, I wanted that so badly. Wanted his hands all over me, on my chest, on my cock, or, God, in my ass. Or maybe he'd let me go down on him. Fuck, that gave me a jolt, the thought of caressing Gray's cock—newly confirmed as *massive*—in my hands, running my tongue along that smooth skin, parting my lips around it and letting him fill my mouth.

I stroked myself faster. Fuck, I could see myself naked, getting down on my knees in front of Gray, holding the base of his cock in one hand, sliding him in between my lips. Jesus, I'd never given a blow job before, but holy shit did I want to, now. I wondered what he'd taste like.

I could almost feel the heat of Gray's body, feel his hands on my shoulders, on my neck, tangled in my hair. And all the while, he'd whisper softly to me, tell me how good I was. And then, just when he was ready to come, he'd pull me off and up. He'd spin me around and push me down onto the bed, or a desk—any horizontal surface, really. Just like that guy in the video.

My breath came shorter and faster as I pictured Gray rubbing his cock against my stomach, my thighs, my ass. I'd moan as I felt that hot, firm length press against me, knowing it was me he wanted. He'd tell me how good he'd make me feel and I'd whimper in pleasure—hell, I was whimpering now in bed.

And as I watched Gray thrusting into that guy in the video, as I imagined him bringing his cock to *my* hole, I held my cock with my left hand and slid my finger down to my hole and circled it. I could see Gray pressing into me, practically feel it, and as I pushed my finger inside, all I could think of was Gray whispering my name.

I came. Hard. I stroked myself with shuddering movements, my body shaking from the force of it, and I panted for minutes as I came down from that high. Jesus, I hadn't come like that in—I couldn't even remember how long.

A hot rush of a million feelings swept over my body at once. Shock, desire, satisfaction, shame. God, did I really think I might not like guys? Was that really a possibility anymore?

I grabbed a tissue to clean up the splatter of cum from my stomach and then stopped, my eyes caught by the video still playing on my phone. The guy—the bottom, I guess he was called—had just come, and Gray had pulled out, was standing over the guy and stroking his cock hard. As I watched, Gray came, ropes of cum landing on the bottom's stomach while the guy lay there and watched, his mouth open and his eyes wide.

Something hot and metallic felt like it was constricting around my chest, and it only got worse as Gray bent down and kissed the guy, first lightly, then deepening the kiss and claiming his mouth.

Jesus. I closed out of the video and turned my phone over in frustration. I was not allowed to be jealous of a stupid guy Gray had fucked in a porn like, three years ago probably.

For one thing, it wasn't real, it was goddamn porn. For another, I had literally no claim on Gray. And most importantly, I wasn't looking for one.

I was trying to get my life back on track and that did not include developing a baby-gay crush on my costar just because he was *nice* to me. He'd never like me anyway—too young, too dumb, too not-actually-a-good-person.

But it didn't matter. Because I wasn't interested. I didn't have time to like someone, didn't have time for a relationship with—

Ugh. Relationship. Where the fuck had that word even come from? Being in a relationship was the worst thing an actor could do for himself—especially someone in my position who was trying to get their life back. Who the hell was talking about a relationship?

No one, that's who. I rolled over onto my side and closed my eyes forcefully. Relationship. Bullshit. I was done thinking about this, and I was going to sleep, going to be ready for shooting tomorrow.

But as I lay there in the dark and tried to think of other things, Gray's blue eyes lingered in my mind far longer than I would have liked.

~

"Dylan?" Wyatt sounded surprised, almost shocked, when Dylan almost smacked into him in the woods. Dylan stopped short, breathing hard. "You're not supposed to be here."

This was it. It wasn't the moment Dylan had expected to see Wyatt—he'd thought he'd have the grounds to himself, with everyone else away on the trip. He'd taken the run as an excuse to calm his restless mind after their conversation last night at dinner.

But now Wyatt was here and Dylan didn't want to wait anymore. He was sick of holding himself back, sick of the constant buzzing jumping on-edge gonna-die might-throw-up feeling in his stomach. Because last night, things had changed.

And now Wyatt was here, right in front of him.

Dylan had to make this moment count.

All of that flashed through his mind in the seconds it took for him to steady himself, to take a step back and blink up at Wyatt, to lose himself in those blue eyes again, and smile.

"Hey," Dylan said, and he knew that Wyatt would attribute his shortness of breath to the fact that he'd been running—just as surely as he knew that that wasn't true. It was Wyatt who made Dylan constantly feel like he was in free-fall. "I didn't—I didn't go on the trip," he finished. He blushed.

"What? But you—I have the list," Wyatt protested. "Of everyone who's supposed to be gone. You're on it."

"I know," Dylan said, a smile creeping onto his face. "But you can't take a kid with the stomach flu on a weekend trip off campus, can you?"

"Jesus, you're sick?" Wyatt said, instantly concerned. Dylan loved that about him—his concern, his care. It was part of what made Wyatt so wonderful—and so frustrating. "What are you doing out here? Should you be running?"

"I'm not sick," Dylan said, the smile growing broader, undeniably a grin now. "They just think I'm sick. I couldn't sleep last night, not after we—well, anyway, it seemed like a shame to leave, right after that. So I figured, might as well put the insomnia to good use. It's not that hard to fake throwing up. Once in the bathrooms on our floor, once in the infirmary, and now you're looking at the only senior who's not in New York this weekend."

"And now you're out running? That hardly seems like something a sick kid would do. Aren't you afraid someone will realize you're faking?"

Dylan shrugged. "I went out through the greenhouse. No one saw me leave. And no one uses this trail anymore, not since that oak fell across the path back by the river." He gestured at a spot behind Wyatt's shoulder. "See that beech tree over there? I do my reading here sometimes, sitting underneath it. Hours go by and you never see anyone."

Wyatt followed his gaze and they were silent for a second, and Dylan wondered what Wyatt was going to say, and then realized he knew what Wyatt was going to say, knew it exactly, and he didn't want to hear it. He was sick of waiting.

"So," Dylan said, "I figured I'd run, clear my head, shower—and then make a miraculous recovery and come find you during your planning period." He took a step forward and Wyatt, as usual, took one back. "We left things kind of unfinished, you know?"

"We—what? Dylan, no. You can't—I told you last night, this has to stop. We can't... do... anything."

Wyatt stepped back again. Dylan followed him. It was like the world's slowest tango and it was impossible to tell who was leading, but soon they were underneath the canopy of the beech tree, the coppery leaves filtering the morning's sun down onto them in a shifting kaleidoscope of light.

"Can't?" Dylan asked, taking another step. He wished he could wipe the grin off his face, wished he could look cool and mature and sexy, but dammit, it was too hard. He was giddy and he couldn't hide it. "Or shouldn't?"

"Both."

"Fine," Dylan said, and even though he sounded petulant, childish, he could tell that Wyatt was shocked he'd given in so easily. If only Wyatt knew.

"Fine?" Wyatt repeated.

"Yeah." Dylan bit his lip. "Just tell me you don't want me, and I'll leave."

Wyatt frowned immediately. "That's a ridiculous ultimatum. I'm just going to walk back."

"Great," Dylan said, shrugging his shoulders. "I'll walk with you. I'm sure no one will have any questions about what a sick student and his Calc teacher were doing out in the woods together at 7:30 in the morning."

"That's not fair."

"You know, I can almost remember someone telling me recently that life wasn't fair," Dylan said, cocking his chin to the side. "God, who was that? It's the strangest thing..."

Wyatt glowered. "I don't want you, Dylan."

It felt like a punch to the solar plexus. Dylan blinked, then stared at Wyatt, uncomprehending. He couldn't mean that. Not really. It was just something he was saying to get Dylan off his back.

Dylan's eyes narrowed and he waited for Wyatt's expression to change. He couldn't really mean it. Every interaction they'd had til now told Dylan that Wyatt was wrong, that Wyatt was lying because he thought it was what he was supposed to do—the 'right' thing to do.

But that was bullshit, because what was right was everything between them, every atom in Dylan's body that was pulling him towards the other man, that had them tethered, and he knew Wyatt could feel it too.

But Wyatt didn't say anything, and slowly, that certainty inside Dylan's chest folded and crumpled like a sandcastle slumping over, succumbing to the tide. A new brew of feelings bubbled its way up in Dylan's body. Fear. Shame. Anger. He wanted to shake something—Wyatt, himself, anything—to dislodge those feelings, but he couldn't. They were taking up residence.

"Fine," he spit out. "Fine."

He turned away angrily, cursing himself for the tears he felt forming in the corners of his eyes.

"Dylan. Wait."

Two words. Barely even that. Three simple syllables. And yet they held Dylan as surely as an iron cage.

He turned. He saw Wyatt's face—a mask of pain and anguish, regret and self-loathing. And he knew he couldn't wait any longer.

Dylan took two quick steps to Wyatt, reached up to place both hands on Wyatt's face, and pulled him down for a kiss. Wyatt's lips froze in shock at first, unmoving, but his hands, Dylan noticed, went around Dylan's waist immediately.

It was hard to kiss someone, though, if they wouldn't kiss you back, and even though Dylan could feel the warmth of Wyatt's breath, his hands holding Dylan to him, could smell the soap Wyatt used this morning, taste a hint of coffee on his lips, Wyatt was moving like he was in a stupor, and suddenly Dylan felt foolish, and realized he was being unfair.

"Sorry," he said, breaking away. He looked down. That had been a shitty thing to do. Wyatt had said no, and then Dylan had forced the issue. What kind of person did that? "God, sorry, I shouldn't have—"

But then there were fingertips under his chin and he looked back up to see Wyatt's eyes, deep and blue, pupils blown wide. He saw one second's worth of desire pulsing deep within them, and then Wyatt was pressing his lips to Dylan's and all Dylan could do was feel.

He closed his eyes and let himself surrender. Wyatt's heat, Wyatt's strength, Wyatt's passion knocked him over. He parted his lips as Wyatt pivoted them and pressed Dylan back up against his beech tree.

Dylan's hands went to Wyatt's neck as he tasted Wyatt's tongue, letting Wyatt into his mouth. Dylan groaned, arched his back, pushing up off the tree and against Wyatt's body as one of Wyatt's hands slid up underneath Dylan's t-shirt. It made Dylan bold, made him brave enough to drop a hand, to palm the hardness he swore he felt inside Wyatt's jeans.

And suddenly, Wyatt pulled back.

"We can't do this," Wyatt said again, and Dylan's mouth fell open, his eyes widening in silent, confused protest, but before Dylan could speak, Wyatt continued. "Here, anyway. We can't do this here. Anyone could come by."

"I told you," Dylan said. "No one will. I could build a three-story treehouse in this tree and no one would ever notice."

"Still," Wyatt said, "it's not worth the risk. And I have class. Jesus, I don't even know what time it is."

"7:45," Dylan said, still a little breathless as he glanced down at his running watch. "First period doesn't start til 8."

"I have to go," Wyatt said. "I have to get ready, I have to— dammit, I came out here to clear my head and now I'm more muddled than I was before. God, how the hell am I supposed to teach Trig right now?"

Dylan laughed. "You think you have it tough? I have to fake being sick for the rest of the weekend."

"Poor kid." Wyatt rolled his eyes. He started to take a step back, but Dylan grabbed his wrist.

"I can see you later, though, right?"

Dylan didn't know why he was so nervous. He'd just made out with his fucking Calc teacher, stroked Wyatt's hard-on through his pants. So why did he suddenly feel so shy, so vulnerable?

"Yeah." Wyatt nodded ruefully. "Yeah, you can see me later."

And as the sunlight landed around them, lighting up their faces in green and gold and copper, Dylan realized he'd never felt anything more perfect than this.

"Cut!" Violet yelled.

The sound knifed through the trees with startling force and Dylan—no, me, Tyler, I wasn't Dylan anymore—I breathed heavily.

Gray stepped away from me, holding out a hand, and I let Gray pull me up away from the tree.

"Thanks," I said, blinking rapidly. It was taking a moment to come back to myself—longer than usual. I always sank into my characters but with a script this good, it was taking a bit more effort to separate myself from the person I'd been pretending to be.

Well, that, and the fact that I'd just kissed Gray. And while that might have been in the context of a scene, it's not like my lips knew the difference. Or my heart. Or really any part of my body, apparently.

Fuck, that had been... I smiled slowly to myself, looking at Gray out of the corner of my eye, trying not to let him see me staring. That had been good. Gray's lips were soft but strong and he'd kissed me like—well, like he meant it.

It had been so good, it scared me a little. Because if I'd liked it that much—well, there went my plausible deniability.

Even after my extra-curricular activities earlier this week, as I'd watched Gray's porn online, it had all still felt a bit theoretical. Jerking off to a scene of Gray fucking another guy was still in the realm of fantasy. But kissing Gray? Kissing him for real?

If I knew I liked it, didn't that mean I was gay? Or at least bi?

Why did that thought make my stomach turn a somersault? I knew there was nothing wrong with it, nothing bad about not being straight. But somehow—I don't know, somehow it felt different when it came to me personally. I wasn't sure I was ready for what it all meant.

It was just a fucking scene. Get a grip.

I shook myself and looked around the clearing. It felt like it had been a good take. A long one, but Violet said she wanted us to do it in one if we could handle it. I glanced over at her, as much to force myself to look away from Gray as to ask her a question.

"Verdict?" I said, keeping my fingers crossed.

"Fucking amazing," Violet said, grinning broadly. "I could kiss both of you. Though I imagine you've maybe had enough of that for now."

I laughed weakly.

"Really?" Gray said. "It was—it was good?"

"You gotta stop thinking you're terrible, Gray," Violet said with a laugh. "You've been great this whole week, I don't know why today would be an exception."

Gray flushed as Violet turned and consulted a PA briefly, then looked back at us.

"Let's pick up back in the dining hall for the next scene," she said. "Tyler, you'll need to change. The extras should start arriving soon and if everything keeps going well, knock on wood, we'll be able to wrap the next scene by midafternoon."

~

"What's up?"

I looked up from my phone in confusion and stared at Gray. I hadn't heard him walk over to me. I'd changed out of Dylan's running clothes and into his school uniform. After a week of filming, this school uniform was beginning to feel as comfortable and familiar as my actual clothes. I'd picked up my phone as I'd walked into the huge old hall that we were using as a stand-in for the cafeteria in the movie.

I'd missed a call from my father.

"Sorry," I said, feeling a little light-headed. "What did you say?"

"Just asked what was up," Gray said. His voice sounded muted against the buzz of activity around us, like maybe my hearing wasn't working quite right. "You look like you've seen a ghost—or more specifically, like what *I* would look like if I'd seen one."

"I uh—it's my dad," I said slowly. "He—he called me." I held my phone out to Gray as evidence.

"Shit. Did he leave a message?"

I shook my head. "He never does. He always says he's too busy for that.

Gray frowned. "You gonna call him back?

I glanced at the time. They were still setting up the boom mics and Violet was wrangling the extras. I knew I should wait and call later. But I was afraid I wouldn't be able to concentrate if I were worrying about my dad through the next scene.

I looked at Gray. "Do you think I have time?"

"Go for it," Gray said with an encouraging smile. "If we need to stall, I'll just say I forgot my lines."

"Bad news for ya, buddy," I said, shaking my head. "After this morning's scene—after this whole week, really—I don't think you can play yourself off as the nervous ingenue anymore. You're way too good for anyone to believe you don't have your shit down cold. But, uh... thanks."

Gray waved my apology away and then walked over to talk to Danny, clearly trying to give me space. I looked down at my phone and took a shaky breath, then walked over to one of the deeply recessed windows in the dining hall. I hopped up on the ledge, then drew my knees into my chest and pushed the call button next to my dad's name.

It barely even had a chance to ring before my dad picked up.

"Tyler!" he barked. His voice was so loud he might as well have been standing next to me.

"Uh, hey, Dad," I said, immediately feeling myself wilt a little. He was pissed—there was no mistaking that tone—and I had an instinctual urge to apologize. "I'm, um, sorry I missed your call. We were shooting and—"

"You're damn right you're sorry," my dad interrupted. "What the fuck were you thinking?"

"I, uh—I thought—"

"You *weren't* thinking," my dad interrupted again. "Clearly. That's the only explanation. Just Tyler the Idiot making another one of his mistakes."

"But Dad, I—"

"Don't 'but Dad' me, unless it's 'But Dad I'm a moron for not thinking this through.' Have you seen what they're saying about you online?"

I hadn't, actually. Partially because, at the group home, they'd talked about how reading what people said about you was looking for external validation or something, and how bad that was. But mostly I was just sick of reading stories about myself. They were never good.

"I've been trying not to—I mean, I don't really—"

"They're saying you're gay now, you know that? Either that, or that you're an asshole for taking this part away from a gay man."

"I know, but it's—"

"So which is it?" my dad demanded. "Are you an asshole, or are you actually gay?"

His tone left no doubt as to which he considered worse.

"I'm not—not sure," I said weakly.

I hated myself. So much for thinking about coming out. So much for being proud of my work on this movie, so much for not caring what other people thought about me. I couldn't even tell my dad the truth. Why the hell had I thought any of this was a good idea?

"You're dropping out," my dad said. His tone made it clear that this was a command. "Today."

It felt like something was gripping my heart.

"I can't—I can't just quit," I stammered.

"You certainly can if you know what's good for you. You want to be pigeon-holed as a gay actor from now on? As a slut? You want to never get any work again?"

"I'm not sure it's—"

"If you ever want my help again, you will quit this movie," my dad continued. "I swear to God Tyler, drop out today or this is it, we're done."

It landed like a kick to the stomach and I sucked in a breath. I knew it was probably stupid. Maybe Luke was right, maybe I shouldn't still care what my dad thought. We hadn't talked in over a year.

But some part of me had still been holding out hope that somehow, some way, I'd be able to make that right. Fix things. Make him talk to me again. That maybe he'd at least approve of me going out and finding a role, getting a job on my own.

But my dad was right. I was an idiot. Taking this movie was never going to get me back in his good graces. I should have known he'd never be okay with this—hell, I had known, and I'd done it anyway. Because I was selfish—because I was immature.

Because I'd *wanted* to, and I'd somehow thought that what *I* wanted was more important than making good business decisions. Thinking with my—well, I didn't want to say heart, that made it sound more pure than it was. Thinking with my dick, or anything, really, except for my head.

"Do you hear me Tyler?" my dad snapped into the phone.

"Yes, Dad," I said quietly. "I'm just not sure I can actually—I mean, we've started filming and everything. Are you sure I can't—"

"Tyler?"

"Yeah?"

"Call me when it's done."

And then he hung up, leaving me staring at the phone in my hand.

*O*ne look at Tyler was enough to show that the phone call did not go well.

Tyler was sitting on the window ledge, unmoving, staring at the phone in his hand. He looked so lost. That protective urge inside of me swelled like a wave and as it crashed and broke over me, I took a step forward. I could at least ask him what was wrong, couldn't I? No harm in being a concerned friend.

I nudged him with my knee gently when I reached him and Tyler looked up in surprise.

"How'd it go?" I asked.

"It... went." Tyler's voice sounded small and uncertain, like paper blowing in the wind.

"You wanna talk about it?"

Tyler just stared up at me, mute. The hurt in his hazel eyes was like a knife ripping through me.

"He wants me to quit," Tyler said slowly.

"Oh." I paused, taken aback. "Oh."

I felt a million things all at once—worry, about what would happen if Tyler did quit; anger, at Tyler's dad for asking that of him; but above all, sadness. Sadness at the thought of having to do this movie without Tyler. It was only the first week, but still—I couldn't imagine having to finish this without him.

"Yeah." Tyler looked around the room as it filled up with people and shook his head.

"What are you—what are you going to do?" I asked, afraid of the answer.

"What *can* I do?" Tyler said. "I don't think I can quit—not now that we've started. It's in our contract. It would be messy."

But he still looked so unhappy.

"Do you... want... to quit?" I asked.

This was the answer I was actually dreading—the thought that even if Tyler stuck with it, that he didn't want to be here. He'd become this sort of beam of sunshine in my life this past week and I hated seeing him sad. But if Tyler didn't actually want to be here, I didn't want him to feel stuck.

Tyler glanced around the room again and then back up at me.

"No," he said, and he almost seemed surprised by his answer. "No, I don't."

Relief flooded my system. But that was reasonable, wasn't it?

No matter how well Violet thought the week was going, I was only able to do so well because I had Tyler acting against me in almost all my scenes. If Tyler left the production, I'd be screwed. They'd have to recast his role, I'd start acting shittily, then the movie would perform shittily, and the whole thing would be a disaster.

That was why I cared.

And yes, also because I liked the guy—because I'd already started thinking of Tyler as a friend. But just as a friend. I was definitely *not* thinking about what it had felt like to kiss him this morning, what his slim body had felt like beneath mine as he'd writhed against me under that tree, what his lips had tasted like, or how that lemon scent of his still lingered in the air.

"Good," I said forcefully. Maybe more forcefully than I'd meant to. Tyler looked up at me in surprise. "If you're not here, who the hell's gonna keep the ghosts away?" I added.

"Yeah, good call," Tyler said, hazarding a smile. But his heart clearly wasn't in it.

"Anything I can do?" I asked.

Tyler snorted. "I don't know, can you convince me that somehow this wasn't a terrible decision and isn't going to backfire on me? Or better yet, do you have a time machine so I can go back to 15 months ago and never end up in this position? Or fuck, go back 15 years and stay home that Saturday morning instead of auditioning?"

"Hey, you're gonna be fine," I said. My hand darted out to squeeze his shoulder but I moved it back when he jumped in surprise. "You're gonna be better than fine, you're gonna be great. You're an amazing actor and that's what people are gonna take away from this movie."

"Maybe," Tyler said, making a face. "But that's not enough, you know? You also have to be smart, and make good decisions. Be strong. And I'm none of those things. I just... suck."

Something inside me twisted, listening to Tyler say that. I hated that he thought so little of himself. He clearly thought there was something wrong with him, that he was irredeemably fucked up.

And yeah, I couldn't deny that he'd fucked up a few times in the past. Maybe more than a few, from what I'd gathered at dinner our first night. But all I'd ever seen from Tyler was kindness, curiosity, and a ready smile. Whatever had happened this past year, he'd clearly changed—if he'd ever been that bad to begin with.

But how to put all of that into words—without seeming creepy for how much I'd been thinking about him?

"I mean, I disagree. But if you want me to call you an asshole, I can do that. If it'd help."

"Thanks," Tyler said wryly. He sighed and stood up. "Might as well get this over with. At least Dylan's supposed to be fucking depressed in this scene. I should call my dad back and thank him for getting me into the right head space."

Tyler pulled himself together for the rest of the day, but he was quiet and moody between takes. The big lunch scene took forever, because the principal, the Spanish teacher— pretty much every character except for Wyatt was in it.

That, and because Violet, I was learning, was a perfectionist.

A lot of *Foresight* was running on volunteers. Former students of Violet's, or fans of the book who'd been so excited about the movie that they'd volunteered their time to help as runners, PAs, or extras. A few of them even won tiny speaking roles in the film, based on the tiers of different crowdfunding levels.

But despite the fact that the set was full of non-professionals, Violet's standards weren't slipping and she held everyone to as high a standard as she did herself, calling for retakes as needed and insisting on getting it right. But she was kind, I realized—thanking everyone, encouraging people, coaching her actors until she got what she needed from them.

She was, I saw, immensely good at working with people. Making them feel appreciated, but more importantly, making them *want* to do their best for her. It was amazing to watch, since I could still remember when one of her jobs was literally mopping up after we'd filmed a four-way sex scene.

I supposed it was probably because Violet had worked her way up that she had respect for everyone in all positions. Each person on a film crew mattered and Violet took the time to show everyone that their contributions were valued.

The last scene of the day was a wordless one of Dylan wrestling with his emotions as he watched Wyatt from across the room. We'd already finished shooting my part and Violet was working on a series of close-ups with Dylan. I stood to the side, watching as a complex storm of emotions crossed Tyler's face, in awe of how easily he could summon that up.

Violet frowned at the end of the first take, then looked back at the camera.

"Want me to do it again?" Tyler asked.

Violet pursed her lips. "I'm honestly not sure. Come here for a minute," she said, beckoning Tyler to come behind the camera with her. "Tell me what you see," she said as she replayed the shot for him.

"Me looking like I'm about to ugly cry?"

Violet laughed. "Yeah—but that part's perfect. I don't think *you're* doing too much, but I'm thinking I might want to try—"

"A medium shot?" Tyler asked.

"Yeah. Emphasize Dylan's isolation a bit more," Violet agreed. "You game?"

"Sure," Tyler said. "You're the boss."

"Good." Violet nodded. "Alright, let's do it one more time."

That, I realized, was Violet's secret. She involved people in the process. She had reasons for everything she did, but she valued other people's input as well.

And, I noticed, Tyler had seemed more animated and engaged in that conversation than he had any time he was off camera all afternoon. Once the scene was over, though, he was back to looking resigned and quiet again, even though I could tell he was trying to hide it.

That pensive mood of his lasted through the weekend and

clear into the following week. I asked Tyler if he wanted to talk about anything a couple more times, but he just shrugged and shook his head. Clearly he wasn't quitting, but just as clearly, he wasn't happy about how things stood.

I wondered if he'd talked to his dad again, but didn't know how to ask. If he didn't want to talk about it, it wasn't my place to bring it up. But I didn't like seeing Tyler, that ray of self-deprecating human sunshine being replaced with Tyler, slim, small human raincloud.

That Tuesday, Violet invited both of us out to dinner with Dave and Andrew, but Tyler declined.

"Just gonna read up for tomorrow," he said, smiling apologetically.

Highly suspicious, if you asked me, because Tyler always had his lines memorized after reading them only one time. I knew I was being stupid when I begged off of dinner too, citing a headache I didn't have. But something in me felt like I didn't want to leave Tyler by himself that night.

When I got back up to my room on the second floor, I had a text from Micah.

MICAH: Hey so remember when I told you nothing was going to go wrong and you could totally leave the bar in my hands and everything would be completely fine?

My stomach dropped.

GRAY: What happened?

GRAY: It's barely over a week

GRAY: Please tell me you didn't burn it down

MICAH: Omg haha no. Nothing that dramatic.

MICAH: Just a billing question. Charterhouse Brewing dropped off the new keg today and said there's some paperwork you need to sign.

GRAY: Jesus don't scare me like that

MICAH: See, but now you're thinking "oh all it is is just a little paperwork" instead of "jfc i have to drive all the way back to the city tonight"

MICAH: Aren't I brilliant?

GRAY: You're annoying. But fine. It's been a while since I've checked in anyway. I'll see you in an hour

I changed into a pair of beat-up jeans and a t-shirt, then headed out the door. And in what was beginning to seem like a pattern, I paused at the top of the stairs and then doubled back until I was outside of Tyler's door. There was no way he was actually reading over his lines.

I knocked.

"Who is it?" Tyler's voice was slightly muffled by the door.

"It's me," I said. "Um, Gray, that is."

I heard Tyler get to his feet and when he opened the door, he gave me a wry smile. "I know who '*me*' is."

I shrugged. "I didn't want to assume."

"Please, you think I'm not gonna recognize the person I've spent 99% of my time with up here?" Tyler rolled his eyes. "What's up—did you wanna run lines or something?"

"Actually, no," I said, shifting my weight and leaning against the doorframe. "I was going to ask you if you wanted to come into the city with me tonight."

Tyler's smile dropped a little. "You don't have to babysit me, Gray. I'll be fine."

"What? It's not babysitting at all."

Tyler just looked at me and cocked an eyebrow.

"Okay fine, maybe it's a little bit babysitting."

"I knew it," Tyler said with a triumphant grin.

"Sue me for caring, asshole," I said with an answering smile. "I really do have to go into the city—there's some paperwork I need to take care of at the bar—and I was gonna grab a quick dinner while I'm in there. And I'm afraid if I do go, by the time I get back, you'll have convinced yourself once and for all that you need to quit and then I'll be stuck doing this movie by myself and I'm gonna suck really badly without you. See," I said, poking his shoulder. "It's actually totally selfish on my part and not babysitting at all."

Tyler frowned up at me. "Maybe," he said, his eyes looking suspicious. "But you've gotta stop thinking you're terrible. And I'm not gonna quit. Even if I wanted to, I couldn't."

"Sound more excited, jeez."

"Sorry, sorry." Tyler laughed lightly. "I'll try."

"Come on, come into the city with me. Take your mind of things. What are you gonna do if you stay here all night anyway?"

"Eat a depressing ham sandwich from catering and contemplate my many failures?"

"God, well, good point. A night in the city definitely can't compare to *that*."

"Oh, shut up."

"I'll shut up if you come with me."

Tyler studied my face for a moment and finally, he sighed. "Fine. I suppose it won't actually kill me."

"Your enthusiasm is flattering," I said with a grin. "Now come on. Let's try to actually get there before sunrise, huh?"

"Oh my God," Micah said as we walked up to the bar an hour later. He smiled brightly at Tyler. "I can't *believe* Gray didn't tell me he was working with you. I mean, I can, because Gray's no fun and probably got off on keeping your identity a secret from me. But, seriously, let me thank you on behalf of all gay-kind for being in this movie. I'm so glad they actually cast someone cute."

Tyler's eyes widened in surprise at Micah's greeting and I sighed.

"You'll have to forgive Micah," I said. "He's never really understood basic concepts like *manners* or *not being incredibly forward*."

Micah glared at me. "Just because I choose not to subscribe to outdated and useless social mores is not reason to judge me." He turned back to Tyler. "And it is with the utmost respect and admiration that I tell you I can't wait to see you get fucked on screen. Even if it is by Gray," he added, making a face.

"Jesus, Micah," I said, exasperated.

"No, it's—it's okay," Tyler said with a weak laugh. "It's actually kind of nice to hear that someone doesn't hate me. I thought people were mad I'd been cast in this role."

"Oh whatever," Micah said, waving his hand like he was swatting away the notion. "People just like getting mad about stuff. It'll blow over. Now, you guys want a drink?"

Tyler's face fell a bit. "Um, actually—"

"Actually, we're gonna go grab a bite at Alejandra's," I broke in, "so we're not staying. I just wanted to stop by to take a look at that paperwork first."

"Ugh, so boring," Micah grumbled. "Okay, wait here and watch the bar, I'll be right back."

He turned and hurried off towards my office.

"Sorry," I said, looking at Tyler. "I didn't even think—you know, like, coming to a bar. I should have asked you if this was okay."

"Nah, it's fine," Tyler said. "Alcohol was never really my drug of choice. I'm just trying to be careful." He looked around the room and smiled. "Honestly, I couldn't tell you the last time I've even been in a bar, but this feels loads nicer than any of the awful, trendy places I used to go to in LA with their overpriced drinks. I usually just ended up getting high in the bathrooms instead."

I laughed. "Well as long as you're here, your drinks, alcoholic or otherwise, are on the house."

"We can stay if you want," Tyler said quickly.

"Okay, well, secret confession time," I said, lowering my voice conspiratorially. "Alejandra's is this Venezuelan place right around the corner and they have a two-for-Tuesday deal where you buy one arepa, you get the second half off. It's pretty sweet."

Tyler laughed, loudly this time, and looked at me in amusement. "Dude, you *own* a bar. In SoHo. You're like, *not* poor."

"Old habits die hard. I *was* poor for a very long time. Besides, it's too good a deal to pass up."

Tyler glanced around the room again. "How'd you end up with the bar, if you don't mind me asking?"

I smiled sadly. "It was Maggie's."

Tyler's eyes opened wide. "Oh shit. Is this place *called* Maggie's?"

"Yeah," I said, cocking my head. "Why?"

"My brother comes here sometimes," Tyler said. "He says his friends love it."

"Oh, cool. Who are his friends?" I asked. Not that I expected I'd know them, but maybe they'd turn out to be some of our regulars.

"These guys Ben and Adam? I don't really know them that well but—"

"Shit, yeah!" I interrupted. "I know them. They're actually good friends of mine." Micah came back out from my office with a sheaf of papers in his hand.

"What's all the excitement about?" he asked.

"Tyler knows Adam and Ben," I said. "Or his brother does, anyway."

"Cool." Micah grinned and looked at Tyler. "Who's your brother?"

"Luke?" Tyler said. "Luke Wolitzky?"

"Oh my God, yes," Micah said. "I totally know him. Blond. Hot. Must run in the family."

"Jesus, see?" I said to Tyler. "No manners whatsoever."

"Hey, it was a compliment," Micah protested.

"It's also sexual harassment," I said darkly.

"Whatever," Micah said. He looked at Tyler, tilting his head to the side. "Wolitzky? Not Lang?"

"Yeah," Tyler said with a rueful smile. "Lang's my mom's maiden name. And my dad figured 'Tyler' would sell better than 'Timothy,' which is the name I was born with."

Micah frowned and studied Tyler. "Hmm. Timothy Wolitzky. Nah, I'd probably still think you were hot."

"Just give me the damn papers already and stop hitting on my friend, you creep," I said, glaring at Micah.

The thing was, Micah was right. Tyler was hot. But I was trying *not* to think about that. Not only because we were working together but because at 21, Tyler was nine years younger than I was. He was smiling now, and it was his real smile, warm and relaxed so maybe he wasn't offended by Micah. But that wasn't an excuse for me to go around being creepy, too.

~

"You know, I don't think I've ever had an arepa before," Tyler said, picking his up. "Looks good though."

He bit into it with gusto and smiled, then yelped when sauce started running out of it and down his wrists.

"Sorry," I laughed. "I should have warned you."

Tyler was frantically trying to lick the sauce off his skin and it was disturbingly suggestive. *Stop it,* I scolded myself. *Get your mind out of the gutter.*

Tyler made a beatific face as he licked up the last bit of sauce off his pinky finger. "So worth it."

I had to smile. "Glad you approve, Mr. Wolitzky." I looked around the tiny restaurant with its exposed brick walls and colorful tablecloths. "I haven't actually been to Alejandra's in a while, but I used to come here all the time with—well, all the time."

With Ethan, I finished internally. But it wasn't like Ethan got the restaurant in 'the divorce'. I was still allowed to come here.

Tyler made a face at me using his last name. "It's not at all fair that you got born with the most screen-ready name ever. Who's named Grayson Evans? You sound like a law firm."

I snorted, "Trust me, you wanna trade families, I'm in."

Tyler's face fell. "Sorry," he said, stricken. "I didn't mean—"

"Don't worry about it," I said, jumping in. "I hardly think about it anymore."

But Tyler looked at me long enough that I had to drop my gaze.

"It's been a long time," I said finally. "It's not—I mean, it's never gonna be a great situation. But I can't change the past."

"If it makes you feel any better, I really would trade you my dad," Tyler said. "But I don't think you'd want him."

"Yeah." I winced. "No offense, but your dad—"

"Seems like a dick?" Tyler finished for me.

"I mean..."

"It's okay," Tyler said with a smile. "I know. Trust me. He—he kind of is."

"So then why do you—" I stopped before I finished my question, because what was I actually going to say? Why do you let him get to you? Why do you listen to a single thing he has to say? Why do you let him make you feel shitty about yourself when you deserve nothing of the kind?

Why don't you see how amazing you are?

I flushed. *You're trying to be* less *creepy, not more.*

"Nevermind," I said, finally. "You don't have to talk about it. I know family's weird."

Tyler looked into middle distance for a moment, then looked back at me with a sad smile.

"I know he can be a jerk sometimes," he said. "But he's also —he's the only father I've got. And he took care of me. He uprooted his whole life to move to California. He's always been there."

I refrained from pointing out that his dad clearly hadn't always been there, if he was coming out of nowhere now to yell at Tyler after not talking to him for a year. Because much as I wanted to say it, I didn't want to upset Tyler anymore.

"I don't think it has to be a death sentence, though," I said instead. "You doing this movie, I mean. I actually think— God, stop me if this sounds dumb but like, the listening thing? Ever since you explained that, it just feels—I don't know, I just feel like this movie is going to be really good. God, I'm rambling, I'm sorry."

Tyler laughed. "It's okay. It's—I mean, I think you're right. Thanks."

But as he took another bite of his arepa, his eyes drifted off into space again and that pensive look came back.

"Is there—is there something else that's bothering you?" I asked as gently as I could. God, I hated feeling like I was prying but I couldn't seem to help myself.

Tyler blinked at me in surprise, then blushed. "It's stupid."

"I'm sure it's not."

"That's because you don't know what it is yet," Tyler said. "What if I'm about to say that I've been thinking about your 'socks with lasers' idea and I've got a great investment opportunity for you."

"I'd probably give you all my money, please."

Tyler rolled his eyes. "It's just—God, this is so dumb, but it's the coming out stuff."

"Ohhh." I hadn't thought about that—hadn't even considered that that might still be bothering him. "Yeah, that's hard."

It was hard, coming out. Or at least, it could be. I'd been outed when I was in high school and my whole town, tiny as it was, had known within a few days. I couldn't imagine what it must feel like to have to come out when you felt like the whole country was watching.

But at the same time—Tyler *was* in the movie. So he kind of had to know people would wonder—or assume. Right?

"I mean, is it insane that I just don't wanna like, talk about it publically?" Tyler said, his voice plaintive.

"No," I said decisively. "No, it's not at all." I paused. "But it is... I don't know, I guess I was gonna say it's something that sorta comes with the territory. With doing this movie." I snorted. "It's kind of funny in a way, though. There are plenty of straight guys who do gay porn—"

"Wait, what?" Tyler broke in.

"Yeah." I nodded. "I mean, it pays better. And no one really bats an eye at it. It's just sex and hell, you're taking Viagra anyway to make sure you're hard, and what feels good, feels good, you know?" I laughed. "And arguably, *Foresight* is even more removed from reality than porn. There's an actual plot. And yet, it feels important that the guys in it actually be queer, you know?"

"I just don't see why it has to be such a big deal," Tyler burst out. "Like, can't it be about the story, about the characters, and not about me? I'm fucking sick of everything being about *me*."

I was quiet for a moment, thinking that over.

"I mean, it's complicated, right?" I said finally. "On the one hand, you're right. But there's also—I don't know, maybe it seems different coming from your perspective, if you've mostly been playing straight roles. But it's just, most roles in TV and movies are for straight characters. There's so little representation of gay and bi and pan or whatever men in general. So when there finally *are* queer characters, to have those opportunities get snatched up by straight actors, and then have them applauded for doing something '*edgy*'? It's fucking frustrating."

I realized I was kind of ranting and looked apologetically at Tyler. He flushed.

"Sorry, not that that's the case for you, obviously," I said. "It's just—"

Tyler snorted. "I think you're giving me credit for having purer motives than I actually do. Don't think I didn't consider that option—just going the '*edgy role for a straight guy*' route."

"Hell, you could probably get away with it," I laughed. "It's just—you can see where the frustration comes in, right? People get protective of these things. And God, that's not even getting into how hard it is for actors of color, actors with disabilities, or don't fit the typical beauty standards." I shook my head. "Trust me, I know I'm kind of a hypocrite, saying this as a white dude who still goes to the gym all the time, but... you see how it can come off, right?"

"Yes," Tyler said with a groan. "Ugh, I keep fucking up. Even when I'm trying to do the right thing."

"I don't think you're fucking up," I said, not quite sure why Tyler was beating himself up over this. "Even if you don't want to officially come out, it's fine. You're amazing in the role, and honestly, anyone complaining is going to get over it when the movie comes out and they see how great you are."

"Yeah, but I don't wanna be an asshole. I just—why do people care so much? Why do I have to label it?"

"I mean, you don't have to," I said, trying to figure out what it was that was bothering Tyler. "Some people care a lot about labels, because they fought for those labels to be recognized. But you have to do what's right for you."

"I just—I don't want to get it wrong. What if I—like what if I say one thing and then it turns out I'm wrong?"

I frowned, trying to make sense of what Tyler was saying. What did he mean by getting it wrong? How the hell *could* he even get it wrong, unless—oh.

I blinked at Tyler, sure I was wrong but also unable to think of what else he could mean. Jesus, had I completely misinterpreted everything from the very beginning?

"Tyler, are you—are you *straight*?"

Tyler flushed and I immediately regretted the question.

"Fuck, sorry," I said. "That was awful. God, here I am trying to tell you that it shouldn't matter and no one will care and then I ask you that. Fuck, forget I said anything."

"No, no, it's okay," Tyler jumped in. "I—I like guys," he stammered. "I'm just not like—you know—ugh, I'm just not like, the *most* experienced. When it comes to... that stuff. It's just —it's like, it's hard enough to date when you're in the public eye and I knew my dad wouldn't have wanted me to come out so I just—"

"No, I totally get it," I said, still wincing at my stupidity. What a shitty thing to ask someone. How would I have reacted if someone had asked me that, point blank, before I was out all the way? "You don't need to justify anything to me. I can't imagine how hard it is, in your position."

Tyler must have felt like he had to keep all of his relationships a secret. How would you even find someone to date, to be with, if you felt like you couldn't even be seen with them in public? It made me sad to think of Tyler living in fear of someone finding out.

God, and he was so young. I had to remember that. Tyler was still going through things I'd dealt with over a decade ago.

"Don't say anything you're not ready to say," I said emphatically. "And don't let anyone push you into doing anything you're not ready to do." I laughed. "If you need me to fight Andrew and Dave for you, I will."

"Thanks," Tyler said with a laugh. "Honestly, I think Danny would also volunteer to be my defender, so between the two of you, I think I'm set."

And oddly enough, despite how awkward I felt, Tyler actually seemed like he was in a better mood for the rest of dinner. I still felt like an asshole, but he was smiling, and I supposed that was what I'd wanted from the beginning. By the end of the meal, I was even feeling like less of a blundering idiot myself and laughing as Tyler suggested asking Alejandra's to cater the rest of the film shoot.

"That might be a *little* bit out of Dave and Andrew's budget," I said with a chuckle as we stood up. "But I suppose we could always—"

I stopped. Stopped speaking, the unfinished sentence hanging in midair, and stopped moving. Stopped being aware of anything happening around me, because all I could see was the table four rows down from where Tyler and I had been sitting.

Ethan was there. Leaning in and kissing someone with long brown hair. Kissing Christie, I realized, when they pulled apart. Ethan was kissing Christie.

8

TYLER

*G*ray stopped walking so abruptly that I accidentally smushed my nose into his back before I realized he wasn't moving anymore.

"Shit, sorry," I said, taking a step back and rubbing my nose. "Also, ow. Anyone ever tell you your shoulders are like semi-trucks?"

But Gray didn't respond.

I frowned up at him. "What's wrong?"

He still didn't say anything, but I noticed then that his eyes were wide and staring at something. I followed his gaze to where it landed on a man and woman kissing—or if we were being technical about it, making out so enthusiastically that I was a little worried someone was going to end up with an arepa in their lap—at a little two-top four tables down from us.

They were a cute enough couple, I supposed, though it was kind of hard to see their faces, given how mashed up against each other they were. And I had to admit the guy with his artfully messy blond hair was calling my attention a bit more than his brunette date. But Gray wasn't looking at them like they were cute. Or even looking at the guy in a 'that dude's hot, I want to stare, but probably should pretend I'm not,' kind of way that I was so used to.

He was staring openly, and he looked upset.

"Gray. Gray, hey, what's wrong?" I put my hand on Gray's arm—a light touch, not trying to startle him—and he looked down at me in surprise, like he'd forgotten I was there.

I tried not to let that bother me.

"It's—that's—that's my ex?" His voice was so lost, his answer almost sounded like a question. "That's Ethan."

"Oh." My eyes darted back to the couple. "Oh. God. I'm sorry."

"I didn't—I didn't know he was..." Gray said, so softly that I wasn't sure he knew he was speaking out loud. "I didn't know there was anything—I thought they were just..."

"Shit."

It was all I could think of to say. It had never occurred to me until that point that Gray's ex might be bi. I barely even remembered that Gray was. The possibilities tumbled around my head like marbles in a washing machine while I watched as anguish crept across Gray's face, the shocked expression that had previously registered there dissolving like sidewalk chalk in the rain.

So this was Ethan. The ex. The guy Gray had been with for

years, had loved for years, who he'd given so much up for. Watching him kiss that woman—who could have been a lovely person, for all I knew—righteous anger coursed through me.

How dare this guy have thrown Gray over? For the woman he was with or for anyone, for that matter? How dare he treat Gray the way he had over the years and then drop him? How dare he bring someone here, to the place he and Gray had shared—how dare he even bring someone into Gray's neighborhood?

Gray brought you here, a voice whispered in the back of my mind. But that was different. Gray and I were friends—barely. More like coworkers. And that's all we ever would be, which I was completely fine with.

I was.

But that didn't stop me from wanting to punch Ethan in the face. Even if he did look like he had 20 pounds on me.

"I don't know what to say to them," Gray said, looking down at me helplessly.

I didn't need to look at them to know what he was talking about. The restaurant was tiny. There was no way to reach the front door without having to walk right by their table—no way to avoid having to talk to them.

"Come on," I said, jerking my head in the other direction. "We can go out through the kitchen."

"The kitchen?" Gray blinked. "But they're working back—we can't just do that."

"I used to do it all the time," I said with more confidence than I felt. "Come on."

Restaurants in LA were definitely used to accommodating celebrities on the few times they *didn't* want to be seen by the paparazzi. I wasn't sure that was the case in New York. But quick talking, and quick walking, could probably get us through the door and out into the back alley before anyone stopped us.

But no sooner had I grabbed Gray's hand and begun to pull than I heard the sentence I dreaded most in the English language.

"Oh my God, are you *Tyler Lang*?"

Usually when I heard those words, what bothered me most was the tone of voice. I'd sift through layers of prosody, hearing the subtle signs of judgement that the speakers thought they were hiding. But tonight, the problem was purely one of decibels. Fucking hell.

The speaker, a girl with curly red hair in a bright blue t-shirt sitting one table behind us, had spoken so loudly that the entire restaurant had looked up. Granted, that was only about 20 people, but I winced as I slowly swiveled my head back towards the front of the room.

Ethan and his date slowly unhooked their mouths from each other. I couldn't shake a sudden vision of them as two goldfish as they looked up at us, jaws still agape. The woman locked eyes with me in surprise and then curiosity. But Ethan only had eyes for Gray.

Everyone started talking at once.

"You are!" said the redhead. "You *are* Tyler Lang. Aren't you supposed to be in jail or something?"

"Yeah, hi," I said, turning back to her, trying to keep my voice friendly but brisk. "That's me. Not in jail, just grabbing a bite. So sorry to say hi and run, but we actually need to—"

"Gray? What are you—I thought you were—I didn't know you'd be here."

That voice came from behind me. I didn't recognize its flat, crisp tones but I knew it had to be Ethan. His voice sounded exactly like what you'd expect from an entitled douchebag. Having been an entitled douchebag for quite a while, I considered myself something of an expert.

And then Gray's voice.

"I—I have to go."

Gray was already past me, then brushing by Ethan who'd begun to stand up from his table, before I could say anything to stop him.

But what could I have said? I couldn't do anything to fix the situation. And it was pretty fucking arrogant to think that Gray would want me to, anyway.

Still, I had the urge to follow him. Especially because now Ethan was pushing away from *his* table, mumbling half-formed excuses to his date, gesturing for her to *Just. Stay. There.* as he hurried out the door after Gray. I don't know what I thought was going to happen, but a jolt of fear flashed through my body at the thought of the two of them alone.

"I'm sorry," the redhead said behind me. "I didn't mean to—did I do something wrong?"

"No, no, you're fine," I said, pulling a smile onto my face and launching into self-deprecating mode. "Old friends. We just didn't expect to run into each other—didn't even know we'd be in the city until a couple hours ago and now we're running late to get back to the set and it's a whole, very boring, thing. I'm so sorry, but we really have to—"

"Oh my God, set?" The girl's eyes lit up. "Holy shit, for that movie? The gay one? Oh my God, I heard about that. Are you really doing that?"

"I—" I started, but the girl wouldn't let me get a word in edgewise, just kept talking.

"I read about that online but I was like, '*No way* would he do that'. Like, I mean, I know things were like, kind of bad for you there for a while and no one wanted to work with you, but like, even rock bottom can't be *that* bad, right? Like, I can't even imagine why someone would do *gay porn*. I mean, eww, right?"

I blinked, my smile about to crack and crumble off my face like plaster.

You'd think I'd be used to people passing judgement. I'd been acting since I was a kid. It hadn't always been as negative as it'd been for the past few years, but even well-meaning people who tell you how much they love you are still basically telling you, *'I love this very specific version of you and feel like I own it in some way. Do not change if you want to continue pleasing me.'*

Lately, of course, it'd been a little bit harsher. Okay, a *lot* a bit harsher. But nothing had prepared me for this. For someone laughing off what they'd heard about me as a crazy rumor. Something so *low* and *mortifying* that even I, who could usually be counted on to make dumb decisions, could be trusted not to do it.

I don't know what I'd been expecting. This was exactly what my dad was trying to warn me about. Exactly what I'd known would happen.

But somehow, talking to Gray tonight had made me forget all that. Made me feel like maybe people wouldn't be so quick to pass judgement, so quick to condemn. Talking to Gray, I felt safer, saner. Talking to Gray, I felt like maybe being myself wasn't the worst thing in the world.

But now Gray wasn't here—and not only wasn't he here, he was dealing with his own *actual* crisis while I was in here feeling stung because a total stranger had—gasp—the gall to have an opinion about me and share it.

Welcome to the world, Tyler. It doesn't magically change and decide to be nice to you, just because you decided you didn't want to be an asshole anymore.

For that matter, I hadn't actually changed either. I was still in here whining about my feelings getting hurt when, if I were an actual friend, I'd be outside looking for Gray.

"Actually, I am doing the movie," I said, letting the smile fade from my face. The girl's eyes widened and I wondered if it was because of what I'd said, or because I'd broken celebrity code and actually let my frustration show through. "And it's a beautiful story, with a team I'm proud to be a part of, and I think it's going to be an amazing project."

"Oh. I mean, I didn't—"

"But we really *do* need to go," I added. "It was lovely to meet you—" if by '*lovely*' you meant '*unsettling*' and '*meet*' you meant '*have you tell me about your disapproval*' "—and if you're still curious about the movie, you should really grab the book it's based on. *Foresight* by Danny Wilson. It's amazing!"

I even pulled my smile back onto my face as I waved good-bye, though I let it drop as I walked past the rest of the tables and out the front door.

I wondered if I'd have to walk far to find Gray. Wondered if he'd still be talking to Ethan—even had a brief vision of the two of them kissing passionately, Gray pushing Ethan up against a wall the way he'd pushed me up against a tree last week, pinning my body with his.

Jesus, get a grip.

But it turned out they hadn't gone far at all—only two store-fronts down the street before they'd stopped. And there they stood on the sidewalk, Gray and Ethan, two feet apart, staring at each other like they were the only people in the world.

I felt hot and uncomfortable, like I was intruding by just standing on the same block as them. My grand plans to—what? Stand up for Gray? Intercede on his behalf? Get my ass kicked by Ethan? Whatever my grand plans had been, they wilted as I looked at them looking at each other.

I started to turn around, not sure where I was going to go—not back into the restaurant, that was for sure—but desperately not wanting to be on that sidewalk anymore either.

"Tyler, no." Gray's voice stopped me short, like a sharp tug on a leash. "Ethan and I are done here. Let's go."

I turned, still feeling like I needed to apologize. "I can just—"

"No," Gray repeated, walking towards me and reaching out a hand. I moved to take it, then darted away. We were on the street, in the middle of a perfectly pleasant New York evening. I probably shouldn't be holding Gray's hand, even if part of me was suddenly very curious what that would feel like. "We're going."

"Gray, wait." Ethan's voice cracked through the air and I swear I saw a shudder roll through Gray's body. "Please. Please let me explain."

"You can't," Gray said, shaking his head.

"Yes, I can," Ethan insisted. He stepped forward, too, laying a hand on Gray's right shoulder. There was no denying the shudder that time. I could feel it—Gray's left hand was still inches from mine and I swear the very air moved, passing some kind of current back and forth through Gray's body.

"You can't," Gray repeated. "Not in a way that's gonna make this any better, anyway."

"It's not that serious," Ethan said, his voice taking on a pleading tone. "It's just—I don't know, what was I supposed to do? You know I'm no good at being alone."

"How long?" Gray asked, his voice disturbingly even.

"What?"

"How long did you manage to be on your own this time? When'd it start? A week after you dumped me? Two?"

"That's not fair, Gray. You know things with Christie are complicated."

"Right. Sure." Gray rolled his eyes. "They're not *serious*, but they're *complicated*. Whatever it takes to get me to stop being mad at you, right?"

"That's not what I meant." Ethan glared at Gray.

"How long?" Gray asked again. His voice was quiet this time, almost resigned.

Ethan let go of Gray's wrist. Put his hands in his pockets and looked down. "It's been three months. We ran into each other that night at Jason's party and—"

"Three months." Gray shook his head. "God, I skipped Jason's party because I wasn't sure I was ready to see you only *two days* after you'd dumped me. You got together with her *that night*?"

"It wasn't like that. I didn't plan this. It just... happened." Ethan shrugged uncomfortably. "I didn't bother telling you because I didn't think it was that serious." His eyes snapped back up to Gray's. "It doesn't have to be that serious, you know. You're the one who's making such a big deal out of this."

That urge to punch Ethan came back really strong. That or like, say something really rude and cruel—except the dude was obviously hot and pretty clearly rich too, so there weren't really any easy targets for cutting him down. But I just hated his tone, hated his whole attitude.

I almost wanted to drape myself over Gray and say something like, *'You're right, it's really not a big deal because he's totally over you and fucking me instead.'* If I'd been braver, I would have. But I didn't have quite that much courage. Because of course I didn't.

"Pardon me for taking more than two goddamn days to get over someone I dated for eight years." Gray's voice was full of disgust. "Jesus, I can't do this, I can't talk to you anymore."

"Gray, come on. You're being—"

"What? What am I being?" Gray's eyes bored into Ethan's. "Unreasonable? For deciding I don't want to keep talking to someone who's been lying to me for three months? And not just lying to me—unless you're telling me Christie *knows* about all the times you've invited me out since we broke up, or asked me to come over, and told me how much you miss me—how much you miss us being together."

Ethan's eyes flicked to me, of all things, at those words, like he was embarrassed and angry that I'd heard that.

"Yeah," Gray said. "I'll take that as a no." He looked over at me then, too. "Come on, Tyler. Let's go."

He stalked off down the sidewalk, anger radiating off his back. I took one last look at Ethan, who was staring after Gray with a look of obscure pain on his face. Then I hurried to catch up to Gray's retreating back, silhouetted by the setting sun.

"So that was... awkward," Gray said apologetically as his car swept out of the Lincoln tunnel, curling up and around the cliffs in Weehauken before getting onto the highway. "I'm sorry you had to, you know, hear all of that."

"Oh my God, no," I said, glancing at him in confusion. "Don't apologize at all. I'm sorry I barged in. I was just worried that you'd like—I don't know. It doesn't matter."

Just worried you were playing tonsil hockey with your super hot ex-boyfriend. No big deal.

"I wouldn't have left you," Gray said. He glanced over at me, seeming concerned that I knew this.

"No, no, I know," I said, uncomfortable now, because I sure as hell wasn't going to explain what I actually meant. I couldn't even explain it to himself.

"I'm really sorry," I said after a moment. "About Ethan. That just... sucks. A lot."

Gray was quiet, and I wondered if I'd said something wrong. And of course, because I was nervous, I kept talking, even though I knew what I should really do was shut the hell up.

"I just—you're like, actually maybe the nicest person I've ever met," I babbled. "Like, you've been so fucking nice and understanding about me and my bullshit and like, trying to help me and never making me feel bad about myself and aside from the fact that I think there might *actually* be something wrong with you because that much niceness really isn't normal and you should maybe go to a doctor and get that looked at, I just, I don't know, it just sucks that your ex is such an asshole." I winced. "Sorry. Fuck. I didn't mean to say that."

Gray laughed, the sound low and rumbly like an engine revving across a highway. "Which part? You kind of said a lot."

"The part about Ethan being an asshole. I mean, I don't

really know him. Like, at all. So, I don't know, maybe he's secretly amazing, but he sure seems to be *acting* like an asshole." I gave Gray a side-eyed smile. "Trust me, I spent like, the last five years acting like an asshole. I'm pretty good at recognizing it."

Gray laughed and shook his head. "Well, trust me, you're fine. I just—fuck, I just feel so dumb. Overreacting like that. I should have just said hi, made nice, and then walked out of the restaurant like I didn't care. Instead, I was a giant baby and caused a scene and now he *and* Christie probably both think I'm fucking immature."

"Okay, well, no offense but... why do you care what *either* of them thinks?" I asked, looking at him askance.

Gray looked at me helplessly. "I know I shouldn't. I just... do. Ethan, at least. It's stupid, right?"

I thought about that for a moment.

"It's not stupid. It's just... I don't know, he doesn't seem like he deserves you caring about him, if he's gonna act like he doesn't care about you." I snorted. "I mean, most people are assholes, if you ask me. So why let someone who's being a dick take up any space in your brain? Like, why let him win, you know?"

"I can't decide if that's the most cynical read on human nature I've ever heard, or the most true," Gray said, wrinkling his nose. "Maybe both."

I laughed. "I mean, I'm probably not the best person to be taking advice from. I am, after all, an asshole. Also, a total hypocrite, because what I actually kinda wanted to do was make Ethan feel really shitty by pretending we were dating."

Gray looked over at me in surprise. "What?"

I flushed. "I don't know, I mean, it's dumb. But it did kind of cross my mind to pull you in for a kiss and then like, hang all over you and be like, *'Oh my God, is* Ethan *your ugly, dumb, bad lay ex boyfriend you told me about? Haha, I thought he'd be* hotter. *Oh well, anyway, shouldn't we get going back to your apartment so you can fuck me into the mattress seven times before sunrise?'"*

Gray practically yelped. "Jesus Christ, Tyler."

"Or, you know, something like that." God, my cheeks were on fire.

But then Gray laughed, and everything was okay again.

"God, I almost wish you had," he said. "Just to see the fucking look on his face. You know he thinks you're hot, right?"

"Wait, really?" I blinked.

"Oh don't pretend you don't know that," Gray said. "Everybody thinks that about you."

I felt a flutter in my chest but forced myself to just arch an eyebrow and ask, all cool and calm, *"Everybody?"*

"Shut up," Gray said. "You know what I meant."

"Well you're fucking one to talk," I shot back. "Mr. Highest Paid Gay Porn Actor of All Time."

"Somebody's been doing some research," Gray laughed.

"Fuck you. Just trying to learn about my costar."

Gray snorted. "Anyway, thanks for the thought. I don't think Ethan would have believed it though."

"Why not? Weren't you just reminding me how great an actor I am?"

"Uh, because we've known each other for less than three weeks?"

"Um, haven't you ever heard of love at first sight?" I said, trying to sound as offended as possible. "Or first onscreen handjob, I suppose, in our case."

Gray laughed. "We haven't had our first onscreen handjob."

As though I didn't know that, as though I weren't critically aware that we weren't getting to that until next week. As though the sex scenes on the filming schedule hadn't been branded onto my brain.

"Ethan doesn't know that, though," I said. "For all he knows, you've already proposed to me and we're engaged."

"Wait, I'm the one who proposes in this scenario?" Gray asked. "Don't I get a say in this?"

"No," I said brightly. "But don't worry, it was very romantic. You dressed up like a clown, to match the clown theme of my room at Bailey Park, and then jumped out of the closet, brandishing a ring at me."

"Well that's fair. Definitely sounds like me."

"Obviously. And because I know how much you love them, our engagement photos are going to be ghost theme. And we're going to be hosting the wedding at a Taco Bell in Vegas. But it's black tie."

"Naturally," Gray said with a laugh. "Because what else would one wear?"

"Right? I mean, we're not heathens."

"So where are we honeymooning?"

"I can't decide," I said. "Either our house on the Vineyard or the Maldives."

Gray squinted of into the distance for a second in thought. "The Maldives," he said. "We're renovating the Vineyard house, remember? To add a ball pit and make room for our menagerie of giraffes."

"Oh God, yes, of course." I grinned. "And to put a sex dungeon up in the attic."

"Wait, why's our sex dungeon going in the attic? What's wrong with the basement?"

"The basement's where we're putting the moonbounce, honey."

"Ah, yes, the moonbounce. How could I have forgotten?"

"You're probably just stressed from doing the paperwork for the 10 children we're adopting." I waved my hand airily.

"Hence the moonbounce," Gray said with a smile.

"Oh, no, the moonbounce is adults only. In fact, the whole Martha's Vineyard house is. We ship the kids off to camp while we summer there."

"I'm really glad to hear that we're such responsible parents," he added.

"With the great examples of parenting we both had, how could we be anything else?"

We drove the rest of the way in a warm kind of silence. Gray sighed as he pulled off the highway and I leaned my head against the cool glass of the passenger side window. We'd be back at Bailey Park soon. I wasn't sad about it. But this night, despite all of its weirdness, had actually been one of the best nights I'd had in—God, I actually couldn't remember a time I'd felt so... good.

And that was because of Gray, I realized.

God, was this what it felt like to have a friend? Someone you could actually be yourself around? Someone who accepted you for who you are—and not just because they have to or because they're your family?

I looked over at Gray with a smile, but the smile ran off my face when I saw Gray's pensive look.

"I.O.U. for your thoughts," I said.

"I.O.U.?" Gray asked.

"I spent all my money on JetKicks, remember?" I said with a shrug. "Luke's setting up my direct deposit, though. I'm totally good for it. And you know where I live. For the next few weeks, anyway.

Gray sighed again. "I just feel like an idiot."

"Why?"

"Ethan," Gray said, not elaborating.

"It's not your fault he decided to start dating some woman two days after breaking up with you, and then lied about it for three months," I pointed out. "That makes him a dick, but it doesn't make you an idiot."

"Yeah but—" Gray stopped, shaking his head and rolling his eyes. "God, I'm so dumb. I actually thought we were going to get back together."

"Really?" I asked, surprised.

Gray'd never mentioned that before. Not that he was supposed to. Not that I had any right to know, or to feel bothered by that idea. And yet, I was.

"Yeah," Gray continued. "Like I said, it was dumb." He made a disgusted noise in the back of his throat. "Ethan used to—even after we broke up, he'd still call me, text me, ask to hang out. Never with Christie, obviously. I guess he only did it when she was busy. But God, he knew me so well. All it took was like, one hand on my wrist when we were out at dinner. One casual 'I miss you' and I was right back to eating out of his hand."

"Jesus," I said. "But he—he's the one who dumped you, isn't he?"

"He is," Gray said. "Which only makes me dumber, right? What was I thinking? That somehow he'd change his mind about marriage? Or maybe it was just one more thing I was willing to sacrifice to be with him." His voice took on a self-loathing tone. "Yeah, knowing me, that's definitely what it is."

"What do you mean?"

Gray turned and looked at me. "You told me at that Thai place that you were pathetic, but I think I've got you beat."

"Oh please," I said. "Like, I'm sure you're proud of your patheticness and that's cute and all. But come on, Gray. You're JV-level pathetic. Varsity, at best. I'm on the fucking Olympic team."

"Wanna bet?" Gray said, smiling.

"Yeah." I turned my head to look at him. "I do. What's so pathetic about you?"

"Try giving up my dream to be an actor because Ethan said he didn't think I had the right personality for it. Oh, and that he'd break up with me if I left for a three month shoot in Vancouver, the one time I actually got cast in a real part in a movie."

"Shit."

"And accepting his excuses about how much his family would judge him as his reason for not coming out, don't forget that," Gray added. "And also accepting those same excuses for why he had to 'pretend' to date Christie for years —because she was a family friend and he had to do it 'just for appearances.' All the while never letting me even meet his family."

"Fuck."

"And just in general, for believing him when he told me that he really was going to come out, he really did want to be with me, he really did love me and want to get married and have a house in the suburbs and a fucking minivan, because I'm a goddamn cliche who just wants a family."

"Wow," I said slowly. "That's... shitty. Of him, I mean, not you," I added. "There's nothing wrong with wanting all of that. But that's really fucked up, what he put you through."

"Yeah," Gray said. "Yeah, I guess when you look back on it, it kinda is."

I was quiet for a minute, then smiled as a thought occurred to me. "If only we'd met a year ago."

"How do you mean?" Gray asked.

I laughed. "The car I got arrested in—the one with all the cocaine in it?"

"Yeah?"

"It was a minivan. So if that's all you wanted..."

"Oh God, that's priceless," Gray said, laughing. "I'm just picturing you leading a high-speed chase in a Toyota Sienna."

"Honda Odyssey," I corrected him. "I dunno, my dad was the only person who ever used it, but he always said it got good gas mileage."

"I'll keep that in mind," Gray said with a wry smile. He sighed again, scrubbing a hand over his face. "Sorry, this is probably really boring to listen to."

"What? No, really, I don't mind."

I'm just hanging onto your every word like a total weirdo, fantasizing about making your ex think we're dating. No big deal.

"Yeah, but it's so fucking stereotypical. It's not even interesting. I'm sure you have ex stuff too, this is nothing new."

"Right. Yeah."

What the fuck was I supposed to say to that?

Sure, I have ex stuff too. As long as there are no follow-up ques-

tions, I've got 20 fucking exes and they're all super hot and still in love with me.

"I just can't help thinking," Gray said after a moment, "about how dumb I am. I kept telling myself that somehow, this was as good as break-ups got. I mean, it sucked and it hurt and I hated it, but I told myself that I didn't blame him. If he didn't want to get married, that wasn't something to blame him for."

"Well, right," I objected, "but if you'd told him what you wanted before that, and he'd always said he wanted it too—"

"I know," Gray said, "But sometimes you don't know how you're going to feel until you're in a situation, you know? You might think you want something, right up until the choice is in front of you, and suddenly you realize you want something completely different."

He shook his head. "Maybe it was just me being stupid, trying to make excuses, but I kept telling myself, *'It's fine, he doesn't want to get married, this doesn't invalidate what you had together, it just means you don't have a future.'* But if he started dating Christie—two days after he'd broken up with me? He must have fallen out of love with me a long time ago."

Gray made a sort of growling noise and his hands gripped the steering wheel tightly. "Fuck, for all I know, they'd actually dated before and Ethan just never told me. Like, how many months do you think it was, me thinking that we were in love, we were going to be together, forever, while he was already making plans to end things? I feel like a goddamn idiot."

"It's not your fault, though," I said, wishing I could say

something more helpful. "It really isn't. It's his fault, not yours."

"I just thought I was going to get my happy ending, you know?" Gray said. "All the sacrifices, everything I gave up, was going to be worth it."

I was quiet for a moment, an idea forming in my mind.

"You know what?" I said after a minute.

"What?" Gray asked.

"We need to make our own fucking happy endings."

Gray cocked an eyebrow. "Go on..."

"Shut up, not what I meant." I blushed furiously.

"You sure?" Gray said. "Because I'm pretty sure that's actually exactly what this movie—"

"Okay, okay, fuck you," I said, rolling my eyes. "What I meant was that we have to like, seize the day or whatever."

I turned and looked at Gray as he pulled onto the street Bailey Park was on, suddenly feeling it was immensely important to say this before we got back, before this car ride, this evening, was over.

Gray was my friend—my goddamn only friend, maybe, but that wasn't important at this juncture—and I needed a friend right now. And as far as I could tell, so did Gray.

"Tell me," I said. "Gun to your head, right now, what's your goal for the next year?"

"Honestly?" Gray gave me a pained look as he drove down the street, the car slowing steadily as he approached the driveway. "Tyler, I'm not even sure I have one. Just like... living, I guess?"

"Bullshit," I said decisively. "You have to have one. Everyone has something they want."

"You sound like Micah," Gray said with a groan. "He fucking loves reminding me that I'm in a rut."

"Okay, so then get out of it," I said. "What would getting out of a rut look like for you?"

"I don't know! That's—that's the fucking problem."

Gray turned into the driveway and my eyes swept over the expanse before us, the grounds, the mansion, the woods beyond. I thought about all the scenes we'd shot so far, how Gray kept blowing everyone away, and turned to study him.

"You said you wanted to be an actor once," I said.

"Yeah." Gray turned the wheel as he followed the curves of the driveway down to the old stables.

"Do you still want to be?" I asked gently.

"What? No," Gray said. "No, God, no, I gave that up years ago."

"But you didn't give it up. I mean, you're here."

"I'm here as a favor to Violet."

"You're here because you're good at it," I countered. "You could have said no. You probably had a million reasons to turn it down. But you didn't."

"Maybe I just missed fucking mouthy little twinks on camera," Gray said, and I practically had a heart attack.

Fucking mouthy little... Jesus Christ, I needed to get a grip. Gray was just joking, he had no idea how much that sentence tied my stomach up in knots with nerves and worry and, fuck me, desire.

"Or maybe," I said, refusing to let myself dwell on the feeling in my stomach. "Maybe, you're here because you realized that this is something you always wanted to do." I turned to Gray as Gray pulled the car to a stop in a parking space. "What if you could be doing this, a year from now?"

"Sitting in a parked car with a pushy bottom harassing me?"

"Yeah," I said with a grin. "But then after that, what if you got *out* of that car and stepped onto a red carpet to go accept an award for giving the performance of a lifetime in a movie that the entire world loves, and you knew that this was what you got to do for the rest of your life?"

Gray was silent for a second and I wondered again if I should shut up, stop pushing. But I couldn't. Or wouldn't. Because I was sure of it now, completely sure.

I knew people. I was good at reading them. And I could tell that Gray was excited by what I was saying. From the way his nostrils were flaring and his hands kept fiddling with his keys and he couldn't stop glancing at me and then looking away.

I'd figured Gray out. And it was ridiculous to let him keep lying to himself about what he wanted, especially when I could see how good he could be.

"Come on, Gray," I said, my voice taking on a pleading tone. I didn't care. Hell, I wanted it there. I'd always been good at wheedling. "You're a natural. I don't know why you stopped trying for this, and I can't—*you* can't go back in time and change it. But you can decide from this day forward that this is what you want. To pursue this. To take charge of your own future."

Gray finally turned towards me, holding my gaze this time, and the look he gave me was impossible to read. "Yeah?" Gray said. "And what do you want to be doing a year from now?"

"I wanna be back in LA," I said, without hesitation. "Working again. With people's respect. Actually picking my projects carefully. Working with directors and writers whose vision I agree with. Being in charge of my own damn fate." I glared at Gray. "That's what we both should be doing."

Gray arched an eyebrow. "Why do I have the feeling you're going to tell me we have to slice our palms open and make a blood pact or something?"

"Um, probably because that's exactly what I'd do if I had a knife on me and if I weren't concerned about the upholstery in your car."

"Then I'm definitely not going to mention that I carry a pocketknife," Gray said with a snort. "So, what? We pinky swear?"

I burst out laughing. "Pinky swear? God, I haven't—I don't think I've ever actually done that in real life. Is that a thing real people do?"

Gray rolled his eyes. "Yeah, like 12 year olds. I wasn't being serious."

"Too late, man," I said, shaking my head. "We're pinky

swearing. This is my inaugural one, you're not ruining this for me."

"What are we even swearing about?" Gray asked with a sigh.

"We're swearing," I said, unbuckling my seatbelt and turning inwards so I could face Gray head on, "that we're not going to let ex-boyfriends or asshole dads or really anyone in general prevent us from getting what we want. We're swearing that we're going to go after it. And we're taking our lives back."

"I feel... distinctly nerdy doing this," Gray said. "But fine. If you insist."

"I do," I said, and I realized it was true. I felt like I was on fire, like something was propelling me to say this, almost speaking for me. I felt more alive than I had in so long. I held up my pinky for Gray. "Don't leave me hanging."

"Fine," Gray said, his voice dry and amused. But he brought his hand up to meet mine. His pinky, larger and stronger than my own, curved around my finger as he looked me in the eye. "I swear that I will try not to care about what Ethan thinks and like, look into acting again seriously. Or something. Whatever."

"That's not quite the wording I would have chosen, but fine," I said, grinning impishly back at him. "And I swear that by this time next year, I'm gonna be back in LA with five projects under my belt, awards buzz, and calling you from my fucking private jet to congratulate you on becoming the next James Bond."

"Sure," Gray said, rolling his eyes.

"I mean it."

"You know," Gray said after a moment, a small smile playing upon his lips, "of all the people I've ever met, you're the one I most believe could make that all happen."

"Good," I said, looking back up into his blue eyes, an inky black in the darkness surrounding us. "Because I will."

～

The room Violet was using for Dylan's room on set was one floor below the hall where Gray and I were staying for the month. But aside from the conspicuous lack of clowns in this one, it looked a lot like my own. There was a biology textbook from God knows where opened to a section on mitochondria on the artfully messy bed and a Calculus book in the corner along with some massive kind of calculator I'd never seen before.

Granted, my schooling had maybe been a little lax. Well, not maybe. Definitely. But school had never been my focus, and getting tutors to coach me through my classes on the set of Shoestring Miracles hadn't been cheap, so my dad hadn't asked for more than the bare minimum for me.

It's not like you're going to college, he'd said. *I'm not wasting my money on Calculus when you'll never use it.*

It was strange, feeling nostalgic for a life I'd never had. AP Calculus. Boarding school. A family that actually cared about me—like Dylan's family did, in the movie.

I looked over at Gray, who was lounging up against the wall as we waited for Violet to get the cameras set up right. With the budget as tight as it was, Violet was acting as both director and director of photography and, when she deemed the shot important enough, camera woman as well.

Gray looked totally calm. I wished I felt the same, or even anywhere close to calm. Instead, I felt like I was going to jump out of my skin.

Today was hand-job day. The first 'sex' scene of the movie, and—in my mind—the final test. After this, there'd be no denying that I was into guys. If I was. God, I thought I was. And fuck, if I wasn't, that was going to be incredibly awkward.

I honestly wasn't sure what I wanted to happen. Not enjoy it, not be into it? Realize I was straight after all? Get to take the easy way out... but still have to find a way to get through the rest of the movie?

Or would I rather enjoy it—love it even? Have it confirmed, once and for all, that I wanted this. And then have to deal with everything that came after—accepting that I wasn't straight, and figuring out what to do with that.

Too many questions raced around my mind. What if I came too quickly? What if I couldn't come at all? What if Gray could tell, somehow, that this was the first time another guy had touched my cock?

I mean, there was no way he could be able to, right? It's not like my dick had some flashing neon sign that said 'gay hand-job virgin' on it. But that didn't stop me from worrying about it.

To distract myself, I stood up from the desk chair where I was sitting and walked over to Gray, who was in the process of grimacing at his phone and shoving it back into his pocket.

"Anyone exciting?" I asked.

Gray made a face. "Ethan. So, no."

"Boooooo," I said. "Boo hiss grrr. What the hell's he calling you about?"

"I dunno," Gray said, shrugging. "I ignored it."

I glanced up at him, pursing my lips. "You talk to Tiana yet? She said she was going to call you."

The morning after our bizarre, impromptu pinky-swear ceremony, I'd been willing to chalk the whole thing up to me being in a weird mood. Surely Gray would rather me drop the whole issue. But surprisingly, he'd asked me that afternoon what his next steps would be, if he really were going to try to get back into acting.

I'd told him I'd talk to my agent, and after calling Tiana and explaining the situation, she'd agreed to keep an eye out for some potential roles for Gray, and promised to call him later this week.

"She did, yeah," Gray said.

"And?" I asked.

Gray looked uncomfortable. "And she, uh, left a message."

"What?" I blinked. "And you haven't called her back? Gray—"

"I will, I will," Gray protested. "Give me a minute."

"Right, because you've been soooo busy here, going back to

your room every night and playing Snake on your old-person flip phone."

Gray's eyes narrowed and he gave me a long look. "Where's all this coming from?"

"All this what?" I asked. "Me taking an interest in your future? My apologies."

"No," Gray said slowly. "You being all pushy, like you're trying to start a fight." He tilted his head to the side. "Are you nervous?"

"Nervous? What?" I blinked. "No. I'm fine."

"Liar," Gray said, the corner of his mouth quirking up in a smile.

And just like that, he cut through me, cut through defenses I didn't even realize I'd raised.

"Ugh, fine," I sighed. "Maybe a little."

"You're gonna do great, I promise," Gray said. "It's just like jumping off the high dive at the pool for the first time each summer. It's nothing you haven't done before—it's just a new context, you know?"

Right. Nothing I haven't done before. Because I get hand-jobs from guys—from super hot, strangely nice ex-porn stars, no less—all the fucking time.

"You guys ready?" Violet asked, and we both swung around to look at her.

Gray glanced down at me and waited for me to respond.

"Yeah," I said, hoping I sounded confident. "Yeah, we're ready."

We got back into position to resume shooting the scene. I sprawled out across Dylan's bed and Gray took up his position by the door. The boom mic operator stepped forward and Violet walked behind the camera, checked to make sure we were all in place, and then called, "Action!"

And suddenly, I was Dylan. All it took was a few deep breaths and I was out of my own head and into Dylan's— who also had a perfectly good reason to be nervous, since what he wanted to do with Wyatt right now would also be a first for him.

"If you think I'm going to pass you just because we—" Wyatt *began from the corner, but then stopped, blushing.* "Well, I won't. You have to study."

"I am," Dylan *said with a sly smile, eyeing Wyatt up and down.* "I'm studying right now."

"I mean it. This isn't something you can mess around with. This is your future," Wyatt *said, folding his arms as he leaned back against the closed door.* "I'm not leaving until I see you crack that book open."

"Then I guess we're at an impasse, aren't we," Dylan *said.* "Unless you're willing to incentivize the situation."

"Dylan—" Wyatt *warned.*

"Dylan," Dylan *repeated, smiling and sitting up slowly. He licked his lips as he balanced, bracing himself against the mattress with his wrists.* "Dylan, Dylan, Dylan."

He pushed himself up off the bed, standing and walking slowly towards Wyatt, who stiffened and looked like a deer frozen in panic as Dylan approached. Dylan put his hands on Wyatt's chest, meaning to pull Wyatt down to kiss him.

But Wyatt wouldn't move, so instead, Dylan just stood up on his tiptoes and kissed Wyatt's jaw, then his neck, then parted the two sides of his button down shirt right above the top button and laid a kiss on Wyatt's chest there. Wyatt inhaled sharply and looked down at Dylan.

"What are you—what are you doing?" Wyatt said, his voice hoarse.

"You wanted me to work, didn't you?" Dylan said. "This is my incentive."

He started to kneel, letting his hands trail down Wyatt's sides as he sank to the floor—but Wyatt grabbed his wrists and pulled him back up roughly.

"No," he said, sounding hoarse. "Just no."

Dylan looked up, hurt.

"I thought you—I thought you wanted—"

"Not like this," Wyatt said, his voice raspy. He pulled Dylan in, pressed a rough, hungry kiss to Dylan's lips. When he pulled away, he gave Dylan an unreadable look. "You kill me, you know that?"

"I don't know anything," Dylan said, knowing he sounded petulant, unable to stop it, and pissed about that, all at once. "Obviously."

Wyatt traced a finger along Dylan's cheek and smiled at him. Dylan didn't know what to make of that smile. It was sweet, tender—and a little sad.

"Come here," Wyatt said, taking Dylan's hand gently and pulling him towards the desk. He pulled out the chair and smiled. "Sit."

Dylan looked at Wyatt suspiciously. Was Wyatt really just going to make him sit and then leave? But Wyatt's lips were still curled in that smile, and Dylan found himself sitting anyway.

Wyatt moved behind Dylan, his hands coming to rest on Dylan's shoulders. He squeezed them once and Dylan shivered, despite the warmth radiating from Wyatt's body into his own.

"Chapter 5," Wyatt said. His voice was soft but rough, like waves crashing on a distant shore. "Page 142."

As Dylan opened the book, Wyatt's right hand slid down onto his chest, rubbing him once there and then trailing his fingers lightly across Dylan's Adam's apple. Dylan sucked in a harsh breath and tried to steady himself as he looked at page 142.

"Third problem set," Wyatt said, his left hand moving lightly to Dylan's neck, not even applying pressure, just caressing his skin, while his right hand dropped down again, brushing across Dylan's chest until it fell onto his lap.

And then I was me again—not Dylan—and Wyatt was Gray and holy fucking shit, I was completely pulled out of the scene, because Gray's hand was in my lap and I could barely breathe.

What the hell was happening? Why was I so shaken? I couldn't remember the last time I'd come out of a scene in the middle like this.

I struggled to get my head back into the scene. I didn't want to ruin this take. It was fine—everything was fine. I didn't even have lines right now, thank God, I just had to listen to Gray—to *Wyatt*—say things about 'integration by parts' and 'finding limits' and weird calculus stuff I'd never actually learned in real life.

And Dylan was supposed to be sort of losing it too, I figured, as I tried to steady my breath. It was just—fuck. I wasn't prepared for this. How—how present I'd feel. And fuck, how good *it* would feel. How good *Gray* would feel.

Jesus Christ I was hard. Gray's hand was still only brushing me lightly, but my cock was stiffening rapidly, responding to his touch. So much for my worries that I wouldn't be able to get hard. Apparently *that* wasn't going to be a problem, at least.

Gray's hand—fuck, no, *Wyatt's* hand—stroked my cock through the fabric of the running shorts I was—*Dylan* was wearing. I let out a moan at the firm, steady touch, and in response, I felt Gray's—*Wyatt's*—fuck, Gray's lips make contact with my neck. God, I couldn't do it, couldn't keep myself from thinking of Gray as himself and me as me. It was too real.

Dammit, we'd rehearsed this. Blocked it. I knew both of our lines cold and we'd run through the outlines of the scene multiple times. But Violet had wanted a spontaneous feel and I realized now how stupid it had been for me to think I knew what to expect.

Gray pulled his hand away and I whined at the loss of contact, not even faking a tiny bit. I started to look up, but Gray just laughed lightly in my ear.

"If you want me to keep going," he whispered, "you know what to do. Those limits aren't going to find themselves."

Groaning, I picked up a pencil and forced myself to lean forward, staring down at the textbook. It was a good thing Dylan wasn't actually supposed to solve these problems because they might as well have been hieroglyphics to me.

But the camera sure as hell wasn't lingering on the fucking notebook page under my hand, so I just began writing random strings of numbers and letters.

As soon as I put pencil to paper, Gray's hand returned to my cock, stroking me again.

"Fuck," I moaned.

"Shh," Gray whispered, his lips ghosting across my cheek. "Shh. If you want me to keep going, you gotta be quiet. Can you do that for me?"

"Okay," I whimpered, sounding like I was falling apart and actually on the verge of doing so. God, it was hard to keep myself together under Gray's attentions. I nodded and looked down at the textbook again.

"Good boy," Gray growled in my ear, and my cock fucking twitched in his hand.

Good boy? That sure as hell wasn't in the fucking script, but there was no denying the effect it had had on me, and Violet wasn't calling for us to cut.

And then Gray's hand dipped down into my shorts and took hold of my cock, guiding it out from under the fabric. It bounced free before Gray took me in hand again, and I thought I might melt right there, right that minute.

Skin on skin, hot and smooth, in that firm grip of Gray's that somehow felt so different, so much better than my own hand. Or anyone else's, for that matter. I stole a glance down into my lap and my cock twitched again at the sight of Gray's hand circling it.

Fuck, that was hot. Gray stroked me, his hand pumping up

and down on my shaft, then twisting up and playing with the head. I started leaking pre-cum and Gray swiped his fingers across my slit, using it as lube and slicking my cock with it. It felt dirty, and Jesus Christ, was it turning me on.

"Fuck, fuck," I breathed, struggling to keep myself under control. I couldn't have told you how long the scene had been going—a minute? an hour?—but I knew I was on the edge. "I can't—fuck, you're gonna make me come. I can't—can't concentrate."

It was true—I could barely get the words out. But evidently Gray had decided that Wyatt had seen enough effort from Dylan to reward him, because he didn't stop stroking me. Instead, he tilted my head back with his left hand, exposing my neck, and brought his mouth down to it, worrying the sensitive skin there with his teeth.

I let the pencil fall from my hand, gave myself over to just *feeling*, letting Gray guide my body on this cresting wave of pleasure. My cheeks were flushed and I had half a second's thought for what I must have looked like on camera right then before I shoved it away. Thinking about that—thinking about anything, really—wasn't something I wanted to do right now. All I wanted to do was feel.

Gray stroked me faster and trailed his lips back to my shoulder where he bit down.

"Fuck," I moaned. I tried to turn around, suddenly desperate to taste his lips with my tongue, but Gray caught my chin and turned my face back towards the desk. It was bossy and demanding and fuck, it was hot. I couldn't handle it anymore—everything had built up too much. I couldn't hold it off any longer.

"I'm gonna—fuck, I'm gonna come," I gasped, and Gray sucked down on my shoulder, and my orgasm knocked me flat. I tipped my head all the way back, hungry, needy breaths and moans escaping from my lips as I came into Gray's hand, pleasure rolling through my body.

I felt limp, like jelly, like my limbs no longer worked. I let Gray cradle my head, let him support me completely, and just tried to keep myself from disintegrating entirely.

It occurred to me suddenly that I was supposed to say something. Jesus, what the fuck was my line? I couldn't remember it for the life of me. I wasn't entirely sure my brain hadn't liquified as I'd come, leaving nothing but soup.

"Fuck," I whispered. And then it hit me—that *was* my line. Goddamn Danny Wilson and their brilliant, beautiful brain had somehow known I'd be so fucking incoherent that I wouldn't be able to talk right now.

"Language, Mr. Jones," Gray said, using Dylan's last name. "I'd hate to have to give you a demerit after all of that."

"You wouldn't," I breathed, looking up at him in exhaustion. The dialog was beginning to come back to me, but it still felt dreamy, like I couldn't be sure it was actually me talking.

"Depends," Gray said with a smile, "on how you do on the exam tomorrow." And then he kissed me on the cheek and began to walk back towards the door.

"You're leaving?" I said, my voice confused and desperate. I didn't know if that was Dylan, desperate for Wyatt, or me, desperate for Gray. "You can't just leave. Not after—not after that."

"Study hard, Dylan," Gray said with a grin. And then he slipped out through the bedroom door.

"Cut!" Violet called.

I let my shoulders slump, closing my eyes. I felt like I should be moving, should be doing something. Cleaning myself up, if nothing else. But first, I just needed to breathe.

Jesus, what the hell had just happened to me? I hadn't been ready for that. At all.

Gray stepped back into the room and flashed me a quick smile before moving to talk to Violet. A runner came over with a box of tissues, handing it to me. The general hum of discussion and activity started up again and I realized, both embarrassed and relieved, that no one was paying me the slightest attention at all.

For Gray and Violet, at least, this was nothing special. Just another day at the office. But for me...

For me, I thought, this day might be the fulcrum on which the rest of my life balanced. The before part, the part where I wasn't sure what I wanted, wasn't sure *who* I wanted—and everything that came after.

Everything I'd thought about maybe being into guys, about it not being a big deal, about it being 20 goddamn 17 and none of this mattering—all of that had been exposed as nothing more than the artful objections of someone trying to hide from himself.

It was no longer a hypothetical that I liked guys. I knew that now. And suddenly, everything was different. I was gay. Or not straight, at least. I couldn't deny that anymore—not to myself, anyway. And now I had to figure out what came next.

I cleaned myself up, then pulled my shorts back on. Still sitting, not quite ready to get up and talk to anyone yet, I turned and glanced at Gray where he stood talking to Violet. Maybe he felt my eyes on him, maybe it was just chance— but he looked over and shot me a smile that went right to my heart.

God, he was perfect.

And God, was I fucked.

Because it wasn't enough to have realized I liked guys. No, I had to go and make it even worse by realizing I liked one guy in particular. Way more than I wanted to. Way more than was smart.

I needed a friend right now, not a stupid crush. I was moving back to LA when this movie was done. And Gray would never be interested in me anyway. Besides, that wasn't what I wanted.

I didn't want Gray.

I didn't.

But no matter how much I repeated that to myself, my eyes kept finding their way back to his face, and his smile kept on twisting through me like a knife in my heart.

9

GRAY

"*R*eady?" Violet asked, looking over at me and Tyler with a grin on her face.

My stomach flip-flopped. I was as ready as I'd ever be, I supposed, to see myself acting on screen. I looked over at Tyler and winced. He shot me a quick smile, then looked away.

Another thing that was making my stomach flip-flop. Tyler had been acting a little bit weird for the past few days. Not angry, not even sad. Just... distracted somehow. Or not quite there. Whenever we talked, it was like Tyler was simultaneously thinking about, and carrying on, an entirely separate conversation I couldn't hear.

"Ready," I said, and Tyler nodded.

Violet clicked play and we all drew in close to watch the first footage from *Foresight*, edited. Not even a trailer, but a teaser Violet had cut together for promo purposes.

It wasn't much—just some gently propulsive string music

beneath shots of Dylan looking pensive, Wyatt looking nervous. Oh, and there was their fight in the library. Shit, and the two of them out in the woods. Dylan upset, Wyatt calling his name. And then Dylan launched himself at Wyatt and kissed him—and the screen cut to black, *Foresight* scrawled across the screen in white letters.

"Holy shit," I said.

"Good, right?" Violet said with a smile.

"Good?" I repeated. "Vi, are you sure that was us? Me, anyway? That looked... that actually looked real."

"Dummy, I've been telling you for weeks that you're actually good."

"I know, I know," I said, shaking my head. "I just—I never thought I'd actually see it for myself."

Violet glanced over at Tyler. "What did you think?"

"Amazing," Tyler said without hesitation. "Violet, it's perfect. You edited it so well."

Violet laughed. "Thank you for saying that, since I spent all last night putting it together."

"All of last night?" I blinked. "We were shooting til midnight."

"Yeah."

"And its 6 a.m. now."

"Yeah."

I stared at her. "Did you get *any* sleep?"

"Eh, I'll sleep when I'm dead," Violet said. "Or when this

movie's done. Whichever comes first." She grinned over at Dave and Andrew. "But we're planning a little release event for the end of the week and we wanted to have something done for it. It's not perfect, of course. We need a better score, for one thing. But that's a problem for post-production-Violet."

"I still can't believe it," I said. "It just seems so... real?"

"We *have* actually been filming you this whole time, you know," Violet snorted. "Not just pretending."

"Do you—do you think people will like it?" I asked, hating how uncertain my voice sounded.

"Gray, they're gonna love it. Trust me."

"They already do," Danny put in. I swiveled to look back at them. "I've been posting updates on my blog and literally every time I put a photo up from set, people go nuts."

"They're not—are they still mad about..." Tyler trailed off.

"Pssh," Danny said. "Sure, some people might complain, but you can't please everyone. The people who were excited about *Foresight* still are, and they're pulling in new people every day. I've gained two thousand more followers in the past three weeks. Not even exaggerating."

"Shit," Tyler said, his voice impressed.

"Yeah," Violet agreed. "Shit is right. People are going to love this movie because you two are fucking amazing and Danny wrote a great screenplay and we're going to take over the goddamn world." She grinned at all of us. "So yeah, get ready for everyone to lose their collective shit about you when this teaser comes out in..." she glanced down at her phone, "three days. But," she said, looking back up at me, "enough of collectively jerking ourselves off. Gray, I wanna get the tree-carving scene in before we lose the early morning light. You good to go?"

"All set."

Everyone stood up to file out of the room, but I jogged to catch up to Tyler and snagged his elbow.

"Hey," I said. "You got a sec? I know you're not in this scene and probably just wanna go back to bed, but—"

"What?" Tyler looked up, almost as though he were surprised someone was talking to him. "Oh. Yeah. What's up?"

"Well, that's actually what I was going to ask you," I said as I settled in next to him, walking down the hall. "You just seem —well, I dunno. Is everything okay?"

"Yeah," Tyler said. He pulled a smile onto his face, but it felt like it was stretched too sharply and was warping at the edges. "Totally."

"Really?"

"Really," Tyler said. He gave me a wry look. "I promise, Gray, I'm fine."

I glanced at him suspiciously. "Did your dad call again?"

"What?" Tyler barked a laugh. "No. God, no." He shook his head. "That, I suppose, is one thing I'm *not* actually going to have to worry about again. Not anymore. Since I didn't quit this film, I'm pretty sure he's officially disowned me by now."

I didn't know what to say to that but before I had to come up with an answer, Tyler spoke again.

"Speaking of phone calls," he said, giving me a significant look. I knew he was just trying to change the subject, but he wouldn't stop staring at me and finally I gave up.

"I know, I know," I said, raising my hands defensively. "I'll read the scripts and call Tiana back, I promise."

True to her word, Tiana had sent me a bunch of scripts, just to look at, she'd said. To help her get a feel for what kind of roles I'd be interested in. But so far, I'd just ignored the email and let it sit in the bottom of my inbox.

It was dumb, I knew. But somehow, as long as I didn't open it, it wasn't real. I didn't have to read the scripts, didn't have to actually start pursuing things, auditioning—and getting rejected.

I still couldn't imagine anyone would want to cast me in anything, once they knew my background. My age. My lack of experience. But as long as I didn't actually put myself out there, no one could say no to me, I figured.

Tyler yawned as he followed me outside. "Tired already?" I asked. "Or were you up with Violet?"

Tyler laughed. "Nah, I just haven't been sleeping so great lately." He looked away from me and I wondered why. "Fuck, I wish I *had* been up working with Violet, then I'd have an excuse to be this exhausted."

Was that really all it was? Just Tyler being sleep deprived?

"Yeah," I said, keeping my voice light. "But then you'd have to, you know, work on editing and stuff."

Tyler shrugged. "Honestly, that could be kinda fun. Violet was showing me the dailies a couple days ago and it was cool, watching her talk through her process." He glanced over at me. "I dunno, I know what happens in theory, but that's an aspect of filming I've never actually had a chance to see up close before. Usually people just wanted me off set and out of their hair."

"Well, Violet adores you, so you don't have to worry about that."

"Pssh, that's nothing compared to what she thinks about you," Tyler said. "I don't even come close."

"Why don't we just agree that she loves both her children equally and could never pick between us?" I said with a laugh.

"Whatever," Tyler said with a sly grin. "You know you've always been Mom's favorite."

I shuddered. "I think I regret this metaphor. It's way too weird to refer to you as my brother given, you know, the scene we're shooting this afternoon."

"Oh," Tyler said, his eyes widening. "Yeah. Right."

And then he glanced away again.

"Wait a second. Is *that* it?" I said as an idea hit me.

"Is what what?" Tyler asked, giving me a confused look.

It had just dawned on me—Tyler had been acting weird ever since we'd shot that hand-job scene. God, how could I have missed that?

"Is it the sex stuff?" I asked. "Is that what's making you

uncomfortable? Like, being on camera. Oh God, or is it me? Is it something I did? Fuck, I can't believe I didn't think of this sooner. I'm sorry Tyler, I didn't realize—"

"What? Jesus, no, Gray, calm down," Tyler said. "Nothing's wrong. I promise. You certainly didn't *do* anything wrong."

"And you're not uncomfortable with filming? I know sometimes things can feel different once the camera's on you."

Tyler laughed and it had the strangest sort of resigned sound to it. "Trust me, Gray, the camera is the least of my worries right now."

"You're sure?" I asked, scrutinizing his face.

"I'm sure," Tyler said, those hazel eyes meeting mine and gleaming in the sunlight. "Now get out to those woods before Mom gets mad at you."

I really did work on letting it go. If Tyler said everything was fine, I should listen, shouldn't I? I didn't want to be obnoxious. At this point, if there really were something wrong, he clearly didn't want to tell me.

Still, when I walked into the room we were using as Dylan's on the main floor that afternoon, I couldn't help wanting to check in with him. Tyler was looking at something on his phone as I came over.

"Hey," I said, sidling up like everything was totally casual and I was coming to talk to my friend with no ulterior motive. Which it was, and I was. Because I wasn't going to ask him again. Really. "What's up?"

Tyler looked up with a smile. "Danny wasn't kidding. They've been posting pictures from set with updates about how things are going, and the comments are insane. They're getting like, a thousand likes on Instagram, even if it's just a picture of donuts over on the catering table. Look."

He held his phone out to me and scrolled through picture after picture from the past few weeks, each one followed by tons of reblogs, likes, and emoji-filled squealing.

"Damn," I said.

"Yeah." Tyler's eyes grew wide as he looked at me. "I guess people are actually excited about this? I've been trying to stay away from the internet and what people are saying about the movie but... this is intense."

"Is it—I mean, does it bother you at all, that they're posting—"

"Gray, I swear to God, if you ask me if I'm okay one more time, I'm going to slip in this next scene and use my teeth."

I looked at him in horror. "You wouldn't."

"Better not test me," Tyler said with an evil smile—but then his face softened. "I promise, I'm fine. Pictures of us online, the sex stuff—none of it bothers me, okay? I'm just... tired. That's it."

So what else could I do but believe him? Even if something in my gut told me there was actually something bothering Tyler, he clearly didn't want to talk about it. I studied the bed on the side of the room in thought. He said it wasn't the sex scenes getting to him—but just in case, I decided, I would do the best I could to make this scene feel as safe as possible.

I'd been thinking a lot about what Tyler had said, about listening and responding to your scene partner instead of just concentrating on lines. Oddly enough, it wasn't all that different from doing scenes in porn, except in those scenes, I'd been reading someone's body language and responding to that, not their words.

The scene we were about to film was a pivotal one in the book. Wyatt walked into Dylan's room planning on blowing Dylan, not at all prepared for Dylan to flip all of that on its head. And he couldn't deny how hot it was, Dylan wanting him that bad. So he ended up letting Dylan blow him— because Dylan had that much power over him, because he couldn't say no to anything Dylan wanted.

My stomach tightened, thinking about Tyler down on his knees in front of me. I felt a little queasy about how much that turned me on. I didn't want Tyler to do anything he didn't want to—but I couldn't deny the way my cock stirred at the thought of Tyler taking me in his mouth.

I didn't want to think about what that might mean. Tyler was my friend—I hoped—but nothing more. He certainly didn't want anything else from me. So no matter how much my cock might be responding to the rogue thoughts about Tyler that were drifting through my mind, I had to push that down.

That hand-job scene from last week had been intense. I hadn't known what to expect from Tyler. Even though we'd become friends—just friends—I still hadn't known what Tyler liked. How he wanted to be touched, how he'd respond to me.

I shivered, remembering the way Tyler had fallen apart in my hands. I still wasn't sure how much of that had been Tyler acting as Dylan and how much was just Tyler being Tyler. But I couldn't forget Tyler's moans, seeing him melt, feeling the heat of his body, smelling his skin as I'd buried my face in his neck.

But I wasn't going to get caught up in that today. This was Tyler's first on-camera blowjob. The important thing was making sure he felt in control.

"Just remember," I said, trying to sound off-hand. "You can stop the scene at any point. Violet will understand if you need to—"

"Gray," Tyler said, a clear note of warning in his voice.

"Okay, okay," I grumbled. "Shutting up."

I gave him a tiny salute, nodded to Violet, and stepped back out into the hallway. I could see Tyler moving over to the bed just before a camera guy followed me out into the hall and shut the door. I walked down the hall til I found my mark and waited, setting my face into a half-nervous, half-excited expression that wasn't all that different from how I felt anyway.

On my cue from the camera guy, I began walking, my eyes glued to the door. I knocked twice, quietly, and then threw a glance over my shoulder, looking both ways before silently opening the door and slipping inside.

Tyler was already standing up from the bed and I only got one step into the room before he launched himself at me. He pushed me back against the door, pressing it shut with the combined weight of our bodies as he kissed me.

"You're late," he said when he broke the kiss, looking up at me with accusing eyes.

"Department meeting ran long," I said, trying to get my breath back. I smiled down at him, put my fingers under Tyler's chin, and tilted it up, brushing my lips across his mouth lightly before pulling back. "Let me make it up to you."

My hand dropped to Tyler's shoulders, then slid down to find his waist, my other hand already stroking his ass. His hips were slim and perfect in my hands.

"You're damn right you're gonna make it up to me," Tyler breathed. "Lock the door."

My heart thumped as I fumbled for the door behind me, finding the lock and flipping it with my fingers. As soon as I'd done it, Tyler tugged me towards the bed. My eyes widened in surprise—well, not surprise, but, you know, in *Wyatt's* surprise—and I smiled as Tyler pushed me around and thrust me down onto the mattress.

I tried to pull Tyler down on top of me, but he pulled back and gave me a stern look.

"Strip," he said peremptorily.

"What?" I asked, doing my best to sound taken aback by the command.

Tyler was already pulling his shirt off over his head and he glared at me once he was free of the fabric.

"Strip," he repeated. "If you want to make it up to me, that's a start."

I looked up at Tyler, taking in the broad, lean strength of his shoulders, the grace of his collarbones, the thin but powerful chest, lithe and beautiful.

I tore my eyes away just long enough to pull my shirt off, then let them return to feast on Tyler's skin again as I fumbled for my belt. Tyler was shimmying his jeans down over his hips and soon enough he was standing naked before me, thin but defiant, with all the arrogance and insecurities of youth, as though he were daring me to look—or to look away. He stroked himself, but his eyes were glued to my face.

I hurried to kick off my shoes, slide my pants to the floor. Jesus, I was almost painfully hard. No need to worry about that. My cock pushed up against the fabric of my boxer briefs and bounced with relief as I kicked those off as well.

"Come here," I said, holding my hand out to Tyler.

It wasn't like I hadn't seen Tyler's cock before, wasn't like I didn't know how good it looked—long and pink and smooth, but fuck, I needed it in my hand again, needed to feel him. And I'd never seen Tyler like this—proud and gorgeous, owning his body and, by extension, owning me. So much for him being uncomfortable.

Tyler blinked in surprise as I pulled him down to straddle me. Did he think I was just going to let him get right on his knees? No, I wanted—needed—to feel him against me. His slim form in my lap fit as though he'd been made to go there and my hands stroked the deep V of his hips, the curve of his ass, the length of his cock.

This wasn't exactly in the script. Wyatt was supposed to try to pull Dylan down onto the bed, and Dylan refused and knelt instead. But dammit, I couldn't help wanting to have Tyler on top of me for a little while longer. He felt so good, his weight on me so right, and he moaned as I stroked our cocks together.

Fuck, I loved how responsive Tyler was, how eager. He was already leaking pre-cum and I slipped my finger across his slit, then slicked his cock as I pumped up and down his shaft.

Tyler bent down and pressed a hot, hungry kiss to my mouth, nipping at my lower lip before trailing kisses across my jaw to my ear.

"What," he asked, angling his face away from the camera, "are you doing? You're supposed to let me blow you."

His breath heaved in his chest and he groaned again as I stroked him, giving no indication that he'd asked me a question.

I tilted my chin up and licked a long stripe up Tyler's neck, then traced my way over to his ear.

"So do it then," I growled, my voice just loud enough for him to hear.

Tyler's cock twitched and I had to stifle a chuckle. God, this was actually fun. I could do this forever.

Tyler gave me a stern look, then pulled back, letting his feet down to touch the floor. I gave him my best confused look and as Tyler knelt down in front of me, parting my legs, I frowned.

"No," I said. "No, I'm the one making this up to you, remember?"

"You are," Tyler said with a smile.

"But—"

"Wyatt," he said sharply. "I've wanted to do this since the first day I saw you. I've dreamed about it. Do *not* tell me I can't do this now. Or you really *will* have something to make up to me."

He pushed my legs open, sliding himself in between them, then brought one hand to the base of my cock. I sucked in a deep breath of air and Tyler smiled up wickedly at me, a hint of a challenge still lingering in his eyes. All I could do was look back at him, drinking in the heat coming off of Tyler's gaze. Finally, I let myself smile.

As if that were what he'd been waiting for, Tyler leaned in and licked a long stripe up the underside of my cock. I shuddered at the contact, the smooth, slick touch, then shivered again as Tyler licked his way around my shaft. His eyes stayed glued to mine, though, and that fact—the contact, the spark between us—was hotter than anything he was doing with his tongue.

Tyler continued his circuit of my cock and by the end of it, I was practically jumping out of my skin. Jesus, Tyler was taking it slow. Not that I was complaining, but we hadn't exactly talked about drawing the scene out this much. Evidently Tyler had decided to enjoy himself.

Finally, *finally*, he brought his lips to the head of my cock and I nearly convulsed as he sucked the tip into his mouth. I let out a low moan and Tyler hummed approvingly, sucking down more of my length.

God, that was hot. I knew I was big. And maybe it was sleazy, but the sight of my cock filling Tyler's mouth, looking so large that he could choke on it, sent throbs of pleasure through me.

Tyler got me warm and wet before pulling off, stroking the base of my shaft with his hand as he swirled his tongue around the head, then sliding back down and taking even more of me into his mouth this time. He looked up at me with wide eyes as my cock slid down his throat and I felt myself twitch. Jesus, he looked good like that. I wasn't going to last long if he kept that up.

Tyler began to build up a rhythm, sucking and stroking me. He wasn't overly coordinated, but he was eager. If I hadn't known better, I'd almost have thought he'd never done this before—which, I supposed, was the point. This probably was *Dylan's* first blow job. Tyler was just committing to character.

Still, what he lacked in experience, he made up for in enthusiasm. His mouth was wet and sloppy and fuck, the noises he was making, these little moans like *he* was the one getting pleasure, were driving me wild. He massaged my balls with his left hand, then pulled his mouth off my cock to lick them. When he moved back to my tip, he brought my own hand to the back of his head.

"Fuck," I breathed, letting my hand tangle in Tyler's hair.

God, did Tyler have any idea what he was doing to me? Maybe this was normal for him, guys losing their fucking minds when he blew them. It probably happened all the time. An irrational stab of jealousy went through me at the thought of Tyler with other guys, with any other guy, but I shoved it away.

It was probably just because it had been so long since I'd

gotten any kind of attention other than the kind that came from my own hand. Not since Ethan and I had broken up. And Tyler was different from Ethan, of course. Not as confident—though that could just be him in character, I reminded myself—and smaller, slimmer.

And there was something about Tyler that I couldn't quite find words for—not that words were particularly easy to come by, in my current mental state. Something that made my stomach tighten when I looked at him, something that made me want to protect him. Cherish him.

With Ethan, everything had always felt like a performance, like he wanted me to know he was doing me some kind of favor. With Tyler, everything just felt... sweeter?

Jesus, what the fuck was happening to me? *You're having an orgasm, dumbass, not having a religious experience.*

Besides, this actually *was* a performance. It wasn't real. This wasn't *Tyler* looking up at me like he needed me, like he'd die without my touch, like he wanted nothing more than to be with me forever. He was just *acting*.

And then Tyler moved his mouth back onto my cock and swallowed me down even further than before, getting almost all of my cock into his mouth. I could feel the tip hit the back of Tyler's throat and heard—*felt*—Tyler gag in surprise. My cock twitched.

"Fuck, Ty-Dylan," I moaned, correcting myself at the last second. Jesus, I'd almost lost it there, but no one said anything and Tyler was still going so apparently we weren't stopping.

"Baby, baby, you're so good,"

Baby was safer. And honestly, it fit. It wasn't a word I'd used before. But with Tyler, something about it felt right, fit the way I wanted to take him in my arms, take care of him.

Tyler looked up at me again, his hazel eyes golden and open in the light, his mouth filled with my cock and as we locked eyes, Tyler deliberately sucked down and gagged on my cock.

"Fuck," I groaned. "Fuck, baby, I'm gonna come."

I meant that as a warning. I was used to coming on a guy's chest or face and it wasn't until Tyler didn't move that I realized we'd never clarified how this scene would end. I'd just assumed.

But instead of pulling off of me, Tyler kept sucking me down. His face was covered in spit and pre-cum and as he pumped his hand in time with his mouth, I could feel my orgasm building, my whole body tightening, and suddenly I was over the edge, coming into Tyler's mouth.

Tyler's eyes widened in surprise for a second and I wondered if I should have pulled out after all. But then he kept going, milking out my orgasm as I released into his mouth. God, and then Tyler pulled back and let a trickle of cum run out of the corner of his mouth and down onto his chin and my cock tried to empty another load right then and there—if I hadn't been completely empty, that sight alone would have been enough to make me come.

I couldn't help it—I pulled Tyler up and off of me, then pushed him back down onto the bed so I could take his mouth with my own. I could feel his hard cock pressing up against me and even though I knew the scene was almost over, I couldn't help grinding my hips down onto him.

Tyler's lips, his tongue, were wet and sloppy and no, we hadn't planned this either, but God, I needed to taste him, needed to taste myself on his tongue, tangy and sweet.

I licked the dribble of cum off his jaw and then pressed a kiss to Tyler's forehead, trying to convey in some way how fucking perfect he was, how grateful I was, how... fuck, how much I wanted to thank him and hold him, me, myself, not Wyatt, not anyone else.

Except that was stupid, I knew. Tyler was acting—we both were. Tyler didn't care what *I* felt or what I wanted to show him. And so with a final kiss, ghosting my lips over his, I pulled back and returned to the script.

"You're perfect," I said. "You know that?"

It was my line—and it also happened to be exactly what I wanted to say at that moment.

Tyler grinned up at me. "Well, I'm punctual anyway. Unlike some people I know..."

I laughed. "Hell, if that's what I get for being late to meet you, maybe I need to start making that a habit."

Tyler reached up and took my chin between his fingers, tilting my face down to look at him as one of his legs curled up and over mine. "Don't even think about it."

I grinned at him and kissed him once more. "Lucky for you I can't think about much of anything right now."

"Yeah," Tyler said, his eyes alight. "Lucky me."

"Cut!"

Violet's voice sliced through the room, through the moment,

and brought me back to myself. I smiled down at Tyler, who smiled back. It had felt so real for a second there, so right for the two of us to lie here tangled like this.

But it wasn't. Real or right. We weren't doing this because we liked each other. Or, at least, Tyler wasn't. I had to remember that—make sure I knew why I was doing this as well.

I shifted off to the side, feeling suddenly awkward, and let Tyler slide out from under me. He pushed himself up and scooted to the edge of the mattress, bending down to find his clothes on the floor and pull them on. He was still hard, I couldn't help noticing out of the corner of my eye, as I sat up and began doing the same thing.

I was fairly comfortable being naked in front of strangers—hazard of the trade, I suppose—but something about that scene with Tyler had felt so intimate. Getting dressed felt like putting on armor, and for some obscure reason, I felt like I needed that.

"That was great, guys," Violet said. "Really great. Just let me replay the footage and check to see if—"

A crash from down the hall cut her off. All of us turned towards the door. The camera guy closest to it stuck his head out into the hall. "What was—"

"Violet?!" Dave's voice came from the far end of the hall, followed by Dave himself, huffing and puffing. "Violet, one of the other cameras—we need—can you come—in the dining hall?"

Violet's eyes widened. "Fuck." She turned to Tyler and me. "Can you guys hang out here for a second?"

"Sure," Tyler said with a shrug. I nodded. We'd need to wait anyway, in case she wanted to reshoot any parts of that scene.

Violet hurried off down the hall, followed by the second camera man and the sound tech. As the room cleared out, Tyler flopped down onto Dylan's mattress with a sigh, lying on his back and folding his arms behind his head.

I glanced at him, then glanced away, feeling suddenly awkward now that the two of us were alone. Jesus, what was *wrong* with me? I'd gotten hundreds of blow jobs on set and I'd *never* felt this mix of nerves and excitement and happiness before—especially not *after* the scene was over.

"God, it says something about how tired I am that this bed actually seems comfortable," Tyler said, flopping back down onto the bed.

"No," I said, shaking my head disapprovingly. "You're not allowed to lie down, or you're gonna make me wanna lie down, and then I'm gonna go straight into a post-orgasm coma."

Tyler laughed and I glared at him. "I'm serious," I said. "The better the orgasm, the deeper the coma. I won't wake up until tomorrow morning."

"That good, huh?" Tyler said, arching an eyebrow as he looked up at me.

"Um, obviously."

Tyler flushed. "Just checking."

"Pssh," I snorted. "You know it was good."

Tyler shrugged and curled up on his side. "Good," he said, looking very self-satisfied.

"Alright, shove over, then" I said, squeezing myself into the space between the wall and Tyler.

Tyler immediately flipped onto his back again and and sprawled out, letting his right arm and leg flop over me gracelessly.

"Oh, no you don't," I said, picking his arm up and pushing it off my chest. "You have to share."

"I'm the sleep deprived one here," Tyler grumbled. "Maybe this is just how I sleep, ever think about that?"

"Right, I'm sure everyone loves sharing a bed with you when you sleep like this."

"Hey, you don't know." Tyler laughed. "Maybe people love having the privilege of getting elbowed in the stomach by me when they share my bed."

I snorted. "Tempting as that sounds..." I shifted up to balance on my elbow and rolled Tyler back onto his side. "You take that half. I'll take this one."

"Pushy," Tyler said, but his voice didn't have any bite. If anything, it sounded drowsy. Maybe he really *was* sleep deprived.

"You're the pushy one. I'm just standing up for myself."

He didn't respond, and eventually I lay down on my back and stared up at the ceiling. Tyler was right—this bed wasn't particularly comfortable. I supposed he'd have figured that out already, given how many scenes he'd had to shoot here in Dylan's room.

I glanced over at Tyler, watching the slight movements of his body as he breathed in and out. It was gentle, rhythmic, and I wondered if he'd already fallen asleep.

I smiled as a thought occurred to me—as long as it had been since I'd gotten a blow job from someone, it had been even longer since I'd *slept* with someone, in the original sense of the word. Ethan had stopped spending the night with me long before we'd broken up.

He'd claimed he was no good being around sick people, and since I'd moved into Maggie's apartment by then, I'd said I understood—no matter how much I'd needed him, no matter how much it felt like I was losing him and Maggie at the same time.

God. No fucking wonder. Looking at it now—he'd already stopped loving me, hadn't he? And I hadn't even noticed.

The weight of that—the sadness, and the shame—settled into me as I lay there, like rain falling on parched earth. I'd been trying to avoid thinking about Ethan since the night we'd run into him in the city. Avoiding his calls, ignoring his texts. Seeing them, thinking about him—it just made me hurt. And I was sick of hurting. I'd thought I was done with it.

I knew I should get over it. But it was hard to shake it off what had happened—Ethan dumping me, Ethan immediately moving on, Ethan probably moving on even before he'd broken things off—when it just confirmed what I'd always known.

I wasn't good enough. No one had ever wanted me, no one had ever wanted to keep me. Not my mother. Not my foster families. Even Maggie had left me—not that that was her fault, of course. But it didn't make me feel less alone.

Ethan had been the one thing I had left. The one person who I'd thought might love me, the one person I'd hoped I'd be good enough for. And so I'd held onto hope that he might still feel something for me, like a fool. All because I was afraid of looking the truth in the face.

Tyler had asked me where I wanted to be in a year, what I wanted from my life. And sure, acting was as good a goal as any, even if I couldn't really believe it would ever amount to anything. But it had been easier to say that than the truth.

The truth was, all I wanted was to stop hurting. To have somewhere I belonged, some*one* I belonged with. And I wasn't sure I'd ever get that.

I knew 30 wasn't exactly old, but where I came from, most people were married with multiple kids by now. I'd spent years of my life with Ethan and it was hard not to feel now like that was time wasted.

Hard not to worry if I'd missed my chance at happiness. Hard not to wonder if I'd ever had one, or if I was just one of those people who didn't get a happy ending. Not everyone could, could they? Life wasn't like the movies.

Tyler shifted in his sleep, his leg brushing back against mine, followed by his body, and suddenly he was pressing up against me. I froze, hesitating for a second, before giving in, letting my body curl around Tyler's like it wanted to.

It didn't mean anything. Nothing at all, other than that I was tired, and Tyler was tired, and his body was warm against mine.

But I *was* tired. Tired of thinking, tired of caring, tired of hurting when I didn't think I could hurt anymore. I brought my arm around to the front of Tyler's chest. It felt good to hold him close, felt good to let him fill my arms, to tuck my chin in against his neck, feel the softness of his cheek.

It felt good to stop thinking.

And with that, I drifted off to sleep.

~

"Hey!"

Tyler's voice was bright and cheerful as he stuck his head into the door of my room at the end of the week.

"Whatcha doin'?"

I looked up from my laptop and smiled.

"You wouldn't believe me if I told you."

"Really?" Tyler said, finally letting the rest of his body join his head in my doorway. "Now you've made me curious."

"I'm looking," I said, gesturing to my laptop where it sat on the mattress next to me, "at the scripts Tiana sent."

"Holy shit, Gray. That's awesome!" Tyler crossed the room to my bed and plopped himself down next to me. "Can I see?"

"Uh, sure," I said, feeling suddenly bashful. Tyler knew so much more about this stuff than I did and for some reason, him looking through these scripts made me feel like a fraud, like he'd see that these projects were all out of my reach. "I wouldn't get too excited. Just because she sent these to me doesn't mean she thinks I'm actually any good. She's prob-ably just doing this as a favor to you."

Tyler rolled his eyes impatiently as he reached over and grabbed the computer. "Gray, agents don't work out of the goodness of their own hearts. If Tiana's sending you anything, it means she thinks you have a shot at something. She makes money if you make money, remember. Now, what are you looking at? Oooh."

As I watched, Tyler skimmed the email Tiana had sent and then began clicking his way through the attachments, talking slowly to himself.

"*Archers* looks good. I know the screenwriters, Greg and Karma, from back when they punched up the script on *Konterra Rising*. They're great. Hmm, *Ticonderoga* is definitely worth checking out. If Brian Luther's attached to that, you want to get on his radar. He's legendary among directors. Ooh, and *Chevron* looks interesting. I think that's been on the Black List for like, two years running. If someone's finally producing it, that could be great."

"The Black List?" I asked blankly.

"Oh, it's this list of like, the most liked screenplays that haven't been produced yet," Tyler said absentmindedly as he continued scrolling. "Usually it means a good project that just has some logistical challenges getting funding. But everything's great quality."

"How do you *know* all this stuff?" I said, looking at Tyler with open amazement now. "It's just—how do you keep it all in your head?"

Tyler shrugged and his cheeks flushed. "I don't know. I

just... do? I like this stuff, you know? Plus, like, the industry is really all I know. I can barely spell my own name or calculate tips, but if you wanna know who the gaffer was on an arthouse romcom from 1979, I could probably tell you."

"So *that's* why you kept getting me to pay for things, isn't it?" I said, elbowing him lightly. "It's just because you don't know how to figure out the tip on a bill!"

"What? No. Definitely not. It's totally because I enjoy your company and not because I'm using you at all," Tyler said, his eyes way too wide and innocent. "Frankly, I'm shocked and hurt, to the core, that you could think such a cruel and callous thing about me."

"Okay, you almost had me, until the tears," I said, snorting at the tears welling up in his eyes.

"Dammit." Tyler grinned. "I overplayed my hand, didn't I?"

"Just a tad. Anyway," I said, looking at him with curiosity. "What's up? Or did you come here just to try to guilt me into things by looking like a kicked puppy?"

"Eh, it wasn't important," Tyler said. "I didn't mean to interrupt if you wanted to keep looking at these." He gestured down to the laptop screen.

"I'm happy to be interrupted. All I'm doing now is reading these things and feeling shitty and insecure about myself. Really, interrupt me. Please."

Tyler bit his lip. "Well, I was gonna ask if you were doing anything tonight, but—"

"Why?" I asked, cocking my head to the side. "Did you want

me to buy you dinner and teach you how to calculate 20% on the bill."

"Very funny. Actually, I was going to ask you for an even bigger favor. Specifically, if you by any chance felt like going into the city tonight... and maybe driving... so that maybe I could hitch a ride with you."

I laughed. "First you use me for my math skills, now for my wheels. When does it end, Tyler?"

"Hey, I warned you I was a spoiled asshole from the start. You walked into this with open eyes."

"I suppose I did, at that." I thought about it for a moment. "Yeah, I could go in. It's been a while since I've checked on the bar and if I don't stop in every now and then, who knows what Micah's going to do to the place."

"You're the best," Tyler said. "Have I told you that yet? The absolute best."

"Yeah, yeah, I know. But the deal is, you have to do something for me in return. Are you meeting up with people in the city?"

"Just my brother. Why?"

"Because as payment for the ride, you have to spend the trip in and the trip back out telling me everything you know about the scripts I got sent, and the directors, and help me figure out what I'm actually supposed to do now."

"Deal," Tyler said with a laugh. "And actually, I'm not even supposed to meet up with Luke until like, 7, so if you want, I can hang out at Maggie's with you for a while."

"You sure? We could go somewhere else."

"Positive. Any awkwardness about it being a bar is offset by the fact that it's the one place where I know the owner and can run and hide in the back room if I have a nervous breakdown. Besides, getting to show off all my useless knowledge and pretending I'm actually good at something for once sounds fun."

"Perfect," I said with a grin. "Just let me get my keys."

The thing is, though, Tyler's knowledge wasn't useless. In fact, once we were tucked away into a booth in the back corner of Maggie's and I'd pulled my laptop back out, I felt like I was getting a crash-course in everything film-related as Tyler sifted through the scripts I'd been sent.

"Definitely go after this one," he said about *Rubicon*, which was apparently a sprawling war epic. "That director's amazing, her action sequences are fantastic, and all of her past features have gotten award nods."

"Jesus," I gulped. "I'm not sure I'm up for that."

Tyler rolled his eyes. "Gray, the first thing you need to know about being an actor: no one ever thinks they're good enough, but you're not supposed to say it out loud."

"But you tell me all the time what a fuck-up you are."

"Yeah, but that's different. You don't count," Tyler grinned.

"You wound me."

"Shut up, you know what I mean. You're not a director. If I tell you I'm terrible, the worst that happens is you realize one day it's true." He frowned back down at the laptop screen. "Anyway, this looks like an ensemble cast and it's not the lead you'd be reading for, so if it makes you feel any better, you'd probably get like, a total of 20 lines. But good exposure. Think about it, anyway."

"How about you just be my agent?" I said with a smile. "You clearly know more about this than I do."

"You'll learn. That's the whole point of me telling you this stuff." He glanced down again. "Honestly, I kind of think you should go out for all of these. If you're just starting out, you're gonna be getting lots of rejections anyway—"

"Oh, delightful—"

"So you might as well not limit yourself by not trying for everything," Tyler finished. "Besides, sometimes weird things happen, financing falls through, the studios decide to shelve a project."

"They can do that? Even after they've gotten everyone on board?"

"Oh, God yeah," Tyler said, his eyes widening. "Studios make decisions entirely based off of bottom line calculations and if they think a movie's not actually gonna help them, they'll pull the plug on it, or keep it in limbo, or even film the damn thing and never release it." He shook his head. "What we're doing with *Foresight* is... not normal. Violet and Danny having this much control over every decision, with Dave and Andrew mostly just providing the money? Definitely not common."

"Oh." I paused. "I guess... maybe I should have realized that."

"I mean, I hope it moves more in that direction. Movies really are getting cheaper to make and if you can cut out the long chain of middlemen and reach your audience directly, you don't *need* to spend as much money on marketing. I'd love it if more projects were like that."

I smiled at how animated Tyler was getting, his eyes lighting up and his hands waving wildly as he talked. "You should produce movies, then," I said.

"With my five thousand dollar paycheck from *Foresight*?" Tyler said, arching an eyebrow. "Right."

"We're gonna get royalties, aren't we?"

"The amount of money we're talking though..." Tyler made a face. "Whatever, it doesn't matter. It's not gonna happen."

"Well I guess it'd be a shame anyway, depriving the world of your acting ability," I said, trying to cheer him up.

"Trust me," Tyler snorted. "If that's all it was... God, it would be so nice to not be in front of people's faces all the time."

"Then do it. What's stopping you?"

Tyler waved my question away. "Nevermind. It doesn't matter."

"No, seriously. Tyler, if you wanna do something different—"

"Drop it, Gray."

The tone of Tyler's voice made it clear I'd stepped on a nerve, but I couldn't figure out why the hell Tyler was so set against the idea.

"I need a refill from the bar," I said after an awkward silence, holding up my empty bottle. "You want anything?"

Tyler looked stricken. "Shit. Sorry. I didn't mean to snap at—"

"Dude, you're fine." I tried my best at an encouraging smile. "You sure you don't want anything?"

"Um. Seltzer, I guess?" Tyler still looked uncertain.

"Coming right up.

Micah was swamped with people when I got to the bar so I just waved at him and slid behind the bar myself, grabbing another beer and getting Tyler more seltzer. I was gone for less than a minute, but when I turned around, I saw someone talking to Tyler at our booth.

It was another guy, with longish, shaggy brown hair. Not someone I recognized. And Tyler was smiling. I pushed down an irrational surge of jealousy and started back towards the booth.

I set the beer and seltzer down on the table and the guy talking to Tyler jumped when he realized I was there for the first time. Then his eyes widened.

"Oh my God," the guy said. "It's both of you! Holy shit, I can't believe you're both here. Of all places. This is insane, I just saw the teaser today and now you're in my favorite bar."

"The teas- oh." I stopped, blinking. "God, I'd completely forgotten about that."

"Me too," Tyler said with a laugh.

"You guys are amazing," the guy continued. "My friends and I are so excited about *Foresight*."

"We are too," Tyler said," smiling brightly.

But it was his public smile, I realized now. Until that moment, I couldn't have told you that I knew Tyler had two different smiles—but he did, and the one he was using on this guy was completely different from the one he used when—well, when it was just the two of us. It wasn't strained looking or anything—it was just... opaque, somehow. Like he wasn't letting as much of himself shine through.

"Is there any chance—" the guy stopped and flushed. "Oh God, this is so embarrassing, I can't believe I'm asking this, but is there any chance I could get a picture with you guys?"

I looked over at Tyler, deferring to him.

"Sure," Tyler said, and the other guy smiled like he was having an orgasm.

"I keep forgetting that you're famous," I said with a laugh when the guy finally left.

"Uh, hate to break it to you, buddy," Tyler said with a wry glance, "but you're famous too now."

"Yeah, but I was still just an afterthought for that guy. It wasn't *me* he was jizzing his pants to meet."

"Thanks for that image."

"Do you ever get used to it?" I asked after a minute. "People wanting to talk to you, or take your picture?

Tyler frowned as he thought that over. "In a way, yeah, you do. That doesn't mean you start *liking* it, but you can get used to it."

"Why'd you tell him we'd take a picture then?" I asked,

confused. "I mean, if you didn't want to, we could have said no."

"Yeah, we could have. But then *that* becomes the story, you know? Like, if your ultimate goal is to minimize public attention, you have to think about what takes more energy —just saying yes to the damn picture, or saying no, then having to explain or defend your decision, and then having that guy tell all his friends that we're assholes, and then that becomes a whole thing."

"Who cares if they think we're assholes. Let 'em. You should do what you want."

Tyler smiled sadly. "I wish I were that good at not caring."

"Sorry," I said wincing. "I feel like I keep saying the wrong thing, somehow."

"No, Gray, seriously. You're fine," Tyler said, his voice insistent. "You're like, the one person I actually feel like I can just be myself around, and it's because *you're* being *your*self. Please don't change that."

"Well, as long as you don't change that either."

Tyler was quiet for a moment and when he spoke again, his voice was soft. "I'm sorry," he said. "I know I've been kind of weird the past couple weeks."

"What? No, you haven't."

I said it automatically, even though, okay, yes, he definitely had. And Tyler knew I thought so because I'd been bugging him about what was wrong. But he clearly hadn't wanted to talk about it and I didn't want him to feel like he had to explain.

"I have been," Tyler said, giving me a stern look. "And it's... God, it's complicated and stupid and—"

"You don't have to talk about it, Tyler."

"It's just—it's not—just, know that it has nothing to do with you," Tyler said, like he was struggling to find words to say what he meant. "It's not about you, and I want you to know that. I'm so fucking thankful to have you as a friend—God, I mean, if that's not too much to say. Ugh, is that weird?"

"That's not weird at all," I said, feeling my face warm as I smiled at him. "And I completely—"

But I didn't get to finish my sentence because out of nowhere, a chorus of *'Hey's!'* surrounded us. I looked up to see my friends, Ben and Adam, descending on our booth, along with their friend Nick, and some blond guy who looked vaguely familiar who Tyler was standing up and hugging, so I assumed that must be his brother, Luke. Suddenly our booth was filled with people.

"What the hell are you guys doing here?" I asked as Ben and Adam squished in on my left. Luke and Nick pushed Tyler in across the table so now all six of us were crammed into this booth, Tyler sitting directly across from me, looking surprised but not unhappy.

"Well, Tyler said you were here," Luke said. "So I figured I'd just come over and meet you guys. And then I ran into these three," Luke said, gesturing to Nick, Adam, and Ben, "on my way over, and when I told them where I was going, they decided they had nothing better to do and tagged along."

"Um, excuse you," Ben said, "we were wrapping up events of

vital importance and you just happened to come along at the right time."

"Events of vital importance as you sat eating hot dogs on the High Line?" Luke said with a smirk.

"Extremely important," Adam said, his tone earnest. "If you'd come by even five minutes earlier, we would have been much too busy to even say hi."

"Doing what?" Luke asked.

"Grilling Nick about his love life," Adam said with a grin. Nick, sitting across the table, buried his face in his hands. Adam smiled as he gestured to him. "As you can see, it continues to be a very intense and important conversation."

"It's really not," Nick said, his voice pained as it emanated from behind his hands. "And I will buy everyone a round of drinks if you agree to drop it."

"Um, I'll buy everyone a round of drinks if we *don't* drop it," Tyler said with a laugh from the corner. "This sounds fascinating. I'm Tyler, by the way," he added, waving at the rest of the table. "We haven't actually met, I guess."

A flurry of 'Hi, How Are You's' took over the table for a moment as Adam, Ben, and Nick said hi to Tyler and Luke and I awkwardly acknowledged that we'd probably met before and completely forgotten it.

It was great to see them all. Ben and I had been friends for awhile, but I'd only met Adam more recently, right around when the two of them had started dating. They were both musicians and I took an obnoxious amount of pride in the fact that I'd helped those two lovable idiots figure out how made for each other they were.

I didn't know Nick as well, but he'd always had a warm, calm presence that I just liked. I was pretty sure he was in school to become a minister, if I remembered correctly, so maybe it was divine forbearance that let him put up with the way Adam and Ben were shamelessly ribbing him.

It turned out Luke had gone to college with Ben and Adam, which explained how he knew them. I kept watching Tyler's face for signs that he was uncomfortable with having his evening with his brother crashed by a bunch of other people. But he actually looked happy and at ease, and I wondered how long it had been since Tyler had just been able to relax with a group of people where he wasn't the center of attention. Maybe it helped that in certain circles, Ben was at least as famous as Tyler.

"You good?" I asked him quietly while the rest of the guys went up to get drinks from the bar. "I can get the other guys to leave you two alone if you just wanted time with Luke."

"What?" Tyler blinked. "Oh. Nah, I'm good." He smiled at me in surprise. "That's really nice of you though."

"Is this where you comment on how strange that is again?"

Tyler laughed. "I'll try to restrain myself." He looked over at the bar, then back at me. "I don't know, it's actually kind of nice, being with these guys. Like, they don't care that I'm Tyler, the fuck-up actor. To them, I'm just Tyler, Luke's little brother."

"So," Luke said as they all sat down again. "I believe we were about to find out all of Nick's deepest darkest secrets?"

"Yeah, sounds about right," Adam said.

"Oh my God, it's not even that interesting," Nick groaned. "I promise."

"See, that's what he's been saying all afternoon," Ben explained to us, "but he won't say anything else, so you know there's a story there."

"There's no story," Nick insisted.

"Is too," Adam said stubbornly.

"Fine, then you fucking tell it," Nick grumbled, crossing his arms in front of his chest.

"Basically," Adam said, turning to the rest of us and grinning, "a month ago, Nick was head over heels for some mystery guy named Eli—"

"After having quite possibly the most adorable meet-cute in the world," Ben put in.

"And then he gets all busy so we don't see him for a while," Adam continued, "and now, when we finally do and we ask him how it's going, he says nothing ever came of it, they never even went out, and they never will—*but* he won't tell us why, what happened, who called it off, or anything."

"Because there's nothing to tell," Nick protested. "It didn't work out. I called, we texted, it came to nothing."

He glared uncomfortably at Adam, who cocked an eyebrow and looked right back. "Did you actually ask him out?" Adam demanded.

"I don't want to talk about it," Nick said dourly.

"Okay, better idea," I cut in, feeling a little sorry for Nick at this point. "How about I buy the next round of drinks and instead of torturing Nick, you guys catch us up on everything we've missed while we've been out in Jersey this past month?"

"Depends," Ben said. "Do you have enough scandalous teacher-student romance stories to make it worth our while?"

"Wait, what?" Nick asked, looking up in confusion.

"Oh, don't worry," I said quickly. "Until a few weeks ago, I'd never heard about it either."

"Heard about what?" Nick stared at me. "I'm lost. Are you... teaching now?"

"No, it's their movie," Luke cut in. "The movie they're doing is based on a book and it's a teacher-student romance and it's—you know, it's complicated. But I can lend you the book if you want. I just bought it myself."

"Wait, you bought the book?" Tyler asked Luke in surprise. "I thought you said you hadn't read it."

"I hadn't," Luke said, his cheeks coloring slightly. "But once you got the part, I kind of figured..."

"Oh my God," Tyler said, grinning. "I would have thought you'd be too highbrow and perfect to read something the unwashed masses enjoyed."

"Cute," Luke said, making a face as Tyler stuck his tongue out at his brother. "I mean, I'd already finished this week's *Economist* and I needed something to read on the treadmill so—"

"Jesus, I take back my compliment," Tyler said.

"You didn't actually compliment me, asshole," Luke said before turning back to Nick. "Anyway, if you ever wanna borrow it—"

"It's teacher-student?" Nick said doubtfully. "And that's supposed to be romantic?"

"Oh, don't be such a prude," Adam said. "Just because you're practically a minister doesn't mean you have to be boring."

"It's not *that*," Nick said, his tone somewhat huffy. "It's just... you know, there are power differentials there. And it's—I just feel like it's not really responsible for—"

"Drink your beer and stop ruining our fun," Adam said, making a face.

Ben looked over at Tyler and smiled. "So what's it like acting with Gray? Please tell us he has all sorts of embarrassing pre-shoot rituals that we can tease him about."

Tyler laughed. "Nothing pre-shoot. He is completely terrified of the ghosts he's convinced live in the mansion where we're filming, but—"

"Hey," I objected, kicking him lightly under the table. "I told you that in confidence."

"Sorry, I'm drunk," Tyler said with an unrepentant grin. "It just slipped out."

"You're drinking seltzer."

"I know." His eyes danced. "You should see me on actual alcohol. I'd be spilling all kinds of secrets."

"See, this is why I recommend doing all your embarrassing shit in public," Adam said, nodding sagely. "It's mortifying, but then at least you've got nothing left to hide."

"You know, that's not a bad way to look at it," Tyler said with a laugh.

"Speaking of public," I said, "You guys have any more shows coming up?"

Adam and Ben had played together for the first time about a month ago—actually, right after I'd first talked to Violet about *Foresight*—and I'd been hoping to be able to see them play together again soon.

"Um, maybe," Adam said, looking down. "I'm not really sure."

"We're actually taking a little break from that," Ben said, throwing his arm around Adam and kissing him on the cheek. "Just for a bit, anyway. Plus, it gives us a chance to write some more stuff together."

"You working on anything new?" Luke asked.

"Eh." Adam made a face. "Kinda. I sort of hate everything I've written for the past few weeks."

Across the table, Tyler's eyes narrowed speculatively. He turned towards Adam and Ben. "You wouldn't happen to be in search of inspiration, would you?"

"Depends," Ben said, cocking his head to the side. "What did you have in mind?"

"I was just thinking," Tyler said, looking over at me now. "Wasn't Violet just complaining that she and Dave and Andrew still hadn't figured out what they were gonna do about music rights?"

"Yeah," I said slowly. "But I don't know if—"

Tyler grinned back at Adam and Ben. "You guys wanna write original songs for a crowd-funded gay porn?"

"Well, when you put it like that, I'm sure—" I began, but Ben and Adam were already laughing before I could finish my sentence. They looked at each other. Ben shrugged. Adam shrugged back, smiling.

"I mean... it's not the worst idea I've ever heard," Ben said.

"It wouldn't pay much," Tyler said quickly. "But I honestly do think it's gonna be an amazing movie and if you guys wanna come to the set and meet the director or the producers, or if you wanna see clips of it or something, I'm sure we could work that out. And it would seriously be such a cool thing to be a part of, like I think you'd get a lot of good press and—"

"Tyler, Tyler, relax," Ben said with an easy laugh. "You don't have to sell us that hard."

Tyler flushed and I felt the urge to take his hand and squeeze it. I had to physically stop myself. God, I needed to stop treating Tyler like he needed protection. His *actual* older brother wasn't even all that protective around Tyler, so why the hell did I find myself wanting to do that?

"Yeah," Adam said with a snort. "Ben's fucking rich, and I just mooch off of him, so the money thing isn't an issue." Ben rolled his eyes and Adam snuggled up closer to him. "And actually, it sounds kind of interesting. At least better than banging my head against a wall for inspiration and writing crap all day."

Ben looked concerned. "Babe, the stuff you're writing—"

"Is boring," Adam said. "Being in a loving, trusting, committed relationship is all well and good," he added with a frown, "but it's hell on my creativity. I was writing a lot better when I was unhappy."

"So sorry to ruin things for you," Ben said.

"No you're not," Adam laughed, leaning over and kissing Ben on the temple.

"You're right," Ben grinned. "I'm really not."

I couldn't help but be amazed at Tyler as he talked through logistics with Adam and Ben. He really *was* good at this kind of thing—the behind the scenes work in the film industry—even if *he* didn't think he was. And it was nice to see him in his element, see him confident around people. He looked happy, and for whatever reason, seeing Tyler happy made me happy.

Eventually the conversation drifted back to Nick's romantic prospects and, still feeling for the guy, who clearly didn't want to talk about whoever Eli was anymore, I nudged the conversation in a different direction.

"Enough of Nick," I said, poking my finger at Ben and Adam. "Delightful as it is to grill Nick, your single-minded focus means we're ignoring everyone else at the table. Luke, for instance," I said, raising my eyebrows at him. "We haven't grilled him about his romantic prospects at all."

"Ooh, Gray makes an excellent point," Ben said, turning to Luke. "Come on, tell us all about your most recent conquest."

"Okay, A, gross," Luke said. "And B, there's no reason my brother needs to hear this."

"But we're not your brothers," Adam pointed out.

"And we demand to know," Ben finished. "Earmuffs, Tyler."

"No need," Luke said. "There's no one... important."

"Ooh, but there is *someone*?" Tyler said. "Come on, bro. Take a hit for the team, give me a break and be the Wolitzky brother who gets gossiped about for a change."

"To be fair," Ben said, "there's always *someone* with Luke. He's banged all of Morgan Stanley by now and is probably halfway through Goldman Sachs."

"Hey, no slut-shaming," Luke objected. "Not fair. First you tease poor Nick for not sleeping with this Eli person, now you bully me because I'm not ready to settle down and get married immediately? Is nothing ever enough for you?"

"No," Adam said with a grin. "Not when it comes to making fun of you."

"Delightful as it is to hear about my brother's sex life," Tyler said, "I actually have to pee. You guys mind letting me out?"

Tyler standing up led to everyone standing up, and after watching him walk towards the back of the bar for a second, I reminded myself not to be a giant fucking creep and follow him.

Just... thought you might want some company. While you pee. What? No, that's not weird at all. You're being weird.

What did I think he needed my help with, holding his dick? I'd just forced myself to turn around and was going to ask everyone if they wanted more drinks when Micah hurried over.

"Gray, Ben, hey," Micah said to me and Ben, who was standing next to me, as he skidded to a stop in front of us. "Gray, do you have a sec?"

"Sure, what's up?" I asked.

Micah's eyes were wide and excited and he was clutching his phone in his hand. "Caro just had her baby!"

"Oh, shit, Micah, that's awesome," I said, smiling. "That's really fantastic."

"Is there—" Micah winced. "I know this is a shitty thing to ask but is there any chance you'd mind me taking off for the rest of the night, if I can get Kellie to come in and cover my shift? I already called her and she's free, so she could be here in 15 minutes. Caro just asked if I could come meet The Bean and I was kind of hoping—"

"Yeah, no, that's totally fine," I said. "Honestly, Micah, you're been better at managing Maggie's than I ever was. Just do what you'd do if I weren't here—if Kellie can cover your shift, no worries."

Micah beamed. "Gray, you're a treasure and I take back every mean thing I ever said about you."

"Yeah, yeah, save your promises for sometime when you're not on cloud nine," I said with a snort, shaking my head as Micah practically floated back to the bar.

"He seems excited," Ben said.

I smiled. "Caro and Micah have been best friends since— you know, I actually don't know? I think grade school or something. And she and her husband asked him to be a godfather, so... that's actually fairly subdued, for Micah." I glanced back towards the bar. "Maybe I should go lend a hand until Kellie gets here. I can get you guys some more drinks, too."

"So, how are you, really?" Ben asked as he followed me the bar. "Seriously, it's been a while since we've talked. Things are good?"

"Yeah," I said, nodding slowly as I slid behind the long wooden surface. "Never thought I'd end up here, but yeah, they actually are."

"What's it like working with Tyler Lang?" Ben asked, leaning his elbows on the bar and giving me a funny look.

"Um... normal?" I shrugged. "I honestly had no idea who he was at first, but he's actually just... really great."

"Yeah?"

"Yeah. He's really—" I smiled and tried to figure out how to put what I thought about Tyler into words. "I mean, he's been through a lot and it hasn't always been easy for him, but he's trying, and he's funny and smart and I'm really glad I've gotten to know him. He's just got this—I don't know, this way of making things seem possible. And just... better? Somehow?" I snorted. "And he puts up with a lot of weird shit from me— watching me deal with this Ethan bullshit, for one. My ex—" I said, in response to Ben's confused look, "and listening to me whine and just be generally awful and he's just... he's great."

Ben didn't say anything, just propped his chin up on his hand and gave me a slow smile.

"What?" I asked, looking at him suspiciously.

"Nothing," Ben said, even though, whatever it was, it was definitely not nothing.

"Seriously, what? You're creeping me out."

"Just remembering."

"Remembering what?"

"Remembering a conversation we had a few months ago," Ben said, giving me a speculative look. "When I was here. And so was Adam. And Nick. And they were getting breakfast."

My eyes narrowed as I tried to remember what Ben was talking about, then widened in comprehension. Ben had been so annoyed at Nick at the time, and confused about why that was. He had somehow never considered the idea that he might be into—or, rather, *in love with*—his best friend, Adam, and jealous of Nick. It had turned out that neither Adam nor Nick was interested in the other, but somehow Ben had needed that kick in the pants to realize his true feelings for Adam.

And now Ben was suggesting...

"No," I said, shaking my head resolutely. "No. He's just a friend."

"A friend you really like," Ben said. "A friend you basically just described to me like he's the second coming."

"I didn't mean it like that," I clarified. "I'm not—it's not—that's not it. I'm so much older than him."

"So?"

"So he wouldn't be interested in me. He wouldn't be anyway, even without the age thing. He's—he's—"

"He's someone you're completely head over heels for?" Ben suggested.

"No. I just meant he's—he's *someone*, you know? And I'm no one. I'm no one, and I'm not that kind of—not the kind of person he'd end up with."

Not the kind of person anyone ends up with. I'm the kind of person people keep around for a while until they get bored. Until they find the person they want to stay with forever.

I'm nobody's forever.

"Gray," Ben said gently, "those are reasons why Tyler shouldn't like you. But they're not reasons why you don't like Tyler."

I frowned—and realized what Ben was saying was true.

"I just—I don't—that's not how I feel about him," I said lamely, wishing I could articulate this better, wishing I didn't suddenly feel hot and like I was having trouble breathing. "He's not—he's a friend. And sure, he's attractive, but that doesn't mean—what are you doing?" I asked as Ben brought his phone out.

I watched in silence as he opened up a browser and went to Danny's blog, pulling up a picture they'd posted.

It was me and Tyler, curled up and napping on the bed in Dylan's bedroom. Danny must have shot it that afternoon after the blowjob scene. I hadn't even been aware. Danny had captioned it: *Working hard or hardly working?*

Something in my chest constricted, then expanded as I

stared at that photo. At first, I thought it was because I was seeing what had been a vulnerable moment caught on camera. But the more I looked—and God, I couldn't pull my eyes away—I realized it wasn't the fact that Danny had caught a glimpse of us, or even put it online, that bothered me. Not at all.

For the first time, I was seeing myself from the outside. And what I saw as my eyes devoured that picture was the way my arm curved protectively around Tyler, the way my nose was pressed into his hair, the way my eyes were resting gently, my forehead relaxed, as I slept next to him. What I saw was someone who cared deeply, profoundly, for the person in his arms.

The person in his arms. Tyler.

"Fuck," I whispered.

Ben gave me a smile. "I mean..."

"Fuck, fuck, fuck. This isn't good."

"What?" Ben said. "Wait, what's not good about it? I thought —Gray, it's so sweet. The way you smile at him, the way your eyes light up when he looks at you—that's a good thing."

"It's not a good thing at all."

"Why not though?"

"Because—because it can't happen," I stuttered. "It's not—I can't—he can't—we can't do anything. And he's not —oh, fuck."

"But why can't you? And how do you know he doesn't feel the same way about you?"

"He doesn't," I said, my voice rougher than I'd meant it to be. "Just trust me, I know he doesn't. He wants to move back to LA and get back to work. And Jesus," I said, my eyes widening as another thought occurred to me. "He's been acting strange ever since we started shooting sex scenes. Fuck, what if he knows how I feel, and *that's* why he's been so awkward? Because he's been trying to make it clear that he's not interested in anything else?"

"Don't you think that's jumping to conclusions a little bit?" Ben asked. "I really don't think this is the apocalyptic situation you're making it out to be."

But at that moment, Tyler came back out from the bathrooms, caught sight of me, and waved. And as he walked over towards me and Ben and my heart started beating a million miles an hour, I knew Ben was wrong.

This was very much apocalyptic. Because I *did* have feelings for Tyler. I hadn't realized it before, I'd been too blinded by Ethan—which was insane, because Tyler was a thousand times better, kinder, sweeter, than Ethan could ever be.

But there was one thing the two of them did have in common. Neither of them wanted me. Neither of them ever would.

Only one other thing was certain: I was completely and utterly fucked.

10

TYLER

I wasn't nervous.

I wasn't.

I know you might think I'd be nervous. That spending this afternoon getting fucked for the first time by a man with a truly giant cock on camera might have set my heart the tiniest bit aflutter, but you'd be wrong. I wasn't nervous.

I was fucking terrified.

I kept trying to tell myself that this was actually good, in a meta kind of way. That it would make for a great story later about how actually, I'd lost my virginity—well, my gay virginity, which I guess was the kind I actually cared about —to an ex-porn star with a monster cock while pretending to be a teenager doing the same damn thing.

I also tried to tell myself it was good for verisimilitude. That I was just being really *method* about my craft. That I was, in fact, lucky to be able to sacrifice my butt-ginity on the altar of Truth in the temple of Art. That it would, at the very least, lessen the mental leap that I had to make to get into Dylan's head.

Except for the fact that everyone thought I'd already done this like, hundreds of times—thought that because I'd let them think it, because I'd gone ahead and basically said as much. So if something went wrong, if it wasn't good, if any of the nightmare situations I couldn't stop envisioning came to pass, I'd be fucked. Literally *and* figuratively.

I'd never wanted to get high as badly as I did in the days leading up to this scene. God, just imagining slipping into blissful unawareness, that chilled out state of not really giving a fuck what happens to you because you're too busy marvelling at the webbing in between your fingers or wondering about the true nature of carrots, was painful. What I wouldn't have given to just fuzz out and wake up next week with the scene behind me.

Except, of course, that I didn't quite want that either. Because the other thing was this—after today, we only had six more days of filming. Six. And then the whole movie wrapped. And I wasn't anywhere close to being ready for that.

Because once the movie was over, once I had to go back to my real life—well, that was the problem. My real life. Where I had to actually deal with this whole holy-shit-I-think-I'm-gay thing and decide what to do about it.

I didn't want to lie to people. I didn't want to lie to myself, either. But I also couldn't think of anything I wanted less than one more reason for people to pick and pry and poke at me, dissecting every piece of my life until it resembled steak tartare.

Plus, filming being over meant that I wouldn't see Gray every day anymore. And as much as I just wanted to get back to work after we wrapped this movie, as much as I wanted to move to LA and get my life back—and as much as I'd spent the past few weeks repeating all the reasons I *couldn't* like him and *did not* have a crush on him and just saw him as a friend, *goddammit*—I wasn't sure I was ready to go from seeing Gray every day to seeing him not at all.

Gray was the best thing in my life right now, and I wasn't ready to say goodbye.

The worst part was Gray was being impossibly nice to me, so solicitous, and I just wanted to yell at him to stop. But I couldn't, because anything I said would just lead to me having to say everything. It was all tangled and connected like a skein of yarn after a particularly vicious kitten had gotten to it. But I knew one thing for sure—I didn't want to have to tell Gray I'd never done this before.

It wasn't even that I didn't want to do the scene. Or more specifically, have sex. With Gray. Because I did, actually, though you couldn't have paid me to admit that to him, and remember that you're talking to someone with a checking account balance of basically zero.

But I was also completely fucking freaked out of it hurting, or going badly, and I didn't think it was exactly fair that while everyone else's awkward and possibly painful first times got to be lost to the mists of time, mine was going to be recorded for millions of eyeballs to watch. The fact that I had only myself to blame for this situation did not make me feel better.

The annoying part was, in theory, Gray was *exactly* the guy you wanted your first time to be with. He was experienced, so you knew that he knew what he was doing. He was fucking hot, which certainly didn't hurt. But most importantly, he was sweet. And kind. And fucking perfect, and you just knew that he'd be the kind of guy to make your first time amazing—*if* he knew it was your first time.

But I couldn't tell him—couldn't tell him what I felt or what I thought, so instead, I'd spent the past few weeks being a prickly asshole and probably just pissing Gray off, getting him on his last nerve, which was exactly what I wasn't trying to do but couldn't seem to help. In fact, in the week since we'd gone into the city and met up with Luke, he'd actually been a little distant. My fault, entirely. But I didn't know how to fix it.

"All set, Tyler?"

Violet's voice pulled me back to reality, back to the fact that we weren't even filming that fucking sex scene yet, that we still had another scene to get through, first. This one was going to be the penultimate scene in the movie, actually, and it was wordless, just Dylan alone in the woods.

It wasn't supposed to take too long to film, unless I fucked things up, but part of me kept wanting to, wanted to draw this out and do as many takes as possible. Anything to put off the sex scene that came next.

I glanced over my shoulder at Violet. Danny was standing next to her, but Andrew and Dave weren't on set today. They were meeting with Ben and Adam, actually, to talk about music, but the woods were still filled with the usual techs and grips.

The only other person who was missing, really, was Gray. I

shoved down that obscure sense of sadness that arose inside me anytime he was gone. He wasn't in this scene, after all. There was no reason for him to be here.

Only, well, I'd gotten used to it. Used to that gruff sarcasm, that wry amusement. That solid, warm presence that I felt like I could wrap myself up in like a blanket.

It was just comforting, really, having Gray there, and I'd gotten used to him hanging out on set, even during scenes he wasn't in. I had this nagging feeling like I'd left my phone at home or forgotten to turn off the oven—this small, insistent urge that something was not right when Gray wasn't around.

He's probably just sick of you being an asshole. And honestly, can you blame him?

I'd acted for years with no Gray. And once *Foresight* wrapped, I'd have to go back to doing that. Gray was a friend but nothing more. Might as well get used to his absence.

"Yeah," I said to Violet with a smile. "Yeah, I'm good."

I walked back down the path to my mark, rolled my shoulders out once, and breathed deeply. Whatever emotional baggage I was carrying, I could put it aside for now. That was Tyler's baggage, and for this scene, at least, I got to leave it behind. I wasn't Tyler anymore. I was Dylan.

"Action!"

Dylan jogged forward, picking up speed as he rounded a bend, and by the time his beech tree came into view, he was sprinting. He went hard, throwing his body into the run, forcing his lungs and legs to work to exhaustion, and by the time he reached the tree, he thought he might burst.

He came to a stop, bent over, and supported himself, hands on knees, as he caught his breath. It had been a shitty run. He'd barely even made it a mile and he already felt like he was dying.

Stupid, dumbass idea. Like you can run away from your problems. Like running can change anything.

He frowned as he looked over at his tree. Maybe coming for a run, coming out here, hadn't just been to take his mind off things. Maybe it was even dumber than that. Because some part of him couldn't help feeling heartbroken that Wyatt wasn't standing there under that tree, waiting for him. Ready to give him some explanation. Ready, at least, to say goodbye.

But no. Wyatt wasn't there. Wyatt was long gone, just like they'd told him, and he'd left without saying anything to Dylan.

Well what did you expect? That you meant something to him? That Wyatt felt the same way you did?

He'd never said the words. And no matter how many times Dylan had tried to convince himself that words didn't matter, that Wyatt's actions made it clear that he loved Dylan, he knew it wasn't true.

Wyatt could never feel the same way. Why would he? Dylan was a fucking teenager. Wyatt would never see him as an equal.

And now you'll never see him again.

Tears welled up in Dylan's eyes as he realized that and he slumped back against the tree. The same tree where Wyatt had first kissed him, pushing him up against the trunk and pressing their bodies together. Images cascaded through Dylan's mind as he sank to the ground, unable to stop replaying all the precious moments he'd captured and stored, like a squirrel hiding berries and nuts for the winter, like some part of him had known, even from the beginning, that he'd need that cache someday.

And now that these images were all he had left, they were already starting to take on the quality of a dream. Were they even real? Who was to say, when only he and Wyatt had experienced them, and now only Dylan was left? They might as well evaporate like morning mist over the river.

Dylan opened his eyes and blinked up at the sky, willing the tears that distorted his vision to clear. He was not going to cry. He was going to get up, finish his fucking run, and go back to school. Somehow, he was going to force himself through the rest of the fucking day. And month. And year.

He put his hand on the tree trunk as he turned and rose, steadying himself with his palm against the bark, and then paused. There was something rough slashing across his palm, like a canyon gouged into the trunk. When he looked down, his mouth dropped open.

Carved into the tree inside the shape of a heart were the letters 'CH + VC,' and below that, 'E Kita Xio.' And underneath it all, a date.

The tears Dylan thought he'd pushed away came flooding back as he smiled down at the tree trunk. Wyatt had remembered. Remembered his stupid made up language, remembered how Dylan had traced that onto his body.

And the date. Wyatt had carved that yesterday. The day he'd left. He'd finally told Dylan what he needed to hear. And he'd said goodbye.

He'd said goodbye.

Tears streamed down Dylan's cheeks, and he smiled.

"Cut!"

I stepped back from the tree and looked over my shoulder at Violet, wiping the tears off my cheeks.

"One-take Tyler," she said with a grin. "That's what we should call you."

"You don't wanna do it again?" I asked. "I thought I might have overdone it a bit with the water works."

"Nah, it's perfect." Violet looked over at Danny. "Thoughts?"

Danny grinned. "Yeah, Dylan's a fucking crybaby. That was great."

"Cool." I sniffed and tried to dry my tears on my t-shirt.

It was weird. I knew I wasn't actually sad right now, or dealing with the end of my illicit teacher-student love affair, but I still felt all those emotions coursing through my body. They'd drain out eventually, but for now, I felt raw.

And now there was nothing but a tiny lunch break standing between me and the afternoon's scene with Gray.

Perfect.

My hands were wrapped around a turkey and cheese sandwich when my dad called. Again.

I let it go to voicemail. Also again. It wasn't like he was going to leave a message.

For a while, I hadn't heard from him. And I'd been fine with that. I felt shitty and guilty enough as it was, I didn't need to be reminded about how, according to him, I was fucking up not just my life but also his. But then last week, things had gotten worse.

He'd texted to tell me that he'd seen the trailer and maybe this wasn't the worst decision I'd ever made, that maybe we could "salvage" this—if I called him back, of course. And then he'd started calling again. Every day.

Turns out, my dad being positive about me doing *Foresight* weirded me out as much or more than him calling me an idiot. I knew I should respond. I knew I'd have to, eventually, but I didn't feel quite ready to deal with all of that yet.

I'd just picked my phone up to slide it back in my pocket when I got a text from Luke.

LUKE: Hey you got a sec?

I glanced around the room, checking to make sure that everyone else who'd be filming the next scene was still hanging around and I wasn't already late.

TYLER: Like literally A sec, then I gotta get to the next scene

TYLER: What's up?

LUKE: Oh shit

LUKE: Is today D-Day?

I frowned in confusion.

TYLER: Do I even want to know what D-Day is?

LUKE: Dick Day. Well, dick in ass day, to be more specific. I guess context is important, on a movie like this

LUKE: ;)

I flushed, deeply regretting ever telling Luke anything about this shoot. But since I couldn't really talk to Gray about it, and no one else *was* talking to me, I hadn't really had any choice, and last week, I'd finally broken down and told Luke how nervous I was.

TYLER: Jfc DO NOT winky face me

TYLER: You're my goddamn brother, it's creepy

LUKE: Sorry

LUKE: >:)

LUKE: Better?

I snorted.

TYLER: Barely

LUKE: Also you didn't answer my question

TYLER: And now we're back to you being creepy

LUKE: ...

TYLER: Ugh fine yes. Today is D-Day. Happy?

LUKE: How are you feeling about it?

TYLER: That depends. Is that a real question, or a segue to you making more dick jokes?

LUKE: Real question. Brotherly concern. I promise

I eyed his text with some skepticism. But since I also felt like I might explode from nerves, I decided to take it at face value.

TYLER: So terrified I think I'm about to give myself a heart attack

I was still freaking out about all the same stuff, but now I'd had the added benefit of eating lunch by myself, instead of with Gray like I usually did. Which meant that I hadn't seen him since yesterday, which was kind of odd for us. So of course, my brain had decided he was avoiding me, which was just the cherry on top of my nervous breakdown sundae.

TYLER: So, you know, normal Tuesday kind of stuff

LUKE: You sure you don't want to talk to someone? You know, tell them why you're nervous?

TYLER: And shut down production because everyone gets concerned about me and whether or not this is okay and it becomes this giant thing and suddenly everyone on set and soon the entire world knows that I'm a giant virgin who's never done this before?

TYLER: Thanks but no thanks

LUKE: Okay okay don't bite my head off, jeez

TYLER: Sorry. Just tense. Anyway did you actually need something?

I looked around the foyer and noticed our grips tossing out the remains of their lunches. Crap. I was going to have to get over to Dylan's bedroom soon.

LUKE: Actually, yeah. So you know how you got me added to your bank account as a co-manager?

TYLER: Because I'm a child, yes, I remember

I'd specifically asked Luke to add himself. I knew it was pathetic, but after everything that had happened over the past few years, I just didn't trust myself with money. And now that I'd gotten part of my paycheck for *Foresight*, I didn't want to actually be responsible for that money. If I didn't have someone else watching it, who knew what ridiculous things I'd spend it on?

LUKE: Okay so this is hard to explain over text but

LUKE: I went in to check and make sure the direct deposit had actually gone through

LUKE: Sometimes things can be wonky when you first set that up

LUKE: And I noticed that you've got a monthly transfer set up to what looks like some kind of third party investment account?

What?

TYLER: I do?

LUKE: Yeah. You do. You didn't know?

I felt my face heating up again. My day for embarrassment, it seemed. I failed at being a reasonable adult in all facets of life.

TYLER: I mean, I guess. Dad set a bunch of stuff up years ago. I never really paid attention to that kind of thing

LUKE: Jesus

LUKE: You really should

LUKE: Do you realize you've been transferring two hundred dollars a month to Graylance Investing for at least the past 3 years?

TYLER: What? Seriously?

LUKE: And normally I'm all for putting your money to work, but when you don't even have a healthy emergency fund cush-

ion... I don't know, I just think you might want to be a bit more liquid

I had to force myself to read that text four times before I thought I might understand what Luke was saying. I had an almost physical aversion to thinking about money stuff. After the way I'd fucked up my finances, just talking about it made me feel itchy and like I wanted to run away.

And of course Luke had to bring this up now, when I had to be on set in like, five minutes, and I was supposed to be trying to feel more calm, not less. I knew it was childish to blame him, but I mean, duh, this is me we're talking about.

TYLER: Ok

TYLER: So like... what should I do?

LUKE: I mean, there are lots of options

LUKE: You don't even have to change anything right now

LUKE: But we should sit down sometime and talk about the big picture.

LUKE: Do you have other investments that you're funding like this?

I groaned out loud.

TYLER: Ugh Luke, I literally have no idea

TYLER: I know that's pathetic but I just...

TYLER: I don't know, I'm not good at this stuff

TYLER: Can't you just like tell me what to do?

TYLER: I kind of have to go, so...

LUKE: Tyler you have to be more involved in this stuff

LUKE: I know you don't like it, but it's part of being an actual grown up

LUKE: Look, if you want, I can try to get a full picture of your accounts and come up with some possible strategies for money management

LUKE: But you need to promise we'll actually sit down together and you'll make an effort to understand this stuff ok?

TYLER: Ugh you're the worst

TYLER: I CAN'T BELIEVE YOU WON'T JUST DO EVERY-THING FOR ME IS THAT REALLY SUCH AN UNREASON-ABLE THING TO ASK?

TYLER: But fine, ok, I guess we can do it your way

LUKE: I know, I'm a monster

TYLER: You really are

LUKE: But if you really want me to tell you what to do...

TYLER: GOD yes please that is ALL I want

LUKE: Use lube

LUKE: Lots

LUKE: ;)

◦∾◦

"Hey! How'd it go this morning?"

I looked up at the sound of Gray's voice as he walked into Dylan's room 10 minutes later. He looked so completely cheerful and normal that I felt like an idiot for thinking he'd been avoiding me.

Why would Gray do that? Gray, unlike me, wasn't a child. He wouldn't avoid me just because I'd been an inadvertent jerk to him. Gray was a professional and an adult, two things I was beginning to think I'd never be.

"Good," I said, feeling my cheeks heat up.

"Violet was showing me the footage from this morning over lunch," Gray said. "It was so cool—I ended up spending all of lunch in the edit bay."

"Ohhh." I wished it didn't sound like I cared so much, wished I weren't so relieved to hear Gray give a reason for missing lunch.

"I still can't believe you can cry on command like that," Gray said.

I shrugged, trying for nonchalance. "Everyone needs a talent, I guess."

"Oh come on, that's hardly your only talent."

"Right."

I regretted the word as soon as it was out of my mouth. I'd wanted to come across cool, collected, but somehow I just sounded like an asshole.

Gray flushed. "I just meant—"

"No, it's fine, I didn't mean—"

Gray stopped and laughed, shaking his head as he looked at me. "God, you wanna just erase this conversation and try again from the beginning?"

"Yes. *Please*," I begged, for once not caring how pathetic I sounded.

I walked over to Dylan's bed and sat down next to Gray, putting my elbows on my knees and my head in my hands. We'd shot everything leading up to this scene in the past week, so today we really only had to shoot the sex itself. At the time, I'd thought that would make it easier, but now I found myself wishing I had something else to help me ease into this.

I glanced over at Gray and gave him a sheepish look. "Sorry for jumping down your throat. I'm just—I don't know what's wrong with me these days."

Lies. I knew exactly what was wrong. A sexual orientation crisis. An inconvenient crush on my impossibly handsome, smart, sweet, funny coworker who happened to be my only friend. And losing my virginity. On camera.

But I couldn't say any of that.

"It's okay," Gray said simply.

But it wasn't. I wanted nothing more than to just vomit everything I was feeling at Gray. Or, failing that, for this to just be done, for it to be tomorrow already. I didn't even care if it was terrible and it hurt or I looked like a complete idiot on camera. I'd take any of that in exchange for not actually having to go through with this right now. To stay in my fucking nervous wreck of a body one more second.

"You guys good?" Violet asked.

Gray looked at me and I smiled wanly back at her. "Yeah." I hoped she heard more confidence in my voice than I did.

"Alright." She peered down at a laptop sitting on a chair next to her where footage of everything just prior to this scene was displayed. "So you guys are in the center of the room. Dylan's hands on Wyatt's shirt, Wyatt's hands on Dylan's face. You guys know the blocking. Dylan walks Wyatt back to the bed and you take it from there."

We got into position and I wondered if Gray could feel my heart beating, wild and erratic, like an animal throwing itself against the bars of its cage. I fisted his shirt in my hands and used that position to create an inch of separation between our chests.

Gray's hands came to my face and he pulled me in, resting his forehead down on mine. I could see the silent question in his eyes—eyes so impossibly blue and impossibly warm. Eyes that made me want to tell the truth. *'Are you okay?'* they asked.

'Yes,' I lied back with my own eyes. *'Completely. Never better.'*

Yes, I'm okay.

I had to be. This was happening.

I'm okay.

"Action!" Violet called, and Gray's eyes closed, releasing me from their spell, and then his lips were on mine, soft and demanding and pulling me close and I could taste him, I could smell him, I could feel his body against mine, all heat and strength and desire and fuck—

I am not okay.

I knew it the moment his lips touched mine, knew it even as I balled more of his shirt into my fists and took my first step backwards towards the bed. Knew it in the little gasp I gave when I felt the bed hit the back of my legs, stumbled, and Gray caught me.

Gray—*Gray* caught me. That was the first sign that something was wrong. I couldn't think of myself as Dylan at all, couldn't get out of my own head. Couldn't see Gray as anyone other than who he was. But perfect as he was—and oh God was he perfect—I could tell I wasn't okay.

Gray laid me back down on the bed gently. God, everything about him was gentle. This should have been good. This was sweet, this was tender, this was exactly like it was supposed to go in the script, his hands in my hair, his lips on my neck, my arms on his back and my legs parting slightly to let one of his thighs slide in between.

Everything was perfect. So what the hell was my fucking problem? This was a literally picture-perfect scene of someone losing their virginity, and I was doing it with someone who wanted nothing more than to make sure I felt comfortable, secure, and safe. I couldn't ask for better than this.

So why the fuck was I freezing up? Why did I feel like my limbs were full of lead, like I couldn't get enough air, like I might be having a heart attack?

I closed my eyes, not wanting the camera to catch any of the hundreds of things flashing through my mind right now, as I felt Gray's lips travel back up my neck and across my jaw to my ear.

"You okay?"

My eyes popped open in shock when the same words that

had been running through my mind were suddenly whispered into my ear. Gray was looking down at me in concern, his body blocking the cameras from seeing my face as his hands worked up and down my body, still moving, not ending the scene.

I nodded, a tight, jerky little movement, and tried to smile. I think it must have come out looking like a grimace because Gray's face got even more concerned, so much so that I worried he was going to break character and stop the scene, and then he'd want to talk about this and then we'd have to start all over again and this scene would never end.

So I did the only thing I could think of. I pulled him down and kissed him, hard, like if I got my tongue far enough into his mouth I could somehow burrow into his body and stop having to live inside my own.

Gray kissed me back, his left hand coming up to stroke my cheek, and somehow that touch, that warm, gentle touch, made things even worse. It was the kind of thing you'd want someone to do, someone who cared about you, someone who loved you, someone you were giving yourself up to. And all of a sudden, I realized that that was what I wanted. I wanted that kind of touch for real—I wanted Gray to want me like that for real—and I hated myself for it.

Gray broke the kiss and smiled, pulling back to strip his shirt off over his head, before bringing his hands down to the bottom of my shirt. He pulled it up a couple inches, pressing a kiss to the exposed skin of my stomach. I had to squeeze my eyes shut again at the tenderness of the gesture, at how much it hurt that this was just a scene.

Gray pushed my shirt up until it was bunched around my

chest. I was supposed to sit up now, let him strip it off me. Then pull him back down, kiss him again, keep the scene moving. I knew what I had to do next.

But I couldn't move. It was like someone had tied my arms down to the mattress, like they weren't even part of my body any more, like I couldn't communicate to any part of myself that I had to *Move, goddammit. Sit up and take off your fucking shirt.*

And suddenly I felt lightheaded and kind of swimmy, like maybe my head was resting on a bed of jello and the light around me started going funny, kind of dark around the edges. Gray gave me a strange look, then picked my arm up for me and my first thought was of how fucking grateful I was that Gray was going to move my arms for me, how embarrassed I was that I couldn't move them myself, before I realized he was bringing it to his lips, kissing the underside of my forearm while gripping my wrist with two fingers.

And then his eyes widened, he dropped my wrist, and pushed back from the bed. I couldn't see where he'd gone, could barely see anything beyond the tunnel that my vision had narrowed to, but I heard a door slam and footsteps pounding down the hallway.

"Cut!"

Violet's voice knifed through the room and it was like it cut through the curtain of darkness around me, too. Suddenly, I could see better, could breathe better. Before I even realized my arms worked again, I'd pushed myself over onto my side to survey the rest of the room.

"Go see if he's okay," Violet was saying to one of the runners, and he took off down the hall after Gray.

"What happened?" I asked, still a little fuzzy.

Violet frowned. "I don't know," she said. "Hopefully he's okay."

I realized with surprise that she was talking about Gray. That she hadn't realized I'd asked the question about myself as well. Because I wasn't sure what had happened with Gray, but I also wasn't sure what had just happened with me.

Something odd, though. I knew that much. But no one else seemed to have noticed and I didn't want to cause problems, so I just sat up and tried to act like everything was normal.

Two minutes later, Gray walked back into the room, looking shaken and unsteady.

"Sorry, Vi," he said, sounding remorseful. "I should have said something earlier. I woke up feeling kind of queasy. Hoped it would go away if I didn't eat lunch. But I guess—ugh, I need to go brush my teeth."

"You're sick?" Violet asked.

Gray nodded regretfully. "I'm sorry."

"Don't be," Violet said briskly. "You can't control these things. Just concentrate on getting better." She looked down at her phone and pursed her lips. "You know what? I've got some editing I wanted to finish up that I haven't yet. Let's take the rest of the day off."

"Shit, Vi," Gray said. "I didn't mean to put us behind schedule."

"You're not," she said firmly. "Honestly, I'm amazed we made it this far into the month without any disasters. And we've all been working really hard. I'd say everyone deserves the afternoon off. And you—" she pointed at Gray "need to go straight to bed and sleep, okay? I'll send someone up with gingerale and stuff for you in a bit, but it's bed rest for you."

"Thanks, Vi," Gray said. He looked over at me. "Tyler, you mind walking back up with me?"

"What? Oh. Yeah, sure." I shook my head to clear the left-over cobwebs from it.

We walked through the halls quietly. I watched Gray with concern as we went up the stairs, but he seemed steady enough on his feet. God, had he really been sick all morning and I'd totally missed it? How self-absorbed was I to not have noticed?

"You uh, want me to get you anything?" I asked as we got to Gray's door.

"No, I'm fine," Gray said, giving me an unreadable look.

"Okay." I shrugged, still feeling a little confused by the past five minutes. "Well then, I guess—"

"Tyler?" Gray's voice was firm.

"Yeah?"

"I'm not actually sick."

"What? But you just—"

Gray laughed ruefully. "I lied."

"But why?" I asked, frowning in confusion.

"Well, for starters, because I'm pretty sure you were having a panic attack in bed down there."

I blinked. "What?"

Was that what had happened? Was that what I'd felt? I hadn't... Jesus Christ, that's exactly what that had been. I just hadn't felt that in—God, not in ages.

I used to get panic attacks when I was a kid, whenever my dad would talk to me about my numbers, tell me I wasn't doing well enough, that I needed to work harder, be better, be smarter. My last panic attack had been the night of the Emmys when I was 16 and our show was up for Outstanding Drama Series, and when Gil had offered me some pills to calm me down, I'd taken them without question.

Fuck, no wonder I hadn't recognized what was happening just now. I'd been self-medicating for so long I'd forgotten what it felt like to deal with a panic attack while sober.

"How did you... know?" I asked Gray slowly.

"A few different things," Gray said. "Your eyes looked a little off—like you weren't quite there. Your breath was coming in kind of short—and not in like, a good way. There's a difference, you know? And then I felt your pulse and it was racing and I realized—

"I can't believe you noticed that."

"Tyler, I—I care about you," Gray said. He cleared his throat. "As your friend, I just want—well, I wanted to make sure you were okay."

"So you stopped production? For me?"

"Well, it didn't seem like you were going to do anything about it," Gray pointed out. "So I figured..."

I just stared at him, feeling like such a fucking idiot, feeling ten million things all at once. Amazement, once again, at how fucking kind and *good* Gray was, especially when all I'd done was be a jerk to him. Gratitude. Affection.

And ladled over it all, this sense of loss, remembering that after we wrapped, I'd have to say goodbye to him. Gray'd been nothing but perfect and I'd still never even told him the truth.

"Well, anyway," Gray continued, probably taking my silence for reticence to talk, "you don't have to—"

"I've never had sex before," I blurted out.

Gray's eyes widened. "What?"

"With a guy, I mean," I said, wincing. "Though, I mean, barely with women either, really. Like, I'm not the most experienced person all around but I just—that's what—I—ugh." I looked up at the ceiling, wanting to die. "That's sorta what I was freaking out about. Back there. And like... the past few weeks."

"Oh." Gray's expression was inscrutable. "Oh."

"Yeah. So." I looked down, still not ready to really meet his eyes.

"Do you, uh—do you want to come in?" Gray said slowly. "To talk?"

He stood back from the door and I finally met his gaze. Gray's eyes were full of concern, still, but there was none of the disgust or anger or even annoyance that I'd been sure I'd see.

"Really?" I asked.

Gray nodded.

"Um." I closed my eyes for a moment. "Okay. Uh, thanks."

I stepped into Gray's room and he closed the door quietly behind me. I felt awkward suddenly, even though I'd been in here more times than I could count. Gray sat down in his desk chair, gesturing for me to make myself comfortable on the bed. I climbed up onto it and scooted back until my back hit the wall, hugging my knees up to my chin.

"Why didn't you tell me?" Gray asked after a minute. "Or, well, someone? I mean, it didn't have to be me, but—"

"I was afraid I'd get fired," I said. "Or that, if I told you, you wouldn't want me to go through with it. And I needed this job. And then I thought, like—" I paused, shrugging my shoulders— "you know, like, realism and all that? It's supposed to be Dylan's first time, too, so I figured..." I trailed off because Gray was staring at me incredulously. "I know it's stupid," I finished.

"It's not... stupid," Gray said, like he was thinking out loud. "It's just very..." he laughed and looked at me. "It's very *you*, that's for sure. Committing two hundred percent to something without maybe thinking through the consequences all the way."

"Yeah, well, when you put it like that," I said with a wry laugh.

"Can I ask..." Gray paused, looking cautious.

"Go ahead," I said. "Anything."

It felt good, honestly, to finally be saying this out loud. It felt good to say it to Gray. To not be lying to him anymore. I might as well tell him whatever he wanted to know.

"The other stuff we've done. Blowjob, hand job, all of that. Was that the first time you'd—"

"Yeah," I said, flushing. "God, that's embarrassing. Was it that obvious?"

"It's not embarrassing," Gray said quickly. "And no, it wasn't *that* obvious. It's just—Tyler, are you sure you really want to be doing this? I mean, you told me before that you weren't sure you wanted to come out. If you're still figuring out your orientation—"

"It's *not* that," I interrupted. "I like guys."

"It's okay not to know," Gray went on. "Really, it is. This stuff takes time to figure out. But if you don't know what you want—"

"Just because I'm inexperienced doesn't mean I don't know what I want," I shot back.

Gray winced. "You're right. Sorry. No, you're completely right. I shouldn't have doubted you."

It was Gray's chagrin, really, that made me want to be more honest. Because all he'd ever done was be nice to me and I'd been so weird and prickly and it wasn't fair—Gray shouldn't feel bad about himself, not ever, not when he was pretty much the best person I'd ever met.

"You're not—you're not wrong, though," I forced myself to say. "To be honest, if it hadn't been for this movie? I don't know, I mostly just tried not to think about this kind of stuff. Like sexuality or whatever." I sighed. "Everyone assumes that just because you're famous, you're some kind of huge player, that people throw themselves at you all the time and you sleep with anything that breathes, but it's not—it's not easy, you know, trying to actually find a meaningful connection in all of that, trying to figure out who you can trust."

"I can see how that would be really hard," Gray said.

"Well then take that, and then multiply it by growing up in public, where you have this image to maintain, and then multiply *that* by realizing that you're not really into the gender everyone assumes you're into, that you don't actually really want to do anything with any of the women who you know, but that it would be a huge scandal and tank your marketability if you so much as kiss someone you *are* actually into..."

"I'd never thought about it like that."

"My dad always told me it would hurt my numbers if I were gay. I don't think he knew, it was one of those things that he just ranted about, but I knew he'd be pissed if he ever found out the truth about me." I sighed. "But then he stopped talking to me, and then *everybody* stopped talking to me, and suddenly I couldn't think of a single reason why I shouldn't do *Foresight*, and maybe I'd get to find out for the first time if all these feelings I'd had my whole life were real."

I gulped, then took a deep breath before launching into the next part, the part I was dreading saying out loud. But I wanted to say it—I wanted to be honest with Gray.

"I think part of me was hoping that they wouldn't be. Those feelings, I mean. That I'd try it and find out that it wasn't really my thing. And I could just go back to being who I was before, instead of having to wrestle with this whole new identity and everyone having a fucking opinion about it and wanting me to come out and be this proud gay actor, or, if you're my fucking dad, to not come out and to keep plausible deniability, and I don't know what I'm supposed to fucking do now."

I buried my face in my hands.

"I'm sorry for being such a fucking asshole the past few weeks," I said, my voice muffled. "I shouldn't have taken all of this out on you."

"You didn't take it out on me," Gray said. "And it's a lot to deal with. Shit, it took me years to come to terms with the fact that I was bi, and I was a fucking mess. You're trying to make sense of all of this new stuff *and* make a movie at the same time? I honestly don't know how you've kept it together this well."

I laughed. "I don't know how you're defining *well*, but thanks."

"You're gonna be okay," Gray said, and his voice was so warm, so sure, that I almost believed him. "You're gonna get through this, one way or another. And you don't owe anybody anything. You don't have to make any decisions. Hell, you don't even have to do this scene."

I snorted. "Gray, I appreciate the *'Chin up, champ,'* speech, but we do actually have to film this scene." I shook my head. "At least we've got til tomorrow. Think Montclair has a sex shop? Maybe I can go buy a dildo and—"

"Tyler, you really don't," Gray interrupted. "We can talk to Violet. Explain—or, well, tell her something anyway. Maybe we can work around this scene. Or get body doubles. There's gotta be something. You should *not* have to have sex for the first time on camera."

And that was when it hit me.

As soon as the idea popped into my head, I knew it was the solution to my problems. Well, a solution, anyway, to one of them, at least. But I also knew, somehow, that Gray was going to object.

"You're right," I said, staring at Gray, trying to figure out the best way to propose this.

"I'm right?" Gray blinked. "Since when? I was really expecting you to argue with me more here."

"I mean, you're still wrong about most things—"

"Phew, I was worried—"

"—but you're right that my first time doesn't have to be on camera. My *second* time, maybe. But my first time..." I paused and gave Gray a direct look.

Gray's chin came up as his eyes narrowed suspiciously. "Tyler..."

"Come on," I said, my tone wheedling. "It's not the worst idea, right?"

"I don't know if—"

"I mean, if you're willing to fuck me when the cameras are on, I don't know why it should be so different when they're off."

"Jeez, so romantic," Gray said, his voice gruff.

"I'm not completely repulsive am, I?" I scooted forward on the bed and made puppy dog eyes at Gray.

"That's not fair. You know that's not why—"

"Why not, then?" I pouted, knowing I looked ridiculous.

But honestly, it's not like I could get any more ridiculous looking than I already did, confessing my virginity, my panic over coming out, and now begging my much older, much hotter, much more experienced costar to fuck me. What was a little pouting, compared to all of that?

"It's just—I don't know, you don't think it would be weird?" Gray arched an eyebrow. "I mean, I consider you a friend and sometimes, things like this..."

I had to push down a little squelch of something excited and full of yearning when Gray said that, implying that our friendship could get complicated if we did this. Because I was *not* looking for those complications. I *wasn't*.

"Gray," I said instead, trying to make my voice plain and serious. "I am not asking you to marry me. I am not asking you to bring me home to your—well, not your mom, but you get the drift. I am asking you to do me a solid, one bro to another, and swipe my V card. Or, well, A card in this case."

"A card?"

"Ass?" I said with a lopsided grin.

"Okay, first rule of gay sex," Gray said. "Never say that again."

"Does that mean you're saying yes?" I asked, giving Gray my widest, craziest grin. "Because if it does, then yes, I promise."

Gray gave me a considering look. Finally, he stood up and came and sat down on the bed next to me. I tried to ignore the fact that my heart was racing and that my wildly fluttering pulse was probably visible in my neck, and turned to face Gray, sitting cross-legged.

"I'll consider it," Gray said, "if you answer me honestly when I ask this next question."

My stomach turned a somersault and I wondered what Gray was going to ask. As much as I felt like I'd poured my guts out to Gray, I'd really only scratched the surface. I hadn't told him I'd jerked off to his porn. Or that I'd fantasized about him telling me I was a good boy ever since he'd done it that one time on set. Or that, honestly, I struggled to think about anyone who *wasn't* Gray when I jerked off now.

"Well that sounds ominous," I said, trying to keep my voice and my smile light.

"That's my offer," Gray said. "Take it or leave it."

"God," I grumbled, "what ever happened to just getting wasted and hooking up in a night of passionate bad decisions?

"You don't drink," Gray said, his voice dry and amused.

"Believe me, I've never regretted my sobriety more," I said with a snort. But Gray was still watching me with those serious blue eyes piercing into mine every time I looked up. Finally, I sighed. "Okay, fine. Yes, I promise, I'll answer you honestly. Ask away."

"What are you afraid of?"

I looked at Gray in confusion. "That's all? That's all you want to know?"

"Well pardon me," Gray laughed. "Did you want to give me

the last four digits of your social security number and your bank account number too?"

"Joke's on you, buddy, because I don't even know that shit. I have to have Luke do it all for me."

"Well fine, then, if it's not such a big deal," Gray said, "then you shouldn't have a problem answering me honestly. What are you afraid of. What is it that scared you so much, downstairs? Because something made you freeze up. And I'm not even going to consider doing this with you if I don't know what that is."

"Um, you really wanna know?"

"Yes."

"Okay, well, you asked for it. I guess, to be perfectly honest, I'm nervous it'll hurt. And I'm nervous it wouldn't actually hurt a normal person but like, there's something wrong with me, so it'll hurt me, and then everyone will think I'm weird. I'm nervous your cock is too big and even if it feels good, it's gonna like, make me bleed and I'll hemorrhage like that scene in *The Bell Jar* and I'll have to go to the hospital and then they'll be like *'Jesus, you're bleeding from your asshole, why do you still have a boner?'* and I'll have to explain. I'm nervous it won't feel good and I won't be able to come, I'm nervous it'll feel *too* good and I'll come too soon. I'm nervous I'm gonna make weird faces, I'm nervous I'm gonna like, actually lose my mind and forget where I am, I'm nervous it'll feel good for me but not for you, I'm nervous you're gonna think I'm fucking terrible in bed and judge me, I'm nervous that there's some secret butt sex curse that I don't know about where if you have bad sex your first time, you're doomed to have bad sex for the next seven years. Oh, and I'm nervous that I'll fart. I think that about covers it."

Gray was staring at me, biting his lip and clearly trying not to laugh by the end of my speech.

"Just go ahead," I said. "I know you want to."

"I'm not laughing *at* you..."

"Oh, you 100% are, but it's fine. I assume this is how all gay sex begins? With the ritual humiliation of the bottom? So we're off to a great start here."

"I mean, I get it," Gray said, still chuckling. "I've had each and every one of those fears." I cocked an eyebrow and he grinned. "Okay, maybe not *The Bell Jar* part, because I haven't read it, but the general idea? I was totally worried about that my first time."

"Yeah, but most of these are concerns that are pretty specific to bottoming—"

"Well, right, but I've bottomed."

"You—what?"

Gray laughed. "Of course! You can't get through too many years in porn without doing it at least once. Hell, sometimes I've done it just for fun."

"Holy shit, really?"

"Yeah." Gray squinted at me. "You know that these roles aren't like, written in the stars at the moment of your birth. Bottoming once doesn't make you a bottom for life or whatever."

"I just never thought..." I paused. "God, what else have you done that I don't know about?"

"What is this, *Never Have I Ever?*" Gray snorted.

"Uh, no, because I would lose in a heartbeat. Obviously."

"Don't be so sure," Gray said. He gave me a sly smile. "Never have I ever been brave enough to tell a potential sexual partner all of my fears up front."

"Eww, gross. No fair."

Gray reached out and took my hand. I shivered and looked at him in confusion until I realized he was folding one of my fingers down.

"Since you don't drink," Gray said, that smile still playing on the corners of his lips, "we'd have to play the ten fingers version. And see, you're already at nine."

I rolled my eyes but Gray put his hands down on the mattress, fingers splayed out in front of him, and looked at me expectantly. I realized, suddenly, that Gray wasn't doing this out of some obscure urge to play a teenage drinking game, but because he was trying to take his time and make me feel more comfortable.

And dammit if that wasn't the nicest fucking thing anyone had ever done for me. Ugh, fuck. I was *not* going to get choked up over this.

"Ugh, okay, fine. Never have I ever, um, topped," I said, clearing my throat gruffly.

"Too easy, at least try a little," Gray said, but he put a finger down.

"You're gonna take cheap shots, so am I." I smiled sweetly at him.

"Fine. Okay, never have I ever... hmm. Never have I ever kissed someone on TV."

"Oh come on. Just because porn isn't technically TV..."

"Hey, it's hard enough to find something that I honestly haven't done," Gray complained. "And then I have to pick something from that category that I think you *have* done? Nearly impossible."

"Great, way to set me at ease," I grumbled. "So you've bottomed. You've topped, clearly. Umm, never have I ever had a threesome."

Gray arched an eyebrow. "Specify the genders."

"Does it matter?" I shot back.

Gray barked a laugh. "Actually, I guess not." He folded a finger down. "Okay, never have I ever been in a legitimate dramatic production, before this movie. Like, something people watched for purposes other than just getting off."

"Excuse you, are you trying to tell me people haven't been getting off to watching me cry on camera for years?" I said with a smile. Gray just gave me a level look. "Fine." I put down another finger. "Never have I ever been involved in any kind of like, double-penetration situation."

Gray folded a finger and my eyes widened.

"Seriously?" I asked. Gray shrugged and I narrowed my eyes.

"Bondage?" I said, before I could stop myself.

Gray folded another finger.

"Public sex?"

Another finger went down.

"Jesus, really?" I blinked. "Breath play?"

Another finger.

My eyes widened. "Is there anything you haven't done? Whips? Chains? Daddy kink?"

"What did you do, read Wikipedia's list of kinks and fetishes?" Gray asked.

"Stop trying to avoid the question," I said. Gray rolled his eyes but he did fold down his fingers. "See, I told you. I never stood a chance of holding my ground against you."

"Never have I ever been completely fucking adorable," Gray said, "worried that I'm somehow not going to be good enough or measure up, when it would be physically impossible for that to be the case."

I blinked, trying to wrap my mind around that sentence, but then Gray was leaning forward, pushing up on his knees and kissing me, and my eyes flew open, then closed, as Gray's hand slid around to my back.

And fuck, that was good. I'd kissed Gray so many times by now, but somehow, it felt different. We weren't on set. It was just the two of us. And just when I was telling my mind to shut up and go with this, Gray pulled back.

"See," he said with a crooked smile. "Told you you wouldn't necessarily lose."

My thoughts couldn't stop racing. Gray had kissed me. *Gray* had kissed *me*. By choice! Fuck. What the hell was I supposed to do now?

I did the only thing I could do. I pushed myself forward and kissed him again.

Because I didn't want to stop and analyze, didn't want to think about what this meant. It didn't mean anything. Gray wasn't seriously interested. And even if he were, I couldn't be. We were just friends. That was all.

And God, what did it say about me and my pitiful sexual history that this was the hottest thing that had ever happened to me and we both still had all our clothes on? Gray brought his hand to my shoulder, running it along my arm, and I leaned into it, letting him pull me with him, slide me up the bed and then push me down onto my back gently. He pulled away again with a smile.

"You don't have to kiss me," I said, flushing as I looked up at him. "I mean, I know this is just—"

"Shh," Gray said, brushing a finger across my lips. "Kissing's nice."

I started to laugh but Gray cut me off by leaning back down and catching my mouth in a kiss. And okay, yeah, it *was* nice. More than nice.

And yes, I knew it wasn't real. But somehow, the fact that it was just us here, the fact that I didn't have to try to be someone else, that it was just me and Gray with no one else around—I felt like I could relax for the first time. Just be myself.

And Gray—Gray seemed to like who *myself* was. And for the first time in a long time, I let go of that extra layer of consciousness, that part of me that was constantly monitoring, constantly checking the reaction of everyone around me and wondering what they thought of me.

When I was with Gray, just the two of us, I got to feel what it was like not to wonder. Not to worry. Not to hate myself.

Gray's lips traced down my jaw to my neck and started sucking on my skin there and I couldn't help moaning as my hands scratched down his back, reaching for the hem of his shirt and slipping up underneath. I wanted to feel skin, Gray's skin, Gray's body against my own.

Gray shifted, bringing his body directly on top of mine and I felt a moment of utter panic when I realized Gray could feel how completely hard I was, how desperate I was for him, and I worried that I was giving myself away somehow. But then I felt Gray's erection pressing down against my thigh and warm sparks shot up my spine.

Gray wanted me too. He wasn't in character, he wasn't performing, and he wanted me. I decided not to think about the fact that Gray could be thinking about anyone else right now, that Gray probably knew how to get himself hard no matter who he was with, because fuck it, I was not ruining my first fucking time with an extra scoop of self-doubt. I already had a double-scoop cone of self-loathing—no need to go and add sprinkles.

Gray pushed up and back, resting on his knees, his legs on either side of me, as he stripped his shirt off over his head. My eyes widened. Goddammit, he was hot, and before I could shame myself out of doing it, I reached up and ran a hand down his muscular chest and onto his abs.

"Fuck." It came out involuntarily, my voice a whisper.

Gray just smiled, leaned down, and kissed me again. I struggled to get my arms into position, shimmying them underneath Gray until I found the bottom of my shirt and began to tug it up. But once he saw what I was doing, Gray put a hand on my arm and stopped me.

"You don't have to," he said, looking into my eyes.

I snorted. "Right, you're just going to fuck me with all my clothes on. That'll work real well, I'm sure."

Gray bent down and kissed my forehead. I blinked and looked back indignantly.

"I just meant that there's no rush," he said. "You don't have to prove anything."

He thinks I'm going to freak out again.

The idea made me want to laugh. Things were so different now. Gray knew, now, all my secrets. Well, most of them anyway. And he hadn't pushed me away, hadn't judged me. Gray was kissing me, for Christ's sake, which didn't make sense on any planet but it was happening and how the hell could I explain to Gray how night and day it was, being in that bed downstairs and being in this bed now, without sounding like a total fucking sap?

"I know," I said with a grin, settling on sarcasm as the safest response. "Maybe I just don't want you coming on my shirt."

"Give me *some* credit," Gray said, sounding almost offended.

"You may be an expert porn star," I said, curling my back up off the mattress and pulling my shirt off overhead, "but some of us are a little newer to this and maybe aren't quite as trusting."

"I don't come on guys' shirts unless I'm supposed to," Gray grumbled.

"Just shut up and kiss me," I said, throwing my shirt to the ground and grabbing Gray's arm, pulling him back down.

He did kiss me, his lips hot and demanding, but only for a minute before he was moving south again, tracing his way down my neck, licking my Adam's apple and making my stomach flutter. And okay, I never would have thought of myself as a nipple guy but Jesus, whatever Gray had learned in Porn Star Academy was *not* a joke because holy hell, that felt good.

I moaned as Gray's tongue circled my nipple, lapping at it, teasing it, and then yelped when he bit down. But it wasn't a bad yelp, God, not a bad yelp at all. My back arched up off the mattress towards Gray as my hands skimmed across his back, reveling in the heat of his skin.

I was getting harder by the second and by the time Gray pressed a kiss to the skin of my stomach, right above the waistband of my pants, I thought I might short circuit.

"Okay if these come off?" Gray asked, running a hand up and down the fabric on my legs.

"Yeah."

It came out as a breathy whisper, nowhere near as cool and nonchalant as I'd have liked. But fuck it, who was I kidding? Gray already knew I was a mess.

I helped him slide my pants off my hips, dragging my boxers down too. Gray's eyes flashed up to mine, widening for a second, and I wondered if I was supposed to leave those on. But we were having sex, weren't we? It's not like they could stay on forever, right?

God, I wished I didn't feel like such a fucking idiot all the time, but before I could sink too far into mortification, Gray pressed a kiss to the soft skin of my hips as he ran a finger up the inside of my right thigh. I moaned and my cock, lying hot and hard against my stomach, twitched. Gray laughed and looked at me with a knowing smile and all I could do was flush and smile back.

"You make," Gray said, pressing another kiss to my skin, even lower this time, "the *best* noises."

"Shut up."

"I mean it," Gray insisted. "I thought at first it was just something you did for the cameras." He grinned up at me lasciviously. "Apparently not."

"Oh my God," I groaned, bringing my hands up to my face. "Kill me."

"Hey," Gray said, nipping lightly at the skin of my left thigh. "I didn't say it was a bad thing, did I? I like it."

And before I could say anything else, Gray grabbed the base of my cock, brought his lips to the head, and slid it into his mouth. A low, keening moan escaped my throat like it was being ripped out of me because *fuck*, that felt good. And okay, yeah, maybe I'd only ever gotten like, three blowjobs in my entire life, including this one, but I was suddenly certain that I could have been blown by a hundred different guys before today and this would still be the best, by far.

Gray took me all the way down in one gulp and then pulled off slowly, letting his tongue linger and trail up the sensitive underside of my cock. By the time he was all the way back to the top, tracing a circle around the tip with his tongue, I was practically shaking.

I'd watched a lot of porn in preparation for blowing Gray. Like, *a lot*. And even so, I'd been nervous, and when I'd actually gotten Gray to come, I'd felt pretty proud of myself. But it was clear within 30 fucking seconds of Gray teasing me now that I'd had no fucking clue what I was doing. Gray, on the other hand...

He was driving me crazy, sucking up and down on my cock, refusing to establish a pattern. He flattened his tongue out as he licked up and down my shaft, then pointed it to tease my head, then sucked me all the way in and hollowed out his cheeks, leaving me writhing in pleasure and fisting the sheets of his bed.

Gray's hand toyed with my balls and he pulled off my cock briefly to lick them, still pumping my shaft with his hand. I moaned as Gray slipped one wet finger down behind my balls and widened my legs to give him better access. My stomach tightened in excitement. Fuck, this was actually going to happen. But when I felt Gray's finger stroke past my hole, I couldn't help tensing up.

Gray kissed my thigh gently as he looked up at me. "Tyler, what's wrong?"

"Nothing," I said quickly, looking away. It *was* nothing. I was *not* going to let this be something, not going to freak out now. "You can keep going."

"Tyler," Gray said, his voice kind. "Please understand that by now, I can tell when something's wrong." He kissed my other thigh.

"Yeah, well fuck you for being so understanding." I glared down at Gray. He just smiled back at me. "It's so fucking stupid," I said with a sigh. "It's not like I haven't tried putting my own fingers up there. It's just, I don't know, I'm nervous that I'm going to ruin this somehow. Like I have an asshole of doom or something that can't get off from other guys— and not only that, but it like, proactively ruins their orgasms, too."

"That is," Gray said, stroking a hand over my hip, "bar none, the sweetest, silliest thing I've ever heard. And it's not true."

"You don't know," I protested. "I could have some kind of cosmic, orgasm-killing ass."

"I promise you, you do not," Gray said. He gave me a speculative grin. "What would you say if I asked you to turn over?"

My eyes narrowed. "I'd ask you why."

"Because I want to eat your cosmic, orgasm-killing ass, obviously."

"Oh." I bit my lip. "Oh. Ummm."

"Only if you want me to. But if you're nervous about it, let me promise you that yes, I really do want to and no, it's not gross, and yes, I do know what I'm doing."

"I didn't say you didn't know what you were doing," I protested. "I just... I don't know, I've never done it before."

"Tyler," Gray said with a smile, "you haven't done anything before."

"Hey."

Gray slid up the bed, bringing his face even with mine, and

kissed me, nipping on my lower lip and pulling it out before releasing it.

"I'm kidding. And I completely understand if you don't want to. But," he said, kissing me again quickly, just a little peck, "I'd love to be your first. If you're open to it."

I closed one eye and squinted at him. "I want you to know I remain highly skeptical of this whole idea. But I *suppose* if you *really* want to, then I *guess* it's okay."

"Your faith in me is heartwarming," Gray said. He reached down and pinched my waist. "Now turn over."

I did—and immediately felt exposed. Gray stood up to pull the rest of his clothes off and I couldn't shake the feeling that I was on display. This was actually the position we were supposed to shoot the scene from today, but somehow, not being able to see Gray anymore unless I looked over my shoulder heightened everything by fifty, maybe a hundred percent.

My nerves were standing on end. But as Gray knelt back onto the bed, straddling me and kissing the back of my neck, I realized that this position heightened the excitement, too. I could feel Gray's hard cock pressing up against me and, yeah. The excitement for sure. And the pleasure.

So I surrendered, letting Gray kiss my cheek, my neck, my back, as he moved down slowly. I spread my legs obediently at a tap of his fingers, feeling completely vulnerable but Jesus, turned on as hell. I ground my hard-on into the mattress below me.

Gray nipped at my ass, kissing both cheeks, and then brought his hands to either side and spread me apart.

Before I even had a chance to think about how exposed I felt, he licked a long strip up my crack and across my hole, and I shivered. That felt *good*.

Gray alternated between long, flat licks with the pad of his tongue and quick swipes across my hole, before twirling his tongue in circles around it and then doing—whatever the hell it was he was doing to create suction and oh fuck, I couldn't help pushing back against his mouth.

Then Gray pushed his tongue inside me and I thought I might actually die of pleasure right then, or at least faint, because Jesus Christ, that felt good, hard and soft at the same time and wet, so wet. My cock was so hard now and I was torn between rutting down into the mattress and pressing back against Gray's tongue.

I felt completely suspended in pleasure, helpless but somehow safe at the same time. Maybe it was just how good it felt, or maybe it was because it was Gray—because I knew he'd take care of me—but I felt myself beginning to slip away as my orgasm built. But just as I'd begun to let myself go, Gray pulled away.

I whined—actually *whined*—when I felt his tongue leave me and turned my head to the side to see Gray grab lube from the bedside table.

"What's that for?" I asked.

"Well, Tyler," Gray said with a broad grin. "This is called lube. Short for lubricant. And we use it for—"

"Shut up, asshole," I said. "I know what it's *for*, I just meant, like, what are you going to do to me?"

"What do you want me to do to you?" His grin grew wicked.

I bit my lip, feeling my face flush as a sudden wave of shyness overtook me. But maybe Gray could tell, because he came back to the bed, straddling me as he brought his lips to my ear.

"I'm going to use it to finger you, until you're basically just a puddle on my mattress," he said, nipping at my earlobe. I shivered. "If that's okay with you, of course."

"Um, yeah. That's, uh, okay with me," I choked out. Jesus, more than okay.

Gray laughed, all throaty and deep. "Good."

He squeezed my shoulder once before moving back to where he'd been before, between my legs, and I realized I'd just left them there, gaping open that whole time. So much for shyness. Gray kissed my ass once more and then I heard the cap on the bottle flip open.

The next thing I felt was Gray's tongue on my hole one more time, pressing into me before it pulled away and was replaced by something cool and wet—lube, I realized, barely registering it before Gray's finger started pushing into me.

And okay, it's not like I hadn't fingered myself before, but there was something mentally very different about letting someone else do that to you, about letting any part of someone else's body penetrate you, and I couldn't help tightening and tensing up as Gray's finger slid in.

Gray rubbed my ass with his free hand and placed a kiss on the small of my back.

"Just relax, Tyler. It's okay. I'm gonna take care of you, I promise. Just relax."

I tried. It didn't hurt. It was just a pressure and fullness that took some getting used to. Gray's finger was bigger than any of mine, and he was able to get further up inside me than I ever could. But then he started pulling it out and *fuck*, okay, that felt different. That felt good.

I moaned as Gray began pumping me, sliding his finger in and out of my ass, building this frictionless rhythm. It wasn't long before I was hipping back against him.

"How's that feel?" Gray asked, kissing my back again. "That feel good?"

"Fuck, yes," I groaned.

"You ready for another one?"

"Yes, please," I gasped.

I'd barely gotten the words out before Gray was sliding his finger out all the way and then pressing it back in, joined this time by a second digit. And Jesus, it was a stretch, it was a lot, and I wondered for a second if I should ask Gray to stop and again, like he could read my mind, Gray's fingers stopped as soon as they were inside me. He just left them there as he kissed my back, my ass, stroking me with his free hand.

"Just breathe, okay?" he said. "You're doing so good. Just let me know when you're ready."

I nodded, breathing deep, waiting until I felt adjusted, and then experimentally pushed back onto Gray's fingers and oh fuck, yes, that was good. That was better than before and once I'd started, I couldn't stop fucking myself back onto his fingers. I didn't care what I looked like, what I sounded like, how slutty I must seem, how much I must look like I was losing my goddamn mind.

"More, please, I need more," I begged, and Gray obligingly added a third finger.

I felt wanton now, just grinding my ass down onto Gray's hand before rutting forward onto the mattress, seeking friction for my cock. But I didn't care, and Gray was lavishing praise on me, telling me what I'd longed to hear, how perfect I was, how good I was doing.

And then Gray did *something*, I wasn't sure what, but it was like he pressed on something and I screamed in pleasure, seeing stars. Gray's deep, rumbly laugh floated up from behind me.

"Holy shit," I gasped. "Holy shit, what was that?"

"That, my friend, was your prostate."

My eyes went wide. I'd heard about prostate orgasms before but I'd never been able to find my own and had sort of been hoping they weren't all they were cracked up to be. God, I'd been so wrong. So, so wrong. But I wasn't sure how much more of that I could handle without coming, and I definitely didn't want to come now.

"Please," I groaned, looking over my shoulder at Gray. "I'm ready. I want—I want you to fuck me."

I don't know what I expected. Some kind of protest maybe, Gray telling me that I wasn't ready, actually, that I had to wait. But all I saw were Gray's eyes, pupils blown wide, as he smiled at me.

"Turn over," he said, sliding his fingers out. I hated how

empty I felt when he did that.

"But we're supposed to—I mean—this is the position we're gonna—"

"If you think I'd fuck you for the first time without being able to see your face—" Gray shook his head, then reached up and turned me over with his hand until I was lying on my back. "Tyler, the whole point of this is to make it good for you. I want to be able to see you, okay? To know that you're alright."

I nodded, not trusting myself to speak. I was *not* going to cry goddammit, no matter how much I felt like I was suddenly on the verge of doing so. Gray bent down and kissed my forehead again, then grabbed a condom and unrolled it along his length.

"Jesus," I whispered. Gray looked at me in curiosity. "You're just—fuck, you're so big."

"You're gonna be fine," Gray said, picking up my hand and lacing his fingers with mine. "I promise. We're gonna go slow, there's no rush, and you're gonna be fine. You can do this."

My stomach felt like it had dropped through the bottom of my feet and into the basement but I nodded. "Okay. I—I want to."

Gray smiled, then helped me get into position, spreading my legs and bringing himself in between them. For a second it almost felt clinical, but then he was back, lying down on top of me and pressing kisses everywhere, my lips, my neck, as his hand reached in between us to stroke me, and everything was okay again.

I could feel Gray's cock pressed between my legs and I knew I needed him right that second.

"God, Gray, fuck, do it already," I moaned.

"Pushy," Gray said. He shook his head, smiling. "I don't know why I'm surprised."

"Well if you weren't going so slowly, maybe I wouldn't have to be pushy," I said, arching an eyebrow. "Jesus, it's like it's your first time or something."

"Mouthy too," Gray said, and he nipped at my nose. "You're lucky this *is* your first time or I might have to punish you for your lip."

"Oh right, I forgot," I said with a laugh. "Because you're *super* experienced with BDSM."

"I am," Gray said, his blue eyes sparkling. "So behave."

And then he moved his cock to my hole and I could feel the head pressing against me, and any thought of teasing him went out the window. Gray brought my hand to my own cock, wrapping it around my shaft.

"Just remember to breathe," he said, his voice low and soft. "And keep stroking this. And know that I'm not going to give you more than you can handle, okay?"

"Okay," I said, giving my cock an experimental tug. And yeah, it felt kind of good, Gray's tip resting against my hole, ready to push into me. It made me feel vulnerable, but it was hot, and I nodded. "I'm ready."

Gray began to push in. Fuck, that was a lot. So much, holy shit, so, so much. So much more than his fingers, it felt like his whole fucking fist was going inside me and Jesus it was a stretch.

"Breathe, baby," Gray said, and I did, taking in a shuddering gasp and blushing because I needed to be told. "You're doing great."

I wondered if Gray were bored, or disappointed in me, in the fact that I couldn't take him all the way, couldn't take him like—well, like a porn star. "You can—you can keep going," I said.

"Don't rush it, remember," Gray said. "We don't have to rush anything."

He leaned in to kiss me and even that motion shifted the angle of his cock pressing into me, pushed him in just a little further. I hissed, but then Gray's tongue was on mine, pushing into my mouth, and his hand closed around my hand where it circled my cock.

Gray started pumping me up and down, his hand still on mine as he kissed me. I took in another gasping breath, overwhelmed by the sensation. It wasn't bad though, and the longer we kissed, the more I stroked myself, the better it got.

And slowly, alternating between Gray pushing into me and then resting, touching me, caressing me, making me feel safe and fucking cherished in a way I hadn't even realized was possible, Gray worked his way inside. He never seemed frustrated once, never looked impatient. And then he was all the way in and I could feel his hips nestled up against me.

"Holy shit," I breathed. "God, you're so big."

"You did so good," Gray said, brushing a kiss across my lips. "I told you you could do it."

"Holy shit," I said again.

What else could I say? The stretch was enormous and part of me wanted to beg for Gray to take it out but the other part of me wanted him to stay there forever. Part of me felt like for the first time in my life, I was coming home. Like I was finding who I really was, discovering that that person wasn't the man who everyone else saw—it was the man I was right now, right this minute, with Gray.

I felt tears roll down my cheeks and Gray's eyes went wide with concern.

"No, no, it's not bad, it's not—" I stammered, feeling like an idiot, feeling *everything* so much right now. "It doesn't hurt, that's not why—oh fuck, this is embarrassing, I'm sorry."

"You don't have to apologize" Gray said, his voice gentle. "You're perfect. This can be an emotional thing."

That was an understatement, but since I wasn't about to tell Gray, *'I think I've finally realized what I've been missing all my life and you've given a piece of me back to myself that I didn't even know was missing, and also please never leave, don't go anywhere, don't ever go anywhere ever again,'* I just smiled.

"Okay."

Gray kissed me again and pressed in just a little. I gasped, but it was a good gasp, a stretch I was ready for. God, being filled, feeling complete, was like something I'd never known was missing sliding back into place. Like turning the lights on in a room inside of myself I hadn't known was there.

Gray started slow, just pressing up against me, changing the angle of his hips rather than sliding in and out, but it was so good that I was panting and whimpering with every thrust. Gray was so attentive, his eyes searching mine with every move, watching to see how I was doing. I tried to concentrate on breathing, on feeling, on telling myself that no, this wasn't too much pleasure, no I wasn't going to get swept away.

But it was hard to concentrate on anything once Gray started pulling out and pushing back into me, even just the littlest bit. I started moaning and couldn't stop, didn't even want to because it was just so good and Gray kept telling me how good I looked, how great I was doing. I pulled his mouth down to mine frantically, trying to communicate through kisses what I didn't have to words to say, how grateful I was, how good I felt, how I might be about to die from pleasure and needed to say thank you before that happened.

"Fuck, Gray," I moaned as he thrust into me. "I can't—it's too good. Fuck, it's so good."

"You're doing great, baby," Gray said, pumping into me and picking up speed. "You're perfect."

I felt a pang of something, wishing Gray wouldn't call me baby. That was what he called me on set. If he called me baby, I wanted him to mean it, and since I couldn't have that, I'd rather he just call me by my name.

But I pushed the feeling away. Who was I to complain, when Gray was taking me somewhere I'd never been, doing all of this for me. And he was really fucking me now, like honest to goodness fucking, the kind you saw in porn, and I couldn't really believe this was me, this was happening, this was my body taking all of this pressure and pleasure.

I had a vision of myself from above for a moment, a flash of what I must look like. How helpless, how small and vulnerable I must seem underneath Gray. But instead of feeling scared, it just made me feel safe, knowing he had me.

"Fuck, Gray, I'm gonna come," I moaned. "Jesus, if you don't —fuck, I'm gonna come."

"Come for me," Gray said, kissing my neck. "Come for me."

"No," I panted, shaking my head. "No, it's too soon. I don't want—I don't want this to stop. I want to wait—until—until you're—"

"It's okay, Tyler, I promise," Gray said, his voice ragged.

"Are you—are you gonna—"

"I've been two seconds away from coming since the moment I first kissed you," Gray said, moving his hand to my cock and stroking me. "You don't need to worry about me."

I wanted to cry, because what a sweet idea that was, that Gray wanted to kiss me, that Gray actually liked me, that kissing me meant something to him. But I knew he was just trying to be nice, knew it didn't mean anything, and I shook my head, trying to push the idea out of my mind.

"It's okay, baby," Gray said, catching my lips in a kiss. "It's ok. Just let go. I've got you."

And fuck, it felt so good, letting him call me baby, letting myself believe it. And so I did, I let go. Gray's hand was still pumping me, his cock still filling me, and everything just felt so right. I came and I saw stars, felt like I went to the goddamn moon as I felt Gray shudder inside me, pumping a few more times before coming to stillness. I realized he'd come too and somehow that was important, that made everything better.

I wanted to protest when Gray pulled out, but clamped my lips shut so I didn't seem too needy. Gray pushed himself up, threw the condom in the trash, and then came back to bed. He took me in his arms and kissed my cheek, right up next to the corner of my eye, and I felt something wet and realized I was crying.

"God, sorry," I gasped, trying to wipe the tears away. "Jesus, I can't stop—what the fuck is wrong with me?"

I knew what was wrong, but I couldn't say it out loud.

"Nothing's wrong with you," Gray said, squeezing me tighter. "Don't apologize for that. Don't ever apologize for who you are."

I knew he was just saying that because it was what you were supposed to say, but God, it was nice to imagine he meant it. And so I let myself close my eyes, let him hold me a little while longer.

I knew I should get up and move, knew I should go back to my room. It was only afternoon, after all. But I was so tired, and so warm, and dammit, for once in my life, I felt so safe. I'd told Gray everything—close enough, anyway—and he hadn't hated me. In fact, remarkably, Gray still seemed to like me.

My last thought as I drifted off to sleep was that this must be what it was like, to feel like you were enough.

11

GRAY

*W*ell that was... *different.*

And really, really good.

I looked down at Tyler as he slept in my arms. It was the middle of the night now. We'd fallen asleep in my bed and at some point, we must have pulled the covers up.

Tyler was still sound asleep. But me? I'd woken up with my heart pounding, sure that everything that had happened had just been a dream, something cooked up by my brain to make everything seem that much worse when I woke up and discovered it wasn't true.

Except here Tyler was, still naked, still pressed up against my body. I could feel the soft flutter of his breath on my wrist where it lay in front of his face, my arm curved protectively around his body. Tyler's body. That he'd just shared with me. Opened up to me. Trusted me with.

Would he have done that, if he knew what you were hiding from him?

I struggled to push the thought away. Tyler had asked me to help him—as a friend. There was nothing wrong with what we'd done, nothing wrong with me not vomiting out my feelings first and probably just making Tyler feel worse. He didn't need to know how I felt. It wouldn't have helped him —wasn't what he'd asked me for.

Still, I couldn't shake the feeling that I'd messed up. Like Tyler would be pissed if he knew what I felt for him, if he had any idea that the memory of this afternoon was seared onto my brain—that I'd replay it every night, as far into the future as I could see.

Tyler, head thrown back, panting beneath me. Tyler, soft and open, no longer prickly, no longer holding himself back. Tyler, letting himself be vulnerable—and be seen.

The sheen of sweat on his forehead, the scent of his skin. The deep V of his hips and the flat, taut skin of his stomach. Those thin, muscular thighs, parting for me. The way he'd taken me inside him.

No, I wouldn't be forgetting that any time soon.

I knew I should probably wake Tyler up. Help him back to his own room. At the very least because it would be more complicated for him to get back tomorrow morning, unseen.

But waking Tyler now meant ending this moment, this sliver of infinity where he slept in my arms, the moon ghosting through the window and kissing his skin silver, this stolen piece of another universe where Tyler was mine, where this made sense, where this was ours forever. Where I meant something to Tyler—something, anything, close to what he meant to me.

What does Tyler mean to you?

It had taken me by surprise, a knife in the dark, the realization that I had feelings for Tyler. I'd spent the past week trying to put them aside, ever since that night out in the city. I hadn't felt ready, still didn't feel ready, for the way the ground dropped away beneath me every time I saw him.

I hadn't thought it was possible to develop feelings for someone new, not when Ethan still had his fishhooks in my heart, so I hadn't been on my guard. And now it was too late. I didn't want to care about Ethan anymore, was doing my best not to, but every time he called or texted, I felt a sharp stab of pain that told me that wound wasn't fully healed. And yet, I couldn't deny what I felt for Tyler.

When I looked at him, I felt the way I did on those few, rare mornings when I was up with the sunrise. When the sun painted everything it touched a molten gold and the world seemed new and unbroken. Tyler made my heart feel full, feel hopeful in a way I'd forgotten, until now, that I could feel.

But Tyler didn't want me like that. And why should he? I was old, uneducated, messed up from my ex, a fucking pornstar for Christ's sake. I was nowhere near his level. I should be grateful Tyler saw me as a friend at all.

At least you know him. At least you got to have him in your life—in your bed—for this little while.

The movie was going to wrap soon and then all of this would end. Tyler would move back to LA. I'd stay in New York. None of the auditions I went on would turn into anything, I was sure. No one would want someone as washed up as me, someone with my background.

But at least I'd know Tyler was out there, now. That counted for something, didn't it? At least I'd get to smile every time I saw him in something. Remember this month. Remember this night.

But still, Tyler would be gone.

And that alone was reason enough for me to lay my head back down, to pull Tyler back against my chest. That alone was reason enough to keep him close, for as long as I could.

I closed my eyes and pressed a kiss to the back of Tyler's neck. For tonight, this was enough.

"How're you feeling?" Violet asked me brightly at lunch the next day. "Any better?"

She'd filmed another quick scene with Tyler this morning—Tyler, who'd woken up sheepish and blushing in my bed, but who'd seemed sweeter and less self-conscious than I'd ever seen him. I'd had to fight the urge to kiss him again before he whispered a hasty, '*Well, um, thanks,*' and slipped out the door.

"Yeah," I said, smiling back at Violet. "Much better. Just a 24 hour bug, I guess."

"Good," Violet said judiciously. "Glad to hear it."

"Purely out of concern for my health, I'm sure," I couldn't resist adding.

"Oh, absolutely," Violet said, her face solemn. "The well-being of my actors is paramount. Staying on schedule is only a distant, secondary concern." But her face cracked as she glanced down at her watch.

"I'll see you in there in a minute," I said, standing up to put my plate away.

Tyler rushed in as I finished throwing out my trash, coming from another quick costume change. In the past few weeks, I'd gotten so used to not knowing which Tyler I was going to get—the prickly or the easy-going—but his face lit up with a smile when he saw me.

To think that *he'd* been the one nervous about what I would think of him, all this time. God, I wished I could take him in my arms all over again and tell him how little any of that mattered—how all I cared about was that he was happy. But saying something like that—words that had come so naturally to my lips in bed yesterday—just seemed awkward and out of place now.

"Hey," I said, suddenly at a loss for words when Tyler reached me. Goddammit, why was I acting like a middle-schooler with a crush all of a sudden?

"Hey," Tyler said, grinning brightly.

And then we just stood there, looking at each other and not saying anything, each of us apparently waiting for the other to speak, until Tyler started laughing, and then I couldn't help laughing too.

"Is this weird?" Tyler asked, his smile lop-sided. "I mean, now that we've—"

"I have no idea," I said, shrugging helplessly. "I don't think it has to be. I just... didn't know if..."

Didn't know if I'd given myself away—if you'd realized how painfully obvious my feelings for you are.

"Yeah. Same," Tyler said, chuckling. "Let's just decide it's not weird then."

"You got it," I said, forcing myself to smile like a normal person and not someone who was about to choke on his own heart as it tried to climb its way out of my throat and throw itself at Tyler. "You uh, you eat yet?"

Tyler wrinkled his nose. "Nah. I figured if I was going to freeze up again, at least it should be on an empty stomach so I don't barf all over people."

"How considerate of you."

"The world for you, Gray, the world for you." But he did grab an apple as we passed by the craft services table on the way back towards Dylan's room.

"How are you feeling about everything?" I asked. "I, um, I hope I'm allowed to ask that again."

"You're definitely allowed to ask," Tyler said. "And I'm really working on not being a dick, so like, hit me or something if I slip up and say something asinine to you." He shrugged. "I'm actually feeling good, oddly?"

"Good. Me too."

Tyler shot me a surreptitious look as we walked down the hall. "Thanks again for last night. That was—I mean, it was, um—well, you know."

I laughed. "Yeah. I know."

God, it was nice to have this back. This feeling of ease

between us that I hadn't felt since—well, since we'd started shooting the sex scenes. Now that I knew what Tyler had been struggling with—probably still *was* struggling with, honestly—now that we'd talked about it, Tyler seemed happier, and that made me happier.

I can be happy for him as a friend, I yelled at the voice in the back of my mind that was telling me how creepy I was. *That's a normal friend thing to do. Nothing weird about that at all.*

Right.

Just like there was nothing weird about pushing my friend down onto a twin bed five minutes later, grinding my cock onto him as the cameras whirred and the lights began to make us sweat and the rest of the room watched silently.

Nothing weird about kissing his lips, or sucking on the skin of his neck, hoping to leave a mark, or palming his erection through his pants. Nothing weird about stripping his clothes off and letting my eyes roam across his thin frame, feeling my cock tighten at the sight of him lying there before me, waiting for me, asking me to come in.

Okay, fine, so... maybe a little weird. But Tyler seemed okay with everything—more than okay. I'd seen him last night, and I'd seen him the morning before that. There was none of that rigid, plastered-on smile, the wide, terrified eyes, the short, panicky breaths.

That Tyler had scared me. I'd had no idea what was happening, what I was doing to make Tyler react that way. All I'd known was that Tyler was very clearly shutting down and just as clearly was not going to do anything to stop the scene. So I'd done the first thing I could think of to bring it to an end.

I didn't like remembering Tyler like that. But last night? And now? It was like he was a different person. Pulling me towards him, his eyes focused on me and me alone. All I wanted to do was make sure he never felt that fear, that panic, ever again.

And so I kissed him, gently at first, then rougher as his lips demanded it, ravaging my own. Tyler's body was so warm as it twisted and pressed and tangled with mine, his hands seeking every inch of my skin with abandon. And his eyes, those rings of gold like halos under his long dark lashes, locked onto mine and wouldn't let go.

It was so easy to fall into him, and so hard to remember that there were cameras there, that it wasn't just the two of us, reliving yesterday afternoon, the green and golden sunlight splashing through the windows, the air filled with the sounds of our breathing. I didn't want to think about angles and poses, didn't want to calculate the position of the cameras in relation to our bodies. I just wanted to lose myself in this.

Tyler pulled my face down close to his, kissing me deeply, and I had to force myself to pull away, to begin trailing kisses down his chest and move the scene along. Had it been my choice, I could have just kissed him for hours.

Not that I wasn't perfectly happy to take his cock in my mouth again, too. I loved the way it smelled, tasted, and felt in my mouth. And I loved how responsive Tyler was, his hands rubbing my neck as I sucked him in and out, then tangling in my hair as I began to fuck him open with my fingers while he moaned and sweated.

I wished he didn't have to turn over, wished I could see his face again like I had yesterday, but in the book, Wyatt took Dylan from behind. After Tyler turned over, I brought my body down on top of his, covering him completely, wanting him to feel warm and safe.

I kissed the side of Tyler's jaw and whispered, out of sight of the cameras, "Everything okay?"

Tyler nodded, almost imperceptibly, then groaned audibly, pushing back against me and driving my throbbing cock along the tight channel between his ass cheeks.

"Please," he begged, his voice ragged. "Please, Wyatt. I need you."

Wyatt. Right. I needed to remember that. Tyler didn't need me at all—and even if I was having trouble remembering that we were acting, he wasn't.

Still, as I sank into Tyler, watching my cock slide deep inside him, I couldn't help thinking that some part of this had to be real. Because this was the same Tyler who'd been in my bed yesterday, the same slim body taking me in. The same moans, the same breath, the same heartbeat. And even if there were nothing deeper between us, even if we were just friends, some part of Tyler had opened himself to me yesterday, and was doing it again right now.

God, he looked so small beneath me, like he could break apart at any second. But there was nothing delicate about the way Tyler pushed back onto my cock, begging for more until I was all the way inside him. I brought my hands up to meet Tyler's where they gripped the mattress, laced our fingers together, and waited, just breathing in time with him until he pushed back again and I knew I could start thrusting.

And Christ, it drove me wild, watching Tyler moan as he took my cock, arching his back and bucking backwards, begging, groaning, panting. It was all I could do not to come immediately—but I needed him to come first. Not just for the scene, but for Tyler himself. I needed him to know he'd always come first, with me.

Seeing Tyler come apart in my hands, it felt like something was unraveling inside of me. He was so beautiful, so perfect. And I knew, for the first time, that the way Tyler moved, the sounds he made, the way he asked for more—that wasn't just for the camera. That was all Tyler—the real Tyler.

My Tyler.

That was a dangerous thought. But before I could worry, before I could shove it away, Tyler was gasping that he was going to come and that became my only concern, making this moment perfect for him, giving him what he needed.

"Come for me, baby," I said. It slipped out, calling him that, and it was a dangerous thought.

He's not your baby.

And he never would be. But for today at least, for this little while, couldn't I just pretend? Tyler begged and moaned and finally came, releasing into my hand as I stroked him from behind, and I let myself finish in the condom inside him. No porn ending here, coming on his chest. I cared too much for Tyler to do that unless he asked. Besides, it felt good, releasing inside him.

And then we collapsed together onto the bed. I wasn't even sure when the scene ended exactly—I didn't remember Violet saying *'Cut.'* But suddenly people were handing us tissues and water bottles and Violet told us to catch our breath before we resumed the scene.

After getting cleaned up and pulling our underwear back on, we slid under the sheet on the bed, pulling it up so we still looked naked for when we started filming again.

I turned onto my side and smiled at Tyler. I wanted to reach out, stroke his shoulder, touch him in some way. It felt strange not to do that, after what we'd just shared. But I wasn't sure he'd want me to, so I just smiled.

"How are you doing?"

Tyler laughed. "I think we need to get you a button or something that you can push instead of asking me that every time."

"Humor me," I said, catching his eyes, trying to communicate without words that I really wanted to know.

"I'm good," Tyler said, seeming to understand. "Really." And then he reached out and took my hand in his own, squeezing it. "Thanks."

He didn't say what for, but he didn't need to. I knew, somehow, that it was thanks for asking, thanks for being concerned, thank you for last night and thank you for just now, all mixed together. Tyler's cheeks flushed pink as I watched him.

"You're welcome," I said, finally, when I trusted myself to speak.

"You ready for the rest of the scene?" Tyler asked, propping himself up on an elbow to glance around the rest of the room.

"I think I might need another minute before I can get back into Wyatt mode," I said honestly. "Still a little..."

"Yeah," Tyler chuckled. "Me too."

Tyler had told me about how he tried to sink into his characters, losing himself in them, and I'd been trying to do that too. It was impossible during the sex scenes, though. I was too attuned to Tyler, cared too much about how he was doing to see him as anyone other than himself. But I could try it for our other scenes.

"Maybe we should have gone really method for you," Tyler said with a sly smile. "Taken you down to Mississippi to really sink into Wyatt's past. Let you marinate in the Gulf Coast for a while."

"Well, if that's all it takes, then the last scene should at least be a little better," I said with a grin. "Maybe I'll go down early and sleep on some fishing docks for a while to get a feel for the place."

Next week—our final day of filming—we'd be heading down to the Chesapeake Bay to shoot the last scene of the movie. It wasn't quite Mississippi, which was where Wyatt was supposed to wash up at the end of the book, but it looked more like it than anywhere in the New York area.

Since it would be our last day of production, Dave and Andrew had decided to host a wrap party and celebration that night. We were all staying in some divey motel near the bay and anyone who'd contributed to the movie's crowd-funding had been invited to join in.

"God," Tyler sighed. "I can't believe we're almost done. This is all going to be over so soon."

"Yeah, but hey, that's good, right?" I tried for an encouraging smile. "That means you can move back to LA. Get started out there again."

"Yeah. Yeah, I guess." Tyler grinned. "And you'll be on your way to becoming a movie star."

"Something like that," I said with a wry smile.

Tyler looked for a second like he was going to say something else, but he ended up just laying his head back down on the pillow. I settled in next to him and told myself not to notice how warm his skin was, how much of him was touching me. Not to think about how much I wanted to wrap him up in my arms.

"You guys good to move on?" Violet asked a few minutes later. "Don't want to lose all the daylight."

"Sure. Gray, get back on top of me," Tyler said with a commanding tone that was only somewhat ruined by the giggle that slipped out as he turned over onto his stomach.

I moved to straddle Tyler, draping my body across his, and waited for Violet to cue us into action. I was Wyatt. I was with Dylan, the man I loved, and all I wanted to do was show him that.

"Action!"

Wyatt leaned in to kiss the back of Dylan's neck, then slid off of him, pulling him close.

"Fuck, Wyatt," *Dylan said, throwing his head back and laughing.* "Fuck, is it always like that?"

Wyatt smiled at him, catching Dylan's chin between his fingers and kissing him. "No. No it's not always like that."

Dylan frowned for a second and Wyatt kissed his cheek, his neck, his shoulder, before continuing.

"It should always be good, of course. You should always be with someone who cares about you. But... no. That was—I mean, you're—it's—" *he stammered, feeling his face growing red.*

"My God, Wyatt," *Dylan said, a grin spreading across his face.* "Are you trying to tell me I mean something to you?"

Wyatt's cheeks went from pink to scarlet. "You know you do."

"Sometimes I wonder." *Dylan laughed, to show he was joking, Wyatt realized, but his eyes told a different story.*

"Hey," *Wyatt said, propping himself up on one elbow to look down at Dylan as he lay on his back.* "You can't mean that. You know I—" *he broke off again.*

"See?" *Dylan said, his tone caught between playful and hurt.* "You can't even say it. You're not exactly Mr. Forthcoming, you know. It's hard to tell with you."

Wyatt's eyes widened as he fought the urge growing inside him to tell—to shout—how much he loved Dylan, that he'd loved him since the moment he saw him, that he cared more about Dylan than he did himself and that Dylan was the person who made him feel alive, who gave him a reason to get up in the morning.

But it was because of that love that he couldn't say anything. How could he, when he knew it would ruin Dylan's life? How could he say anything to Dylan to make him think they had a future together, when Wyatt knew how futile that was?

What kind of future could they possibly have? An alcoholic high school teacher dating his former student? What, would Dylan share the tiny room Wyatt had in the staff section of the school? Would they get an apartment in town and Dylan would just avoid his former schoolmates? Or would he go away to college and come home for breaks, back to the small, depressing life that Wyatt led?

No, Dylan needed to go to college and forget about Wyatt. Wyatt had been selfish enough already, giving in to what he wanted instead of holding Dylan at arm's length like he should have. It didn't matter that Dylan wanted it too—it had been up to Wyatt to say no, and he'd failed.

So Wyatt said nothing and kissed Dylan deeply instead. But when he pulled back, he could see the hurt, the fear and sadness in Dylan's eyes.

"What's wrong?" Wyatt whispered.

"Nothing. Forget it."

Dylan turned inwards, hiding his face in Wyatt's neck, and Wyatt knew he was doing that so Wyatt couldn't see his expression, knew he was afraid to tell Wyatt what he was thinking. He should have pressed him—except he knew what Dylan wanted to say. So he held him instead.

"What are you doing?" he asked a few minutes later, still cradling Dylan in his arms, still just breathing in the scent of him, savoring this impossible, untenable moment.

"*Drawing,*" *Dylan said, tracing his finger along Wyatt's bicep.*

Wyatt smiled. "*Drawing what?*"

"*Guess.*"

Wyatt closed his eyes and tried to concentrate on the shape Dylan was tracing onto his skin.

"*Is that a sine wave?*" *he asked with a laugh of recognition.*

"*Maybe.*" *The smile in Dylan's voice was audible. He brushed the palm of his hand over Wyatt's arm as though he were erasing something.* "*Here, guess this one.*"

Again, Wyatt closed his eyes and tried to focus his brain on the nerve endings lighting up in his arm at Dylan's touch. It was hard, given how distracting the rest of Dylan's body was. He was silent for a long while.

"*Wait, is that... are you trying to draw an asymptote?*" *Wyatt asked.*

Dylan laughed. "*Took you long enough.*"

"*Don't think this gets you out of studying for the next exam,*" *Wyatt said with a snort.*

He closed his eyes again, waiting to feel what Dylan would draw next, but when Dylan's finger came back to dance along his skin, it wasn't a shape this time. It was letters.

"*Wait, go slower,*" *he said, pressing a kiss down onto the top of Dylan's head.* "*I can't keep up.*"

"*Sorry, old man,*" *Dylan grumbled.* "*Want me to go grab your bifocals, too?*"

"*Hush, you.*"

Dylan went back to drawing, the letters he traced burning into Wyatt's skin.

"C?" *Wyatt asked.*

Dylan nodded, then wrote the next letter.

"U?"

Dylan nodded again.

"I swear to God, if you're writing 'cum'..."

"You'll what? Suspend me?" *Dylan said, grinning up at him.* "Because I can definitely think of something of yours I wouldn't mind being suspended on."

"Cute." *Wyatt frowned, trying to make out the next letter.* "Is that a K?"

"Yep." *Dylan's finger continued tracing.*

"Y?" *Wyatt guessed. Dylan nodded and traced one more letter.* "M?" *Dylan nodded again.* "C-U-K-Y-M?"

"Obviously," *Dylan said.* "It's like you've never heard that word before."

"Cukym?" *Wyatt frowned.* "Fine, I'll bite. What does it mean?"

Dylan turned his face up towards Wyatt and smiled. "It's my name."

"It's your—how?" *Wyatt's brow wrinkled.* "Like a code or something?"

Dylan blushed. It was adorable, of course. "When my brother and I were little, we invented what we thought was a secret language. Every consonant, you replace it with the consonant *before it in the alphabet. Every vowel, you move to the vowel before."*

"So Dylan—"

"Becomes Cukym. Y's get treated as vowels or consonants depending on what they were in the original word."

"Huh."

"Here, watch," *Dylan said, bringing his finger back to Wyatt's arm.*

Wyatt closed his eyes and tried to make out the letters Dylan was tracing this time. "Vuyss? Is that—oh God, is that my name?" *He looked down at Dylan in horror.* "Why does my name have to sound so ugly?"

"I don't make the rules," *Dylan said with a broad grin.* "I just follow them."

"Except for the part where you literally do make the rules, because you made this language up," *Wyatt grumbled.*

"Stop complaining, old man," *Dylan said.*

He lay down again, his head against Wyatt's chest, and went back to tracing his finger idly across Wyatt's skin. For a long time, there were no words, just patterns, scrolls and swirls that sank into Wyatt's skin like tattoos, his body drinking in Dylan's touch. Wyatt had almost drifted off to sleep when it occurred to him that Dylan was writing again—writing something lengthy along his arm.

E Kita Xio. *Wyatt frowned, trying to parse that.* I Lo-

"Oh, Dylan," *he said simply, when he understood.*

"I do, you know," Dylan said. "I know you don't want me to say it, but I do."

"Dylan—"

"And you don't have to say it back or anything. I just—I just wanted you to know."

Wyatt pulled Dylan closer, bent his head down until their foreheads were touching. "You mean more to me than anyone ever has. More than anyone ever will, I think."

"Oh." Dylan's voice was small, and he bit his lip, then shrugged with a nonchalant smile. "Okay."

Wyatt's heart beat fast—too fast—when he looked into Dylan's eyes. God, why couldn't he just say it? Or if he couldn't, why wasn't he strong enough to let Dylan go? Either way would be kinder than what he was doing to him now.

"You kill me, Dylan," he said, squeezing his eyes shut tight. "You absolutely destroy me."

"I didn't mean—you don't have to—"

"If I don't say things, it's not because I don't feel them, Dylan," Wyatt said, the words wrenched out of him. "It's because I'm trying to keep some shred of myself left, something to hold onto after you're gone."

"I'm not going anywhere," Dylan said, peering up at him. "You know that, right?"

Wyatt was quiet for a moment, not knowing what to say. Should he lie? Or tell the truth.

You will go somewhere, Dylan, and you should. You'll go far away from here. You'll have your whole life, the entire world at your feet, and you won't stay here and waste it on me. I won't let you.

You'll go far away and you'll forget all about me. As you should.

No, he realized. No, he couldn't bring himself to say that. Not when it would hurt Dylan so much. Dylan who he seemed destined to hurt, no matter what he did—but at least he could spare him this. And so he lied.

"Right," he said, bringing his hand to Dylan's back and tracing Dylan's name across it, scrawling it across Dylan's skin to match the way it was carved into Wyatt's own heart. "Right."

~

"Dad, I can't just leave."

Tyler's voice floated out of his door as I passed his room coming back from the bathrooms. It was our last day on site at Bailey Park and I was packing up the last of my things.

"Because we're not done yet and we're shooting off-site tomorrow. I have to go down to Whitcomb, Maryland and we won't be back til Monday." Tyler paused. "Right but I have to—" Another pause. "Yeah, but Dad, I have actual commitments I have to honor. Haven't you always told me to be more responsible?"

I knew I shouldn't eavesdrop, but I couldn't help lingering at the doorway to my room.

"Because I just can't, okay? Look, I have to go. I'll call you when I get back."

I heard a long sigh and then the sound of something being

thrown against a wall. Wincing, I stepped back out of my room and poked my head in Tyler's.

"Everything okay in here? I heard a—" I stopped as I saw Tyler bending down to pick something up off the floor.

"Just my toothpaste," he said with a wry grin. "I wanted to throw my phone but decided at the last second to throw something that would be less horrifically expensive if it broke."

"That's more presence of mind than I would have had." I cleared my throat. "I couldn't help overhearing, um—"

"Me acting like a spoiled child with my dad on the phone?"

"I don't know that those are the words I would have used."

"That's because you're too polite to be honest," Tyler snorted. He shook his head and sighed. "It's fine. It's just—"

"I didn't realize you were talking again," I said.

"We're not. Not really. I just made the mistake of finally calling him back, only to find out he's in New York and wants to see me."

"Oh."

"Yeah," Tyler said, the frustration clear in his voice. "Only, of course, he's only in town for two days, apparently, so he wants to see me now or tomorrow—the two days I couldn't see him even if I wanted to. And yet somehow it's my fault that I'm not available, even though it's for legitimate work reasons. No, I'm back to just being irrational, recalcitrant Tyler, making his life hard."

"That's just bullshit." I tried to keep the heat out of my voice but it was hard—the subject of Tyler's dad never failed to make me angry—at the way he manipulated Tyler, to be clear, not at Tyler himself.

"Yeah, well try telling him that." Tyler scrubbed a hand through his hair. "I was going to take the train back and pick up Luke's car from the shop, which the mechanic *finally* fixed after keeping it for weeks, even though I fucking hate driving and am pretty sure I'd crash the car again on my way down there, but I wouldn't put it past my dad to be waiting for me there somehow, if he's talked to Luke."

"Oh. Well that's simple. Don't go into the city," I offered. "Just ride down with me."

"Yeah, but you can't—"

"What? Can't have company on a boring drive? Can't help out a friend?"

Tyler squinted at me. "Are you sure you don't mind? I don't want to put you out. I can just get a rental car or—"

"How would me driving you to a place I'm going to anyway put me out?" I asked.

Tyler flushed. "Okay, well when you put it that way. Are you sure it's okay? Do you want me to pay for gas or—"

"Tyler?"

"Yeah?"

"Shush. It's going to be great."

And it was, actually.

Mostly because it was an excuse to spend more time with Tyler. The shoot was going to wrap tomorrow, and I'd go from seeing Tyler every day to... well, I didn't know, exactly. He was going to move back to LA eventually, though. And even if he stayed in New York, I wouldn't exactly be able to call him up at 7 a.m. and suggest we spend every waking minute of the day together, like we did now.

Enjoy the time you have left with him. I hated thinking about it that way. It felt so final, so cold. But it was true, wasn't it?

And on a more practical level, when we hit traffic as soon as we crossed the Del Mem Bridge, Tyler was there to take my phone from me and navigate us down to the town of Whitcomb where we were headed.

"Okay, in like two miles, you need to hang a right onto Oxblood Hollow Road," Tyler said. Then he grimaced. "God, that sounds like the beginning of a horror movie, doesn't it?"

"Oxblood Hollow?" I laughed. "Definitely. Hope you've enjoyed your life, because it's about to end."

"What if we get murdered and then come back as ghosts, though?" Tyler asked, poking me on the shoulder. "Will you be afraid of yourself?"

"Hilarious." I gave him my best side-eye. "You'd better hope you get murdered, too, or I will definitely come back and haunt you for taking me down this God-forsaken road."

The right turn from the county road we were on onto Oxblood Hollow didn't look promising. It was a dirt road, rutted and pockmarked with deep potholes, and as it wound through what had looked from a distance like a little copse of trees and turned out to be a veritable forest, it began to twist and descend precipitously.

I arched an eyebrow at Tyler. "Well, it's been nice knowing you but—"

And then I stopped, because the road made a final hairpin turn and broke clear of the trees, leading us out into the most gorgeous sight I'd seen in a long time. Gently sloping fields gleamed golden in the setting sun, with deeply shadowed hills rising behind them. Old, solitary oak trees cropped up alongside a small creek as we drove along.

The fields on the right side of the road were lush and full of wildflowers. The ones on the left side were farmland and as the road meandered along the stream, a house came into view, with white shingles, a wide front porch, and—once we got close enough to see, rocking chairs.

"I take it back," I said, my eyes wide. "I want to get murdered here. Please."

"Seriously," Tyler whispered. "God, could we just stay here? For like, ever?"

"Fine by me."

"There's definitely enough space for those 10 children we're going to adopt."

I blinked, then laughed when I remembered that joke from the night we'd run into Ethan in the city. God, that felt like ages ago. Like both Tyler and I had been different people.

"Honestly," I agreed. "It's pretty much perfect."

Seeing the light dancing across Tyler's face, the way his eyes gleamed, the relaxed smile on his lips—so different from the tense, on-guard expression he'd worn after talking to his father—I wished I really could stop the car and take Tyler into that house, that it could be ours, somehow. There was no universe in which that made sense, but I wanted it more than anything I'd wanted in a long, long time.

"Wait, pull over," Tyler said suddenly. "What does that say?"

He gestured towards a small, gravel pull-off a hundred feet in front of us to the right. I guided the car off the road, then blinked in surprise when I saw what Tyler was pointing at—a sign set back in the meadow surrounding us.

Oxblood Hollow Village Park

"Holy shit, Oxblood Hollow is a village, not just a road?" Tyler said excitedly. "God, and their park is just this random scrap of wilderness on the side of a dirt road?"

"We obviously need to come back," I said. "When we have more time, on our way back to the city, maybe? I feel a strong need to find this village now."

"What if this *is* the village?" Tyler asked, looking around. "Just one farmhouse and a bunch of squirrels."

"Does that mean that all of the other residents are ghosts?"

"I think that's the only thing it *can* mean, Gray," Tyler said. He gave me a serious look. "We have to come back here."

"Absolutely."

"No, I mean like, for real, not just on our drive back, but like, when you're a famous movie star and I'm actually getting work again. Let's wait until we have some huge amount of money and then look up whoever owns that farmhouse and give them like, ten thousand dollars to rent their house for a week and just disappear from the world for a while."

I laughed. "Tyler, I think for ten thousand dollars, we could rent this place for a month. Or longer."

"Well fuck, I don't know how much things cost. Let's do that, then."

"In this scenario, aren't we both like, in demand? How are we going to have time for this?"

Though, on the other hand, why the fuck was I nitpicking this fantasy? It appealed to me more than Tyler knew—why was I trying to pull it apart?

"Yes, but that's what makes it even better," Tyler said excitedly. "Because no one will know where we went and it'll be like, did they ascend to the astral plane? Did they get facial reconstructive surgery and flee to Monaco? It'll be this amazing mystery when we re-emerge."

"You know what? Let's do it," I said with a laugh. "Do we pinky swear on this, too?"

Tyler gave me a disbelieving look. "Um, no. This is much more serious. This calls for an elbow swear."

"What the fuck's an elbow swear?"

"Um, a super sacred, inviolable and binding promise that I just made up right now? Here, give me your arm." He took my right arm and linked it with his left. "Repeat after me. *I solemnly swear.*"

"I solemnly swear."

"To come back to this magical glade with Tyler."

"To come back to this magical glade with Tyler."

"When we're both rich, in my case, and famous, in your case."

"When we're both rich, in my—wait, I mean, your case, and famous, in my case."

"And also Tyler is perfect and right about everything all the time."

"And also Tyler is—wait, hey—"

"Gray, you have to say it. You can't break an elbow curse in the middle. Once you start it, you have to finish it or it's really bad luck."

"You have a weird fixation with bad luck and curses, you know that? Wouldn't your cursed asshole like, balance out this curse so that they'd neutralize each other?"

"Look, it's not my fault that my eyes are opened to a plane of existence all around us that you don't have access to. You just have to trust me."

"And Tyler's alright I guess and is right about some things, some of the time. How's that?"

"Ugh, close enough," Tyler said, shoving my shoulder.

I shoved back, and started laughing at the fight that followed. We were acting like teenagers, but I couldn't stop until I'd gotten both of Tyler's hands in mine and was holding them hostage.

"What?" Tyler asked, giving me a suspicious look. "What are you laughing about?"

"Just... this. Us." I shrugged. "Nothing, really."

Just trying to imagine my life if I had never met you, and realized I can't do it. I can't envision my life without you in it. And I'm about to lose you.

"Oh, shit," Tyler said suddenly, looking down. "Your phone's ringing."

I let go of his hands so he could reach down and pick my phone up from where it still rested in his lap. His face was full of misgiving when I looked over.

"Who is it?"

Tyler winced. "Ethan. You want—"

"No. Hit ignore."

Trust Ethan to ruin a moment. I sighed, then put the car back in gear and pulled onto the road again.

"Okay," Tyler said slowly. He hit ignore, but something in his expression told me he had more to say.

"He won't stop fucking calling," I said, glancing over at Tyler as I drove. "It's like, multiple times a day, now. I know he hates being ignored but you'd think he'd get the message."

"Maybe he just sees what a catch you are," Tyler said quietly. "And finally realizes what a dumbass he was."

"Or maybe he just wants attention," I said darkly.

"Maybe." Tyler frowned. "Oh, he's texting you now. You um —you wanna pull over so you can—"

"Just delete it."

"But I'd have to—I mean, I'd have to read it in order to do that. Are you sure you don't want to—"

"Honestly, I'd rather have you read it than me. Password's 1618."

Tyler punched that in and opened the text message. I couldn't read what it said, but Tyler's face was concerned.

"I don't know if I should delete this," he said slowly. "He says, *'Hey please call me, we really need to talk.'* You want me to respond or something?"

"No. Just... no."

"You sure?" Tyler said. "I mean, what if it's—"

"There's nothing he could possibly say that I want to hear," I said emphatically. Tyler didn't respond, and after a minute's silence, I sighed. "Why do I feel like you disagree?"

"I don't. Not really. I just—I don't know. You guys were together for a long time. I just—as someone who doesn't have a lot of people in his life who actually *want* to talk to him right now... Ugh, I don't know. I don't know what I'm saying."

"You think I'm being harsh?"

"I think..." he glanced over at me. "I think I'd be really sad if I were in Ethan's position right now."

"Well, you never would be."

"Yeah, no, sure. You're right."

He lapsed into silence after that but I felt the need to keep talking.

"Things with Ethan are... I don't know. It's just—it's still a wound, you know? I just—I don't trust myself to talk to him right now. I just kept hanging onto him for so long, hoping he'd turn out to be the person I wanted him to be, that I'm not sure I trust myself not to fall back into that pattern if I talk to him again."

Tyler nodded. "I get that. Change is hard."

"I think I need an Ethan detox."

"Need an ankle bracelet?" Tyler asked with a grin. "To keep you from getting too close? Because I know a guy..."

"Yeah? You mind picking one up for me when you get back to LA?"

"Not at all," Tyler laughed. "I'll just swing by the county courthouse. It'll give me something to do in between getting rejected by casting directors and rebuffed by everyone I used to know."

"You sure it'll be that bad?"

Tyler shrugged. "I want to say it won't be, but you gotta prepare for the worst, don't you?"

"Why go, then?" The question was out of my mouth before I could stop it. "Couldn't you just stay in New York? Or am I being totally naive to think I don't have to uproot my whole life to do this acting thing?"

"No, not at all. Plenty of people are based in New York. It makes total sense if you have a life there. It's just... I haven't lived there since I was six. LA's all I really know. And what's keeping me in New York?"

Me.

Except it wasn't true. Tyler had never given any indication that he thought of me like that. And he never would. And yet, the thought of losing him, even though I'd never had him to begin with, tore me to shreds.

"Fair point," I said instead.

"Plus," Tyler said, "I think my dad has some leads on projects for me. He wasn't really clear on the phone but I think he has some ideas for what we can do next."

"We?"

Tyler shifted uncomfortably in the passenger seat. "I mean, I guess he's been talking to some people."

I sighed, but didn't say anything.

"What?" Tyler asked. "Come on, just say it. I know you want to."

I shot him a troubled look. "Look, I don't know the guy. It's not really my place..."

"But?"

"I just don't like the way he treats you."

"Well what am I supposed to do?" Tyler asked. "He's my father. I can't just... stop talking to him."

"Isn't that what he did to you?"

"That's different," Tyler said with a sigh.

"How?"

"I fucked up."

"So he cut you out of his life?" I said. "And now suddenly he wants you back, now that you're working again? I don't know, it just seems a little bit... dickish to me."

Tyler was quiet and I immediately regretted my words.

"Sorry," I said, shaking my head. "You're right. He's your dad. And I don't know what it's like."

"Eh, everyone's got father issues, don't they?" Tyler said with a rueful shake of his head. "I'm sure mine aren't any worse than yours." But as soon as the words were out, Tyler gasped and clapped his hand over his mouth. "Oh shit, Gray, I'm sorry. I didn't mean-"

"It's okay," I said, trying to smile. "In a weird way, I actually think I *don't* have father issues. I never knew the guy, anyway. Not even sure my mom knew who he was."

"I feel so stupid," Tyler said. "Just focusing on myself. I never even thought—"

"Tyler, you don't have to feel bad for not remembering something I never talk about."

"But I should still—"

"As far as I'm concerned, I'm better off this way," I said, working hard to keep my lip from twisting bitterly. "I'm not saying what my mom did was great. But she was messed up. If she hadn't disappeared, who's to say I wouldn't be worse off now? Maybe I'd never have gotten out of West Virginia."

"Do you ever—have you ever tried to find her?" Tyler asked, his voice small.

"No," I said, shrugging my shoulder helplessly. "What would I say? Hey Mom, thanks for abandoning me, I'm a porn-star now, aren't you proud?"

"You're more than that," Tyler said, looking almost angry. "You've always been more than that. And if you think that there's any reason why she shouldn't—why anyone shouldn't—I mean, dammit, Gray. I'm not going to let you think that little of yourself."

Tyler was glaring at me by the end of his speech and all I could do was stare at him. I'd never heard him talk like that before. I couldn't even begin to sort through all my feelings.

Heart-warmed, that he'd say that about me. Frustrated that he couldn't see reality. Angry at my mom, and then angry at myself for getting angry at her all over again when I'd tried so hard to put all of that away. She hadn't wanted me. So why the fuck was I going to think about her?

But Tyler didn't realize any of that. All he was trying to do was be kind.

"Uh, thanks."

It wasn't enough, but Tyler seemed to accept it for the time being and we drove for the next few minutes in silence. We were almost at the little motel that Dave and Andrew had booked for everyone when Tyler spoke again.

"You'll still talk to me, right?" he said suddenly, his hazel eyes glinting in the setting sun. "Once I move back to LA, I mean? We'll still talk, won't we?"

"Of course," I said, looking at him incredulously. "God, yes. You think I could do this acting thing without you? I'd fall on my face in a second. So if you think I'm not going to be harassing you all the time..."

"Good."

He nodded judiciously and I smiled at how serious he looked.

"You're kind of my best friend right now," Tyler continued after a minute. My eyes widened and Tyler laughed. "Don't look so shocked. I mean, granted, you're also kind of my *only* friend right now. But you still would be, even if I had others."

What to say to that? Calling Tyler my best friend—it wasn't even enough. Tyler was more than that, something much deeper. He'd come into my life so quickly and completely reshaped it. Best friend? That was too banal. After he left, there'd be a Tyler-shaped tear in the fabric of the world—and I didn't even want it to heal.

"Don't worry," Tyler said quickly. "I'm not going to suggest matching tattoos or anything."

"Dammit," I grinned. "I was really looking forward to that."

"I mean, we could, if you wanted. Get *Foresight* scrawled across our foreheads or something."

"That'll really help us both land roles," I snorted.

"Definitely."

"I was going to suggest ghosts, actually," I said with a smile.

"Oh shit, you're right," Tyler grinned. "A little ghost, right over our hearts or something."

"Perfect."

A ghost over my heart to remember Tyler by? I didn't need a tattoo for that. He'd already taken up residence there. And when he left, I knew I'd cling to whatever ghost he left behind.

~

"Cut!"

Tyler stepped away from me on the dock, smiling, but caught his shoe on a loose board. His arms windmilling, he started to fall backwards. I stepped forward and caught him, pulling him close again.

Tyler's arms gripped my shoulders as he breathed heavily, his eyes looking up at me in shock as the dock bounced in the water at the sudden movement.

"Come on, I know we're done filming now," I said with a smile, "but that's no reason to commit suicide by dockboard."

Tyler snorted and then looked over his shoulder. "You get that on camera, Vi? How about it, wanna end the movie with Dylan falling overboard and dying a tragic, watery death?"

"Yeah, sure," Violet said. "I'm sure no one will come to get us with torches and pitchforks if we change the ending and turn their favorite romance into a tragedy."

She took a step away from her camera and glanced around at the crew on the shore and on two other docks on either side of the one Tyler and I occupied in the rundown marina where we were filming.

"That's a wrap, guys," she said with a broad smile. "That's a wrap!"

Tyler grinned at me. "Holy shit. We did it."

"We did," I said, answering his grin with one of my own. "We really did."

It took us both a minute to realize we were still standing

there, clutching each other, but eventually Tyler's face reddened and he let go of me, clearing his throat.

"Shit," he said. "I'd forgotten how good this feels, knowing you've actually accomplished something."

"Pretty awesome."

We walked back down the dock together to the shore. I breathed in deeply. The air was scented with gasoline and motor oil and the setting sun kissed the cattails and lily pads gold where they clustered against the banks. Violet had waited all day to film the final scene of *Foresight* at this exact time.

She pulled the two of us in for hugs once we were back on dry land and I offered to help pack up some of the equipment and get it back to the motel.

Violet just shook her head and laughed. "No offense, Gray, but none of the crew would trust an actor with their equipment. Just go on to the wrap party. I'll meet you guys there."

The wrap party was at a restaurant in the middle of town, a five minute walk or so from the Seagull Inn, the rundown motel that Dave and Andrew had booked for all of us. It wasn't a very big operation, though, so we'd all had to double up and Tyler and I had ended up sharing.

"I need to go back to the motel and take a shower," I said to Tyler as we headed away from the river and in towards town. I was sweaty and gross from hauling fishing equipment around for the past hour while Violet filmed me for b-roll footage. "But wanna head over to the party after?"

Tyler made a face. "Honestly? Not really. I'm not really big on parties. Not anymore, anyway."

"Oh come on, it'll be fun. And people would miss you if you weren't there."

"Really?" Tyler said doubtfully.

"Yes, silly. In case you haven't noticed, people on this crew actually like you. They're gonna want to see you."

Tyler bit his lip as he looked up at me. "I haven't really been to a party like this since I'd been sober."

Oh. Of course.

"Okay, then what if I promise to glue myself to your side? Would that make it any better?"

Tyler laughed. "Is it really pathetic that I want to take you up on that?"

"Nah," I grinned. "Just flattering."

"Don't let it go to your head."

"Wait, so you're saying I shouldn't interpret it as a sign of your undying love for me?" I asked, grinning. I wondered, fleetingly, if that was going too far, but Tyler just laughed.

"Trust me, Gray, when I confess my undying love for you, you'll know."

Our room was at the back of the motel, looking out over a long, desolate stretch of road and trees. Somehow it even managed to *smell* faded. Not musty or moldy—it just smelled the way an old photo album looked. The wallpaper showed bouquets of dusty pink roses on a yellow background, the bedspreads were covered in an ivy pattern, and there were two large paintings of mallard ducks above the beds.

As soon as we got inside, Tyler flopped down onto his bed and folded his hands behind his head.

"Oh my God, what are you doing?" I asked, my tone scandalized.

Tyler looked at me in confusion. "What?"

"You have no idea what could be on those bedspreads. God, at least fold it down and lie on the blanket."

"Says the man who did porn for a living."

"That just means I know what I'm talking about," I pointed out.

"You're really that worried about germs? We slept here last night, don't you think we'd have picked up anything communicable by now?"

"We didn't sleep on top of the bedspreads," I objected. "We're not barbarians. Or at least *I'm* not."

"Go shower and stop judging me," Tyler said with a laugh.

"Fine, but when you end up with a flesh-eating virus on your skin, don't come crying to me." I gave him a final shudder before moving into the bathroom.

I turned the shower on as hot as it could go and stripped as I waited for it to heat up. I looked at myself in the mirror while I tested the water temperature with my hand.

I wasn't bad looking. I still worked out. But I wasn't the perfect 23 year old I'd once been. There were even a few touches of gray coming in at my temples. And my face, which I'd always thought looked so rough-hewn, almost primitive, compared to Ethan's refined features, was starting to look a little weathered. I had crinkles at my eyes when I smiled now.

Ethan had started getting botox when he was 25. Maybe I'd been naive to think that was crazy. Would anyone really want to cast me in anything, the way I looked now? With my lack of experience—or maybe too much experience, depending on how you looked at it. Who would want someone with my past?

I couldn't help feeling foolish, couldn't help envisioning a string of no's, doors slamming in my face. Who was I, to think I could make a career in acting happen at this point in my life? Hadn't I learned yet that life didn't care what I wanted? That life wanted to put me back in my place, and keep me there?

Shaking my head, I stepped into the shower and let the scalding water run down my skin.

It wasn't til I got out that I realized my mistake. I'd forgotten to bring a change of clothes into the bathroom. Which meant I was going to have to go out there in my towel. And you'd think I wouldn't care about that—it wasn't as if Tyler hadn't seen me naked, more than naked—but somehow this felt intimate. Besides, I didn't want Tyler to think I was trying to—

What? asked the voice in the back of my head. *What are you afraid of? That Tyler will think you're trying to come onto him? Please. The thought would never cross his mind. He's made it completely clear that you're friends and nothing more.*

Rolling my eyes, I wrapped a towel around my waist and stepped out into the main room. It was shadowy now, the night sky outside the window black and starry. Tyler had turned on the TV and a lamp between the two beds, but the volume was low and everything felt still and hushed.

"Jesus," Tyler said, glancing over at me. "Did a volcano erupt in there?"

I smiled sheepishly at the steam rolling through the open door. "Yeah, sorry. It might be a little humid for a bit."

I walked over to my duffel and grabbed a pair of boxer-briefs, pulling them on quickly underneath my towel. Feeling slightly less creepy, I turned around and began dressing. Tyler couldn't think I was coming onto him if I wasn't looking at him, right?

"Sorry," I said as I dressed. "I'll only be a few more minutes."

"No worries. Trust me, I'm not exactly in a hurry."

"What are you watching?" I asked as I pulled on a pair of jeans.

"*Chaos Theory*."

"Never heard of it."

"You know, for someone who wants to be an actor, there's a lot of stuff you've never heard of," Tyler said, giving me a questioning look.

I flushed. "I know. I⁻guess—it's kind of sad, but after I decided I wasn't going to try anymore... it was just easier not to pay attention to any of that stuff, you know? To kind of turn my back on it." I shrugged and then smiled. "Besides, I've got you now, so it all worked out. What's this show about?"

Tyler laughed. "It's an anthology series set around a university science department. Each episode has a different writer and director. This one's written by Robin McGee, who's actually one of my favorite writers working right now. Reminds me a bit of Danny's style, actually."

I smiled as I popped my head out through my t-shirt. "You should tell them!"

"Right," Tyler said. "I'm sure that wouldn't come off condescending at all, me offering my 'expert' opinion."

"You sell yourself far too short."

"Maybe," Tyler said, flicking the TV off and looking over at me. "Dude, why even wear a shirt if you're gonna look like that?"

I frowned, looking down. "What do you mean? It's maybe not the nicest, but I didn't think we had to look fancy tonight."

"Not that, dummy," Tyler said. "I meant that it looks painted on." He shook his head. "Come on, let's go get this torture started."

"See, now you've gone and made me all self-conscious," I said as we left the hotel room.

"Mission accomplished, then. Now we'll both go into this party feeling emotionally fragile."

The night was warm as we walked through the motel parking lot and out onto the road into town. Tyler walked so close to me that his arm kept bumping into mine, but I refused to move. I didn't want to think about the fact that as of tomorrow, this was all going to end.

Tyler just made me feel good, I realized. He was like

sunlight breaking through the clouds, the kind that not only made you happy, but shocked you by showing you how unhappy you'd been until that moment. And now I had to let him go.

Tyler, for his part, kept up a steady stream of observations about the town of Whitcomb as we walked through it, suggesting which houses might be haunted, what he thought everyone had died of, and which places probably had the best ghosts. Until a moth fluttered down the sidewalk and I dodged to get out of its way.

"I don't like them," I said, ready to be teased. "And I'll fight anyone who tries to tell me they're harmless. They're demonic hellspawn sent here to torment me."

"Ooh, this place is definitely full of the ghosts of dead truckers," Tyler said a moment later as we passed by a divey looking bar with neon signs in the window.

"Yeah?"

"Yeah, but don't worry, you could handle them." He grinned at me slyly. "Can't take moths, but you could take dead trucker ghosts for sure."

"Shut up," I said, and my arm had already started moving of its own accord, trying to go around Tyler and pull him to me, before I realized what I was doing. I turned the movement into an awkward shoulder punch at the last minute.

We ran into Dave and Andrew outside the restaurant where the wrap party was taking place—already in full swing, if the noise coming out from inside was any indication.

"Hey, it's our illustrious stars!" Dave said, his face lighting up. "The men of the hour!"

"Ready to party?" Andrew asked, grinning at us lasciviously.

Tyler glanced at me nervously and I thought about squeezing his hand, but just then my phone rang. I pulled it out of my pocket, praying for it not to be Ethan. But it was Micah instead.

Tyler glanced down at my phone screen and then up at my face. "Answer it. I can just go in with them."

"You sure?" My brow furrowed. "I don't mean to—it's just, Micah knows I'm working today, so he wouldn't call unless—"

"I suppose I can survive," Tyler said, giving an exaggerated sigh. "I'll hold this against you for years and years, of course, but I'll survive somehow."

"That's the spirit." I grinned at him. "I promise it'll just be a few minutes and then I'll come in and find you."

I waved the three of them off as they walked towards the entrance, then swiped my phone on, walking a few yards back down the street the way we'd come to get away from the noise.

"Hey, Micah, what's up? Everything okay at Maggie's?"

"Oh," Micah said sounding surprised. "Oh, yeah, no, sorry. Everything's fine with the bar. I didn't mean to scare you. I just…"

He stopped talking, and I waited for him to continue.

"Micah?" I said after a minute, confused by the silence. "Are you still there?"

"What? Oh. Yeah." Micah paused again. "Ugh, I'm trying to figure out the best way to say this."

"Oh God, what's wrong?" A rush of images cascaded through my mind. Micah injured. Micah quitting. A meteor hitting Manhattan.

"No, no, nothing's wrong," Micah said quickly. "God, I'm making a mess of this, sorry. I just—I called you because I thought you'd want to know, and now I'm wondering if this was a bad idea. Maybe we should just hang up and talk tomorrow."

"Jesus, Micah, now you have to tell me." I ran a hand through my hair as I continued walking down the street. Micah'd made me nervous and I felt like I needed to keep moving.

"Ugh, okay. Fine. So, basically, this is going to sound weird, I think, but, um, have you talked to Ethan recently?"

"What?" I blinked. "No. I haven't. He's been calling, but I'm just ignoring him. Why?"

Micah sighed. "I was afraid of that."

"Is me not talking to him *not* a good thing?" I asked, confused. "God, I was taking your advice for once, I'd think you'd be happy."

"No, I know, I know," Micah said. I could almost hear him wince. "It's just—ugh, okay, I wouldn't even mention this if I thought it were something you could avoid entirely, but I think you're going to find out eventually because Ethan came into the bar tonight looking for you and he said he'd been trying to get in touch and I hate to be the one to tell you this, but I figured if I didn't tell you, eventually he'd catch up with you and then you'd be blindsided and I figured you'd rather hear it from me so—"

"Micah, Jesus, spit it out."

"Ethan's engaged."

"What?"

"To Christie. He, uh, he told me that was why he was looking for you."

"He *what*?" I said again, trying to process what I was hearing.

"Yeah," Micah said heavily. "He said he'd been trying to talk to you for weeks now but—I don't know, I told him you were out of town and working and probably didn't want to hear from him but, well, yeah. I just... thought you'd want to know."

I tried to turn it all over in my mind. Ethan was engaged. Ethan was *engaged*. *Ethan* was engaged.

To someone who wasn't me.

"Gray?" Micah said after a minute. "Gray, are you still there? Are you—are you okay?"

No. No, I am not okay at all. In fact, I'm having a fucking out of body experience right now and I'm not even entirely sure I'm still breathing.

I forced myself to exhale, then inhale deeply, and keep walking. I needed to move, needed some kind of forward motion to distract myself.

"I'm... here," I said eventually.

"Gray, I'm so sorry," Micah said. "I know this can't feel good. And I'm fucking infuriated at him and how he's treated you. I just—I thought you'd want to know?"

"Thanks, Micah," I forced myself to say. God, my voice sounded weird. Stilted. Like I'd lost the ability to speak from my chest.

"Is there anything—anything I can do?" Micah asked. "You know, Caro's husband Chris is a firefighter and he's fucking ripped. Want me to ask him to beat Ethan up for you?"

I let out a shaky laugh, then stopped, because it sounded way too close to a sob. "No," I said, "no, I just need to— thanks, Micah. I need to go."

I hung up. I knew it was rude, but I also knew Micah would forgive me. Micah knew—Micah understood. As much as anyone outside of my own head and heart could understand, anyway.

Jesus Christ, I wanted to punch something. To lash out. It was pathetic that I cared so much, that I wanted to cry and scream and tear something apart. Why the fuck did Ethan still have this much hold over me when he clearly didn't give a shit about me?

God, and this whole time, I'd been assuming Ethan was calling me to apologize, that he might even throw himself at me and ask for forgiveness, to get back together. What a fucking idiot. Ethan was never going to do that because Ethan had never cared about being with me in the first place.

Ethan, the man I'd been with for years, the man I'd given up so much for, had sworn to me that he never wanted to get married. To anyone.

And now, four months after telling me that, he was engaged. He didn't have a problem with marriage at all. He just didn't want to be with me.

And after all, why should he? No one had ever wanted me. Ethan didn't love me, my mother hadn't loved me, my foster families had actively hated me at times. Even Maggie—Maggie who told me she loved me every day—had left me. It wasn't her fault, but the end result was the same.

Something about me drove people away—and I ended up alone.

I turned back towards the restaurant and the wrap party, blocks away now, and felt a stab of pain at the thought of going back there. How could I be there and pretend to be happy? How could I pretend I hadn't just been stabbed in the gut?

And fuck, Tyler was in there, and Tyler would know something was wrong. But the last thing I wanted right now was Tyler seeing me like this. Seeing me for the weak, pathetic, broken man I really was.

Because if Tyler saw that, what if he also saw what everyone else did? The thing about me that made everyone want to leave? Tyler was already leaving me—but at least I could pretend that was because of circumstance. That some part of him still cared about me. That someday, in some world, things might be different, and the two of us could be together.

I couldn't look him in the eyes if he saw me like this. I couldn't bear the disgust I knew would be there.

I turned back around. The bar we'd passed, with its buzzing neon lights, called out from the other end of the block. I didn't want to be there, but I didn't want to be anywhere else. I didn't want to go to the party, I didn't want to go back to the motel and have Tyler find me there later.

I didn't want to *be* anywhere right now, but a shitty bar with shitty beer that I was sure Tyler wouldn't enter seemed as good a place as any to disappear.

12

TYLER

I walked into the restaurant with Dave and Andrew, smiling and trying to push down all the fears swirling around inside me. I'd never liked these kinds of events, not even when I was a kid. But no one knew that about me, and I didn't intend for them to find out.

Large groups, crowds of people I didn't really know, or at least didn't know well, always made me uncomfortable. I felt like I had to be *'on'* the whole time, always performing, even though there were no cameras rolling.

The problem wasn't exactly that I didn't know who *they* were—it was that the more people there were in a room, the less I felt like I knew who *I* was.

When I was about six of seven—during my first year in Hollywood—my dad had sat me down and explained to me that I was never really off the clock. You never knew who was in the same room as you, who you might want to impress.

Jobs, fortunes, reputations, careers—all of that came from

nights, from parties like this, and I had to be on, be groomed, be perfect. But being everything to all people left no room at all to be myself. Nights like this, it was like I could barely breathe.

It had gotten easier, in a way, once I'd started getting high. It had made these kinds of nights more bearable, taken the edge off. Except that only worked in the short run, and made the prospect of your next night like this even worse. It had gotten to the point where I'd felt like the walls were closing in on me if I had to go to a function like this, sober.

What was it like, I wondered, to be someone who *didn't* feel anxious at this kind of a party, who didn't wish for that calming wash of euphoria that came from xanax or the giddy freight train of a high that cocaine brought? Or even the unsteady, shaky fizz that came from drinking—never my drug of choice, too unreliable, but it would do in a pinch?

God, the amount I was panicking now was a testament to how much of a wreck I'd been back then, if you thought about it. Not only because I was someone who could buy a ton of cocaine and then forget about it, lie to himself and make believe it wasn't his, but because I hadn't even been able to get through a simple business function sober.

But now, of course, I couldn't use any of that. So here I was, at my first industry party as an adult, sober and fucking terrified. I'd tried to joke about it with Gray, but God, what I wouldn't have given for his solid, steady presence at my side right now.

The restaurant was hot and crowded, conversation and clinking glasses and pulsing music swirling together like a cocktail, spiked with the kind of Dionysian glee that comes from a group of people letting loose after a month of non-stop work. There was still tons to do in post-production, of course, but most of the crew wouldn't be involved in that, and they seemed determined to blow off as much steam as possible.

Dave and Andrew immediately moved towards the bar but I held myself back. Fuck, except now I was alone. Arguably the most famous person in the room and here I was, standing awkwardly in a crowd of people with no one to talk to.

I glanced over my shoulder towards the door as I heard it swing open, hoping it would be Gray, but it wasn't. Dammit. How long was that phone call going to take?

I'd just have to suck it up until Gray got back. I could do that, right? Couldn't I?

It's time to grow the fuck up, I told myself, trying to use the voice my dad used when he was particularly disgusted with me. *Grow up, Tyler, grow some balls, and fucking smile.*

I spread a grin across my face and fixed it in place, heading deeper into the party.

An hour later, I'd made the rounds and talked to everyone at least once. I'd turned down seven different drinks, at least four invitations to join people in a round of shots, and two, possibly three come-on's from already drunk volunteers from the crew. The last one had been a little hard to read, but the first two guys had just straight up asked me if I wanted to go back to their rooms with them.

I'd smiled and blushed. Told them I was flattered but demurred. And sent a series of increasingly frantic texts to Gray, who wasn't responding. Violet wasn't here yet either, so I kept telling myself Gray had gotten pulled into a conversation with her somewhere. But no matter how many times I stuck my head out the door and checked for either of them, I came up empty.

Finally, I saw Danny standing in a corner, observing the room.

"Hey," I said, flashing them a relieved smile as I approached. "Mind if I join you and your patch of wall?"

"Not at all," Danny said, smiling back.

I had the feeling that Danny might have been comfortable standing there in silence for another 45 minutes, but eventually I cracked.

"I can't believe it's over," I said, mostly just to say something, gesturing at everyone celebrating around us.

"Tell me about it," Danny said, shaking their head. "I still can't believe people wanted to make a movie of my stupid book."

I looked at them in confusion. "Your book is fucking amazing, that's why."

"Thanks, man," Danny said. "That's really nice of you."

Somewhat concerned by Danny's lack of affect, I pressed on. "Seriously, though. It is. God, if the rest of your books are anything like that, you should seriously consider shopping them around."

"Really?" Danny blinked.

"Absolutely," I said, not even bothering to hide the enthusiasm in my voice. "Seriously, a lot of production companies will option books before anyone's turned them into a screenplay and with the way you write—I mean, studios might want to turn the heat level down *just* a smidge, but—"

Danny laughed. "Yeah, I could see that being an issue. Honestly, it's not all that important to me. We just kept the sex in this one because of the funding angle."

We lapsed back into silence and after a minute, Danny shot me an amused smile. "You don't have to babysit me, by the way. I'm not going to cry if I'm on my own."

"Oh, I mean—I'll go if you don't want the company. But I—I've never been much for parties. Even ones where all the people in the room haven't seen my orgasm face." I snorted. "So it's kind of nice to have an excuse to just stand to the side and observe, you know?"

"Yes," Danny said, their voice emphatic. "God, yes. Sometimes I think I'd rather people watch my whole life than ever actually have to talk to anyone."

"Same," I laughed. "Some of the time anyway."

My gaze drifted out over the crowd and though my eyes kept straying over towards the door, my obsessive watching wasn't making Gray magically appear. Go figure.

"I used to play a game, sometimes," I said. "When I was younger, as a way to get through parties. I'd pick different people in the room and try to mimic their mannerisms, their stance, the way they talked, and try to figure out what they were thinking and feeling."

"Right on. How'd that work out for you?"

"Pretty good. Sometimes I'd even end up talking to them and just mimic every gesture, every move they made, just to see if they'd notice." I shook my head. "They never did."

Most people, I'd realized, were pretty damn self-absorbed. Myself included. Maybe it had something to do with being in LA.

And I was voluntarily moving back there. What the hell was wrong with me? Only, what else was I supposed to do? I wanted to go back there—or, at least, I was doing it for a good reason. I'd do what I had to do to get my life back on track.

The door from the outside swung open again, but this time it was Violet coming in. A cheer went up and I heard Dave's voice rise over the din, yelling something about shots. I sighed.

"Looking for someone?" Danny asked.

"What?" I'd almost forgotten they were there.

"You keep watching the door," Danny pointed out.

I flushed. I hadn't realized how completely obvious I'd been. Though I had the impression that of all the people in this room, Danny was the last one in the world who'd care or judge me.

"Gray," I confessed after a moment. "He got a phone call right before we got here and said he'd just be a few minutes. I know it's stupid, but I'm starting to worry that something's wrong. He's not answering my texts," I finished lamely. Tolerant or not, I'd probably just managed to convince Danny I was a psycho or stalker or something.

"It's not stupid," Danny said. "You should go look for him."

"Is that weird? Am I being crazy?"

"Last time I checked, I think you're allowed to look for the guy you're dating. Having someone to hang out with at awkward parties is like, the main reason to date anyone in the first place."

"Oh, we're not—" I stammered, "we're not dating. Just, uh, just friends."

"Oh, sorry. My bad."

"No, it's fine," I said quickly, feeling my face redden. Again. Because apparently all I did these days was blush.

It's not like I hadn't thought about it, what Danny was suggesting. I mean, duh. Gray was... pretty much perfect. But even assuming a hypothetical situation in which Gray was interested in someone as young and inexperienced and spoiled and naive as I was, I couldn't—I didn't—I wasn't *ready* for that.

Gray deserved someone who was all in. Someone amazing, who saw how great he was. I pushed away the weird feeling of jealousy that rose inside my chest as I considered this faceless, nameless guy I'd conjured up in my mind. The guy Gray would end up with. The guy who'd be lucky enough to get him.

"Seriously, go find him," Danny said after a moment. "I'll do my best to hold up the wall without you."

I looked at them, biting my lip. "Are you sure—"

"Tyler. Go."

So I went.

It felt good to step out into the night air after the almost claustrophobic heat and noise of the party. The lights in the parking lot threw circles of illumination onto the tops of parked cars and left everything else in shadow. I stepped down to the sidewalk and turned my head left and right.

No Gray. Not that I'd really expected to see him just standing out here waiting for me. But where the hell was I supposed to look for him? I sighed and turned left, heading back towards the motel. If he wasn't there, I'd be shit out of luck.

If I could forget why I was doing it, it was actually sort of pleasant, walking through this strange, tiny town alone. It made me feel small, and almost like a different person. It was nice to imagine for a moment that I wasn't myself, but maybe was someone who lived here, walking home from a dinner party to—whom? A family? A boyfriend?

Gray. I'd be coming home to him.

And for a second, I lost myself in that dream. The idea that in some world, I wasn't going back to a seedy motel but to an apartment we shared, or a little house with a wide porch. I'd have some other job—not on screen anymore, that was for sure. All my fears and uncertainties gone. I'd just get to exist, and no one would care about me or give a shit about my private life. I'd just be able to be. And be happy.

A car came down the street, rushing towards me and ripping me out of my daydream. Instinctively, I stepped into the recessed doorway of the building I was passing and turned my face away until the car had passed. It was a habit I'd picked up over the years, hiding from attention, and even though I doubted the driver was looking, I'd made the move without thought.

After the car was gone, its tail lights glittering like rubies as it sped down the street, I looked up and realized the doorway I was standing in belonged to the dive bar we'd passed on our walk to the party. I peered through the glass pane on the door out of curiosity, ready to tell Gray I'd seen trucker ghosts.

I didn't expect to see Gray sitting there himself.

An empty shot glass lay on its side in front of him at the bar as he spun a beer bottle around on the smooth surface. Anger coursed through me. Gray was at a bar?

He'd abandoned me to—what, drink at a dive bar? He clearly wasn't on the phone anymore, and he just as clearly wasn't doing anything. So why the fuck had he never come in? Why hadn't he even texted me back?

Did he just forget about me? Did I really mean so little to him?

Mad and not caring who knew it, I threw the door open and walked straight up to Gray, who didn't even look up until I was right next to him and then blinked in surprise when he saw me.

"Tyler," he said, and his voice was full of pain and regret.

"Gray." My tone had bite, but I was already dialing it back, my anger ebbing as I took in the state Gray was in.

It wasn't just his voice that sounded remorseful, hurt. His

shoulders slumped defeatedly, his mouth had settled into a grimace of pain and his eyes—

I'd never seen eyes that looked so lost. And it felt profoundly wrong to see them on Gray. My Gray, who was solid and dependable and always *there*, whenever I needed him, as unrelenting as a mountain, as constant and secure as the earth itself. Gray looked uncertain, unsteady. What could possibly have knocked him so far off his axis?

"I'm sorry," Gray said softly. "I didn't mean to—I should have—I know I left and told you I'd come—"

"Gray, what happened?" I asked, trying to make my voice gentle. "What's wrong?"

"Nothing," Gray said. "Nothing."

"Well that's obviously not true."

Impulsively, I put my hand on Gray's shoulder. It was fine, I reasoned, after my hand was already there. Gray needed a friend right now, clearly. That was all I was doing.

"Come on," I said. "Tell me what happened."

The bartender, a pretty woman with spiky black hair and a full sleeve of tattoos came over to our end of the bar.

"Among other things," she said, leaning her arms against the bar, "four shots and two beers happened. You're his friend?"

"Yeah," I said, bracing for impact.

And there it was—her face tilted to the side, her brow furrowed, and she squinted at me. Then her eyes lit up in recognition.

I steeled myself for whatever came next. It didn't matter if it was complimentary or not—I would have given anything to just not have her say anything. All I really wanted to do right now was figure out what the fuck was going on with Gray, who was staring glumly at the circles of condensation that his beer bottle had left on the surface of the bar.

The bartender smiled. "I'm glad you're here. I think he could use a friend to help him get home tonight."

My eyes widened. She knew who I was, I could tell. But she wasn't going to say anything. I could have hugged her—if I hadn't been concerned that Gray was about to slump over so far that he'd slide off his barstool.

"How much is it?" I asked, digging for my wallet.

I owed Gray that much, at least. How many times had he paid for me and never asked for anything in return? Besides, I wasn't quite as poor as I used to be, anyway.

"Don't worry about it," the bartender said with a warm smile.

"No, come on." I pulled my wallet out. "You've gotta—"

"Just make sure he gets home safe," she said. "He didn't say much, but he sure looks like he got the shit kicked out of him."

Feeling a warm rush of gratitude, I thanked the bartender and got Gray on his feet, guiding him towards the door. He lurched through it and stumbled out onto the other side.

"Jesus," I said, "come here."

I pulled Gray's left arm around my shoulder and put my

right arm around his waist to steady him. "Come on, let's get back to the motel."

"I'm sorry," Gray mumbled. "I'm so sorry, I didn't mean to—" The S's of his words slurred together like raindrops on a window pane.

"Shh. Don't worry about that now. Let's just get home."

Home.

The word twisted in my mind. To think that I'd just been having some fucked up fantasy about Gray *being* my home, when Gray was sitting in that bar, apparently ready to drown himself in cheap beer and whiskey over a problem I didn't understand.

What had *happened*? Something with the movie? Something with Micah? I couldn't begin to guess, and it made me so sad to think that maybe, I didn't actually know Gray at all.

Not now, I yelled at the sulky part of myself. *Deal with that later. For now, just try to get back to the motel in one piece.*

The walk back seemed longer, somehow, and I had to keep batting away images of the two of us on our walk to the bar, how good a mood I'd been in, how I'd kept glancing at Gray and wondering if any passersby would think we were just friends, or might think, maybe, the two of us were together, that someone as strong and handsome and perfect as Gray would be with me.

Gray's weight was heavy on my shoulders and he kept tripping over his own feet. I'd never seen Gray like this before. I realized, suddenly, that while I'd seen Gray drink, I'd never even seen him tipsy, let alone drunk. And this felt a level past drunk, even. This was the deliberate stupor of someone drinking to forget things.

I recognized it. I'd been there myself, in the past, when I'd run out of drugs, and self-esteem, and used whatever I had on hand to forget how much I hated myself.

Eventually, we made it back to the motel and I dug the key to the room out of Gray's pocket—no fancy key cards at this establishment—and unlocked the door. I turned the light switch on as soon as we stepped inside to prevent Gray from stumbling even more.

It was a testament to Gray's state that he made a beeline for his bed and collapsed down onto it, right on top of the bedspread he'd been so grossed out by earlier in the night.

"No, no," I said, shutting the door behind us and locking it before following Gray to the bed. "No, you've gotta get up. You'll regret that in the morning."

"Already... regret... this," Gray said slowly, his words slushy.

"I know," I said, pulling on Gray's arms. "But come on, at least this is a regret you can avoid."

Jesus, how could the man possibly weigh this much? I'd felt Gray's weight on me before, his body pressing down against mine, and it had felt nothing like this. Had he been taking care of me even then, making sure not to crush me, or had his body suddenly metamorphosed into lead?

I hauled Gray up into a sitting position and pulled the bedspread, the blanket, and the sheet back, sliding them down to where Gray was sitting.

"Can you take off your shoes?" I asked, looking at him doubtfully.

"Fuck," Gray said heavily, leaning over. "Yes. Fuck."

"Okay, I'm gonna go get you some water. And then maybe you can tell me what happened, yeah?"

I walked into the bathroom and grabbed an unused styrofoam cup, pulled it out of its plastic wrapping and filled it with water from the tap. When I came back out, Gray was still struggling with the laces on his shoes. By the time I got to the nightstand, he'd given up and kicked them off still tied.

"I'm sorry," he said again, his voice plaintive and broken as he looked up. He took the cup of water but didn't drink. "I didn't want you to see—you shouldn't have to deal with me —with this."

He set the cup down on the nightstand and leaned forward, cradling his head in his hands.

"Gray, it's okay."

It was okay. Somewhere along the walk to the motel, my anger at being left at the party had dissipated, leaving behind it just a heavy tiredness. Not knowing what else to do, I knelt on the carpet in front of him, put my hands on Gray's arms.

"It's okay, I don't mind. Can you just tell me what happened, so I can know how to help?"

"You can't help," Gray said. It was muted, the syllables crushed up against his hands, and it took me a second to process the words. "It's not—it's just how I am. It's me. I'm the fucking problem. Please, just—"

He stopped and I bit my lip. I had no idea what to do. It wasn't just that I'd never seen Gray like this before—I wasn't used to being a caretaker. I was the one who was supposed to be a mess. I didn't know how to be the stable one.

God, I'd been so selfish. The whole time I'd known Gray, I'd only ever thought about what *I* needed—what I needed from life and what I needed from him. I'd never thought about what he might need.

I tried to think of what I'd want in this situation, my hands still gripping Gray's arms, and I realized Gray's skin was hot.

"I'm gonna go get a washcloth," I said. "A cool one that you can put on your face, okay?" I stood, then grabbed the cup and pressed it back into Gray's hands. "Please, try and drink some water. It'll help."

Gray was still looking at the cup like he'd never seen such a contraption before as I stepped back into the bathroom.

I wet a washcloth with determination, and frustration. Whatever the hell had made Gray feel this way, I was angry at it. Or them. Because it was clear that Gray wasn't just lost. He was despondent. And it hurt to see him hurting.

I squeezed the washcloth out with more force than strictly necessary, stepped back out of the bathroom and then stopped. Gray was no longer sitting on the bed where I'd left him—he was stretched out on it, lying on his back. And, from what I could see, fast asleep.

I sighed and tried not to feel frustrated that I still didn't really know what had happened. I set the washcloth down next to the still-mostly-full cup of water, then reached over to turn Gray onto his side. He moved easily enough, but he didn't wake up.

"I'm sorry," I said, though I didn't know what I was apologizing for. For not being able to crack this code and make Gray feel better? For not being able to stop whatever had happened in the first place?

You're not the problem, Gray. No matter what happened to make you think that, it's not true. You are many things—kind, and funny, and smart and wise and generous and sweet and caring—so many things. But you could never be the problem.

Realizing I'd done as much as I could tonight, I sat down on the bed across from Gray. I was so tired. The high of wrapping the movie had burned off now, leaving behind only the aftertaste of joy and a brutal exhaustion. It took me two minutes to pull off my jeans and shoes, to brush my teeth, and to turn off the lights.

I was asleep as soon as my head hit the pillow.

I woke up desperately thirsty an hour later, chugged two glasses of water, and tried to go back to sleep. An hour after that, I woke up sweating. I stripped off my t-shirt and tried to sleep again. Another hour later and I woke up again, this time for no good reason other than that my body had apparently decided to wake up.

Gray was still sleeping soundly in the other bed. I could hear the sounds of his deep breathing. I tossed and turned for a while but no—apparently my brain had decided that after a month of getting only five or six hours of sleep a night, it had no sleep deficit to catch up on and no interest in being asleep right now.

I sat up angrily and crossed my arms. What the fuck was I supposed to do? I didn't want to turn on a light and wake Gray, who was already gonna feel pretty shitty when the morning came. With a quiet but dramatic sigh, I threw the covers back and got out of bed, grabbing my phone off of its charger.

There were no streetlights outside so I decided it was safe to pull the curtains back. I dragged a blocky chair from the built in desk against the wall over to the window, then sat down and stared at the inky blackness.

After a few minutes, my eyes began to adjust. I could see the close shapes of the trees and bushes between our room and the parking lot and, beyond them, the fuzzier shapes of the cattails and reeds in the marshy patch of land between the motel and the roadway. I could just make out the flat strip of smooth gray that must have been the road, but everything else was just a blur of shadow.

Except for the stars overhead. They were shockingly bright, even from the inside of a building, through glass. I wished I knew anything about constellations. To me, they just looked like pinpricks of light, scattered across the sky like some cosmic jeweler had tossed diamonds down onto a swath of velvet.

A car drove by on the road in front of me and the headlights stabbed into my eyes, but as soon as it was past, I felt wistful. Where was it going, I wondered? I glanced down at my phone and realized it was 2:00 a.m. Who would be driving now? What could they be doing that had them out at night?

I wondered what it would feel like to be that person, in that car. Where I would go at this hour. It might be kind of nice, being that anonymous, that insignificant. That small, in the scope of the world at night.

I could drive all the way out to LA. Except the more I thought about it, the sadder I got. Not the drive, but the fact that when I got there, I'd be alone.

On a whim, I unlocked my phone and texted Luke.

TYLER: *You ever wonder if everything you're doing in life is a fucking horrible mistake?*

To my surprise, an instant later, Luke texted back.

LUKE: *Welcome to the club, bro*

LUKE: *It's called being an adult and it sucks*

I frowned. What the hell was Luke doing awake?

TYLER: *Really?*

TYLER: *Because you always seem like you have everything worked out*

LUKE: *I'm really good at pretending. Trust me, I have no idea what I'm doing*

Well now this was just weird. It wasn't just a question of why Luke was awake, but why Luke sounded downright depressed. Usually Luke wore being positive and optimistic like a suit of armor.

TYLER: Who are you and what have you done with my normally obnoxiously upbeat brother?

TYLER: Also what the hell are you doing up?

LUKE: I'm drunk

Jesus, was everyone drunk tonight except for me?

LUKE: And I'm looking at my high school yearbook

LUKE: Because, again, I suck at being an adult and really have no idea what I've been doing with my life

I wrinkled my nose. I didn't know what to say. Luke never talked about emotional stuff. I hadn't actually been convinced Luke even really *had* emotions before tonight.

TYLER: Do you... want to talk about it?

Luke's reply was immediate.

LUKE: God no

LUKE: Definitely not

LUKE: Fuck, is it really 2 in the morning? I should go to bed

I shook my head.

TYLER: Night Luke

I set my phone down and stared out the window again. I felt grumpy, all of a sudden, like I'd been shafted in some kind of way. And then I realized why.

Gray, and to a lesser extent, Luke, were the two people I relied on to know what to do in any situation. To *tell* me what to do, if needed. And suddenly, here I was, sitting in the world's most random motel, staring out into the darkness, wondering if I was making the right choices, and I couldn't rely on anyone to tell me what to do, or even to just listen to what I said and make me feel better about my decisions.

And before I knew it, I was spiraling. What the fuck *was* I doing with my life, anyway? For the past month, I'd just been focusing on *Foresight*, telling myself I'd worry about what came after, after. But I think that secretly, I'd been holding onto this hope that doing *Foresight* would somehow make all those lingering questions disappear. That somehow, by the time the movie had wrapped, all my problems—my sexuality, my career, this shit with my dad—would make sense and I'd know what to do.

Instead, all I felt was more confused.

All I knew in life was acting. That was it. It was the only thing I'd ever trained to do, the only thing I was remotely qualified for.

My education was a joke and I'd completely ruined my reputation. I'd spent years high out of my mind and gotten arrested with half a kilo of cocaine in my car—drugs I couldn't even remember buying.

I'd fucked up so badly and I'd been so desperate to get my life back, but now that I was finally on the brink of doing so, of moving back to LA, I hated the thought of it. Going back there, being back in the public eye? It made my stomach hurt.

And then, of course, then I'd gone and done a fucking porno because I was such a fucking genius, somehow thinking that would make things better. I knew it would be a great movie, but let's not kid ourselves—it was still porn.

All it had done was make my life more complicated and honestly, *duh*, who the hell except for me hadn't seen that coming? Of course people had opinions about me doing it. Of course people wanted me to come out. Of course everyone still wanted a piece of me. I was putting myself out there for consumption, wasn't I?

The only person who'd ever made me feel like this wasn't all completely crazy, like maybe I hadn't completely fucked up my life, was Gray. And now I wasn't even going to see him anymore. How the hell was I supposed to manage now?

As if thinking about Gray had stirred something inside him, I heard Gray turn over and when I glanced over my shoulder, he was pushing himself up into a sitting position.

"Tyler?" Gray's voice was rough with sleep. "What are you doing?"

"Nothing," I said, staring at him. "How are you feeling?"

Gray ran a hand over his forehead. "Better than I should be, probably. I didn't keep you up by snoring or anything, did I?"

"No, not at all. I slept for a while, but then my body decided to wake up and refused to go back to sleep."

"So you're just... staring out the window?" Gray said, sounding confused.

"Thinking." I shrugged, hugging my knees to my chest in the chair.

"What about?" Gray asked, pushing himself further upright.

How messed up it is that I'm moving to LA and I'm not sure when I'm going to see you again? How I can't even imagine not *seeing you every day after this? How it makes me hurt, in this physical, chest-cracking-open kind of way, to think that this is ending.*

"Nothing interesting." I laughed lightly. "It's okay, you don't have to pretend to care. Go back to sleep."

Gray shrugged. "I actually feel weirdly awake right now." He smiled. "Talk to me. Bore me back to sleep."

I knew what I wanted to say—to ask, really—but I wasn't sure Gray would answer if I did. So instead I looked out the window. Another car, only the second one since I'd been awake, passed by that lonely stretch of road outside.

"Where do you think people are even driving at this time of night?" I asked absently.

"That's what you've been thinking about?"

"Sorta, yeah."

Gray paused. "I don't know."

"Sometimes I wish I could just get in one of those cars and disappear."

"Really?"

"God, yes. I used to fantasize about that all the time when I was younger. Just being able to drive off somewhere and —*poof!* Old life gone, and I could just slip into some new one."

"Where would *you* go, then?" Gray asked.

I thought about it, then smiled. "Maybe back to our ghost village park."

"I wonder what it's like at night."

"Wanna find out?" I said mischievously.

Gray laughed softly. "I'm feeling sober now, but my blood alcohol level is probably still not right for driving."

And suddenly, I couldn't wait any longer. I had to know. Even if he didn't want to talk about it, I had to at least ask.

"Gray, what *happened*?" I said for what felt like the thousandth time, aware of how pathetic I sounded, like I was begging for scraps of Gray's life. "What did Micah call about? Or if it wasn't the phone call, what—why did you—"

"I'm sorry," Gray said. "God, it was so stupid. It's really not that big a deal. Or it shouldn't be anyway. It's dumb."

And now I was angry again. I knew my emotions were so all over the place, but dammit, Gray wasn't allowed to pretend like nothing happened, like this was a totally normal night. Not after everything went so weird.

"I waited for you," I said, heat in my voice. "For over an hour. You were supposed to come back to the restaurant, and you didn't, and I didn't know where you'd gone, or if something had happened to you, and I was worried and before you say that it was nothing, that whatever happened it was just stupid, just stop and think for a second about what that felt like from my perspective."

Gray looked crushed. He looked down at his hands. "God, Tyler, you're right. I was a fucking wreck after I got off that phone call, and I was embarrassed, and I didn't want anyone to see—didn't want *you* to see me like that. But I didn't think —I didn't think about what you were going through."

He looked up at me then, and that lost, hopeless look was back. "It *is* stupid, but I shouldn't have let that impact you."

He sighed. "Ethan's engaged. To Christie, the woman we—the woman he was with, that night in New York."

"What?"

"Yeah." Gray spread his hands out on his lap and looked at them helplessly.

I stood up from the chair, crossed the room in the dark, went to sit on the edge of my bed, facing Gray. I wanted to hug him, to hold him, to do something more. But I'd practically had to drag this admission out of him. I wasn't sure he'd welcome that from me.

"Gray, I'm so sorry."

"Yeah," Gray said. "Yeah, so am I. Except, you know, I really shouldn't be. I have no fucking right to still be this messed up about it. He's made it completely clear how he feels about me."

"Gray, you dated for years. You're allowed to still care."

"He doesn't," Gray said with a listless shrug of his shoulders. "And I'm sick of caring about him. I honestly am. So why... why *do* I, still?"

I didn't know what to say, because while I was supposed to answer Gray's question, I was just filled with this potent, burning rage.

"What a fucking *asshole*," I exploded. "How the fuck—didn't he tell you he didn't believe in marriage?"

"Yeah," Gray said softly.

"I can't fucking believe—I'm so—God, I could kill him."

"I'm glad *you're* mad, at least. Someone should be. *I* should be, I know. If I can't not care, I should at least be angry instead of just... pathetic and sad."

"You're not pathetic," I said.

"I'm not? Because the way I see it, pretty much my entire life, people have been telling me they don't want to be with me. And I never fucking get the message. But after a certain point, after enough people abandon you, you kind of have to realize—the common denominator in all of this is me. It's me."

"It's not fucking you, okay?" I said, even madder now. "I promise."

I was so angry. How dare Ethan treat Gray like this, lie to him like this? He'd never felt about Gray the way Gray felt about him—never felt about him the way he should have. Gray was so fucking perfect and he deserved someone who saw that—not someone who made him feel like he was nothing, not worth loving.

"I'm sorry," I said after a minute. "I just—I know how much you care about him and it pisses me off that he treats you like garbage."

Gray looked up from his hands and looked at me helplessly. "I don't even—I don't even think it's really about him. Like at this point—obviously he was a shitty guy to date and I just didn't see it. It's less about him and more about... me. Like, what's wrong with me? He didn't want me. No one does. Not even my own mother." He shook his head. "God, that's pathetic, isn't it?"

"It's not pathetic, because it's not true. There's nothing fucking wrong with you."

"I'm 30. I'm unmarried, I don't have a family, I don't even know where my mother is anymore. The only thing I've ever been good at is literally having sex for money, which is pretty sad. What the hell do I have to show for all the years I've spent on this earth?"

"Hey, that's my friend you're talking about," I said, standing up and glaring down at Gray. "You're smart and you're kind and you're funny and you're caring and reliable and nice to people and you're basically the best fucking person I know, so fuck Ethan and fuck your family and fuck anyone and everyone for making you think these things about yourself. And fuck you for believing it."

Gray looked up at me in surprise and before I could stop myself, I put my hands on either side of his face, bent down, and kissed him. Gray froze at first, but then his hands moved to my waist. I thought for a second that he was going to pull me down onto his lap but instead, he pushed me back.

"Tyler," Gray said, tearing his mouth away from mine, "Tyler, what are you doing?"

"I'm kissing you, you moron. I'm trying to show you that there's nothing wrong with you, you dumbass. And I'm trying to cheer you up, you fucking asshole."

Because you're fucking amazing and I hate that you don't see that. And I know you'd never be interested and that's fine—it's fine—because God knows I'm in no position to be with someone, but fuck you if you think I'll let you get away with thinking no one wants you.

"Tyler, no. Don't—we can't do this. We're not—"

"I know we're not anything. I'm not saying we should be, I'm not trying to make this anything other than what it is."

"But you—"

"Listen, you've—you've done a lot for me," I said, biting my lip. 'Let me—I don't know, let me do something for you."

God, I was starting to feel kind of pathetic, now that I wasn't in the middle of the heady rush of kissing Gray, now that we'd stopped and I actually had to think about my motives.

I sounded like I was begging Gray to fuck me. Because I *was* begging Gray to fuck me. God, this was a terrible idea wasn't it?

"Tyler." Gray's voice was so full of sadness that it just about broke my heart. "I don't think..."

He trailed off but I didn't need him to say the words to know where that sentence was going. *I don't think about you that way.* Dammit, why did that hurt so much? I didn't want that, did I? I shouldn't want Gray to want me. And yet, it stung.

He'll never see you that way, I realized. *How could you think he'd want you-especially tonight, when he's thinking about Ethan. You could never compare to him.*

"Forget it," I said, stepping back. "It was a stupid—"

But then Gray was grabbing my wrist and I barely had time to register what was happening before I was falling into his lap. My lips sought Gray's hungrily. Just because I was confused about what was happening didn't mean I was going to stop.

Gray's lips found mine, pressed back greedily, claiming my mouth. His tongue slipped inside and tangled with mine.

He pulled me closer to him and I found myself straddling his lap. I knew I should stop, should pull away, should ask Gray what made him change his mind, but dammit, I didn't want to.

We'd talked enough, hadn't we? We were clear on what was happening. Gray didn't want me as anything other than a physical distraction but I was fine with that. I was. So why slow things down and talk?

Besides, I could feel Gray's cock, long and hard, pressing up against me through his jeans as I shifted my hips on his lap. And dammit, even if Gray didn't *like* me like that, he *wanted* me.

I felt my own cock growing harder, pressing through the thin fabric of my boxers, my erection painfully obvious, but I didn't care. Gray's hands ran along my naked back and chest, but I actually liked it, being nearly undressed while Gray still had all his clothes on. It made me feel exposed and sent a thrill through me.

Gray nipped at my lower lip, pulling it out and then releasing it. I gasped as his lips moved to my jaw, then down onto my neck. My hands scrabbled at the bottom of his shirt, trying to pull it up. Because fun as it was to be the mostly naked one, I also needed to feel his skin on mine.

Our limbs tangled as I pulled his shirt off, then tossed it onto the floor behind me. After a second, though, I leaned over again and picked it up, then dropped it onto my bed.

"If you're creeped out by the bedspreads I'm sure you've got some weird thing about motel floors, too."

Gray made this half-growl, half-laugh sound and gave me a

suspicious look. "I seem to recall you kneeling on that floor a while ago."

"What, is *that* the reason you're going to push me away now?"

"Of course not," Gray said with a smile. "You were wearing pants when you did that. Now you're not. Obviously we're good."

I started laughing, then yelped in surprise as Gray picked me up and pushed me back onto the bed. My hands worked double-time to undo Gray's jeans and push them down as Gray's mouth roved across my skin. Gray hipped up off of me and tugged his jeans down, tossing them over onto my bed next to his shirt.

"You know you lay down on your bedspread while you were wearing those," I said with a laugh.

"Shhh," Gray said. "No I didn't. You're definitely lying."

"I would never—" my protest stalled when Gray's hand found my cock. "Okay, fuck, yes, I was lying. Just... keep doing that."

I groaned as Gray caressed me through my boxers, then dove underneath to stroke my skin.

"Fuck, yes," I moaned as Gray pulled that last article of clothing off of me.

My cock was hard, bobbing against my stomach, and as Gray stroked it, a long line of precum began leaking out of my slit. Gray caught it in his fingers and then brought them to his mouth, then looked at me as he licked them clean. And okay, so that was kind of pornographic, but really, if anyone were allowed to do that... Besides, it was fucking hot.

Gray began to kiss his way down my chest but I was way too full of energy and desire to just lie there and let him suck me off. I pushed him off me, then over onto his back, climbing up to straddle him. I felt slutty, my wet cock tracing against Gray's stomach as I bent down to take another kiss from his mouth.

My hand strayed south, feeling for the outline of Gray's cock beneath his boxer-briefs. God, it was massive. I still couldn't believe I'd taken that inside me—twice. I stroked his length, smiling when my fingers found a wet patch in the fabric of his underwear, pleased to know Gray was as turned on as I was.

It wasn't enough to feel him, though—I wanted to taste him. I'd had fantasies of sucking Gray's cock ever since the first time. I'd jerked off to thoughts of Gray feeding his cock to me, making me slurp it all down, filling my mouth and making me swallow.

I nipped at his lips one more time before pulling back and into a sitting position. I shifted forward then, sitting on his cock, feeling it pressing up against my ass, then rubbed back and forth. Gray moaned as I ran my hands up and down his chest, and held me tight as I rutted against him.

Finally, when I decided I'd tortured him enough, I pushed up onto my knees so I could peel Gray's boxer-briefs off of him, freeing that massive cock. I sat back on his thighs and stroked him, loving the broken, whimpering noises Gray was making. Before long, I was stroking our cocks together, using the precum leaking liberally from both our tips to coat our shafts, my hands creating a slick channel for us together.

"God, you're so beautiful, you know that?" Gray whispered.

I could feel myself blushing and bit my lip, but didn't respond. I didn't trust myself to speak. I just locked eyes with Gray and watched him as I stroked us together.

"Come here," Gray said, reaching up for me.

He pulled me down into a kiss and I had to let go of us, prop myself up with my elbows to keep from falling completely. But that didn't stop me from rutting against Gray, sliding my body up and down against his, trapping our cocks and giving us both the friction we needed.

I moaned as Gray's hand slid down my back to cup my ass, squeezing and rubbing the muscle there before dipping in and running along my crack. I pushed back against his hand when his finger hit my hole, rubbing against it. God, I felt wanton, basically begging Gray to push his finger inside me, but I wanted it, wanted it so badly.

Finally, Gray let a finger rest there and began teasing my hole. I whined in pleasure, pushing back again, even though I knew I shouldn't. We needed lube, I knew I should wait, but it just felt so good. I moaned as I felt his finger push inside me just a bit.

"Christ, baby, you have no idea what you do to me," Gray growled.

Something flashed through me—desire and pleasure at the thought of Gray wanting me, and anger and frustration at that word. *'Baby'* was what Wyatt called Dylan. But I didn't want Gray just reenacting that. I wanted Gray to want *me*, to be in this room with me, right now, to want me more than he'd ever wanted anyone else.

I kissed Gray roughly and slid all the way down his body, grasping his cock in my hand and bringing it to my mouth. I took as much of him inside me as I could in one long pull and Gray groaned loudly.

Yes, I thought, *yes. Know that I'm the one making you feel this good, that I'm the one with you, and no one else.*

Gray's cock tasted salty and tangy from the precum and underneath, a taste all his own, the taste of Gray's skin. The scent always reminded me of cedar and campfires, of being held close and warm by someone under a cool night sky.

Gray's hand drifted to the back of my head and I hummed enthusiastically, bobbing up and down on Gray's cock. It almost hurt my mouth, stretching to get around it. And to think I'd ever actually wondered, hoped I wouldn't be gay.

Yes, my sexuality had come with confusion, but it also came with moments like this, where I was sure of who I was and what I wanted. Sure of what felt right. I began sucking him faster.

"Hey, slow down, slow down," Gray said, bringing his hand to my shoulder. "What's the rush?"

A hot mix of something—shame that I was doing something wrong, pleasure that Gray was concerned about me, that Gray wanted to draw this out—coursed through me at those words. But I was still riding the high from my earlier frustration, so I pulled off Gray's now thoroughly wet, still hard cock, and crawled back up to straddled him again.

"The rush," I said, bending down to kiss his jawline, "is that I want you inside me. Now."

For emphasis, I reached back to take hold of Gray's cock, angled my hips up, and brushed my ass back and forth over the tip, letting the head tease against my hole.

Gray groaned and pulled me down. "I—I want that too," he said. "But I don't have any condoms, or lube, or anything." He laughed helplessly. "I wasn't expecting this."

I felt a flash of frustration. Goddammit, we had not gotten this far just to stop now. I didn't just want Gray inside me, I needed it. An idea popped into my mind.

"Stay there," I said commandingly, poking a finger at Gray's chest. "Don't even think of going anywhere."

"Where would I go?" he asked with a confused smile as I hopped off of him and ran to the bathroom.

I came back out and crawled onto the bed quickly, afraid that even those 15 seconds had been enough time for Gray to change his mind.

"I think I read somewhere that conditioner can be used as lube," I said, holding out the little bottle from the shower triumphantly. "We can just use this."

"Tyler, we can't—"

"What, it doesn't work?" I supposed Gray would know better about this kind of thing than I did.

"No, it does," Gray said slowly. "But we still don't have any condoms."

"Fuck condoms," I said. "We've both been tested. And we

know we haven't slept with anyone else because we've been pretty much joined at the hip for the past 30 days. We know it's safe."

"Are you sure you—" Gray paused and looked up at me. "You don't have to do this, you know. I'll still—God, Tyler, I'll do whatever you want, but you don't have to prove anything to me, if that's what this is about."

"Prove anything?" What the hell would I be trying to prove? "Gray, the only thing I'm trying to prove is how good it's going to feel—for both of us—when you're inside me again." I bit my lip, letting the yearning I felt show through in my eyes. Blinking just a little, getting them nice and wide and glistening, I added in my most pleading voice, "Come on Gray. I—I need this."

I knew it was a cheap shot, but fuck, I wasn't an actor for nothing.

"Tyler—" Gray started, then stopped and shook his head. "You kill me, you know that? You sure you don't mind?"

"Mind? I'm the one who suggested it. Why would I mind?"

Gray shrugged. "Some people think it's a little gross. And I completely respect that."

"Well what if I think it's a little hot, do you respect that too? Or are you one of the people who thinks it's gross?"

"Me?" Gray laughed, then pulled me down and kissed me. "Fuck no."

He started to roll me over onto my back but I put a hand down on the mattress to stop him.

"No," I said, shaking my head. "I wanna be on top."

Gray's eyes widened, his pupils dilated, and I smiled. Gray took the conditioner out of my hand and opened the bottle, squirting some onto his finger.

"Come here, you," he said, pulling me down again.

He brought his hand around to my ass and placed his finger right up against my hole. I pushed backwards, a moan escaping my lips as Gray penetrated me. It felt so good, his finger slipping up inside me, filling me and opening me up. I slid back further as Gray's finger went deeper and when he thrummed against my prostate I whined in pleasure.

"You're so fucking beautiful," Gray whispered.

I rocked back against his hand, then rolled forward, my cock brushing against his. He kissed my neck and I let myself revel in how good it felt. Soon enough, I was begging for more and whining as he pushed another finger inside. I felt like I was being flayed open, stretched and bared, but looking down at Gray, I knew I was safe. And even after he added a third finger, I knew I needed more.

"Fuck me, Gray," I moaned. "Fuck, I need you."

"Take your time, it's okay, it's okay," Gray whispered, but I didn't want to listen.

I didn't care that I was begging, didn't care how much I was pushing the pace. I was desperate to feel that fullness again, that feeling of coming home. I took the bottle of conditioner and squeezed some into my hand, then reached between us to find Gray's cock. It was still leaking against his stomach and he moaned as I pumped him up and down.

I shifted, pushing my knees up as Gray pulled his fingers out, then brought my ass to the tip of his cock, positioning it right against my hole. And then, catching Gray's eyes in the darkness, I let myself sink down.

A loud groan tore from my throat as I felt Gray's cock pierce me, and fuck, I wasn't sure I was ready for this, but it felt so good and I couldn't stop sliding down onto it. There was a stretch, a tiny bit of a burn, but I didn't stop until he was sheathed all the way inside me.

I gasped, trying to breathe, trying to collect myself. I could feel myself stretching around him, accommodating Gray's girth and length, pressed into me. It was different, being on top. It almost felt like Gray was deeper inside me than he'd been before. But I liked the feeling of being in control.

"You okay?" Gray asked, his eyes concerned.

"I'm fucking fantastic." I shifted experimentally, lifting up just a tiny bit before sinking back down, and moaned. "Oh, fuck."

"Oh God, Tyler," Gray gasped. "You're so good, you have no idea, you're so perfect."

That was all the motivation I needed to do that again. Gray telling me I was perfect, Gray praising me, Gray using my name? I could have come right there on the spot. Gray started stroking my cock as I fucked down onto his, taking more of him in and out of me with every stroke.

Fuck, how was it possible to feel so complete, so right like this? And knowing Gray felt just as good as I did, knowing that for now, at least, I could make Gray happy, I could show Gray how perfect and wanted he was? That was all I wanted.

I picked up speed, riding Gray faster now, needing more of

him. Gray's hand on my cock kept pace and the other one gripped my thigh.

"Oh God, baby, you look so good, riding me like that."

"Don't fucking call me baby," I growled, thrusting back onto his cock for emphasis.

Gray's eyes widened in surprise. "I—"

"Use my *name*."

Gray didn't seem to know what to say so I bent down and kissed him, then bit at his lip, and after a second, he started stroking me again. At least he seemed to get that I didn't want to stop. Because I didn't, I just wanted Gray to want *me*, to be here with *me*.

Gray shifted his legs, planting his feet on the mattress so he could thrust into me harder and it was just what I needed to forget my frustration, to forget everything except the pleasure of getting drilled, getting absolutely fucked out of my mind by Gray.

"Fuck, Tyler, you're so good," Gray whispered.

I wondered for a second if he were doing that to show me he'd listened or if he would have said that anyway, but I didn't care, because now he was praising me again, telling me how perfect, how beautiful, how good I was and that was all I needed. And then he was just whispering my name, *'Tyler, Tyler,'* over and over and I was on the edge.

"I'm gonna come," I groaned, "oh fuck, I'm gonna come."

Gray caught my chin with one hand and looked into my eyes as he stroked me and thrust up into me, and the look I saw there made me feel like I was coming apart at the seams, and suddenly I was coming, releasing into Gray's hand and down onto his stomach.

Fuck, it was so good, I almost blacked out with pleasure, feeling Gray still fucking into me, groaning, whispering my name.

"Fuck, Gray, yes, it's so good, give it to me," I found myself begging, chanting almost, until I felt him come, an extra fullness as Gray spilled inside me. It felt filthy and fucking hot all at once, knowing I was taking Gray's seed, like he was making me his.

I'm yours, I wanted to tell him. *I'm yours in whatever way, for however long you want me. Just say the words and you'll have me forever.*

Finally, Gray stilled. I shuddered and collapsed down onto him, but stopped Gray when he started to pull out.

"No. L-leave it. I-I like the way it feels."

Even in the dark, I knew my cheeks were flaming scarlet, but I snuggled down against Gray's chest. I wasn't quite ready to end this moment yet.

It just felt right, somehow, being connected to Gray like this. I felt warm and safe and like as long as I stayed right here, just like this, maybe time would stop and our problems would disappear and I've never have to leave.

Ethan would disappear, my dad would disappear, everything. It would just be me and Gray, together. Simple—everything was simple and right when it was just the two of us.

But then I realized what I was doing. Acting needy—acting

like we were together. Like Gray owed me this. And as soon as that thought slipped into my mind, I started to feel vulnerable in a way I didn't like.

I couldn't treat Gray like this. Like a boyfriend, a lover. Not when I was nothing to him—and he couldn't be anything to me. And as Gray's hands caressed my back, his chin tucked against my cheek, his cock still deep inside me, I knew it had to end.

I forced myself up, kissed Gray once more, and pulled away. I still felt empty as Gray slid out of me, but I made myself keep moving like it was no kind of loss. I reached over and grabbed some tissues, wiped down my stomach and then Gray's. I could feel his cum starting to trickle out of me and caught that with a tissue too. Losing him--any part of him-- was just something I was going to have to get used to.

I dropped the mess in the wastebasket, starting to feel a little uncomfortable at how quiet Gray was being. So when I came back in between the beds, I turned to climb into my own.

"Hey, what are you doing?" Gray's voice stopped me. "Where are you going?"

"Oh." I looked at him in confusion. "I didn't know if you wanted—"

"Of course I want you to sleep with me. Don't be silly. Come here." He arched an eyebrow. "Assuming you want to, that is."

"I mean—" I flushed. "Only if you—"

"Just shut up and get over here."

He held the sheet open for me and I climbed underneath it, let Gray wrap his arms around me. It was nice. Too nice, really. The kind of nice that could trick you into thinking this could be real, that this was something you could actually have.

I couldn't, really. I knew that. But for tonight, I wondered, was there any harm in continuing to pretend? The damage was already done, wasn't it?

I let Gray draw me closer. The damage was done. And this felt so good. So right.

I might as well sleep.

13

GRAY

I woke up in stages.

First, it was the gray hint of dawn that did it, imperceptibly lightening our room and casting the whole thing in silver-gray like the seashore or the chrome of an old movie. Tyler was still in my arms, smelling sweet, his light weight pressed against my chest. He didn't stir as I twisted and gulped down the rest of the water in the cup on the bedside table.

The clock on the nightstand said 5:05 a.m. Tyler had left the curtains open, I realized, and I thought briefly about getting up to close them. Anyone could walk by and see us in bed together. But before I could work up the energy to get out of bed, I'd fallen back asleep.

The second time I woke up, the light in the room was golden and the clock told me it was 7:00 a.m. I shifted and remembered with disappointment that my water cup was empty. Again, I thought of getting up—to close the curtains, refill my glass—and again I couldn't bring myself to.

Tyler was closer to wakefulness that time and he turned, burrowing closer to my chest. That alone was enough to make me decide to stay put. Tyler was here, and this was not something I could bear to break, this perfect moment, this perfect morning, just the two of us.

Once we got up, we'd have to talk. Tyler had made it clear last night, just as he had so many times before, that he felt nothing for me. And I'd made the mistake of bringing him to bed anyway. All because I'd been feeling sad, self-indulgent and self-pitying.

Pathetic.

I should have known better. But Tyler had been right in front of me, so beautiful, so insistent, and I hadn't been able to say no.

And it had been good—and for a few moments, I'd even been able to forget what this was. I'd been able to convince myself that Tyler cared for me. The way he'd reacted when I'd called him baby had shattered that illusion.

He didn't want me to think of him that way. He didn't want me, period. Not as anything other than a friend.

I thought of the last time I'd awoken with Tyler in my arms, remembered my fears of what Tyler would think if he knew what I truly felt. I'd felt so ashamed, so convinced that a night like last night could never happen.

But parts of last night had felt so real. Was I crazy, for thinking there was something there between us? Something neither of us was acknowledging? Tyler had said he'd just been trying to take my mind off Ethan, but could it have been something more?

Maybe, just maybe, should I say something? Should I bare my soul when Tyler woke up?

My lip twisted, thinking about Ethan. I was still angry about how he'd acted, but it was a hollow anger. There was no heat to it, nothing left to fuel that fire. I was over him—last night had made that clear to me. The only thing left was the aftershocks.

And maybe I should be grateful, in a way. Ethan was, oddly enough, one of the reasons I'd decided to do *Foresight*, which is how I'd met Tyler. It felt like ages ago. And now Ethan had been the thing that had brought us together again.

Together—for the moment. All that remained now was to decide whether to speak—whether to tell Tyler the truth. And so I lay there, breathing in the scent of Tyler's lemon shampoo and his skin, and turned the idea over in my mind until, still confused, I fell asleep again.

The third time I woke up, it was because someone was trying to beat down the door.

My eyes snapped open and I struggled to make sense of what was happening. For a second, I thought I was back at Bailey Park and was late for a scene, before I remembered that no, we were done with that. We weren't even there anymore, we were in tidewater Maryland. The clock on the nightstand said 8:00 a.m. I was in a motel room—a motel room with Tyler.

Tyler! I looked down at Tyler with wide eyes to find him pushing himself up as well, his hair mussed and his expression confused.

"What's going on?" he asked, his voice thick with sleep.

"I think—I think someone's at the door?" My head felt so fuzzy.

Tyler frowned, then looked over at the door, then over at his bed. His eyes widened as he seemed to realize for the first time that he was lying naked in a tangle of sheets with me. The banging on the door continued.

And suddenly there was shouting.

"Tyler, open this door right now! We need to talk and I'm done with you avoiding me."

"Who's—" I started to ask but my voice faltered when I saw the expression in Tyler's eyes. He was staring at the door now with fear.

"Tyler, I know you're fucking in there, I saw you as soon as I got out of the car for Christ's sake. Leaving your curtains open like you're trying to flaunt it. Disgusting. Now get the fuck up and answer the goddamn door before I wake up this entire shitbag motel and everyone fucking sees you."

I grabbed Tyler's hand protectively. My brain was going from shock to anger and I wasn't going to let anyone talk to him like that—especially not when it left Tyler's face drained of color and his eyes pained.

He didn't pull his hand away, but he didn't move closer either. As far as I could tell, he was paralyzed.

"Tyler—" I began, but the words died on my lips because at that moment, whoever had been standing at the door moved over to the window—the window where we'd left the curtains wide open.

It was a middle-aged man with a large paunch of a belly. A button-down shirt strained to cover his bulk underneath a seedy-looking blazer with ostentatious cufflinks. His thin blond hair was combed over what looked like a bald patch at the top of his head. He glared at us through the window.

"Tyler—Tyler, who is that?"

Tyler's eyes flashed from the window to me, wide and wild. "That's my dad."

The man just stood there, glaring, his hands on his hips. Slowly, Tyler slid his hand out of my grasp and then out from under the sheets. He grabbed his boxers from the other bed and pulled them on quickly, then threw his t-shirt on and ran a hand through his hair as he hurried to the door.

My mind felt like it was stuck in molasses, not quite able to keep up with what was happening. That man was Tyler's dad. Tyler's dad was here, looking for him. And now Tyler's dad knew—had seen—well, enough.

Shit, this was not good. Tyler had told me how scared he'd always been to come out to his father, and now the man was here and, from the sound of it, proving Tyler's fears right.

All I wanted to do was stand up and sock the man in the jaw, but I knew that would only make things worse. Shit, shit, shit. I should have gotten up and closed the curtains. I'd had so many chances. Why hadn't I done that?

My brain had only just realized that maybe I should put on some clothes too when Tyler made it to the door and opened it, at which point I realized I was stuck. My boxer-briefs were on the other bed and I'd have to flash his dad to go get them.

"Hey, Dad," Tyler began weakly, but he cut off when his dad stepped inside the room quickly and shut the door.

"Jesus, Tyler," his dad said, looking around the room in disgust. "Do you have no shame at all? Or is it just a lack of judgement? I suppose I shouldn't be surprised—that's nothing new. But even for you, this is pathetic."

Tyler just stared at him like a deer caught in headlights. He looked so small and I was halfway to standing up and going to put my arm around him before I remembered I was naked.

"Well don't just stand there," his dad said angrily. "Get moving. We have a meeting in New York at noon and I'm certainly not taking you there while you smell like a cheap whore. And for Christ's sake, close the curtains. The whole world doesn't need to see this."

"We—what?" Tyler said. "A meeting?"

"Yes, Tyler, a meeting." His dad's voice was scathing. "You remember what those are, don't you? Professionals who work set them up, and you go and try not to embarrass yourself—or me—and try to convince people to spend money on you again."

His dad glanced down at his watch significantly—one that looked chunky and expensive—and then back out the window. For the first time, I noticed a black sports car idling outside. God, he must have driven down from the city this morning. Was this all because Tyler hadn't agreed to meet him two days ago?

"But what for?" Tyler asked. "I mean, what's the meeting about?"

"About your future," his dad barked. "If you don't ruin it first. Jesus—" he broke off, evidently deciding Tyler wasn't going to close the curtains and stomping over to the window to do it himself. "Well, what are you waiting for?" he spit as he turned back to Tyler. Get dressed and get moving."

"But I don't—I never said I'd—" Tyler's voice quavered. "Dad, what's the meeting actually about? I'm not sure I want to just—"

"Of course you're not sure," his dad said. "You're never sure about anything. If it wasn't for me, you'd never get anything done, because if it wasn't for me, you'd be left to your lazy, fuck-up devices for the rest of your life."

Tyler quailed visibly at that, and it was the final straw for me.

"Hey!" I said, standing up from the bed, not even caring that I was flashing Tyler's dad. Belatedly, I grabbed the sheet and after tugging it free, wrapped it around my waist. I moved to stand next to Tyler. "I don't think I like your tone."

"And I don't think I like you preying on my son."

"*Preying on* him?" I said, incredulous. "I'm not—"

"Don't think I don't know what you're doing." The scathing tone was back. "Grooming him, making him believe he's something he's not. Planning on riding his coattails to fame, thinking everyone will just forget about your past?" He shook his head. "Well it might have worked on my son— God knows he's never been that smart—but you've got another thing coming if you think it'll work on me."

Tyler flushed. "Dad, Gray's not—"

"Tyler! I don't recall asking for your opinion. What I *did* ask for was for you to get dressed, but if you don't want to, you can just get in the car like that. We're not going to be late. I worked very hard to get Isaac Henderson interested in you and we are not wasting this meeting."

"You still haven't even—" Tyler stopped, his mouth working silently as it caught up with his ears. He frowned. "Isaac Henderson?"

His dad nodded. I had no idea who that was, but Tyler seemed to.

"The president of WEV network?" Tyler said, his eyes widening.

"He saw the teaser," his dad said gruffly. "Thought it showed promise. And I managed to convince him to see you before he sees the rest of the movie and the level you've sunk to. Wants to talk about getting you on one of their shows. And if we can get an offer from WEV, we can take that to other networks and shop you around. We might just be able to salvage your career—if we can get something inked before this filth of yours comes out."

"That's—I don't—I mean, that's a—" Tyler stammered and emotions warred across his face. Excitement, shame, confusion, and wariness. He glanced from his dad to me and back again.

"Why—why are you doing this?" Tyler asked, finally. "I mean, you abandoned me for all of last year. I thought you were done with me. After they found the drugs. You never answered any of my calls or anything—" His voice broke, and something inside me broke too, because I knew he was about to cry and I didn't know how to stop it.

And Tyler's dad—well, his face didn't soften, exactly. That implied a gentleness that I didn't think he possessed. But it did go from angry to... slightly less angry. A mix of frustration and disgust. When he spoke, his voice was rough.

"You needed to learn a lesson about responsibility. I had to cut you off to teach you how to stand on your own."

I blinked, realizing that this begrudging, still somewhat threatening tone was what Tyler's dad thought passed for kindness. And worse, Tyler seemed to be buying it.

"But you seem to have grown up. A little bit, anyway," his dad continued, sounding like the 'compliment' was being ripped out of him surgically without any anesthesia. "You sniffed this project out, anyway, and disgusting as it is, it's getting a lot of buzz. You always did have a nose for controversy, I'll give you that."

He gave Tyler a long, assessing look. "Tyler, I know you're trying. And I believe you when you say you've changed. I know you're clean. I listened to all your messages last year. Every single one. I know you're doing your best. But come on, you know we're a team, and you do best when we're working together."

Tyler's eyes were still scared, still hurt, and when he looked from his dad to me again, all I wanted to do was protect him. That's all I'd ever wanted, really, from the moment I'd met him. But when I opened my mouth, the look Tyler gave me said 'No' so strongly he might as well have said it out loud.

So I said nothing. Because Tyler didn't want me to. And no

matter how angry I was that anyone would treat him this way, most of all his own father, I would do what Tyler asked.

Instead I just looked back at him, trying to communicate all the concern and care and affection for him that filled my heart, trying to communicate strength, and the belief that Tyler didn't need his dad, didn't need to go back to him.

Tyler smiled, and for a second, I thought maybe he was going to do it, going to say no to his dad. But the smile didn't reach his eyes—they were still haunted and hurt. And I knew what he was going to say before he spoke.

Tyler's dad, to his credit, seemed to have read our silent conversation like a book.

"Meet me outside," he said to Tyler. "Five minutes. I mean it. We've got to get going."

"Okay," Tyler said meekly. "I'll be there."

His dad turned and walked out the door, shutting it so firmly behind him that the walls rattled.

Tyler turned back to me. "Don't be mad at me."

"Tyler, how can you—" I stopped, not even sure where to begin.

"I have to," Tyler said heavily, moving over to where his duffel bag lay on the floor. He began tossing clothes into it.

"Do you? Really?"

"I do." Tyler grabbed his jeans from the bed and pulled them on. "My dad's managed to do more in the past few weeks than I've done this entire past year."

"But you've barely even started looking," I protested. "Just give it time. Besides, are you sure you even want this? From what you've been saying recently, I thought you were maybe reconsidering being in front of the camera anymore at all. Tyler, Jesus, at the very least you shouldn't be working with someone who treats you like that, who clearly doesn't approve of your sexuality, who fucking abandoned you last year."

"He was trying—I know it's hard to see, but he was trying, in his own way, to help. I know he's not an easy guy to like, but—"

"Easy to like?!" I exploded. "Tyler, Charles fucking Manson would be easier to like than that guy. How are you not—how can you—don't you see how he talks to you? Were you not in the same room as me just now?"

Tyler winced. "I know it's—I mean, I'll tell him—I'll make it clear you weren't trying to—I mean, you weren't taking advantage of me—that it's my choice."

"I don't care what he thinks about me. I care what he thinks about you. Which, from the looks of it, is not much."

When Tyler spoke again, his voice had a hint of bite in it. "I don't expect you to understand—"

"Well good, because that's never gonna fucking happen."

"Fine. Fine, then forget it. I'll just get my shit and go." He turned and started searching the floor. "Jesus, where the fuck are my fucking shoes?"

"Fuck, Tyler, no," I sighed. "I'm sorry, that's not—that's not what I meant."

I cursed myself inwardly. Of course Tyler was defending his

dad—the man was emotionally abusive. Even if Tyler could see what was happening, I wasn't sure he could admit it. I needed to be kinder, understanding and supportive, not condemning him and making him feel worse than he already did.

"It is what you meant though, Gray," Tyler said, looking up from the floor, his shoes in hand. "And I get it. Trust me, I know what you must think of me. Weak, naive. Just a stupid kid."

"Tyler, that's not—"

"But you know what? I never pretended to be anything different," Tyler went on, shoving his feet into his shoes and grabbing his duffel bag. He walked to the door. "I told you upfront that I was a fuck-up and if you ever thought I was something more—well, that's on you."

"Jesus, Tyler, wait. Stop." I grabbed him by the arm as he got to the door, then turned him gently to face me. "Please. I don't want to fight about this. I don't even know why we're fighting. I just—that's not what I think about you, okay? Please, just—you have to know that. You can do whatever you want, but you have to know that."

"Yeah?" Tyler's eyes were flinty. "Then what *do* you think of me?"

I think I'm in love with you.

The words popped into my head unbidden and only shock kept me from saying them out loud. My mouth hung open in surprise.

I was in love with Tyler.

But Tyler was staring up at me, angry and hurt and confused. I didn't want to make things worse and I was pretty sure telling him that wouldn't help. Confessing your love to someone who was about to go back into business with his homophobic father, who wasn't sure he wanted to come out, who'd barely had a chance to experience the world...

God, that was a terrible idea. Tyler wouldn't want to hear that. And I was a fucking idiot for falling in love with yet another man who was unavailable.

"Nevermind," Tyler sighed. "Clearly, if it's taking you that long to answer—"

"I think you're amazing," I said. "I think you're the most amazing person I've ever met. I think you're kind and you're honest and you're sweet and you're funny and you're strong and you're smart—and I think you deserve more than working with someone who judges you for being who you are—which, in case you've forgotten—is amazing. But most of all, I think you deserve to be happy. You deserve to get what you want. So if you really want to do this—"

"What other options do I have?" Tyler said. I'd never heard him sound so defeated.

Stay with me. Just stay with me and we'll figure this out.

But that wasn't a real answer. Tyler needed more than that —and also less. More support, less of my unwanted, inconvenient feelings.

"I'm sure there's something," I said lamely. "We can figure something out."

Tyler laughed sadly. "Gray, have you met me? Since when

have I ever been able to figure anything out? My dad's right. I don't know how to make good decisions—I don't know how to make decisions, period. I can't commit, I fuck things up through my inaction as much as anything else." He shrugged helplessly. "Maybe this is the path of least resistance, but maybe that's just who I am. And maybe it's time for me—and you—to accept that. To stop expecting better from me."

"Tyler—"

"Bye, Gray." Tyler turned and opened the door, stepping through it. "I'll see you around."

~

The hotel room felt empty with Tyler gone. And cold.

Any magic that had been here this morning, any spell that had held us together and made everything feel safe, had been broken. And any idea I'd had about telling Tyler the truth was gone.

Maybe it was knowing what that truth was, now, that made it feel so wintry.

I was in love with Tyler. And all I had left were the rumpled sheets, the shadowy room, the shabby wallpaper for company.

When, exactly, had I fallen in love with him? I sat down on the edge of the bed and stared off into space, trying to figure it out. But as I thought back on the past month, I couldn't pick out a single turning point. It was a month filled with Tyler smiling over his shoulder at me, Tyler cracking up when one of us flubbed a line and clutching me as he doubled over in laughter, Tyler watching me intently as I spilled my soul out, Tyler's eyes wide and brave, baring his in return.

Was there ever a moment that I hadn't loved him? Maybe it had only been confirmed last night. But it had started the first night I met him, when he smiled as he came into the taxi cab out of the rain. God, it hurt my heart, thinking back to that night and how badly I'd wanted to protect him, even then.

And now he was gone.

It felt final in a way that didn't make any sense. His dad had said the meeting was in New York, so it wasn't like he was disappearing off the face of the earth. Besides which, Tyler had always been planning on going back to LA. I'd known that. I'd made my peace with that.

But that was before you knew you loved him.

That did change things a bit. And at the same time, it didn't change anything at all. Tyler was still leaving. This was what Tyler wanted. And there wasn't a damn thing I could do about it.

He'd said last night that sleeping together didn't have to change anything between us, and he'd been right. Because no matter what my feelings were, he was moving on and I needed to accept that. Last night wasn't the start of anything. It was an ending.

All that remained was for me to pack up and move on as well.

I tried to push the swirling mess of crap in my heart down as I stood and collected my clothes from yesterday. I knew I should shower. Any self-respecting person would, after the sweat and heat Tyler and I had worked up last night. But I couldn't bear to spend any more time in that motel room than I had to.

And maybe, just maybe, I was pathetic enough not to want to wash the scent of him off my skin.

In the end, I just pulled on yesterday's clothes, shoved everything else back into my bag, and did a quick sweep of the room as I prepared to leave. I'd gotten everything—hadn't had much to start with.

So why, as I stepped outside and shut the door, did I feel like I was leaving part of myself behind?

I walked straight to my car. Dave and Andrew had reserved the rooms for everyone, so I didn't need to check out. I could go straight back to New York—three hours and a world away. Back to my life that was waiting for me. The city. The bar. Everything just the way I'd left it.

Only, I wasn't the same anymore.

Maybe that was why I didn't get on the main road back to the highway. Maybe that was why I decided to retrace my steps—*our* steps—from Saturday and drive back past that little village park on the shores of that creek. And maybe that was why I swerved and turned around at the last minute, pulled the car over in the park's tiny gravel lot, and got out.

I wasn't ready to go back to New York yet, I realized. So instead, I wandered through the field, the tall grass brushing my knees, and headed past the park's sign to the banks of the stream itself. There was a huge tree there, standing all alone, a giant oak that spread its branches with a profligate grace, casting a cool, blessed shade on everything below it.

I ducked underneath, glad to be out of the sun for a moment. It was early yet, but the day was already promising to be hot, one of those October days that feel more like summer than fall. And once I was under the shade of that tree, I couldn't help but walk up and lay a hand on its trunk in a kind of silent reverence.

The tree was massive. Who knew how long it'd been standing there. The things it'd seen. It didn't give a shit about my problems, or Tyler's, or anyone's. We were insignificant before it, and somehow, standing there made me feel a little bit better.

Not quite knowing why I was doing it, I lowered myself to the ground and sat, my back against the tree and my legs stretched out in front of me. I certainly hadn't intended to spend my morning sitting in the dirt, but it's not like I'd been that clean to begin with and it's not like I had anyone waiting on me back in New York.

Only that wasn't true, not entirely. Maggie might not be there for me anymore, Ethan might not give a shit, but there was Micah, who'd been a better bar manager for Maggie's in the past month than I'd been for the whole past year. There were Ben and Adam, who'd made me promise to tell them all about the shoot when I got back.

And then... well, there were the auditions I was supposed to go on. The parts I was supposed to read for. So no, my old life wasn't waiting for me back in New York. But a new one might be, waiting for me to start it. If I were brave enough.

Move on, I told myself. *Move on*.

I'd been stuck in stasis for so long, not swimming with the current or even against it, just treading water and trying to keep my head above the surface. Tyler had helped me be honest about what I really wanted. Tyler had believed in me, even when I hadn't believed in myself. A 21 year old kid had helped me find a kind of courage I didn't realize I had.

So what if he doesn't love you? Wasn't that selfish, to ask for that? Wasn't that asking for too much, when I'd already been given so much?

I had a friend in Tyler—a friend who helped me become a better version of myself. A version that I'd kicked into hiding years ago, but one that had never stopped wanting to come out and see the light. It would be a poor repayment not to try to move forward.

Be his friend. Just be his friend.

Don't blame him for not loving you, don't hold him accountable for something he never promised in the first place. Be grateful for him, and you'll get to keep him in your life, one way or another. Even if he's in LA. Even if he's working with his dad again. You can still have him somehow.

But only if you're willing to move on.

It was time for me to do that. Not just from Tyler. But from everything in the past I'd been holding onto. All the hopes —but also, all the fears. It was time to let that go.

I looked out at the stream before me, trickling only a yard from my feet. Its waters danced and sparkled in the sunlight as it burbled merrily on its way down to the bay, and then to the ocean beyond. Who knew what lay ahead of me? There was no telling. But I wouldn't find out sitting here.

I bent my knees and pushed myself up from the ground. Dusting my hands off on my jeans, I took a final look at that tree. And then, on a whim, I pulled out my pocket knife and took it to the trunk.

When it was done, I folded the knife back up and nodded. I'd done what I needed to do. I slipped the knife back in my pocket, placed my hand on the trunk for a final moment, and then headed back off through the field to my car.

It was time to say goodbye.

14

TYLER

$\mathcal{I}$ walked out to the car slowly and opened the passenger side door.

"Put your bag in the back," my dad said, not looking at me as he popped the trunk. "This is a rental, I don't want to get it messed up."

"My bag's not full of gay germs, you know that, right?"

My dad gave me a hard look. "Tyler, enough with the lip. Just do it and get in the car."

And because I didn't know what else to do, I did.

"Buckle up," my dad said.

I put my seatbelt on numbly. My dad pulled out of the hotel parking lot with a squeal of tires and sped down the street. He didn't say anything else, which would have been fine, except that he kept glaring at me, his hands gripping the steering wheel so hard that his knuckles were white. His silence was somehow more oppressive than if he'd been yelling at me.

By the time we were on the highway, I couldn't stand it anymore.

"So you're just gonna give me the silent treatment til we get back to New York?" I said, knowing I was provoking him and not particularly caring.

"What the fuck do you want me to say, Tyler? That I'm proud of what my son's made of his life at this point? Proud of finding you in bed with another man in a cheap motel? You think I wanna see that?"

"I didn't mean to—" I shook my head and started over. "I'm sorry. I didn't know you were coming."

"Well maybe you would have if you hadn't hung up on me. Maybe I wouldn't have had to come down and get you if you'd come and seen me like I asked you to. You don't think I have better things to do than haul your ass out of some fleabag motel and babysit you to make sure you don't fuck up this meeting?"

"Jesus, Dad, I said I was sorry."

"Yeah, well you'd better be."

We lapsed back into silence as the scenery sped past.

"So you're gay now?" he said, out of the blue, as we were crossing the bridge back into New Jersey.

For a brief moment, I considered unbuckling my seatbelt, throwing the door open, and rolling out of the car and off the bridge into the river below, rather than answering that question.

Except, he knew. So why the hell was I afraid to say it?

Except, also, he knew, so why the hell was he *making* me say it?

Except, also also, he knew I knew, and the longer I sat there not answering him, the more annoyed he was going to get.

"Yes." My voice was quiet, almost embarrassed, and I hated myself for it.

My dad made a noise in the back of his throat like he was trying to hack up phlegm or eject something else disgusting far, far away from him.

"We can hope this is just a phase," he said eventually. "Maybe once I get you away from those influences, you'll realize your mistake."

"It's not—"

"At the very least, no more flaunting it like you did back there."

"I wasn't—"

"I know the PC thing to say now is that you're born this way," my dad said, his tone making it clear what he thought of that. "But Tyler, even if you can't change it, you can still hide it. Use your head. No one wants to see that."

"Dad, the thousands of people who are excited about this movie want to see it at least."

"Kid, that's still a niche audience. It's big enough to tank your other prospects, if we don't do some fast PR work, but too small to sustain you. Think, Tyler—your numbers used to be huge. Don't you want to have that kind of pull again?"

That kind of pull, those numbers—that was the very thing

that had made me feel crazy in the first place, made me panic and wish I could be anywhere else, made me hate the fact that no matter where I went, people knew who I was.

All I wanted now was enough work to sustain me. Interesting projects. People I could stand. But saying that to my dad was a non-starter.

"Honestly, I don't know what you were thinking, taking a role like this. Maybe you felt like you needed to express yourself, but my God, it's going to be hard to cast you now. Until we fix this, anyway."

Those words cut into my skin like tiny knives.

"What's the meeting with WEV about, then?" I asked. "If I'm so uncastable."

"Watch your tone," my dad said. "The meeting's part of the fix."

We settled back into silence. And I couldn't help it—I checked my phone. Hoping to see something from Gray.

Because dammit, this felt shitty. The way I left things with Gray... I'd regretted it from the moment I stepped out the door of that motel and part of me just wanted to run out of the car and go back there.

Except what was to say he'd even be there anymore? Honestly, it'd be simpler to just find him back in New York. It wasn't like I was leaving immediately, right? I hoped. Oh God, though depending on how this meeting went, maybe I couldn't guarantee that.

But then there was the other question—did Gray even want to see me anymore?

That was the other thing that kept me glued to the seat in this over-air-conditioned car, shivering, feeling like shit—the thought that he might not want to see me ever again. Our fight was so stupid—and it was one hundred percent my fault.

Part of me was sure I was overreacting, that I could just send him a text right now and apologize and things would be fine. Another part of me though—a larger part—knew that something about that fight had felt final. That that might have been the last time I'd see him for a long time. 'Til we had to do promo for *Foresight*, maybe. It could be months.

And who knew what could happen in months. People's lives changed so fast. Just look at mine—just look at who I was a month ago.

Would Gray even be the same person in a few months? What if he were dating someone new? Or back with Ethan? Or moving to fucking Oslo for six months to film a movie about Vikings. He might not be mad at me anymore because he just wouldn't give a shit about me by then.

After all, there was no reason why he should. I was a 21 year old, immature fuck-up who picked fights when he felt defensive, who didn't have any other friends because no one else wanted to be around him. Gray might be my only friend —if I could still call him that—but I'd never been his.

What did I ever bring to his life, anyway? It was probably just one of those friendships of convenience. There was no way he was sitting in his car turning over our parting words in his mind. I just didn't matter that much to him.

And yet, I couldn't stop checking my phone.

"Whatever's going on with that guy, you have to stop it," my dad said after another hour of silence. We were well into Jersey by now, hurtling up the Turnpike.

"What?" I blinked, pulled out of my reverie.

"I see you looking at your phone," my dad said. "But you have to end it."

"End—oh. Oh, no, it's not—I mean, we're not, like, together."

"Oh Jesus Christ. So you're just sleeping with any man who propositions you? Great. It's not enough for you to be gay, you're a slut besides."

"No, no. It's not like that either. I'm not—God, you don't have to worry about that. Or anything. Gray and I are just friends."

My dad's eyes were hard. "Good."

"He wasn't—doing any of those things you said," I added. "Grooming me or whatever. I was the one who—" I stopped as my dad gave me a sharp look, realizing I didn't really want to finish that sentence. "Anyway, he's a good guy."

"I'm sure you think that now. But when you're older, I hope you'll realize I'm just trying to protect you. I don't want you to get taken advantage of, and you're too trusting. You need me to look out for you."

"Gray wasn't—he wasn't taking advantage of me." I sighed. "And he probably wants nothing to do with me now, anyway, so you don't have to worry."

"Good," my dad said again, and I wished I could share his

conviction. Because from where I was sitting, things didn't feel good at all.

The meeting got postponed, because of course it did. My dad got a call right before we went through the tunnel and it got rescheduled for Thursday. Three more days with my father sounded excruciating just then, so I told him he could drop me off at Luke's, promised I'd be at the meeting on time.

One look from him told me he wasn't buying that, which is how I ended up spending the next three days on lockdown in a hotel suite with my father. I texted Luke to tell him where I was, since I'd told him I'd be back at his apartment that night. I wasn't even sure if he knew our dad was there.

TYLER: Hey so it sort of slipped my mind to mention this a couple of days ago but did you know dad's in town?

LUKE: Wait what?

LUKE: Seriously?

LUKE: Why?

TYLER: To set up some meeting between me and a network about a tv show? And he's holding me hostage so I'm not gonna be back at your apt til Thursday, looks like

LUKE: Wait, since when is he even talking to you again?

TYLER: It's a long story. I wasn't expecting this though. We were barely talking

TYLER: I wasn't sure if maybe you knew

LUKE: I haven't talked to dad since... jeez I actually can't remember how long

LUKE: He made it quite clear he didn't want me and mom in his life

LUKE: Made it sound like you didn't want us in yours, either

I'd known my parents' divorce hadn't been amicable. My dad had told me at the time that he was just trying to shield me from getting hurt, that he didn't want me to get pulled into the middle of it. Over time, as I'd heard from my mom and Luke less and less, I'd just assumed it was because they didn't want to talk to me.

It wasn't until my arrest and sentencing last year that I'd learned they weren't mad at me for staying with my dad all those years.

TYLER: Well that's not the case. Not then, not now

TYLER: I just need to see how this meeting goes

LUKE: You sure you can't leave? Or do you want me to come get you?

TYLER: Thanks but probably not a good idea. He's pissed enough as it is. Just wanted to let you know where I was

LUKE: You know you didn't do anything wrong though

TYLER: Yeah it's just... it's complicated. Anyway I'll let you know how it goes but looks like I'll be out of your hair for a bit

Luke didn't respond for a while and I thought the conversation was over, but just as I was setting my phone down, it pinged again, and the text this time was weirdly long

LUKE: I really don't mind having you here. And I'm not trying to

tell you what to do but... I hope you're doing things because you want to do them, not because you think you should. And I know it's not really my place to give you advice but please don't feel like you have to make any snap decisions ok? It's ok to stop and think about things

I wasn't sure how to respond. I could almost see the sweat breaking out on Luke's forehead as he composed that. It was clear from what he *didn't* say that he was basically telling me not to listen to Dad's advice. Without coming right out and saying it, because the last time he'd done that, I'd snapped at him.

Fuck. I hated that I'd yelled at him when he was only trying to help. What the hell was wrong with me? Both Luke and Gray had just been trying to help and I'd ended up losing it on both of them. It wasn't fair to expect them to understand why I had to do this.

For about the millionth time, I thought about texting Gray and apologizing before freezing up. God, I wanted to. But what if he didn't reply? What if he did, and told me he didn't want to hear from me? Wouldn't that be worse than wondering?

I'd only known Gray for a month. Granted, it was a month that had completely changed me. But why should I think he'd want to hear from me again?

Luke, though. Luke was my brother. With him, I could at least still try.

TYLER: Thanks. I appreciate it. I'm sorry I've been so fucking weird and probably annoying to deal with—recently and also like, forever. I'm really lucky I have you as a brother

LUKE: Ok well same

LUKE: Mutual appreciation society :)

LUKE: Wanna hang out later this week? Things are kinda crazy with work stuff right now but I'd love to see you before you move back to LA

TYLER: Definitely

Feeling slightly better about things, I did the best I could to wait for the next three days until the meeting. And maybe— I knew it was a slim hope, but maybe—I'd hear from Gray sometime soon? I knew it was a ridiculous thing to hope for.

But I hoped anyway.

≈

The morning of the meeting, I started freaking out. The mechanic who'd been fixing Luke's car had held onto it for weeks, telling me the entire exhaust system was messed up and needed newer parts. I sort of wondered if they might have been scamming me but I knew so little about cars that there was no way to tell. So I'd just swallowed my pride and agreed to pay for it.

But after letting it gather dust for almost a month, suddenly the mechanic was desperate to get it out of their shop. They'd called me every day to ask when I was picking it up, but my dad wouldn't let me leave the hotel. I was praying I'd be able to get it after the meeting.

My dad hadn't even let me swing by Luke's or my mom's to pick up fresh clothes, so while he was doing... whatever it was that he did as his job these days in the office part of the hotel suite, I was trying to iron the worst of the wrinkles out of one of my shirts while blow-drying my least disgusting pair of jeans, which I'd washed in the sink this morning after realizing they were stained.

So I was already sweaty and nervous and frantic when my phone rang and made me jump. My heart leapt to my throat. But when I looked down, it was Danny calling. Not Gray.

Why the fuck would he be calling you, after the way you left things?

I sighed and turned off the blow-dryer to answer. I had no idea what Danny was calling for, but maybe talking to them would help take my mind off the meeting that my entire future depended on now. That had to be worth wearing slightly damp jeans to a meeting, didn't it?

"Hey Danny," I said, standing up and re-wrapping the cord around the blow dryer. I walked into the bathroom to put it back and shut the door behind me. It wasn't like my dad had explicitly told me not to talk to anyone from *Foresight* but I didn't want to risk him getting mad at me about it anyway. "What's up?"

"Tyler?" Danny's voice was warm and bright on the phone. "Is that you?"

"Yeah, it's me."

"Oh thank God," Danny laughed. "I was afraid you had an assistant who I'd have to talk to or something. I hate the phone."

"An assistant?" I barked a laugh. "Danny, do I seem like the kind of person who has an assistant?"

"I don't know," Danny protested. "You're all famous and shit."

"Yeah, and also kind of poor. And a mess. I didn't even have an assistant back when I could have afforded one. But if it makes you feel any better, I hate the phone, too."

"Oh, shit, I'm sorry I'm calling you then," Danny said. "I just —well, you'd mentioned the idea of me shopping some of my books around and now that *Foresight's* in post-production and there's no set for me to hang around anymore... I don't know, I wondered if I could pick your brain about how to do that."

"Oh my God, that's awesome," I said, a genuine smile breaking out across my face—it felt like the first time I'd smiled in days. "Danny, I really think that's a great idea."

"I hope so, but to be honest, I like, don't even know what that means. I'm sure you're busy and don't really want to talk about it right now, but I was wondering if you wanted to get coffee sometime this week and I could kind of—I don't know, find out how this all works."

"Yes," I said, nodding my head enthusiastically. "Yes, yes, yes. Definitely." Then I paused. "At least, I think so. I uh— my schedule's actually a little bit up in the air right now. But I definitely want to talk about it, so we'll just... find a time that works, before I go back to LA. I promise."

"I mean, it's really fine if you're too busy—" Danny began but I interrupted them.

"No." I shook my head, even though they couldn't see it. "No, Danny, this is like, the first thing I've been excited about in —well, it doesn't matter. We're going to make this happen."

God, did that sound weird? *Was* it weird that I was so excited about this? More excited than anything in my own future, whether it was prospects my dad was finding or projects I rustled up on my own? I didn't know. But at that point, the idea of thinking about anything other than myself felt like a wave of relief rushing through me.

"Tyler!" My dad's voice came through the door. "Tyler, get out here. We're gonna be late."

"Shit. Danny, I gotta go but I promise I'll call you back later ok? We can work out a time to meet soon. I should know more about my schedule by this afternoon anyway."

"Sounds good," Danny said. "Everything going alright with you?"

"It's... complicated," I said with a little laugh.

"Well go kick some ass. You deserve it."

Oddly enough, even after I'd hung up with Danny, I was in —well, if not quite a *good* mood, a better one than I'd been in since my dad had shown up. Having something —*someone*—to think about other than myself was just nice. I'd rather spend days helping Danny map out a strategy for shopping their scripts than even an hour in this meeting, I realized.

But maybe, I told myself, if this meeting went well, I'd be in a position where I really could help Danny—and do more than just that. Maybe once I was making money again— serious money—and if I had Luke helping me make sure I didn't spend it all, I'd be able to use it to actually help people like Danny get their projects made.

With that thought in mind, I smiled at my dad and told him

I was ready for the meeting. It didn't even bother me that my jeans were still damp.

～

"So, Tyler," Isaac Henderson said, gesturing to a seat at the conference table after he'd shaken my hand, "it's good to finally meet you."

I took the seat he'd offered and flexed my hand under the table, hoping he didn't notice. Isaac was one of those guys who treats a handshake like a wrestling match and his smile felt as fake as his tan. You could tell that he not only *knew* he was obnoxious, he was proud of the fact.

Actually, when I thought about it, he reminded me of my dad, who clapped Isaac on the back as the two of them sat down as well.

"It's nice to meet you too, Mr. Henderson, I said, making sure that my smile, at least, reached my eyes. It might be fake but I was a good enough actor to put in a little effort. "I've been such an admirer of the direction you've taken WEV in."

"Really?" Isaac said, giving me a long look. I couldn't tell if he was actually surprised or he just wanted to intimidate me.

"Yeah," I said enthusiastically. "In the five years since you became president, your numbers have gone way up. You're first in your timeslot from 8-10pm three nights of the week and when you factor in delayed viewing and streaming numbers, you've pretty much cornered the 18-35 year old market. You've got a real gift for picking promising pilots and giving series orders to successful shows."

The fact that those shows were full of straight white male leads working as doctors, lawyers, and cops, and were written, directed, and produced by more straight white men, *and* were insanely boring was a fact I kept to myself.

Because I'm not a complete idiot. And also because, gross as it was, if I could get onto one of those shows, maybe someday I'd be back in a position where I'd have enough money to try to get better things on the air.

Isaac glanced over at my dad and raised an eyebrow. "You coached him well for this meeting, Vincent."

My dad shook his head and laughed. "That's all Tyler, I swear," he said, which subjected me to the strange sensation of finally getting a true, genuine compliment from my father and managing to feel gross about it at the same time.

"Well, Tyler," Isaac said, "you've got me impressed. I have to admit, most young people don't have anywhere near your level of knowledge of the field."

His teeth sparkled as he smiled and I had to take a deep breath so I didn't bristle at his condescending tone. I forced myself to smile self-deprecatingly.

"Well, I want to be a success," I said. "And the best way to do that is to follow other people who are successful. You're the best at what you do, Mr. Henderson. And I'd be honored to work with you."

Gross, and laying it on a little thick, but the thing about narcissists is that even if your praise strikes them as fake, they still like it too much to hold it against you.

"I like that attitude," Isaac said. "And please, call me Isaac." He turned back to my dad. "I think you were right about him, Vincent."

My dad smiled. "Hey, I told you he was a smart kid. When he gets out of his own way," he added, turning his smile on me and letting a hint of menace in.

"Ah well, we all make mistakes," Isaac said expansively, waving away my dad's comment. He turned back to me and steepled his fingers on the conference table. "In fact, I think that's part of your charm. You're a good kid, but you're not too squeaky clean. Sure, you've made some unconventional choices, but that just keeps you from looking too perfect. And we can capitalize on that."

His smile was predatory this time.

"Um, okay," I said, hoping that that came out seeming pliable and open, rather than guarded and confused, which was what I was feeling. "What uh—what exactly did you have in mind?"

"Tyler, I want to make you a star." He held up his hand as if to forestall my objections, even though I was just sitting there waiting for him to go on. "Now, I know, you're saying, *'But Isaac, I'm already famous.'* And you're right. But right now, you're also *in*famous. Not too much, no, and you haven't done anything people can't relate to. But the fact of the matter is you're a bit of an underdog right now. A good kid gone bad, a child actor who grew up and lost his way. A well-meaning kid struggling with addiction, with his sexuality, with success. You're down, but not out. You're not a lost cause. In fact, you're perfectly poised for what America loves most: a comeback."

"You—wait—what?" I said, blinking and trying to wrap my mind around the mess of cliches he'd just vomited out onto the smooth teak wood tabletop. "So what exactly do you want me to be in? You want me to do a guest arc like that on one of your existing shows? With that as the story? Or..."

"Not a guest arc, Tyler, no. And not an existing show, but a new one. A reality show, with you as the star. *Live Love Lang* or *The Tyler Files*." Again he waved his hand like he was brushing away details. "We're still workshopping the title."

"A reality show?" I blinked. "You want me to do—you want me to be in a reality show?"

"More than just be in one, Tyler. It would be all about you. Your struggle to get back on top in Hollywood. Your redemption arc. You're trying to get your old life back, but with all these new struggles. Searching for love, searching for fulfillment. God, it practically writes itself. We spin this right, throw in a relapse, maybe an overdose, a love triangle, and we've got seasons and seasons of this."

""But I—I don't *want* to be in a reality show," I blurted out. I knew it was a stupid thing to say as soon as I said it, but as Isaac had been talking, so clearly pumped up about this idea that had obviously been in development for weeks before anyone had thought to ask me if I wanted to do it, all I could think was, '*NoNoNoNoNoOhChristNo.*' I could feel my heart beating faster. Sweat broke out on my forehead.

"Now I know, you're probably thinking, '*That's not me,*'" Isaac went on, "and I get it. You're a serious actor, and that's not how you see yourself. But Tyler, when I say seasons and seasons—that means millions and millions of dollars. For doing nothing more than just being yourself. That kind of money—that fuck you kind of money—doesn't come around more than once. This is an amazing opportunity Tyler."

"But that's not—that's not acting. That's not even—I don't—I don't want people watching my life like that," I said, starting to feel like I was sinking.

I'd thought this meeting was about me getting a role on one of WEV's shows—maybe, if I was lucky, getting to be in a new show, make it my own. But a reality show?

The last thing in the world I wanted was more people paying attention to the parts of my life that had nothing to do with acting. And who would even want to watch that?

"Women, 18 to 35." It wasn't until Isaac spoke that I realized I'd said that last thought out loud. "That's our weak spot," Isaac went on. "We win the men in that demographic handily, but our numbers among women are lower, and women are obsessed with you. You've got that mix of boy-next-door appeal, bad boy charm, and God knows women are obsessed with gay men. Can you imagine how much they'd salivate watching you torn between two guys—or a guy and a girl? And maybe the stress drives you to drink a bit, or start using again? And then you have to keep it a secret? An intervention, a detox program... The possibilities are endless."

"But it's—it's lies. And it's manipulating people. And it's—God, I don't want those parts of my life on display, whether they're real or not." I looked between my dad and Isaac. "Is this really the project you wanted me for? This is it? There's nothing else?"

Jesus, I couldn't do this. I just couldn't. I knew I was going to make my dad mad, maybe so mad he'd stop talking to me again. And I hated the thought of facing his anger. But I also knew I'd fucking crumble if I had to do this.

Faking a relapse? If I did this show, I wouldn't have to fake it. I'd relapse for real, within a month of having cameras following me around all the time. I didn't know how I knew, but I knew. I couldn't do this.

God, I was shaking, and I couldn't tell if it was from anger or fear or what. My dad was glaring at me, Isaac was looking at me like I was a four year old throwing a tantrum, and all I wanted was to be out of that room.

"Tyler," my dad said sternly. "This is not a negotiation. This is the offer on the table, and you should be grateful that it's available to you at all."

"Our numbers just don't support you in any other projects at this point," Isaac said, spreading his hands in a fake sincere apology. "You understand—it's just how you test right now, and what we feel comfortable betting on."

"I can understand that," I said, working hard to keep my voice even. "I get it, I really do. Hell, I was shocked you wanted to take a meeting with me, when my dad told me about it." I shook my head. "But no—this isn't me. I'm sorry, but if this is the offer, I have to turn it down."

I took a shaky breath, amazed I'd been able to get that out. How I'd found the strength, I didn't know. I felt raw.

"Tyler—" my dad barked. "This is—"

"No, Vincent, calm down," Isaac said. My dad bristled at Isaac's tone, but he swallowed whatever he'd been about to say and let him continue. "Tyler, I know this isn't what you were expecting. And it's an idea that takes some getting used to. But don't say no to it just yet. Take some time to think about it."

"I don't need any time," I said. God, I was still shaking and I really needed to get out of this room. I pushed my chair back and stood up. "I appreciate the offer, but no."

I turned and walked to the door. Isaac and my dad were both talking, loudly, at the same time, but I refused to listen. I couldn't be there anymore, and I was too afraid that if I stopped, even for a minute, I'd lose my nerve and end up saying yes. I had to get out.

I walked through the office and out to the lobby, pushed the elevator button, and then looked nervously over my shoulder. I expected to see my dad stalking out at any minute and I really didn't want him to start shouting at me while we were still on this floor. He wasn't coming yet, but neither was the elevator, so I gave up and decided to take the stairs.

By the time I got down from ten floors up, some of the shaking had subsided. But it started back up again as I pushed out into the ground floor lobby of the building and found my dad waiting for me.

Fuck. There was no way I was getting out of this conversation. Taking a deep breath, I walked over to meet him.

"Dad, I'm sorr—"

"What the fuck were you thinking?" he barked, not waiting for me to finish. "Do you have any idea how hard I worked to set that up? How long it took to even get him to hear me out, to sell him on this idea?"

"Wait, it was *your* idea? So you knew what he was going to propose?"

"Of course I knew. Not the details, but I was the one who convinced him of how lucrative it'd be for their network, how it would bring in that target demographic. And once we had an offer from WEV, we could have played them against other networks. Upped your price."

"But I don't want to *do* that," I said. "Dad, I just—I can't."

"Tyler, you're being a child," my dad said. "You don't *want* to do that? Surprise surprise. You've always been lazy, I've always had to twist your arm to get you to do anything. You know, you cried the morning of your *Criss-Cross Applesauce* audition, said you'd changed your mind, you were too scared to go out in front of the cameras. You've always been ungrateful. If I hadn't made you go on, none of this would have happened. You'd still be living in Long Island, working at a fucking juice bar for minimum wage. You owe your life to me."

"Well maybe I'd rather have that than any of this," I shouted. "You ever think about that? I never asked for any of this."

"Oh bullshit, Tyler," my dad shouted back. "If you didn't want it, you could have quit anytime. But you didn't, did you? You always liked the perks of being famous—you just never wanted to do any of the work—just run around with your friends, getting high and making an ass out of yourself until you get arrested with a cookie jar full of cocaine."

"That was only because—" I stopped, as my brain caught up with my ears. "Wait. What?"

"I'm trying to say, you don't always make the best decisions. I know you've taken some time. I know you've been trying to take steps to make better ones. But let's be honest Tyler—a movie like *Foresight*? If left to your own devices, you'd be a pornstar by the end of the year, completely throwing your career away. I'm trying to help you."

"That's not what I—" I stared at him in confusion, still stuck on what he'd said a moment ago. "How did you know that the coke was in a cookie jar?"

"They said it at some point. In the papers."

"No, they didn't. I know, because my lawyer told me if I pled guilty, we could keep the details of the case private. And then I had to pay to get the story shut down. It cost the last dollar that I had. But that never came out. So how did you— how did you know?"

My dad didn't answer.

"Dad!" My voice went up an octave and I struggled to bring it back down to normal. "How did you know?"

"Tyler, drop it. It's not important. We need to focus on what's in front of us right now."

"No." I shook my head. "No, it is important. How did you fucking know?"

Because there was only one way he could have known. As far as I could see. I felt like I couldn't breathe.

My dad gave me a long look before speaking. "You're not going to like the answer to that question."

"Tell me." All of a sudden my eyes were filled with tears. Dammit, where had that come from? I was fucking angry, I wanted to yell, not cry. "You have to—"

"You need to know why I did it. There were reasons."

"You fucking—you put it there? The coke was yours?"

"I never intended for you to take that car. If you'd never taken it, this wouldn't have happened."

"Or maybe if you'd never put a fucking half kilo of cocaine in that car, it wouldn't have happened. Jesus Christ, and you let me think it was mine? This whole time? You let me think I'd actually bought it and then forgotten, that I'd been on some bender so big that I'd—what the fuck were you even doing with that amount of coke, Dad?"

"It was for you, Tyler," my dad said sharply. "It was just a side business, very discreet, nothing showy. But I had connections and I had customers. Covering up for your ass, paying people off, getting people to be willing to work with you—that was never cheap, you know. So I sold a little on the side. It was to take care of you."

"To take care of me? You fucking—you stopped talking to me for an entire year. You wouldn't even come see me. Wouldn't return my calls. You just cut me off and the whole time, you were the reason I had to—"

"Oh don't play the innocent here," my dad sneered. "You were off the rails and you know it. If it hadn't have been that, it would have been something else that pulled you up short."

"I can't believe you didn't tell me. I can't believe—how could you do that to me? Know it was yours and just—let everyone think, let me think... I thought I was going crazy. I couldn't remember how it got there and I thought I was losing my mind."

"What was I supposed to do. Raise my hand? Walk into the

police station and tell them it was mine?" He snorted. "Where would that have gotten me? Prison, no question. But you—you were salvageable. You wouldn't suffer the same consequences I would have—and it left me free to keep working on your behalf."

"My behalf? You fucking dropped me. You wouldn't talk to me."

"It was for your own good. You needed to grow up. Everything I do, it's for your own good. All I've ever done is try to take care of you."

"Take care of me?" I repeated, my voice shrill. I sounded hysterical. Because I was.

"Yes, take care of you. From day one, no matter when you made a mess—and you made plenty of messes—I fixed them. Didn't I help you when you broke your leg, jumping off that bike rack? Took you straight to the hospital, got you patched up, even though I'd told you not to do that. The network was so pissed, but I kept you from getting in trouble with them."

You did, I thought. *But you're also my dad. That's what you're supposed to do. And now you're bringing up something I did when I was 10 like it has any bearing on who I am today.*

Suddenly I could hear Gray's voice in my head, telling me that that wasn't fair. That that's not who I was anymore. And I wondered for the first time if maybe, he was right.

"Always keeping you from getting in trouble," my dad went on. "Like that time you and Gil destroyed that cabana bar? You have any idea how much that cost to keep quiet—to pay off each and every person who was working that night, and then bury the story every time it surfaced? But I did that—for you. Because you're my boy and I love you. That's all I've ever been trying to do—to take care of you."

"I never asked you to do that. I'm not proud of it, but maybe I should have gotten punished. But instead, you let Gil take all the blame. I never asked for any of that."

"So what, you want me to stop? You want me to stop helping you? Because newsflash, Tyler—no one else is gonna do it if I stop. You'll be on your own."

"Well that's better than the kind of help you give," I said, clenching my fist in frustration. Tears were still leaking from the corners of my eyes and I couldn't stop them. "You fucking hurt me."

"Oh a little rehab didn't hurt you. You needed some time to sort yourself out anyway."

"Not rehab. Not that part. What *you* did. You let me think for the past year that that cocaine was mine. That I was so out of control I didn't even remember buying it. But you—" I stopped, trying to keep myself from crying, choking on my own tears.

"Everyone kept fucking telling me to take responsibility for my actions, and I didn't know what to do. I knew what they wanted to hear, what they wanted me to say, that I'd bought the drugs, that it was my fault, that it was my choice. But I couldn't fucking *remember*, and everyone thought I was lying and eventually *I* thought I was lying, too. And you just let me doubt my own fucking sanity."

"I never said I was perfect, but when you calm down, you'll realize that this was for the best."

"I can't even—I can't deal with this." I shook my head. "I have to go."

"Tyler—"

I didn't stick around to listen to what my dad had to say. I didn't need to. I already knew it would just be more lies.

~

I walked and walked without any idea of where I was going. My dad followed me down the first block, but I ignored him as he shouted at me, even though he was causing a scene. I didn't care anymore. If everyone was determined to put my life on display, let them try. I wasn't going to play any part in it.

God. I didn't know how to make sense of any of this. My dad —my own father—had been dealing cocaine on the side for, God, for I didn't even know how long. Did it even matter?

On its own, that wasn't what I was upset about. Considering I'd purchased my fair share of prescription drugs to finance my own habit, it'd be pretty hypocritical to blame someone who was on the other side of that transaction.

But the fact that he'd let me take the fall for it. That he'd known, that he'd had so many chances to come forward and hadn't. Even after I'd been sentenced, he could have told me, could have explained. But he didn't. And if he hadn't slipped, I would have gone my whole life without knowing the truth.

I'd spent the past year wondering if I was so deeply fucked up that I'd been lying to myself about that coke being mine. Wondering how far down my addiction ran. If I was that much in denial. Assuming that that made me a horrible person.

And maybe I still was. I'm not saying I didn't deserve to pay for my crimes, or that I didn't need the rehab. I got off lighter than I deserved, I knew that. But I didn't know which way was up anymore, and was afraid I might snap.

I felt like I was going to explode. I felt like I needed to talk to someone, to sort this out. To have someone tell me I wasn't completely crazy.

And without being conscious of it, my feet took me back to Gray.

I looked up and realized I was standing outside of Maggie's. How the hell had I gotten here? I must have walked. But that was a long way from the WEV offices in Midtown.

I felt like I was surfacing out of a fugue state. I pulled my phone out to check the time and saw five missed calls from my father. I didn't even remember hearing it ring. I put it away, then stared at the doorway. But I couldn't go in.

Gray didn't want to talk to me, did he? But who else could I talk to? Luke—except Luke would just tell me that I never should have trusted Dad, that he'd been right all along. And he'd be right.

Hell, Luke would probably want to press charges against Dad and maybe that was the right thing to do. But I wasn't up to discussing that right now, or even thinking about it. I just needed someone to listen.

I needed Gray.

I stared at the door, trying to imagine what would happen if

I walked inside. Would he want to see me? Would he even be there?

I realized I had no idea what his life was like when we weren't shooting. God, how did it feel like we'd wrapped months ago, instead of just days? I desperately wanted to reach out to him, but I felt like I was reaching across an abyss.

And I wasn't sure he'd even be on the other side.

But my only other options were—what? Wandering around the city until I collapsed from exhaustion? Going back to Luke's and having him tell me how stupid I'd been? Going back to my dad's hotel and letting him yell at me?

Or maybe I could just stand on the street for the rest of the day until someone noticed me and called the cops about the creepy guy outside the bar?

So I took a deep breath and forced myself to start walking, stepping down off the curb and crossing the street before I could second-guess anymore. The front room was dim and uncrowded as usual, a couple of people sipping coffees and talking on a collection of low seats. I kept my head down and pushed through the velvet curtain.

And stopped.

Gray was there. Right in front of me, in fact. That wasn't the problem. I could see him clearly, that gorgeous face in profile, his broad shoulders, his muscular arms.

But standing with Gray, behind the bar, was Ethan. And Gray's hand was pressed to Ethan's chest.

In an instant, my whole world turned upside down.

Because as I stood there, watching Gray speak quietly to Ethan, I realized something. I hadn't come to talk to Gray because I needed a friend. Or maybe I had, but that was because I hadn't realized til right now that what I felt for Gray was way more than friendship.

It always had been. I was just an idiot who'd been lying to himself about what he felt.

I was in love with Gray.

And there he was with Ethan.

I turned and fled.

By the time I was at the end of the block, I was running, because it suddenly occurred to me that Gray or Ethan or both of them could have seen me, could want to talk to me, and holy shit, I could not handle that conversation right now.

They were back together—I was sure of it. Something must have happened with Ethan's engagement, because I'd seen his face—more clearly than I'd seen Gray's even. Ethan had that kind of desperately-in-love look that you only got when you were truly gone for someone.

Jesus, I wondered what I looked like right now.

I felt like I might vomit. I wanted to stop moving and I wanted to keep going. Needed to process, needed to get out of here. Needed to figure out what the fuck to do now.

Gray was with Ethan. Gray, my best friend, my only friend. Gray, who I was completely, totally, stupid in love with. All those times I'd told myself I didn't have feelings for Gray, that I couldn't have feelings for him—I wanted to laugh hysterically now.

To think I could control my feelings if I just refused to acknowledge them. They'd only built and grown. But Gray didn't feel the same way. Clearly.

And any chance I might have had to tell him—oh fuck, now I'd never be able to. And I'd have to be happy for Gray and Ethan. Oh motherfucking shit on a stick, this was awful.

My phone rang and I jumped, the noise startling me, but I slowed down enough to pull it back out of my pocket. I couldn't help hoping it was Gray, even though that made no sense—hoping that maybe somehow he'd seen me, that he was calling to apologize to explain, to talk.

I had a vision of myself telling Gray I hoped he'd be very happy with Ethan—God, how petty was I?—but when I pulled my phone out, it was just the mechanic calling. Again. Goddammit, I thought I might scream. I wanted to run away and hide, not go be a responsible adult and pick up this fucking car.

I actually did growl on the sidewalk and people passing by looked at me like I was crazy. Someone across the street pointed at me and whispered to their friend and I had to turn and walk in the other direction or I knew that I *would* scream.

I was so fucking *done* being famous—something that would only get worse if I were on people's TVs every goddamn week eating salad and bitching about some fake, produced love triangle.

It didn't help that my dad kept calling. I was fully fuming by the time I got to the mechanic, who, of course, had managed to add a couple extra charges to the bill. I got in the car, but before I could even start the engine, my phone rang again.

It was Luke. I was tempted not to answer it, because I knew he was gonna ask how things went at the meeting and I wasn't sure I was ready to talk about all the shit that had gone down with Dad. But I also knew Luke was persistent and would just keep calling til he got what he wanted.

"Hey Luke," I said, picking up and forcing my voice to be bright and brisk. "Just getting your car back from the mechanic now. I'll drop it off in like 20 minutes, ok?"

"What? Oh, right, my car." Luke sounded confused. "Sure, whatever. Look, Tyler—please tell me you didn't just ink a new contract with that network and Dad as your manager."

"No, it's—I didn't. It's complicated."

I sighed and waited for Luke to ask what I meant. I was already trying to figure out what I'd say when I realized Luke was talking again and he wasn't saying what I'd expected at all.

"Okay, well, don't. Look, I didn't want to say anything until I knew for sure but um. We really need to talk about Dad. Can you come to my office?"

"Wait, what? Why do I—what about Dad? What do we need to talk about?"

Did he know, somehow?

Luke sighed. "I'd rather talk about it in person, if that's okay. It's... kind of a serious subject. And I know your relationship with Dad is like, different from mine but I—"

I felt something sick twisting in my stomach. "Luke, please —what happened?"

"Are you sure you don't wanna—"

"Luke, just tell me."

Luke was quiet for so long I wondered if he'd hung up or something. Finally, he spoke.

"Okay, well, remember how you asked me to set your paperwork up? And like, keep an eye on things for you?"

"Yeah?" I was starting to sweat.

"Well after I noticed that automated transfer—remember the one I asked you about?"

"Yeah."

"You didn't seem to remember setting it up, which seemed weird to me. So I went back to find out how long you'd been doing that. And the further I dug into your accounts, the weirder it got." Luke paused and I could almost see him shaking his head. "Like, some of the things that looked like investments turned out to just be shell companies? And at first I thought I was wrong, or I was reading something the wrong way, but Tyler, the more I got into it... well, I just got off the phone with a friend of mine who works in fraud detection to see if he'd heard of any of these companies or could give me any more information and basically, um..." He paused again. "I think Dad's been stealing from you."

My heart stopped.

"What?"

"I'm sorry Tyler. I'm so sorry. I hate this. I wish I were wrong.

I would have told you sooner, but I kept hoping there was some explanation for all of this, that maybe it was just Dad rerouting some of your money into accounts that did eventually benefit you but... that's *not* what he's been doing." Luke sighed again. "Once I started looking, I knew I had to be really sure before I said anything, that I needed to document everything before Dad got wind of the fact that someone was checking up on this. But he's basically been taking half of what you've been making—more than half, when you add it up—out of your accounts through various fronts. For years."

I didn't know what to say. Dad had been stealing from me? How could he have—fuck. After everything he'd done, how could I even still be surprised?

And yet, I was.

"How long?" I asked, my voice choked. "How long has he been..." I couldn't finish my sentence.

"I'm honestly not sure," Luke said. "I've only been able to track the past three years, because Dad controlled your accounts completely when you were a minor. But I mean, with what I've seen—I wouldn't be surprised if he's been doing this the whole time."

I could feel tears starting to roll down my cheeks and I scrubbed at them angrily. I didn't want to cry about that asshole. He didn't fucking deserve it.

"So I—" I stopped, swallowed, tried again. "So I've just been letting him..."

"*You* haven't been letting him do anything," Luke broke in, his voice insistent.

"But I've always been shitty with money," I said. "I never learned how to handle it, never checked once. I should have. I should have made sure—"

"Let me guess," Luke said. "Dad said you were irresponsible, right? That's probably why he has access to all your accounts in the first place? Because he said he didn't trust you to do it? And you believed him, because of how he'd been telling you how lazy, how stupid you were for years?"

"How did you—" It was like Luke was reading my mind. Like he'd been there throughout my childhood to see those exact interactions, even though I knew he hadn't.

"Tyler, this isn't your fault. This isn't you being irresponsible. This is emotional abuse, and him lying to you to keep control. You couldn't stop it because you never had a chance. He's probably been doing this to you since you were a kid." Luke made a disgusted growl. "God, no wonder he never wanted me and Mom to come out and visit you, never wanted you to spend time with anyone but him. He didn't want to risk losing complete control over you."

I felt bile rise in my throat at Luke's words and I struggled to keep myself from throwing up. God, he was right. He was completely right.

But it didn't help me feel like any less of a fool, an incompetent, worthless excuse for a human being, who couldn't even see what was being done to him, who couldn't fight back, couldn't stand up for himself and stop it.

Had I ever had a shred of strength? Independence? Had I ever been anything but completely weak and useless?

"Tyler," Luke said after a minute. "God, I'm sorry, I didn't mean to—fuck, can you please just come to the office. Or I can come home early. I just—we can talk about this, figure out what to do. I mean, legal action is the obvious next step, but we'll want to be careful about—"

"Fuck, I can't do this," I said, feeling myself start to shake. "I can't—I can't handle—I can't be here anymore."

"Please, just come to my office."

Fuck, I just wanna disappear.

"Tyler, come on we can figure this out."

I didn't even realize I'd spoken out loud until Luke responded.

"Tyler?" He said again. "Tyler, are you still there?"

"I have to go."

I hung up, took one glance at all the missed calls from my dad, and turned my phone off. I didn't know if I'd scream or cry or throw my phone out the goddamn window if he tried to contact me again right now, but I knew I couldn't handle it. Just like I knew I was supposed to drive to Luke's office and talk to him about this. Like a rational human being.

Instead, I took the entrance to the Holland Tunnel. And within 10 minutes I was driving out of the city.

15

GRAY

"Okay, so this button?" I said to Micah, looking up from the screen in front of me.

I was standing behind the bar, trying to figure out the new POS system. I'd planned on installing it for a while—Maggie had run the whole bar with an old-fashioned cash register and spiral-bound notebooks—but it hadn't actually gotten put in until I was gone, filming *Foresight*.

Micah shifted Bea, the baby he was holding, from his left side to his right as he peered over my shoulder. Even though Bea was only a few weeks old, Micah was babysitting her for a few hours while Caro, her mom, got her haircut.

"No," Micah said, pointing at the screen. "That cancels the order. You need the green one up in the—no, not that one, that one adds guacamole." He turned to the customer standing on the other side of the bar. "I'm assuming you don't want a dollop of guacamole added to your beer."

"Sorry," I added as the customer, an older man with curling gray hair, laughed. "I'm new at this."

"First day?" he said. "I've been there."

"Uh, he *owns* the bar," Micah said while I flushed. "He has no excuses."

"Yeah, I'm just incompetent," I said. I turned to Micah. "You wanna do this while I pour his beer?"

"You'll never learn if I don't make you," Micah replied. But he took my place behind the register while I moved over to the taps. I grabbed a pint glass, poured the guy's amber ale, and slid it over to him on a coaster as Micah rang up the sale.

"See? So easy this one could do it," he said, pointing to Bea as the customer left with his beer.

I frowned. "Are you sure there's no law about having babies in bars?"

"Don't you think you're the one who should know that?" Micah laughed. "Sometimes I'm amazed this place is still open, given how little you know about running it."

I pursed my lips. "About that."

"Oh no." Micah's eyes widened as he shifted Bea over again. "What did I do?"

"Nothing, nothing," I said, trying to calm him down. "Or, well, actually, everything. Which is kind of the point."

Micah eyed me skeptically. "I'm confused. Am I about to get yelled at?"

"No. The opposite, actually. It's just something I've been meaning to talk to you about. You want a beer?"

I moved back to the taps and poured myself an IPA.

"Oh God, now I'm even more nervous," Micah said, "if you think we need alcohol for this conversation."

"Not need, weirdo. I'm just offering."

"Well, as long as you're buying. Sure, a hefeweizen."

I filled his beer and gestured for Micah to pull up a stool at the bar, which he did, deftly balancing Bea on his lap. My phone rang and I pulled it out, on the off chance that it would be Tyler.

It was Ethan. I hit ignore.

Micah arched an eyebrow and I showed him the missed call screen. He made a face.

"I can't believe he's still trying to talk to you. He is the actual worst person on the planet."

I shrugged. "I've honestly given up caring. Hopefully he will at some point too."

Micah gave me a long look. "That's not what you wanted to talk about, is it? Because if he said anything to make you think—if him getting engaged has you going through some soul-searching depression where you've decided you're permanently undesirable or something, I'm gonna hunt him down and kick his ass."

I laughed at that, like his words hadn't hit uncomfortably close to home. "No. Not—well, that's not what I wanted to talk to you about, anyway."

Micah squinted at me, took a sip of his beer, and then nodded.

"Okay. Then lay it on me. Is the bar closing? Are we out of

money? Or are you just packing it up to move to LA?"

"None of the above," I said. "Not exactly. Well, not at all. God, Micah, I don't know if you've actually looked at the books, but we made more money in the past month, now that you've been running things, than we have since back when Maggie was here."

"What? Really?" Micah's eyes widened.

"Really. Micah, you're actually good at this. I... never was. It was never my passion, you know. So," I said, nodding, sure I'd made the right decision, "so, I want to make you an offer. I want you to buy the bar."

"What?" Micah spluttered. "Gray, you can't sell me the bar."

"Why not? You'll do a better job running it than I ever could. You already do. And I'll sell it to you for cheap. Micah, the mark-up on alcohol is so high, you have to be actively *bad* at bar management to lose money on one. The fact that we're still running, even after my mediocre management, is testament to those profit margins. Well, that and the fact that Maggie owned the whole building, and bought it back when real estate in lower Manhattan was cheap."

"But I can't—Gray, I don't know the first thing about owning a business," Micah said. "I wouldn't know how to—"

"I could teach you," I offered. "Everything I know, which, granted, isn't much. But the bookkeeping stuff isn't that hard to learn. Honestly, it would be so easy for you to take over. And if I really *am* going to be trying to do this whole acting thing, it's not fair for me to ask you to keep managing the bar but not compensate you better."

"So pay me more."

"You deserve more than just a raise."

"Gray, you know that the reason I work here isn't just because of what you pay me," Micah said with a sad smile. "It's because I like working here, with you. It wouldn't be as much fun without you."

I frowned and Micah's face grew pained. "Not that I'm telling you not to pursue acting. I just... I don't know, I'm an idiot. I'm pretty sure I'd run this place into the ground."

"You'll be great at it, I promise," I said.

Micah rolled his eyes. "That's the same thing Caro told me today when she asked me to watch Bea. *'You're a natural with kids, you'll be great, I promise.'*" He snorted. "I don't know what I ever did to convince my friends I'm a responsible adult. I really shouldn't be trusted with..." He paused, cocked his head to the side, and then smiled. "Wait—idea."

"Oh no. That's never a good look from you."

"What if you sold me a stake in the bar? But not the whole thing."

"How do you mean?"

"I'll buy the bar from you," Micah said. "I'll buy exactly 50% of it. And I'll take over as manager. And you can become a silent partner. But you have to still *be* a partner," he added. "At least until you become so fucking famous that you can't be bothered with us little people anymore."

"You know that's not going to happen. Probably nothing's going to happen at all and in six months, I'll realize how dumb this was and I'll be the same idiot as before... just this time I won't have a bar to fuck up."

"Please," Micah said. "I've seen that teaser. You're good at this, Gray."

"Debatable." I frowned. "51%."

"What?" Micah said.

"You have to own 51% of it. I'll own 49%. That way, push comes to shove, you have power to make decisions without me."

"You realize I could be a complete idiot with business ownership. This could be a terrible idea."

"I might be a complete idiot at acting. Trying to make that happen could also be a terrible idea. But at least I'm trying."

"You're actually not an idiot, though," Micah protested. "You wouldn't have gotten the role otherwise. Besides, Tyler thinks you're good, and he actually knows what he's talking about."

"Maybe."

Micah gave me a speculative look. "How is Tyler, by the way?"

"I don't know." I shrugged. "Fine, I guess."

"Have you talked to him since you guys wrapped?"

"No," I said, trying to act like I hadn't been thinking about Tyler—and thinking about how I needed to stop thinking about him—every minute of every day.

Dammit, I'd said goodbye. I'd carved it into that fucking tree like a sentimental idiot. I'd put that to rest.

"And that's normal to you," Micah said, squinting at me. "Nothing's wrong? Nothing happened between you guys?"

Micah, despite my best efforts to the contrary, had taken one look at me and Tyler the night we'd been here with the guys and sussed out the lay of the land as quickly as Ben had.

"Yeah." My attempt at sounding nonchalant just came out annoyed. "Contrary to your beliefs, not every crush has to go somewhere." *Crush. That's putting it lightly.* "And not every story has a fairytale ending. Nothing happened. We're just... the same as we always were. Friends."

"Do you believe him?" Micah asked, turning and addressing Bea on his lap. "Do you think he's telling the truth?"

"Micah..."

"What's that?" Micah bent down and brought his ear close to Bea's face. "You think he's lying?" He looked at Bea very seriously. "You know what? Me too. I think he's definitely lying."

"Oh for Christ's sake."

"You wouldn't lie to a baby, would you, Gray?" Micah asked. "Lie to a pure and innocent little beam of light like her? How could you look into her face and do that?"

"I'm not lying," I insisted, my frustration rising. "Everything's fine. We're just..." I trailed off, not sure how to finish that.

"Gray." Micah's voice was gentle. "All joking aside. You've seemed... not great since you got back. Not happy, anyway. And you don't have to talk about it if you don't want to—"

"That's rich," I snorted. "Since when have you ever left well enough alone when someone didn't want to talk about something?"

"Okay, fair. *But* that's just because I'm your friend and I care about you. If you *really* don't want to talk about it, you don't *have* to. But I just—I don't like seeing you hurting. And I think that that's exactly what you're doing right now. Hurting, and trying to pretend you're not."

I sighed and looked down at my beer. What could I even say?

I *was* hurting. But it was my own damn fault, for ever thinking that Tyler might—well, that he might have wanted something he'd explicitly said he didn't want. I should have believed him. Tyler had never promised anything more than what he could give. It was me who'd gotten his hopes up, stupidly.

"We fought," I said finally, looking up at Micah. Well, not at Micah, actually, but at Bea. Her big brown eyes were luminous. "It was stupid. We—we slept together. After we wrapped. It was—I thought—" I shook my head. "It doesn't matter what I thought. I was wrong."

Wrong to think he'd ever want you. Wrong to think there was some world in which you could have a future with him. What the hell were you thinking?

My whole life, I'd carried around this stupid idea that someday I'd have a family. That I'd have someone by my side, someone to go through my life with. Raise kids with. Grow old with.

I smiled down at Bea again, sadly. Ridiculous. I was never going to have kids. Ethan had shown me that. Hell, my whole life had shown me that. I wasn't the kind of person who made people want to stay. And whatever insane dream I'd had about Tyler—it was never going to lead to a white picket fence.

"What did you fight about?" Micah asked quietly. "Did you —did you tell him how you feel?"

"Felt," I corrected him.

"Feel," Micah insisted, and he held my gaze until I dropped my eyes and nodded.

"I didn't tell him," I said. "I—I thought about it, but then—" I shook my head and laughed. "Then his fucking dad showed up."

"What?" Micah yelped. It was loud enough that Bea looked up in confusion and looked like she might start crying. Micah smiled down at her, booped her nose, and bounced her until she started gurgling happily and turned her attention to trying to grab her toes.

"His dad came?" Micah repeated in a softer voice. "When you were—"

"The morning after. He sorta saw us... well, saw the aftermath anyway."

"Jesus."

"Yeah. Not uh—not great. But he'd apparently been trying to get in touch with Tyler, he'd set up some meeting with a network executive and was there to take him back to New York. And I—" I sighed. "I don't know. I kind of lost it. It wasn't good."

"Holy shit."

"His dad's just *such* a dick. And you can tell from the way he treats Tyler that he's fucking horrible, but Tyler goes along with it because he's terrified. His dad's got him convinced he's worthless and that he'll fail without him." I ran a hand through my hair. "So I did the opposite of what I should have done, which was be supportive, and instead I told him his dad was a dick and he shouldn't go with him and he was making a mistake."

"Yikes." Micah winced.

"Yeah. So that... went over about as well as you'd imagine. And Tyler put me in my place—as he should have—and then... he left. And we haven't talked since."

"Jesus," Micah said again. He shook his head. "That's... way more dramatic than I expected. But you're not going to leave it there, right?"

I sighed. "What else can I do?"

"Apologize." Micah said it like it was the most obvious thing in the world. "Literally, that is what you should do. Call him, tell him you're sorry." He stared at me incredulously. "Are you telling me you seriously weren't going to do that?"

"What if he doesn't want to talk to me?"

"Ummm, that is highly impossible. I remember the way he looked at you when you guys were here. That guy is head over heels for you. He might not realize it yet, but once you tell him you're in love with him—"

"I'm not—" I began, but then stopped. I couldn't bring myself to finish the sentence.

"Oh?" Micah smiled expectantly. "You're not *what*?" I sighed and Micah grinned. "That's what I thought." He pulled Bea in and kissed her cheek. "Really, Gray. Think of the example you're setting for the youth of today. Think of Bea."

I snorted. "She's what... not even a month old? She's not going to remember this."

"You never know what she could osmose up from you." He watched me for a minute. "I can't believe we're even still sitting here talking about this. Seriously, what are you doing? Go call that boy and tell him you're sorry, you overreacted, you shouldn't have judged him, but you just care so much because you're, you know, *completely and totally in love with him*. And boom—everything will be—"

I looked up in confusion from my beer glass, not sure why Micah had stopped talking. He was looking over at the door. I followed his gaze.

Standing just in front of the green curtains, hands on his hips, was Ethan.

"What the fuck is he doing here?" Micah said angrily. "Did you tell him to come here?"

"No," I protested, confused. "No, not at all. God, I'm not that much of an idiot."

"Sometimes I wonder," Micah said darkly.

Ethan was looking over at us now, not moving. Micah glared at him like he could push Ethan back through those curtains with the sheer force of his gaze.

Ethan's face flushed and he cocked his head to the side like he was asking me to come join him. I refused, and just watched him, stone-faced. Eventually Ethan walked over to meet us. He said nothing. I said nothing. It was Micah who broke the silence.

"Well," he said, still glaring at Ethan. "What are you doing here?"

"Um, hi," Ethan said, his voice nervous. His eyes darted back and forth between me and Micah before settling on my face. "Can we um... talk?"

I stared at him. I didn't particularly want to talk to him. Not at all. But with the amount that he'd been calling, and the fact that he'd shown up here unannounced, I got the distinct impression that this was only going to get worse until I finally let him say whatever he felt he needed to say.

"Fine," I said. "Talk."

Ethan glanced back at Micah and swallowed. "Um, I was kind of hoping we could do it alone?"

Micah rolled his eyes. "Well, I'm on shift right now, so I'm not leaving."

"Please, Gray?" Ethan said. He bit his lip. "I broke things off with Christie."

Micah whistled in surprise and I blinked. He'd *what*?

"Jesus." I shook my head. "I hope you didn't—"

"Please Gray," Ethan begged. "I just... I need to talk to you. To explain."

I sighed and looked over at Micah. "I'll take over for you up here. I think there's still some payroll stuff to finish back in my office."

I could have taken Ethan back there, but frankly, I didn't

want to give him the impression that I wanted to take him somewhere private, or that I cared about what he had to say at all. I didn't care that he'd broken up with Christie. Except maybe to feel bad for her. At this point, I just wanted Ethan to say his piece and then leave.

"Fine," Micah said. He took a final swallow of his beer and set his glass down, then narrowed his eyes as he stood up, balancing Bea on his hip. "I'll be back there if you need me."

I picked up his glass to bring it over to the dish washer. Micah glared at Ethan once more as he walked away. Ethan watched Micah's retreating back with a mixture of trepidation and annoyance. And then, as soon as Micah disappeared down into the back hall, Ethan came around the end of the bar, walked up to me, and launched himself into my arms.

Or, well, tried to. I'd stopped moving, trying to figure out why Ethan was coming behind the bar, and before my brain could process anything, he was on me. Except I still had Micah's glass in my hands, and I held it in between us like a barrier, frozen in shock as Ethan's mouth sought mine.

"Jesus, Ethan, what the fuck?" I spluttered, stepping back and pushing him away. "What the hell do you think you're doing?"

"Gray, God, I'm so sorry," Ethan said. He took another step forward and I took a corresponding one back. "I know we have so much to talk about but I just can't—I need—I need you."

He moved forward again and I felt the back of my legs bump up against the counter. I held my hand out and pushed against his chest.

"Christ, Ethan, what the hell? I said you could talk, not molest me."

"But you said—I mean, I told you—" Ethan looked at me in confusion. "I broke things off with Christie. There's no reason we can't—"

"There's plenty of fucking reason," I said. "Like how I don't want to." I looked at him as it dawned on me. "Holy shit, did you think we were going to—God, Ethan, no. Whatever you thought was happening here, is just... *not*. You said you wanted to explain. That's all I'm here for—and barely that."

Ethan's eyes traveled down to where my hand was still pressed against his chest and I pulled it back like it burned. I slipped around him and walked to the far end of the bar. From the corner of my eye, I saw the curtains leading out to the front room move. I wondered if I'd just lost a customer because of Ethan's ridiculousness.

"I'm serious. You can say what you want, but you're doing it from... there," I said, glaring at him and indicating the distance between us. "Or you can leave."

"Gray, I—" Ethan's face crinkled into something like anguish. "God, Gray, I'm sorry, I didn't mean to—shit. Fuck, okay." Ethan shook his head and looked up at me. "Okay. I can explain."

I folded my arms across my chest and waited.

"It's—God, okay, I didn't mean to—" Ethan paused and glanced at me. "It's kind of hard to talk to you when you're looking at me like that."

"Like what?"

"Like I'm a days-old used condom you found clogging up your toilet."

I stared at him, uncomprehending. "Jesus, Ethan, how did you think this was going to go? How am I supposed to look at you?"

"I know you're mad but—"

"Mad? Ethan, mad doesn't even begin to cover it. You kept me hanging on for *years* with promises that someday we'd be together, for real, the way I wanted. *Someday* you'd come out to your family. *Someday* you'd tell them you couldn't marry Christie. *Someday* you *would* marry me."

I shook my head in disgust. "And I put up with it—I don't know if that makes me an idiot or just makes you a good liar, but I fucking put up with it and told myself it was enough. Until the second I actually needed you, and then you disappeared. And when I asked you to really commit? Suddenly it's, '*Well actually, I don't really believe in marriage,*' and, '*I'm just not ready for that.*'"

"Gray, I—"

"And you know what? Even then, *even then*, I made excuses for you. It hurt, but I told myself you were just being honest. I told myself maybe you didn't know what you really wanted til you were in that position. And I let you string me along, telling myself that you still cared, that you were still flirting with me all the time, that surely you'd realize you missed me. But then it turns out you've been with Christie since the week we broke up? And now you're engaged? The very thing you told me you'd never be able to do?"

The more I talked, the more upset I got. I'd tried so hard not to think about it because it just made me so angry. Had Ethan really thought I'd be pathetic enough to take him back, after everything? Did he really think I hated myself that much?

And if he did—Jesus, it must be because I'd acted that way. And Ethan must have been counting on me being so grateful that he'd come back to me that I'd just say that all was forgiven.

"Okay, fair," Ethan said after a moment. "I probably deserve that."

I arched an eyebrow.

"Okay, definitely deserved that. But just... hear me out, okay?"

Ethan gave me a hopeful little smile, the corners of his lips just turning up and his eyebrows still drawn together. It was the kind of smile that used to tug at something inside of me but somehow tonight, it was just making me angry. I didn't smile back and slowly, the expression slid off his face like rainwater down a window. Now he just looked apprehensive.

"I freaked out, Gray," Ethan said. "I freaked out completely when you proposed. I... I don't know, I can't really defend it. I know we'd talked about it but in that moment, it just seemed so real and so scary. I mean, Maggie was so sick and I—I guess I was just thinking about how we never know how long our lives are gonna be and I just didn't feel ready to settle down then, you know? And then I didn't want to keep you hanging on for something I knew you wanted, something I wasn't sure I'd ever be able to give you. So I ended it. I know it was shitty timing, believe me, I still hate myself for that. But I just…"

He trailed off and looked up at me, his eyes begging me for some kind of response. But I wasn't in the mood to give him anything. I'd heard all of this before. Ethan seemed to realize that I wasn't going to say anything so he took a breath and kept going.

"Things with Christie… just kind of happened. You know I suck at being alone. And she was just… there. And you know how things are, with our families. It was just… easy. It was nice to just feel happy again, to not feel like a terrible person every time I looked in her eyes, the way I did when I saw you."

My eyes widened. I'd expected… God, I didn't know what I'd expected, but something better than that. I'd expected Ethan to explain some hidden facet of Christie that explained why he'd always kept her around. Something about her that I'd never seen, something amazing that made Ethan want to be with her. But this…

"So you're dating her because she makes you feel like a less shitty person?" I said, my voice flat. "Do you even like her? Or do you just like the way she distracts you from yourself? Do you just like that she likes you?"

Ethan sighed. "It's not that simple."

"Really? Because that's pretty much what it sounds like. It sounds like you felt guilty about what you did and rather than fucking sitting with that and trying to figure out why, you just ran to find the nearest set of holes to stick your dick in and distract yourself. Which… honestly Ethan, fine by me, if that's what you want to do with your life. But getting engaged? Getting married to a woman you've always told me you never even liked, someone who was just a family friend, just months after you told me you never wanted to get married?"

"Well what was I supposed to do?" Ethan shot back. "You barely talk to me anymore. We almost never see each other. We went from spending every freaking day together to me seeing you once every two weeks. You don't think that hurts, Gray? You don't think I miss you? I miss you so much I want to scream."

"That's how it fucking works, Ethan," I said, wanting to claw something to shreds. "When you break up with someone, you don't get to keep seeing them every fucking day. Goddammit, you're the one who broke up with me. You didn't think that was going to change things?"

Ethan sighed. "I just... I didn't realize... I... fuck, Gray, I just miss you. And I was lonely. I lost my best friend, you know."

"Well I lost mine too."

"I'm sorry."

"Sorry? What the hell are you apologizing to me for? *You don't owe me anything anymore,* Ethan. You don't need me to understand. And it's a good fucking thing, because I never will."

Ethan shook his head. "My parents told me I had to get married, Gray. Or I lose my trust fund. You know what they're like. It's not that Christie's so... I don't love her Gray. I never have. But if I hadn't proposed..."

"Jesus Christ." I stared at him. "I can't fucking believe you.

You don't even love her? You just proposed so you wouldn't lose out on your fucking trust fund?"

"But I changed my mind, Gray," Ethan protested. "I broke things off. Don't you get it? I ended things, with Christie, to be with you. It wasn't right and I knew it and I fucking ended it. I said no, to all of that money. For you." He took a step forward, then another. "Gray, I did that before I came here. Before I'd talked to you. Before I had any idea what you'd say, because it was the right thing to do. Because I'm still in love with you."

A wave of... *something* washed through me. Anger, definitely, but something hotter, something that made me feel sicker.

Disgust. That was what it was. Disgust.

"Ethan, I need you to leave," I said quietly.

"What?" Ethan blinked. "No, Gray, you don't understand. It's over with Christie. Fuck, it's over with my family. They're never going to talk to me again, not after the mess I've made. I'm here and I'm willing to do whatever you want. You want to get married? Let's do it. Let's buy tickets to Vegas and do it tomorrow. I'll do whatever you need."

"What I need," I said slowly, "is for you to go back in time and treat me better. Treat our relationship better from the fucking start. Hell, while you're at it, treat fucking Christie better. What I need is for you to realize that just because you're feeling sad or lonely or scared of someone's disapproval, you don't get to treat other people like shit. And failing that, what I need is for you to get out of my bar."

I pointed to the door. Ethan stared at me, but I didn't move.

"Gray, are you really—we have years of history," Ethan said. "You said it yourself. You're really throwing that away?"

"Ethan," I said shaking my head. "You threw it away three months ago. Fuck, you threw it away the first time you lied to me and said you wanted to be with me. I'm not even sure there was ever anything there to start with."

Ethan exhaled and nodded slowly. Pressing his lips together, he stepped back and around to the far side of the bar.

"I understand you're angry right now," he said. "And you— you have every right to be. I haven't handled any of this well. But... Gray, if you change your mind. Or if you just want to talk any more. I—I'll be waiting."

And then he was gone.

It was the strangest thing. The whole time we'd been talking, I'd forgotten we were in the bar, in public, hashing everything out in front of... well, admittedly not the biggest crowd I'd ever seen in there, but still enough people on a Thursday afternoon to make our conversation a little weird. Everyone seemed to be studiously avoiding looking in my direction and yet you could have driven a fire truck through the bar just minutes ago and I probably wouldn't have noticed.

I sighed and picked up Micah's glass for the final time and actually got it into the dishwasher, then walked back to my office—soon to be Micah's, I thought with a rueful smile— and poked my head in through the door.

"He's gone."

"I was wondering what that sudden breath of fresh air was," Micah said, looking up from where he was entertaining Bea on the floor with some large wooden spoons. "How did... things go?"

"They went," I said heavily. "Anyway, just wanted to let you know you could come out now."

"I mean, I'm obviously kind of in the middle of a productivity spurt," Micah said with a grin. "But I suppose I could be convinced to come actually do my job." He smiled down at Bea. "Let's go keep Uncle Gray company." He scooped her up, but Bea made a protesting noise as he left the spoons on the floor.

"Good point," Micah said, bending back down to grab them. "We might need those in case Ethan comes back and we have to beat him off with force."

I snorted as Micah and Bea followed me back out to the bar.

"I don't think he's coming back," I said, sitting down on one of the bar stools.

"Yeah? Why's that? Here, take this one," he added, holding Bea out to me. "I think I need to hydrate before I hear this story."

Bea gurgled happily as I took her from Micah and set her down on my lap, where she proceeded to drool on my arm hair with wild abandon. Micah filled a glass with ice and water, squeezed a lime wedge into it, and then looked at me critically.

"Jesus, you look really fucking adorable with a kid," he said. "It's kind of sickening."

"Yeah, well, any such kids in the future will not be Ethan's," I said, wincing as Bea tried to stick her finger up my nose.

"What did he want?" Micah asked, leaning down on the bar and folding his hands like he was ready for a story. "Please tell me it was really pathetic and you made sure he knew that before you sent him packing."

"It was something, alright." I rolled my eyes. "I don't know, maybe it was pathetic. It mostly just made me realize how pathetic *I've* been for the past few months—years, really. Thinking he'd finally give me what I wanted when he was never going to." I shrugged. "He told me he proposed to Christie to avoid losing his trust fund, but then he broke things off with her because he realized he was still in love with me and that he wanted to get back together and I—well, I told him no."

"Damn." Micah smiled at me. "That's cold. And amazing. And no offense but like, I'm kinda impressed?"

I laughed. "Fuck, no offense taken. Until a week ago, I might have had trouble doing that. But the thought of getting back together with Ethan now just makes me..." I laughed. "Is there a word for grossed out and also just done? Just tired?"

Micah giggled. "The Germans probably have one."

"God," I said, shivering a little at a thought that had just occurred to me. "I'm so glad I didn't pick up any of his calls. If I'd talked to him any earlier, I'm not sure I would have been strong enough to say no."

And then it hit me.

What was different in the past week? It wasn't just finding out that Ethan had gotten engaged. If it had just been that, I'd have been frustrated, sure, angry even. But I might have still *cared* in a way that I didn't now.

Because something else had happened in the past week too. Or at least, I'd *discovered* something else—something that had actually been happening for a long time.

"Fuck," I said softly. "I need to go talk to Tyler."

"Ding ding ding!" Micah said. "You win. Praise Yaweh. Finally. I thought that was going to take a lot longer. Did getting over Ethan somehow make you smarter, too?"

"Shut up," I said, rolling my eyes. I glanced down at my watch. "Do you mind if I cut out early?"

"To go find the man you're in love with and tell him how wrong you were and how much you'd die for him?" Micah said with a grin. "Because if that's why you're leaving, no, I don't mind at all. But if it's for any other reason..."

"No," I said, feeling my heart begin to beat faster. "It's—it's the first one."

It was silly, maybe, feeling like there was some kind of time pressure. But I felt like I'd explode if I didn't find Tyler right this minute. It had been four days since I'd seen him and suddenly I wasn't sure I could go another minute without fixing that.

"Go," Micah said with a smile, reaching across the bar to take Bea from me. "Get out of here."

And I did.

~

I don't know why I felt like I needed to walk out of the bar to call Tyler, but I did. Maybe it was just because I didn't want to be standing where Ethan had just been. Didn't want to think about that anymore.

I stepped out through the front doors, pulled Tyler's number up on my phone, and bit my lip. Then I smiled, that gesture immediately reminding me of the way Tyler looked when he was nervous but excited about something. Pretty accurate representation of my emotional state right now.

The call went straight to voicemail. I hung up and frowned, wondering immediately if I should have left a message. Did anyone leave messages anymore? Did anyone listen to them, if you did?

I texted him instead.

GRAY: Hey so... incoming wall of text warning but basically

GRAY: I'm so sorry about how we left things on Monday, I've been feeling shitty about it ever since and wanting to reach out and apologize. I should have been a better friend and more supportive. I really hope the meeting went well and I'd love to talk to you if you could be convinced to forgive me for being such a dick. There's some stuff I kind of want to talk about

GRAY: So... yeah. Sorry :(And uh, hope you're doing well :)

I stared at my phone for a long moment, trying to decide if I should send one final message. Would it be too much?

But at this point, what did I really have left to lose?

GRAY: I miss you

But the thing about texting is that it's completely unsatisfying if the person doesn't text you back immediately. And if Tyler's phone was off, hence the voicemail, there was no telling when he'd turn it back on. So what was I supposed to do til then?

What any normal person would have done, probably, was go back to the bar and try to keep busy until he called. Work and talk to other people and be productive and try to keep my mind *off* of the situation, since there was nothing I could do in the meantime.

And a semi-normal person, someone maybe only mildly obsessive, might have sent one or two or ten follow up texts to the ones I'd sent. A little much, maybe, but understandable. Maybe engage in a little light social media stalking too.

A completely abnormal person, like me, would decide to walk to his apartment. Which is what I did.

Or more specifically, his brother's apartment, which I'd only been to once to drop him off there a few weeks ago. And yet my brain had apparently committed the address and apartment number to memory and before I knew it, I was standing outside the building in Midtown wondering how the hell I could justify ringing the buzzer for 30J.

What if no one was home? What if Luke was home, and not Tyler? What if both Tyler and his brother were there, but Tyler didn't want to talk, and Luke got stuck in the middle awkwardly?

"Gray?"

I turned around at the sound of a confused voice behind me to see Luke jogging up to me on the sidewalk. He was pulling earbuds out and looked like he was winding down from a run.

"Oh, hey," I said, trying to act like I hadn't been standing paralyzed in front of his apartment building like a creepy stalker for the past 15 minutes. "How are you?"

"Not good, actually." Luke said, wiping sweat from his brow. "Are you here to see Tyler? Did he tell you he was here?"

"I uh—well I thought—I mean, if he doesn't want to see me, I don't have to—" I babbled while Luke stared at me in confusion. "Wait, is Tyler not here?"

"I have no idea," Luke said. "That's why I was asking you. We were on the phone and I gave him some... not great news and he just hung up on me and now he's not answering, his phone's off, and I have no idea where he is. I asked him to meet me at my office but when it was clear he wasn't coming, I ran up here to see if maybe he'd—"

"Wait, you *ran* here from your office?" I frowned. "Don't you work in the Financial District?"

"Yeah," Luke shrugged. "But I don't know, I got kinda worried and it was faster than taking the subway."

"You can outrun the subway?"

"I've been doing interval training," Luke said as if that explained everything. "Wait, so why are you here, if you didn't know if Tyler—"

"Same as you, I guess," I said, starting to feel worried. "I was trying to get in touch with him and I thought maybe he— well, we kind of left things weird the last time I saw him and I thought maybe he was ignoring me so I..."

"Came to make him listen to you apologize in person?" Luke said with a wry grin.

"Well it sounds really creepy when you say it like that," I said weakly.

Luke snorted. "Nah, I'd probably have done the same thing. Here, come on up with me."

He walked over to the buzzer and swiped us in with his key fob. I followed him through the lobby and into one of the waiting elevators. Luke gave me a considering look as we rode up and finally spoke.

"Listen, I know it's none of my business," he said, "but can I ask what you and Tyler—I mean, you said you'd kinda... fought or something?"

"Yeah."

I paused, trying to figure out what, exactly, to say. Tyler's dad might have realized we'd slept together, but that didn't mean that Luke knew—or that he'd approve anymore than his dad did when he found out.

It didn't matter that Luke was gay—you didn't have to be straight to think that your sexually-inexperienced little brother sleeping with an ex-porn star was less than ideal.

"It was stupid," I said finally. "I was being a dick. Your dad came and surprised him with this meeting and I didn't think he was treating Tyler very well and I just—sorry, you probably don't want to hear this, he's your dad too. It's just—"

"Motherfucker," Luke spit out and I winced at the anger in his eyes when he looked at me. So much for him not hating me. But then he kept talking.

"I should have fucking known," Luke continued. "My dad, in

case you haven't figured it out, is the literal worst and ruins everything and has been fucking up Tyler's life for years."

I blinked. That... wasn't what I'd expected at all.

"I uh—I mean—fuck." I laughed for a second, before realizing it wasn't funny. "Yeah, that's more or less it. I mean, he just—is he always like that? The shit he said to Tyler was really fucked up."

"I honestly don't know," Luke said, shaking his head as the elevator doors open. He walked out, talking to me over his shoulder as he went. "I haven't actually seen the guy in years. But he was a dick to my mom and then when Tyler got arrested, he fucking dropped him, just cut him out of his life. And it just pisses me off to see Tyler defending him, because I know it's just that he's being manipulated."

He stopped outside an apartment door. "I hope that doesn't sound bad. None of this is Tyler's fault. It's just... I don't know what to do."

"I one hundred percent believe you," I said, shaking my head. "If you want my opinion, your dad's an asshole."

"Agreed." Luke gave me a long look. "Tyler's lucky to have you, you know."

"Oh, he doesn't—I mean, we're not—"

"Gray." Luke's voice stopped me, but his smile was warm. "I was there at Maggie's. It's not that hard to see there's something between you." He shrugged. "Whatever it is, I'm just saying, I'm glad Tyler has you in his corner."

"Oh. Um." I found myself blushing. "Thanks. He's lucky to have you as a brother, too."

Luke shrugged again, "Eh. I'm alright. I wasn't really there when he probably needed me most. I'm just trying to make up for that as much as I can, now."

With a wry smile, Luke turned the key in the lock, pushing open the door. "Tyler? Are you here?"

He wasn't. It took Luke all of 15 seconds to check the apartment and ascertain that.

"Fuck," he said, throwing his keys down on the coffee table in frustration. "Fuck fuck fuck, this is not good."

"Is there—" I paused. "I know this isn't really *my* place to ask, but is there a reason you're worried? You said you had to give him bad news and I just—should I be worried too?"

Luke grimaced. "I just got confirmation today that my dad's been embezzling from Tyler for at least three years, maybe more."

"Jesus, what? But he—fuck. Are you serious?"

"Yeah," Luke said, looking grim.

"Tyler always said he was terrible with money," I said slowly. "That he'd lost all of his. I know he was afraid he'd do that again, once we started getting paid for *Foresight*. Does this mean that—"

"All of that is actually probably my dad's fault, stealing from Tyler and then convincing him that it was his spending habits that were the problem?" Luke said bitterly. "Getting him to trust himself even less, and giving my dad even more control over his finances? Yeah. That's what it means."

"Motherfucker," I said, using Luke's phrase from the elevator.

"And now I don't know where the fuck he is and I just—" Luke's voice broke and he looked at me in fear. "The last thing he said on the phone was that he couldn't handle this and he couldn't be here anymore. That he wanted to disappear. And I just—I don't think he'd do anything, but I don't know how I'd react in his position and I hate to think—"

It felt like all the blood drained out of my body at Luke's words. If anything had happened to Tyler—if Tyler had done anything, because of this news, because of how his dad had treated him... I could see that Luke wouldn't forgive himself, and I knew I wouldn't either.

"We'll find him," I said. "We will. We have to."

"I don't even know where to look," Luke said, his voice broken. "He's only been back here for a few months. I don't know where he'd go."

I thought for a moment. "Let's start with the obvious places. Your mom lives on Long Island, right?"

"Yeah," Luke said. "Do you think he'd go there? I can call her."

"Do," I said. "And go there. Check anywhere you ever went as kids. Any place he's ever mentioned going in the city."

I turned and started walking to the door.

"Where are you going?" Luke asked.

"I'll start by checking Maggie's," I said. "And I'll call Violet—the director from *Foresight*—and anyone else from set. And if no one's seen him—" No. I refused to think about that. "We'll find him somehow."

"Okay," Luke said, nodding. I hoped my fake confidence was

transferring some real confidence into him, because I felt like I was fraying inside. "I can leave a note here, too, in case he comes back in the meantime."

"Good idea."

Luke and I exchanged numbers as we walked back out to the street and then he stopped and looked at me, stricken.

"What?" I asked.

"I just remembered," Luke said. "When I called him, he said he'd just picked my car up from the mechanic. Oh God, he could have gone anywhere. But where would he—" he turned to me. "I don't even know where to start."

"Wait," I said. "What did he say to you on the phone, again? The last thing?"

"I can't be here anymore?"

"No, after that."

"I wanna disappear."

My breath caught. It was a long shot. It was probably crazy. And I was almost certainly wrong. But the more I thought about it, the more convinced I became that I might just be right.

I needed to get my car.

16

TYLER

*T*hree hours later, the sun hanging low on the horizon like an orange ball, I turned down Oxblood Hollow Road again. I drove slowly through the trees, the darkness engulfing the car like a cave, and then broke out into the valley below. The park was empty when I reached it—I wondered if anyone ever came here, actually —and I pulled to a stop and turned the car off.

I didn't even get out, not at first. Just sat and took in the way the sun was sinking behind the trees on the far side of the creek, turning everything a burnished gold. I wanted to sink into the silence around me, that sense of distance from everything—from my life, from the people I knew. From myself.

Nobody knew I was here. And despite what a shitty day today had turned out to be, a weird sort of peace descended over me.

Finally, I got out of the car, closing the door as quietly as I could. I could hear the gentle hum of cicadas, the croak of frogs in the creekbed, and I didn't want to disturb them, or anything else.

I breathed in the soft air around me. It smelled so much nicer down here—or maybe it was just because, for the first time in a long time, I felt like I could actually breathe, with no expectations, none of the weight of other people's eyes on me. For the first time, I could just *be*.

I walked quietly through the tall grass and sat down next to the stream, right up on the bank so my legs hung over the edge and dangled just inches above the water. It wasn't the world's biggest stream, and the water was low this year, so I could see the way it had carved runnels into the bank on the opposite side.

I looked up, stared at the sky and the leaves of the massive oak spreading above me, making fractal patterns as they moved in the breeze. God, it was nice to just sit here and not have to think for a while. Not have to be in my life.

Except, as I lowered myself down on my back, settling my head against the grass, I knew the moment wouldn't last. Even now I could feel tendrils of anger, of sadness, creeping up inside me. And after mere minutes, I was back to thinking about how fucked up everything was.

My dad had lied to me—had *been* lying to me—for... I didn't even know how long. My whole life? For all I knew, he had been. And I'd trusted him. How could I not have? He was my *dad*, and from age six, he was the only parent I'd had. The only *family* I felt like I had.

It made my blood boil, thinking about how neatly he'd cut all ties that had bound me to anyone other than him. He'd pushed my mom and Luke away. He'd isolated me from my friends. And all the while, he'd told me he was doing it for my own good. Helping me focus, taking care of me, protecting me.

I'd believed him when he told me I couldn't be trusted, couldn't make decisions, couldn't be left on my own. He'd made me feel like I was worthless, and when I'd finally rebelled against him, I'd proven him right.

The sun sank and the stars came out as I lay there, not moving, just trying to let all this anger drain out of my body.

Who *was* I without my dad? If he'd been lying to me this whole time—taking my money, telling me I'd spent it myself, letting me take the fall for things he had done— could I believe anything he'd said about me? But if I wasn't the lazy, stupid, irresponsible person he'd always told me I was—who was I instead?

Was I even anyone? Or was I just nothing?

Tears came then. Hot and fast, streaming down my cheeks. Because the only facts that I knew for certain were that I'd still ruined my own life—through my own choices. What my dad did wasn't right, but that didn't change the fact that I'd taken everything I had and squandered it. That would never go away.

I knew I should move. It was dark now, full dark, and I knew I shouldn't spend all night here. But where was I supposed to go? There was nowhere I wanted to be right now. Or was that even more indication of how stupid, how whiny and worthless I was?

I hated how weak I felt. Because despite everything my dad

had done, there was still a part of me that wondered if he was right to do it. How fucked up was that?

I knew he'd been lying to me, abusing my trust, taking advantage of me—everything he'd always claimed other people would do to me, everything he'd claimed he was protecting me from. And yet a part of me still wondered if he was justified. What if he'd been right about me all along?

I knew Luke would tell me that was wrong, that I couldn't believe my dad. That he'd lied to me and couldn't be trusted. But who was I supposed to trust if *not* my dad? Certainly not myself. He'd made sure of that.

Gray. You can trust Gray.

That thought struck like a knife to the heart. Because though it was true—though the month I'd spent with Gray was the only time in the last few years that I hadn't hated myself—I'd never get that back. He was with Ethan now. And if I'd ever stood a chance with him, if there had ever been a moment where I could have said something, it had passed.

I'd spent the past month denying my feelings, convinced that they were nothing more than complications that could be ignored until they disappeared, and now it was too late. Figured. That was what I'd always done with the uncomfortable parts of myself.

My sexuality? Push it down, don't think about it. The fact that I couldn't stand myself? Shove it away, get high, don't think about it.

But nothing stayed buried forever, and now that I had to deal with it all, I had no one there to help me. I just wanted it all to stop. I wanted to go back and undo the past 15 years of my life.

My dad told me I'd cried on the morning of my first audition, that he'd had to drag me out in front of the cameras. What if I'd refused? What if I'd tanked? What would my life have been like, if none of the past 15 years had happened?

Better—it would have had to have been better.

Except then you wouldn't have met Gray.

That stopped me cold. I didn't want to imagine a world where I hadn't met him, where I didn't know him. Where I didn't get to keep the memory of him close to my chest for warmth. Even if I didn't get to have him, even if he were back with Ethan—at least—at least I'd—

"Tyler? There you are! Jesus, are you okay?"

"Gray?" I sat up and stared in shock.

Had I somehow manifested him by crying hard enough? Or maybe I'd cried so hard that I'd passed out and now I was dreaming. The light of the moon gave everything this sort of hazy quality and I honestly wouldn't have been surprised to find out I was hallucinating.

I put a hand on the ground to support myself and squinted. "Are you really here?"

But Gray hadn't stopped walking the whole time I was staring at him and now he was right in front of me. He held out a hand, I took it, and holy fuck, he was pulling me up and into his arms.

He was hugging me and it was real, *he* was real, or if he wasn't, my brain was way better at dreams than I thought because the soft fuzz of his t-shirt against my cheek and the brush of the hair on his arms as it skimmed against me, the warmth of his chest as he pressed me tight—it was all so real I thought I might die. Gray was here.

"How is this—how did you—" I mumbled incoherently into his chest, but he didn't answer. He just held me tighter and because I'd never been anything but completely pathetic, I let him. Besides, if this was a dream, I wanted to enjoy this as long as I could. I knew I was being gross and weird and I didn't care.

"Luke told me what happened," Gray said, tucking the top of my head under his cheek. He rubbed my back gently. "He told me about your dad and I just—he was really worried. He thought—well, he didn't know where you were. But when he told me what you said—fuck, I was convinced I was going to be wrong. The whole ride down here I was telling myself how stupid I was being. But I couldn't take the chance that you were here by yourself and not have come found you when I could."

"You didn't have to do that," I said into his shirt. God, I was getting it all teary and probably snotty and I knew I should pull away but I didn't want to. It was going to get weird soon, and Gray would move and I'd let him, but until he did...

"Are you kidding?" Gray said. "There's no way I wasn't coming. God, I'm so sorry, Tyler. I'm so, so sorry about your dad. I can't fucking believe he would do that to you."

A warm wave of something like honey and sunshine poured over me, rushing from the top of my head down my spine and radiating through my whole body like pure light.

Gray cared. He was here because he cared about me. Even if it wasn't in the way I wanted, he was still here.

"You don't even know the half of it," I said. I could feel new trickles of tears forming in my eyes and I laughed in an attempt to stop them.

"Wait, what?" And then it was happening, Gray's arms were loosening around me and he took a step back, holding me by the shoulders. I tried to tell myself I wasn't sad at the loss of contact. "What do you mean?"

"I just—" I shook my head and looked up at him. "It's a long story. Do you wanna—" I gestured over towards the tree a few yards away, not really sure what I was suggesting, but Gray nodded and took my hand—my hand!—and walked over with me, sitting down and leaning up against its trunk. I sat down next to him, forcing myself to leave a couple of inches in between his legs, his shoulders, and mine.

"Did something else happen with your dad?"

Gray's voice was full of this angry kind of hesitation that made me want to kiss him. I mean, I'd realized I pretty much always wanted to kiss him, had wanted to since the day I'd met him, probably, even if I hadn't admitted it, but hearing that tone in his voice that made it sound like he wished my dad were there so he could punch him? Yeah, that made me want to kiss him, too.

"He um—" I pulled my knees into my chest and wrapped my arms around them. "He told me—by accident, really, he didn't mean to—but apparently the cocaine that was in my car? The day I got arrested? That was his."

"What?" Gray looked at me sharply. "And he wasn't going to tell you? He let you take the fall for—"

"Yeah," I said, sighing heavily. "Yeah."

"Jesus Christ. I can't fucking believe that man. Jesus I wish he were here so I could drop kick him or something."

"Yeah," I said quietly.

Gray turned and looked at me. I could see his scrutiny out of the corner of my eye, but I couldn't bring myself to look at him, so I just stared straight ahead like I could see the stream or anything other than just shapes in the darkness.

"Tyler, you know this wasn't your fault," Gray said.

"You sound like Luke."

"Well then Luke's right. Tyler, you can't blame yourself for this."

I shrugged. "I can blame myself for a lot of things, anyway, even if not this specific one."

"Tyler—"

I turned and the look on Gray's face was so hurt and confused that suddenly I was crying again. Jesus, like a leaky faucet. But I couldn't see that look on Gray's face and not feel how broken I was, how naive, how stupid I'd been not to admit how I felt about him earlier.

I pushed my face down onto my knees, hugged my arms around me tighter—and then Gray's arms were around me again, pulling me in against him, and I started shaking. And once I'd started, I couldn't stop, and he was murmuring such sweet things, such kind things, and that only made the tears come faster, because I didn't deserve it.

"It's not your fault," he whispered again.

He rubbed his hand up and down my back like I was a fucking child—except that no one had ever done that for me, now that I thought about it. I'd only ever seen it on TV. And that made me cry even harder and then his whispers faded to a kind of gentle, *'Shh, it's okay,'* that I knew didn't mean that he wanted me to stop, it just meant that he had me, and that I could cry until I'd cried myself out.

"I'm sorry," I said, finally, pushing myself upright and away from him again some time later. I wasn't sure how long I'd let him hold me like that, but my face felt sticky from where the tears had dried and I was starting to get a sinus headache. "God, that's—not what I meant to do."

"It's okay."

Gray put his right arm around my shoulders and shifted so that when I lay back against the tree trunk, he was right next to me. God, that felt good.

"It's just—" I tried to figure out how to put it into words.

"I know that it's not my fault. Like, in theory, I guess. Luke's been trying to tell me for months now that Dad—well, that he wasn't being fair to me. Even before we knew about the money thing, or I had any idea about the drugs. And I get it, it's like, intellectually, I know he's right? But then I—"

I shook my head. "The worst part of it is that I keep trying to find reasons to forgive him. To excuse what he did. Like I keep catching myself trying to make it okay somehow, and *that's* what's the most fucked up thing about it. Like he did that to my head, you know? He's still... in there. Making me want to forgive him. And I just hate it. I hate that he did this and I hate that even though I know now, even though I see everything, I still feel this fucking... loyalty to him."

"That really sucks," Gray said. "I can't—I can't imagine how that feels. I wish I could make it go away and I know I can't and I'm just so sorry you're going through this."

"Thanks," I said softly. "It feels good to say it out loud, anyway. In a weird sort of way. Who'd have thought announcing your patheticness would make you feel better?"

Gray snorted. "I don't think it's pathetic. I think you've survived years of someone abusing their relationship with you, and you're only just starting to process that."

"Oh good," I said, my lips twisting. "More ways I'm fucked up. Hooray." I glanced over at him. "Thanks though. I know —I know how you meant it. And I appreciate it." I shook my head. "God, I still can't believe you drove all the way down here."

Gray turned and looked at me, his eyes holding onto mine. "Tyler, I know I can't make it go away but—anything I can do—anything. I will. If you need someone to off-the-record murder your dad, I'll put in some calls. And if you just need someone to sit here with you tonight, I can do that too. I mean it."

"Thanks," I said, trying for a wry smile. "I think Ethan might be a little concerned about you if you don't come home tonight, but I appreciate the sentiment."

"Ethan?" Gray looked confused. "What the hell does Ethan have to do with it?"

Oh God, kill me now. Fuck, maybe he didn't want to talk about it yet and I was making it weird by bringing it up. We had slept together only four days ago and even if it didn't mean anything for Gray, he might not be quite ready to talk about either one of us to the other.

"Nothing," I said quickly, trying to play it off. "Just that I know you—"

"Why the hell would I care what Ethan thinks about me—about any of this?" Gray said.

"Because you—" I stammered, feeling my cheeks heat up. "I mean you're—well, you're—fuck, Gray, I saw you today. I'm sorry, I didn't mean to, I just walked into Maggie's looking for you and I saw you and him together and I just—we don't have to talk about it, it's fine. I get that—"

"You saw me and Ethan at Maggie's today?" Gray said, staring at me in confusion.

"Yeah. I mean, I left as soon as I—I didn't want to barge in on like—your moment or whatever. And honestly, if you've found a way to work things out then I'm—"

"Jesus Christ, Tyler," Gray said. "You really didn't stay for more than a minute if that's what you think happened. Yes, Ethan came to Maggie's today and yes he did more or less throw himself at me but I told him no. You must have seen —God, you could not have picked a worse moment to stick your head in the door."

"Well I didn't know he was going to—I wasn't *trying*," I protested.

"Oh, Tyler, why didn't you stay?" Gray said. "If you had, you would have seen me pushing him away, you would have seen me telling him in no uncertain terms to get out of my bar and leave me alone."

"Oh." I looked up at him, still feeling caught by his eyes. My cheeks were heating up. "Oh."

God, I felt like an idiot.

"Why didn't you ask me?" Gray said. "I would have told you. I wouldn't have—I wouldn't have kept it a secret. None of it."

"I don't know," I said, shrugging uncomfortably. "We left things kind of weird on Monday and I just thought—"

"That I was getting back together with my ex-boyfriend four days after I found out he was engaged to someone else?"

I squirmed. "Well when you put it like that..."

"Tyler, I..." Gray paused and laughed. "I don't really have anyone but myself to blame here." He shook his head. "You know, I only ran into Luke today because I was looking for you."

"What?" I blinked. Somehow in my shock at seeing Gray and after the bathtub's worth of tears and snot I'd expelled from my face-holes, it had never occurred to me to ask how that had happened.

"I wanted to apologize," Gray said. He shifted and looked at me, his hand moving from my shoulders to my upper arm. "I need to apologize. The things I said to you—"

"Were completely true," I interrupted. "You were right. Even if all this other stuff with my dad hadn't happened, you'd still be right. The way he was acting—the meeting—none of it was good. None of it was what I wanted. I was just too scared to—"

I stopped and shook my head. "God, it feels like ages ago now. The meeting got moved til this morning and you wanna know what their big idea was?" Gray's eyes searched mine questioningly. "For me to be the star of a reality tv show. All about my struggles with sobriety and my sexuality and my career."

"Jesus," Gray whispered. "That's everything you—"

"Don't want to have to talk about with people? Don't want the public dissecting?" I snorted. "Yeah. So, like I said—you were right, it was a terrible idea. And that was when I found out about my dad and the drugs and, well, I was actually coming to apologize to you when I saw you and Ethan at Maggie's. I realized I needed to talk to someone about everything and I just—well, if I hadn't freaked out, maybe we could have avoided this little road trip, for both of us."

Gray was still watching me but his expression had gone from one of intent listening to questioning. He wasn't frowning, but his eyes had taken on a kind of faraway look like he was trying to work something out.

"Freaked out?" he said after a moment.

"What?"

"You said you freaked out, when you saw me and Ethan?" He looked back at me again and I blushed. "What about?"

I looked down. "I mean, it wasn't that I—it was just that you were—" I paused and risked a look up at Gray.

He was staring at me like I was some kind of rare species he was encountering for the first time and he wasn't quite sure what to make of me. And suddenly, I just thought, *'Fuck it. You've already cried on him—a lot—made him drive all the way down here to find you, revealed your most pathetic secrets, told him you accidentally spied on him.'* How much worse could it really get?

And so I bit my lip, breathed out, and breathed in.

"I'm in love with you."

I said it quickly, watching Gray's face for any minute reaction, any tell to indicate how he felt about what I was saying. "And I know that's weird and not what you want and I promise, I won't try and make you—"

And then I wasn't talking anymore because he was kissing me. Gray pulled me in roughly, cutting me off and pressing his lips to mine. I couldn't even process what was happening, was kissing him back more out of shock than out of anything else, but when Gray pulled back, my hands were gripping the front of his t-shirt and I wouldn't let go.

"I love you," Gray said. "Tyler, I've been in love with you for —God, I don't even know how long. It took me a while to realize it, but I—I never thought you would—you could feel the same way."

I laughed helplessly. "How could I not? You're... you're everything. You're... Gray you're my best friend. You're the person I need by my side, the one I always want to be with. I didn't want to admit it before, not even to myself, because I was so scared of everything, but seeing you with Ethan—" I shook my head "It made me realize that what I was most scared of was losing you."

Gray smiled and tilted his head down so our foreheads rested against each other. "You could never lose me. In fact, good luck getting rid of me. I'm pretty sure you're stuck with me now."

This time it was me who tilted in further, pressing my lips to Gray's, needing that contact. His hands went around my waist, pulling me in as my mouth opened and I found myself scrambling into his lap as my tongue tasted him, dancing along his own.

Gray laughed, maybe in surprise at my eagerness, maybe just out of happiness, which was what I felt like doing. He shifted, leaning back to brace against the tree trunk. My hands went to either side of his face. I just wanted to kiss him and kiss him, though I could feel myself getting hard and alright, so I couldn't help grinding down against him. It felt good, dammit, and I hadn't thought this would ever happen again and I didn't want it to stop.

Gray pulled back, breaking the kiss. He reached up and brushed the hair out of my eyes. "As much as I'd like to keep going down this path, unless you've got a bottle of conditioner in your car..."

I pouted. "You're no fun."

"The sooner we get back to New York, the sooner I can be all the fun you can handle." He leaned forward and brushed his lips against mine. "We'll have all the time in the world once we're back."

I sighed, knowing he was right. I climbed off of Gray reluctantly, extending a hand to help him up off the ground. As I turned to walk back towards the cars, Gray wrapped his arms around me and pulled me close. His stubble brushed my cheek and I melted a little bit, again.

"I still can't believe you found me," I said, looking up at the sky. "Are you absolutely positive that you're not a dream? Or that I'm not just making all of this up?"

Gray laughed low and rumbly, like the sound of thunder in a far-off storm. "Here, let me show you something," he whispered.

Taking my hand, he turned me around and stepped back to the tree. He placed my hand on the bark. I looked up at him in confusion, then back at the tree when Gray moved my hand over something rough, inlaid in the bark's surface.

I bent down to peer at it closely and Gray pulled out his phone, shining a light for me to see. There were words carved into the bark. *E Kita Xio.* And beneath it, Monday's date—and a heart.

I looked back at Gray, my eyes welling up again. "Why didn't you put our initials in it?"

"I didn't want to speak for you," Gray said with a smile. "But I knew what I needed to say."

We drove back to the city in separate cars, but Gray followed me the whole way, his headlights behind me a steady reminder that I wasn't alone. An anchor, a safe haven, a love letter in the dark.

We drove to Luke's first, to drop off his car. I'd called him before we left, after I'd finally turned my phone back on. I felt guilty for making Luke worry so much and of course, when we got back to his building, he was standing out front to meet us.

"Thank God," he said, folding me into a hug. "I was so worried."

I flushed and hugged him back. "Sorry. I didn't mean to—" I laughed. "I mean, I guess I *did* mean to turn my phone off. But I didn't mean to make you worry."

"It's okay," Luke said. "It's my job as your brother."

"Well then you win the perfect brother award, to go along with the rest of your perfect life."

Luke rolled his eyes and I grinned. "You didn't have to come out to meet us, you know."

Luke shrugged. "I was getting antsy up there. I was doing panic sit-ups and my abs were starting to hurt. Had to get out before I started my third workout of the day"

"Only your third? You're slipping, bro." I held his car keys out. "It took me a stupid amount of time, but I'm finally getting you your car back, good as new."

"Thanks," Luke said with a laugh. "You guys wanna come up? You must be starving by now."

I blushed and Gray cleared his throat. I gave Luke a sheepish smile. "Actually, um, I was going to spend the night at Gray's, so..."

Luke turned bright red. "Oh, right. Yeah, of course. Of course, I didn't mean to—I mean, it's totally—" He shook his head. "Forget it, I don't need to know the details."

Gray laughed wickedly. "Don't worry, we've got a movie coming out in a few months if you change your mind and get curious."

"You guys are horrible," Luke said, still blushing. "Get out of here, both of you."

I'd just turned around, waving goodbye to Luke, when a large, black town car pulled to a stop in front of us on the street. The three of us stopped and stared as the back window on the passenger side rolled down.

My dad glared at us from inside.

"I see I was right about where you'd run off to," he said, giving me a hard look. His eyes flickered to Gray and then back to me. "I thought we agreed you weren't going to see him again."

Gray opened his mouth to speak but I took his hand and squeezed it, giving him a pleading look. I was shaking and it felt like something was clamped around my heart, but I had to do this. I had to be the one to speak, even if it still made me feel a little sick to defy my dad this way.

"I changed my mind," I said, letting out a deep breath. Then I cocked my head to the side, thinking about that for a moment, "Or actually, I didn't. Because I never stopped loving him in the first place."

My dad spluttered and I couldn't help smiling.

"Yeah. Love. I'm sure that word makes you uncomfortable, maybe even angry. But there's nothing you can do about it. Actually, there's nothing you can do about any of it. Because I'm done working with you—in fact, I'm done talking to you."

My whole body was vibrating now, but Gray stepped closer to me and squeezed my hand and I drew strength from his presence—that steady, rock solid confidence that Gray gave me. I could do this. My dad might be awful—I mean, it wasn't a question of might, he *was* awful—but with Gray by my side, I could do this. Even if it hurt.

My dad grimaced. "I know you're upset about earlier today, Tyler, but you're overreacting. Just get in the car and we'll talk about it."

"No." It took all the strength I had to say it, but I did.

"No?" My dad repeated. "I don't think you realize just how stupid you're being. You don't say no to me. You're jeopardizing your entire future here and if you're not careful, I might not be willing to work with you again."

"Fine. Because I didn't want to work with you anyway. Not after what you've done."

"What I've done? Tyler," my dad barked. "We talked about this. That was for your own good. Now get in the car."

"Was stealing from me for my own good, too?" I asked, the words so quiet they might have gotten lost, if it hadn't felt like the whole world had hushed all of a sudden, like it was watching us with baited breath.

"What?"

"Stealing from me," I repeated, trying to ignore the thread of uncertainty worming its way into my stomach.

I knew it was true. I trusted Luke. But suddenly, with my dad's eyes on me, I started to feel queasy. What if I was wrong somehow? What if it was all a mistake, what if there were some kind of explanation? And if my dad really was just trying to help me—how mad had I just made him?

I closed my eyes and braced for a blow. But instead of a

torrent of words, all I got was silence. Slowly, I opened my eyes to see my dad's gaze darting from my face, to Gray's, to Luke's, and then back to me.

He looked nervous.

"I don't know what you're talking about," he said. His voice sounded... God, was that fear? I didn't think I'd ever heard that from him before.

"You do," Luke said, stepping forward. "And we have proof. I've got three years worth of documents showing what you've done. And they'll hold up in court."

My dad's eyes widened at the mention of court and he looked back at me. "Tyler, buddy, what's this about? This is nonsense. Come on, come with me and we can talk this all out."

"I'm not going anywhere with you. Ever again."

"Tyler, I'm your father. I've only ever tried to protect you, to help you."

"I think you should leave now," Gray said, slipping his arm around my shoulders. "Tyler's said he's not leaving with you. And I don't think staying any longer would be productive."

Nothing about his words, or even his tone, was menacing. I didn't actually think Gray had a threatening bone in his body. But my dad didn't know that, and as Gray breathed in and out, his broad chest expanding and his left hand curling lightly into a fist, my dad's eyes widened.

"This is a mistake," he said, and that note of fear was back. "It's all a mistake, Tyler. You'll see that. You haven't heard the last from me."

"Just go, Dad," I said, shaking my head. "Just get out of here."

Slowly, he rolled the window back up and did just that.

Luke let out a low whistle as my dad's town car rolled down the street. I turned and pressed my head against Gray's chest, letting his arms fold around me. I closed my eyes and breathed deeply for a minute, just trying to calm the emotions swarming through my body.

Finally I turned my face in Luke's direction and arched an eyebrow. "Court, huh?"

He shrugged. "I mean, it's up to you. I'm not a lawyer, obviously. But I wanted to scare him. And if you did decide to go that route... well, I've got all the records we'd need. From these last few years anyway. Before that... God, who knows what we'd find."

My eyes widened at the thought. "I don't know," I said slowly. "It's not that I don't want—it just... it seems like a lot. Dragging everything out again."

"Hey, you don't need to decide now," Gray pointed out.

"Yeah," Luke said. "No pressure. You can do whatever you want. We'll support you."

I nodded gently against Gray's chest. "Right now all I want is to go home. Or, to bed, anyway," I said, flushing.

I didn't want Gray to think I was inviting myself to move in with him or anything. But for me, '*home*' was a simple concept. Home was wherever Gray was.

"Sounds perfect," Gray said, and I could hear his smile. "Sounds perfect."

≈

"Home sweet home," Gray said as we walked up the stairs to his apartment above Maggie's. He opened the door for me to walk in.

"I didn't mean—" I blushed. "I mean, back there, when I said I wanted to go home. I just meant like—I mean, not that your apartment is—fuck, I just—"

"Tyler," Gray said. "You can stay here as long as you want. I just spent a month with you, sharing a bathroom, eating together, spending pretty much every waking minute with you. I'm not freaked out by the idea of you in my apartment."

"Yeah," I said, shrugging. "But it's different when it's yours. I just didn't want you to think like—that I wanted to move—"

"Tyler, I swear to God, if you don't get into this apartment right now, that's when you'll see me worry. Okay?"

"Okay," I said, stepping into the space. "God." My eyes widened. "It's huge."

"I could get used to hearing you say that," Gray said with a smile. I elbowed him in the stomach, but he caught my arm and moved up behind me, hugging me and pinning me to his chest.

"I meant your apartment, dummy," I said, tilting my head up and grinning at him.

And it *was* massive. The room we'd just stepped into stretched the length of the building—a huge living room that flowed into a dining room that flowed into a kitchen at the back, with huge windows on either end. A dark metal staircase spiraled up from the side wall in the dining room.

"Well, that too," Gray said.

I turned around and looked at him suddenly, struck by a thought. "Is it weird, at all? That I've never been here before?"

Gray laughed. "Tyler, nothing about our relationship is normal. But that doesn't mean it's bad. Just a little unconventional."

"Like me saying I love you before we go on our first date?"

"Or me offering for you to move in before you've spent the night?"

"Touché."

"And I'll remedy the date thing," Gray said. "As well as give you the grand tour, I promise. But right now, I'm most interested in getting you upstairs."

"Why Mr. Evans, I can't believe you think I'd sleep with you before you've so much as bought me—" I stopped abruptly and Gray looked down at me. "I just remembered that you've actually bought me dinner. Like, a bunch."

"Hmm. Then I guess you're gonna have to pay me back." He looked significantly at the stairs.

I let Gray lead me through the apartment and then push me up the spiral staircase.

"You just wanted to look at my ass, didn't you," I said, grinning over my shoulder at him,

"You got me."

"It looks even better without pants, you know."

"Oh believe me, I know." Gray's laugh was delicious. "And I fully plan on getting that view, too. For the next 36 hours or so. Hope you weren't planning on leaving anytime soon.

"Cheeky."

Gray grinned. "Exactly."

The stairs let out onto a large sort of catwalk that hung over the dining room. Two doors led off of it at the far end. Gray pulled me into the one that led to the back of the apartment and it turned out to be a huge bedroom with old industrial finishings that spoke of the building's past. Two huge windows opened out over a small backyard, a thin balcony connecting them.

But my eyes were drawn to the bed. Partially because I really was tired—it had been a long day, ok? But, well, also for other reasons.

I took one look at that great puffy cloud of pillows and blankets on top of a rustic wood frame, grinned over at Gray, and then flung myself down onto it, sinking deep into the marshmallowy comforter. Miles better than the beds in the motel down in Maryland, lightyears ahead of the beds we'd been sleeping in at Bailey Park for a month.

"Oh my God, I think I'm having an orgasm," I moaned.

Gray laughed and joined me on the bed, pulling me over so I could rest my head on his chest.

"Seriously," I said. "It wasn't the ghosts of Bailey Park keeping you up at night, was it? It was this bed haunting your dreams, its fluffy specter lurking in the darkness, whispering for you to come back to it."

"Maybe I did miss it a little bit. Still, I think the month spent away was worth it."

"Yeah?" I curled my leg over him like a cat. "Why's that?"

"Well, that Thai place was really good," Gray said with a smile.

"Thai food. That's what you're glad to have taken away from that experience?"

"Well not *just* the Thai food. That pizza place was pretty good too."

I pushed up on my elbow and glared at him. "Glad to know that in the order of things you're thankful for, I rank somewhere below tomato sauce slathered on bread."

"*You* are not a *thing*," Gray said. "You're on a separate list entirely." He gave me a wicked grin. "And don't bother being jealous of tomato sauce. I've always liked cream sauces even better."

I blushed furiously when the implications of that statement set in.

"You know, for someone who's led such a crazy life, you're surprisingly easy to make blush," Gray said.

"Yeah, thanks for reminding me. It's really awesome knowing that you're dating someone who's so good at sex that it was his job, and that he's probably fucked tons of guys who're better in bed than you are." I hid my face in his neck.

"Hey," Gray said shifting onto his side. "Hey, look at me." I turned my head and looked up at him. "I love that about you. And I would never want that to change. I don't want anything to change, okay?"

"I mean, I hope you're open to a little bit of change, at least," I grumbled, "and you're still willing to fuck me. I'd rather not *stay* this inexperienced."

"You know what I mean." He kissed my forehead. "If I could show you somehow—I don't even know how to put it into words, how much none of that matters. When I'm with you, you're all I'm thinking about. I can't even remember anyone else. Hell, even when I'm *not* with you, you're still all I think about."

"But you were with Ethan for years. You don't just forget that."

"No," Gray said slowly. "But I'm not the same person I was. Looking back at all that—I know it happened. I know it was me, but it feels like seeing it through glass. Or feeling something through gauze. And I've never—" he stopped and for once, his cheeks flushed. "God, this is embarrassing."

"What?"

"I've never felt like this before. Like I do when I'm with you. The way I have since I met you, really."

"What do you—"

"Like I matter. Like I'm with someone who—who thinks I matter. Like I'm someone worth being with." He looked down. "When I'm with you, I feel wanted."

My eyes pricked. I hated that Gray had ever thought that about himself.

"You matter," I said, choking up. "You matter." Gray leaned down to kiss me and oh God, I wanted to give into it, but I pushed Gray back. I had to get this out. "No, let me say this. You're so wanted. I want you."

God, it was hard to speak around the lump in my throat, but I needed to say this.

"Before I knew you—before I met you—I wasn't really living. I was just... breathing. But my life didn't mean anything. I've spent my whole life trying to perform for everyone, to be who they wanted me to be, but inside, it was like I wasn't there. I didn't even know who I was. And then I met you and you're the first person who ever just *saw* me. You saw me before I even saw myself. You helped me find myself. You matter. You're the most important person in the world. And the best person I've ever known."

Gray's eyes were bright. "I saw you because you're luminous. How could I not see you when you outshine everyone I've ever met?"

He pressed his lips down to mine and I let the warmth of that kiss suffuse me all the way down to my toes. Our movements were slow, almost gentle. Even after we'd undressed, it felt like we were exploring each other for the first time. And it was good—it was fucking unbearably good. But I was impatient.

I felt like I'd been waiting for this my whole life, even though it had been just a week since we were last together, just hours since I'd finally admitted what I felt. As soon as Gray was naked, leaning down on top of me, I reached for his cock, smiling at how hard he was—though, since it had taken us about 30 minutes of slow kissing and stroking to get naked, I might have been insulted if he weren't.

But Gray caught my wrist and brought it above my head, pressing it down into the mattress with a kiss.

"There's no rush," he said. "I want to take my time."

"What for? It's not like we haven't—"

"I know," Gray smiled. "But this time is different."

"How?"

"It's our first time, now that we know. Now that we're together. I want to remember this. I want to remember every minute."

He brought my other wrist above my head and joined my hands together. Then he kissed his way down the underside of my arms, his lips raising goosebumps on my skin.

"So soft," Gray murmured as he made his way onto my neck.

I urgently wanted to move my hands down, to touch Gray, to feel his skin under my fingertips, but I resolved to be good and try to do what Gray wanted.

Who was I kidding, anyway? I'd always do whatever he wanted, even if I'd be impaled on Gray's cock right now if I had my way. I couldn't say no to him. And, I found as Gray's lips continued to take a careful survey of what felt like every inch of my skin, I didn't want to.

I shivered as Gray's tongue passed over my nipples, flicking out to tease them, first one side, then the other, tweaking, nipping, even sucking. He was bringing out sensations I wasn't even aware I could feel and the longer he kept it up, the deeper the stirring in my groin.

I had a sudden image of my body as a violin, being played expertly by Gray, his fingers and lips plucking and strumming sounds and resonances out of me that harmonized into a wash of sensation. I kept my hands up where Gray had put them but I couldn't keep my body from arching up off the bed, thrumming against Gray's. Every inch of me was lighting up.

"Gray?" I gasped as his lips moved to my stomach.

"Yes?"

"Can I please move my arms now?"

Gray looked up at me and smiled, his eyes heavy-lidded with desire. "You know, you look really good like this."

"Disheveled and sleep deprived?"

"No." Gray palmed my cock and I whined, hipping up towards him. "Like that. You look amazing, begging me like that."

"Are you trying to 50-shades me without me noticing?"

Gray laughed, a low, rich chuckle like molasses. "Do you want me to?"

I grinned at him. "I don't know. Seems dangerous. I give you an inch and suddenly it's gonna be erotic asphyxiation and daddy kink from sunup to sundown."

"You have a very active imagination," Gray said. "But yes, you can move your hands now. Only because you asked so politely."

He started to move back down but I caught him and pulled him up into a kiss. I wrapped my arms around him and held him there, just wanting to feel him again. And then, because I'm me and I can't leave well enough alone, I started arching upwards again, feeling my cock slide against Gray's stomach, and alongside his own and goddamn, that friction felt good —but then Gray pulled away.

"Oh no you don't."

"What?" I said, giving him my most innocent eyes.

"You tricked me into moving fast on Monday night. I'm not saying I regret that—not for one second—but I am saying that I want to savor this. I want to savor *you*."

And with that, he slid back down and I had to settle for letting myself be savored. Which, let's be honest, wasn't the worst thing in the world. Far from it.

My hands moved to Gray's shoulders, his head as he kissed the skin around my cock. I moaned and whined as he got closer and closer—Gray wasn't even touching me there but I felt like I might explode. My cock twitched when Gray's hand finally circled my base and his tongue licked long, flat stripes up the side, and I was convulsing from sheer pleasure by the time he'd made his way around.

He looked up at me then, making eye contact, and I realized something. It wasn't just hot—it was intimate. I'd never felt so *seen*. And Gray was taking his time with me because he wanted me, wanted to be with me and no one else.

Gray—*Gray*—wanted me. How was that even possible? But here he was, in bed with me. This was happening, and it had been going on way too long for it to still be a dream, so I had to accept that this was reality.

I moaned as Gray swallowed all the way down around me, then began sucking me in and out, his hand working me in tandem. God, that felt good, and Gray was liberal, sloppy even with his tongue, getting me wet and messy in the most decadent way. As his hand slipped back to tug at my balls, I couldn't help spreading my legs a little, encouraging him to move back further. But no matter how obvious I tried to make it, Gray wouldn't take the hint, and eventually I was reduced to begging.

"Please, Gray, please. I need it."

"Need what?"

I flushed. "I need you inside me."

Gray grinned. "You're going to have to get more specific than that. There are lots of pieces of me. And lots of holes in you. Tell me what you want."

"Everything."

Gray gave my cock a long lick. "Try again."

"I need your—your fingers. Inside me. In my ass."

Gray smiled and sucked me in and out again until I moaned. "There, see. That wasn't so hard, was it? Don't worry, we'll get you caught up and *'experienced'* in no time."

He sucked down around my cock again and it was good, but he still hadn't moved his hand at all.

"Gray, please," I groaned, my fingers digging into his shoulders.

Gray looked up at me speculatively. "You know what?" he said, his hand idling stroking my cock. "If you're going to be so pushy, I have an idea."

I watched in confusion as Gray pulled away, leaning across the bed to open a drawer in his nightstand. He tossed a bottle of lube to me.

"We don't even have to use conditioner this time," he said, wiggling his eyebrows.

I held the lube out to him when he came back to me, but Gray just smiled and shook his head. "No, that's for you."

"What—for me? What do you mean?"

"You're the one who wanted to use his hands." Gray leaned back on the bed, folded his hands behind his head. With his cock laying long and hard against his stomach, he was gorgeous enough to make me drool. "I want to watch you get ready for me. I want to watch you prep yourself."

My eyes went wide. "I—I've—"

I flushed, suddenly feeling very vulnerable. Which didn't make sense. It wasn't like Gray hadn't done this for me before, it wasn't like I hadn't been the one driving things forward. But now, with no pretense between us, only honesty, I felt more naked than I ever had before.

Gray seemed to sense that something was wrong, because he turned over and leaned in, running his hand up and down my side.

"You know what? Nevermind," he said, kissing me gently. "I think I'd actually like to do it for you, if you'll let me."

"No, it's—" I stopped and took a deep breath. "It's not that I don't want to. I just—I don't know, is it really that sexy, watching me finger myself?"

"You have *no* idea." Gray smiled. "But I don't want you to do anything you don't want to."

He kissed my neck, sucking on the skin there as he shifted me onto my back, sliding on top of me and grinding down onto my cock. Fuck that felt good. And if I couldn't do this with Gray... I loved him. And more importantly, I felt safe with him, safer than I'd ever felt before. I squeezed Gray's shoulder, pulled his eyes to me.

"If I'm gonna do this," I said with a small smile. "I'm gonna need some room."

Gray pulled back. "You're so beautiful, you know that?"

"Yeah, yeah, save it for when I've got my finger stuck up my butt."

"You have such a way with words," Gray grinned. "Violet really should have let you improvise more on set."

I stuck my tongue out at him and Gray darted in to kiss me quickly before moving slightly to the side, kissing my neck and stroking my chest but giving me room to maneuver. I uncapped the bottle, squeezed a dab of lube onto my finger, then tossed it aside. Biting my lip, I reached down, my wrist brushing against my cock, searching for my hole.

My mouth opened slightly when I found it, the cool liquid making me gasp, but before I could give myself a chance to freak out, I pushed my finger in. And fuck, okay, that felt good. I'd learned that by now. I loved the feeling of something sliding inside me there.

A moan escaped my lips as I slid my finger all the way in, pushing as far up as I could before resting a moment, then sliding it out. I stopped right before my finger was all the way out of my hole, then pushed it in again.

"God, baby, you're so perfect," Gray whispered—and then I heard a sharp intake of breath. I looked up in confusion to see Gray's eyes focused on me, apologetic. "I'm so sorry," he whispered. "I know you don't like that word."

I hesitated for a second before deciding, well, fuck it. I was already fucking myself open with my fingers for Gray, it's not like I could get any *more* vulnerable or awkward. I might as well tell him.

"It's not the word," I said. "It's just—it's what you said on set, you know? When you call me that, it feels like you're pretending to be someone else, or pretending *I'm* someone else. Like you're not here with me."

"Oh God, that's not—" Gray's eyes filled with concern. "Tyler, I started using that word on set because—" he stopped and shook his head. "Remember when you told me to think of myself as Wyatt, and think of you as Dylan when we were filming?"

"Yeah?"

"I tried. And sometimes it worked. But I could never do it during the sex scenes. I just—I couldn't not see *you*. But I kept slipping and almost calling you Tyler while we were filming. And I didn't want to ruin the take. So I—" he blushed, "I started using '*baby*' instead. Not because I was thinking about anyone else, but because I couldn't see you as anyone but yourself. I just—I don't know, maybe it's weird, but I like calling you that. I've never called anyone else that before, but with you, it feels... right."

"Really?" I looked at him in surprise. "Not anyone?" I didn't say it, but I was thinking of Ethan.

"Not anyone," Gray said, kissing me gently, seeming to get what I meant. "No one but you." He paused and gave me a searching look. "I know some people don't like it in general. But I—I do. If you do."

I smiled. "I do, too."

Gray bent down and kissed me again, sweet and slow, and I grinned into it. I started moving my finger again, sliding it in and out, and eventually Gray shifted so he could watch. I added another finger, then a third, feeling like a complete exhibitionist, but by the end, Gray was in between my legs and I was enjoying putting on a show. I fucked my fingers in and out, letting myself moan, showing Gray how good it felt, as he stroked my cock and his own.

"Fuck, Gray, I need you," I groaned.

"What do you need?" Gray prompted me.

"I need your cock," I gasped, no trace of shame left. "I need your cock in my ass. Give it to me, Gray. I need it."

Within seconds, Gray had coated his cock in lube and brought the tip of it to my entrance. He lowered himself down, brought his forehead to mine.

"I love you." I didn't know why, but I felt the need to blurt it out.

Gray smiled. "I love you too."

And then he was pushing inside me, and fuck he was big. I still wasn't quite used to him, but Gray had been right, it was worth taking our time. Gray sank into me slowly, the pleasure excruciating, building in infinitesimal increments until I thought I might die from it before he was even all the way in and I wouldn't even care.

Until I felt his hips press against me, until I felt him fill me again the way I needed, the way I could never be filled by anyone else, the way I'd needed my whole life but had never known until now, and I realized how wrong I'd been to think I could have died happy before this moment, because this, this right now, was the best thing on earth and okay, now you could really kill me.

Except then Gray was moving and that was even better and fuck, I had to give up trying to grade the different levels of pleasure at that point because it was too hard to concentrate, too hard to even form words in my head when Gray was stroking into me like this. He took my hands in each of his own, then brought them slowly up above my head.

I loved how small that made me feel, how helpless—and how safe I knew I was in Gray's hands. His left hand stroked down until it found my thigh, pulling it up until I hooked it around him. I took the hint and did the same thing with my other leg and holy shit, God, okay, that was amazing.

I felt so much more open, giving Gray complete access, and he started thrusting faster, harder. My head tipped back and my eyes shut. I could barely breathe, couldn't speak, could only whimper and revel in how good it felt, being fucked like this by the man I loved, by Gray.

"Fuck, baby, you're so perfect, oh Tyler, fuck, you're so good."

If my body was an instrument Gray was playing, his words were the melody and I'd never heard anything sound so sweet. It wasn't long before I was on the edge, gasping, trying to hold back.

"Gray, I'm gonna—oh fuck, I'm gonna come," I panted.

My eyes opened to see Gray looking down at me, love shining out of that crystal blue gaze of his.

"I love you," he whispered.

That triggered something inside of me, something warm and deep, and suddenly I was coming. I came so hard I cried, or maybe I was crying already, maybe I'd been crying the whole time, I wasn't sure. Gray's lips found mine as his cock drilled into me harder, faster, until he shuddered and I felt that sweet release inside me. I needed it as badly as he did.

He lingered inside me this time, knowing without me having to ask that that was what I wanted. I never wanted to move again, never wanted to think. Never wanted to leave this bed.

I felt full, and connected to Gray in a way I could only feel when he was inside me, like I was a lock and he was my key. Gray looked at me in delight when I told him that.

"I only feel like I'm home when you're inside me," I added.

"Good," he said. "Because I found my home in you."

I thought Gray would grab a tissue box when he finally pulled out, but instead, he slid down and kissed my chest, then licked the cum off my stomach, which tickled a little and made me gasp. But then he kept going, moving lower, and damn if my cock didn't stir and try to get hard again as Gray pushed my legs apart and his mouth found my hole. He lapped up the cum as it trickled out, his tongue probing and licking until he'd gotten it all. I pulled him back to me desperately after that, crushing his lips to mine. I felt like he'd marked me, made me his, when he'd come inside me, and I wanted to taste that--to taste him.

"I'll go get a washcloth," Gray said softly when we broke apart, but I grabbed his hand and shook my head.

"What's the rush?" I said with a grin. "Like you said. We've got all the time in the world."

"*A*re you ready for this?"

Tyler's eyes sought mine as we made our way out of the back of the theater. Applause still filled the room but an event volunteer had snagged us to get us out before the crush of the audience that would exit a few minutes later.

It was four months since the night Tyler and I had found each other under that tree, had finally spoken the words that had been in our hearts. Four months that we'd been together, and I was still happier than I'd ever known it was possible to be. And tonight, Dave and Andrew had booked a hotel in the city for the premiere of *Foresight*, with the screening in one room and the after-party in a ballroom down the hall.

"As ready as I'll ever be," I said. "You promise you won't abandon me?"

Tyler tilted his head to the side in thought. "You know, maybe I should. You still owe me for abandoning me at the wrap party."

I must have looked panicked because he laughed and squeezed my hand. "I promise. Stuck to your side like glue. You're gonna get sick of me by the end of the night."

"Never."

The volunteer looked over her shoulder, motioning us to hurry up, and Tyler dropped my hand. I didn't mind, not really. We'd been running a press gauntlet for weeks, leading up to the premier of *Foresight*, and I'd told Tyler I didn't want him to feel pressured to come out. All I really wanted was for him to feel comfortable.

After all, we'd just screened a movie in which we'd had explicit sex in front of a couple hundred journalists, industry players, and friends. An entire room of people had just seen, as Tyler put it, his orgasm face. I might be used to that, but he wasn't. We were probably both a little nervous right now.

A reporter from some entertainment TV show I'd never heard of must have slipped out even before we had, because she was waiting for us at the step-and-repeat at the end of the hall, outside the ballroom. I'd felt awkward and over-dressed, standing here before the movie to get my picture taken, but Tyler had assured me it was a normal part of the process and that I'd done fine.

Well, what he'd actually said was that I'd made him want to come in his pants. I was paraphrasing.

"Tyler," the reporter said with a smile, "Gray, how are you guys doing tonight?"

"Felicia, it's so good to see you!" Tyler said, breaking out into his public-persona grin.

He pulled her in for a hug, which seemed to catch her off-balance, and immediately started peppering her with questions about her life. I gathered they'd met before, and by the time Felicia was able to redirect the conversation to actually interviewing us, the auditorium had opened and everyone else was streaming out.

I saw our friends walk by. They smiled and waved, but were clearly content to let us be interviewed and catch up later. Violet got pulled aside by one journalist, though, and Danny by another. Funnily enough, Ben and Adam got snagged by a reporter too. Though I supposed that was justifiable—not only were they arguably more famous than the rest of us—Ben, at least—but they'd written the score for *Foresight*, too.

"Anyway, Felicia said, smiling at Tyler, "I should probably actually do my job. So tell me, was this your first time seeing the finished movie?"

She looked at me, then Tyler, then me again, waiting for an answer. Tyler smiled at me expectantly and I shot him a look that promised he'd pay for making me answer the first question when we got home. Mostly by teasing the hell out of him before I finally touched his cock. But fine, I could answer first.

"It was my first time, yeah," I said, trying to appear as loose-limbed and relaxed as Tyler did. "But you—" I turned back to him, "you'd seen a cut of it before, hadn't you?"

"Oh really," Felicia said, turning her attention to Tyler. "Now why is that?"

"Well, I'm a huge fan of Violet—our director—and all her work," Tyler said, smiling easily and expounding for the camera. "I've always been interested in every part of the filmmaking process. And the group of people working on this film have just been so phenomenal, really. So any chance I had to…"

It never ceased to amaze me, how Tyler could manage to talk up someone else's work and never actually talk about himself at all. We'd done other interviews leading up to the premiere and I'd seen him pull the same trick each time. And at the end, he'd do exactly what he was doing now, turning the question back on the interviewer.

"…I mean, you must feel the same way," Tyler said. "I imagine, at least, you know, you do these interviews, but then they get cut together in post, get edited, have to get packaged right. Don't you find the whole thing just fascinating?"

"I'd never thought about it like that, but, I guess, yeah, it is kind of interesting." Felicia blinked, like she wasn't sure how she had become the interviewee. "But back to *Foresight*, tell me, what was it that drew you to this film? Was it the characters, the issues?"

Another question we'd gotten before. They were all variants on the same theme, Tyler had pointed out back when we started our mini press-junket.

"The movie isn't the story," he'd told me. "They don't give a shit what you think about the writing or what your process is or anything you want to talk about. They're in entertainment journalism, which means they want tidbits about *you*. You are the story."

But Tyler was determined not to become the story again, so he tried to never give them the answers they were looking for.

"Every question is really just trying to get you to talk about yourself, hoping you'll let some juicy piece of gossip or information slip. *'Is there something about this movie that resonated with you?' 'Do you think it's important that we tell these kinds of stories?' 'Was it difficult to put yourself into this character's head?'* Or," as Tyler had said with a smile, "in other words, do you actually like sucking dick?"

And so we got passed around from reporter to reporter—people working for TV, for print, for websites, answering the same questions, and Tyler spent most of his time with each of them trying to get them to talk about themselves. I just tried to get through it and not make an ass out of myself.

It almost got a little boring, by the end of it. I could see our friends through the open doors of the ballroom and I wished we could just go over there and talk to them.

"Do you know everyone here?" I asked Tyler after an interview with some reporter whose oldest kid had just gone off to the University of Wisconsin and for whom Tyler had taken a selfie on the guy's phone.

It looked like maybe that was going to be our last interview of the night, so we started making our way over to the doors of the ballroom.

Tyler laughed. "Most of them. Reporters are in a club, kind of. You do this job long enough, you get to know them, they get to know you. You gotta be nice to them, or they edit you to make you look like a asshole. But you don't have to give them what they're looking for."

I smiled. "I know I've said this before but you're fucking amazing, you know that?" Tyler just shrugged but I put my hand on his shoulder to pause before we entered the ballroom. "No, I mean it. You're so fucking smart, and you're kind, and you want to be nice to people, but you do it while sticking to your principles, and it fucking kills me to think that anyone ever told you you were less than amazing."

Tyler was already blushing, so I really can't be held responsible for what I did next, which was to lean over and whisper, "And the way you look when you're taking my cock is fucking phenomenal."

Tyler went positively scarlet. But if he didn't want me to say things like that, maybe he needed to stop being so adorable.

As soon as we stepped through the doors into the ballroom proper, the noise of the party swelled. That must be why they did the interviews out in the hall, I realized. But before we'd gone even three steps, a younger woman with beautiful curly black hair ran up to us from the hallway.

"Tyler, I'm sorry, do you guys have time for one more interview? I got held up talking to your producers and—"

Tyler smiled, and this time I could tell it was genuine. "Of course, Tansy." He turned to me. "Tansy, you probably haven't met Gray yet. And Gray, you definitely haven't met Tansy, the best reporter out there who also happens to ask the best questions. Four years ago, she started her own website and video series doing film criticism—when she was just 16 if you can believe that—and she's been kicking ass and taking names ever since."

Tansy blushed. "Well, um, actually I've been bought and I'm part of a dreaded online media conglomerate now."

"No," Tyler gasped in shock, feigning a chest wound. "Tansy, not you, too. The future of independent journalism was counting on you."

Tansy shrugged. "My sister got sick and we needed the health insurance. Plus the money's pretty rad, too." She smiled sheepishly. "Sorry, do you mind if I just ask you guys the same old questions I'm sure everyone else already has?"

"Not at all," Tyler said. "I promise I'll even behave."

Tansy beckoned her camera guy over and once he got set up, turned back to the two of us. "Okay, so, tell me, what is it that interested you in this project?"

I trotted out the answer I'd given to everyone else—I'd read the book and thought it was amazing, and I was just so grateful to be a part of this film. True, if a little boring.

"And do you think it's an important movie in terms of representation?" Tansy asked, shooting back a question that we'd heard a million times before. So I used the same answer I'd given a million times.

"I do. I think it's important, that the love story between these two men is beautiful and deserves to be told. And at the same time, I think because it's such a wonderful story, and the characters are so beautifully realized, it's one that can resonate with anyone, no matter their background, orientation, or anything. It's a human story."

Tyler had helped me develop that answer, and I was actually rather proud of it.

"What about you, Tyler?" Tansy asked, and I could see in her eyes that she was as bored of the questions as we were, that she was probably going through the motions for her bosses just like we were going through the motions for Dave and Andrew.

"Oh, I don't know," Tyler said. "I mean, the writing was fantastic, but sometimes I think I just did it because Gray's really hot and I had a crush on him."

I did a spit-take, and I was pretty sure my eyes bugged out of my head as I stared at Tyler. Tansy looked shocked too, but Tyler just smiled like he's said something normal and looked at Tansy expectantly for the next question.

What the hell is he doing? I thought the whole point was not to give them anything useful?

Not that I minded. Not at all—if it made Tyler smile, I was all for it. Hell, I could have given the same answer myself and it would have been just as true. I was just surprised Tyler would open himself up like that, even as a joke.

But Tansy seemed determined not to take the opening he'd given her, almost like she was trying to give Tyler a pass, because the next question she asked him was a total softball.

"So do you see this as a human story, too?"

"Oh, definitely," Tyler said brightly. "I think any story of relationships, of personal growth, is relatable to everyone. I mean we've all had to do it—grow up, learn who we really are, test ourselves. Meet our first loves."

He smiled over at me and my stomach did a somersault when I realized he was talking about me.

"Those kinds of loves can change you," Tyler went on. "Make you a better person, if you're lucky enough to meet the right guy."

He smiled at me again, but then cut his eyes over to Tansy. "Don't get me wrong, there's also a lot of gay sex in there, so, you know... that's maybe a little bit more niche. Though," Tyler said, giving a conspiratorial look to the camera, "I have to say, I recommend it."

I laughed in disbelief. Again, not untrue—but nowhere near the polished talking points we'd been using all night. And this time Tansy didn't pass up the chance to pounce.

"And just what are you recommending?" she asked with a sly grin. "The movie? Or the sex?"

Tyler grinned and waggled his eyebrows. "Both."

Jesus. So much for playing things close to the vest. But God, Tyler was smiling and he was in utter command of the interview. I wasn't complaining.

"Tyler, up until now, some might say you've been a little coy about your sexuality." Tansy pressed. "Are you making a statement one way or another on that?"

Tyler laughed, light and breezy, like sunlight sparkling on water, and he gave her a frank look.

"Honestly, Tansy, I could say something about how sexuality is fluid and we don't need labels—and I'd stand by that. I do think that's true. But fuck it, I'm sick of worrying about this. Yeah. I'm gay. So for anyone who cares, now you know, and for anyone who doesn't care—thank you for not caring in the first place. I appreciate you realizing that I'm really not that interesting."

I burst out laughing, and then Tyler looked at me and started laughing too. It wasn't really funny, per se, but it was just so unexpected and we all knew it and soon enough, Tansy and her camera guy had joined in.

"Sorry," Tyler said when he finally got his breath back. "You're gonna have to bleep that out, aren't you."

"Not most of it," Tansy said, raising her eyebrows. She glanced at the camera over her shoulder. "Alright, well, Tyler Lang, ladies and gentlemen, out and proud actor and one of the most delightful people I've ever had the pleasure to interview. Just one final question," she said, turning back to us. "For both of you. On a scale of one to ten, how good a kisser is the other one?"

My eyes widened and Tyler snorted. "Nice question, Tans."

"Hey, that one's for my long-time followers. Inquiring minds wish to know. So, care to enlighten us?"

I chuckled and thought about it for a second. "On a scale of one to ten?" I smiled over at Tyler. "I'd give him an eleven."

Tyler looked at me, his eyes big and round and full of hurt. "Only an eleven?"

"Um, eleven's amazing. Eleven's literally off the charts. It's better than the best."

"I was going to give you an eleven-thousand," Tyler said, his voice scandalized.

"Well no one told me how much we could break the rules."

Tansy laughed. "So, it sounds like you would recommend that, too, Tyler, huh? Kissing Gray?"

"What?" Tyler blinked. "Recommend it? God no."

I looked at him in confusion—so did Tansy—but before she could follow up, Tyler smiled.

"But that's just because no one else can have him. He's mine."

And he stepped forward, put his hands on either side of my face, and kissed me.

It took my brain a second to even realize what was happening, though my hands flew to Tyler's waist automatically. I was vaguely aware of Tansy woo-hoo-ing in the background. And then someone behind me said, *'Oh my God, look,'* and suddenly everyone was clapping, and Tyler was still kissing me, and I wrapped my arms around him tight and lifted him off the ground to the sound of cheers.

"I thought you were gonna play things close to the vest tonight," I said, breathless, when I finally put Tyler down.

Tyler grinned at me, a little lopsided, his hands pressed to my chest. "I thought so too. But then I realized."

"Realized what?"

"You're fucking amazing." He smiled. "And I wanted everyone to know."

Things got a little busy after that. Suddenly, everyone wanted to talk to us and it was ages before we got a moment to just relax. Finally, Luke made his way over, holding a beer for me and a water for Tyler.

"Well, you certainly created some buzz for the movie tonight," he said with a grin.

"Tell me about it," Micah said, joining in, holding Bea in his arms. "Even Bea cheered when she saw that."

"Yeah, I'm sure she's a real supporter of gay rights at five months old."

Micah laughed. "I have to get the indoctrination started young." He gestured over to a group of three people standing maybe 10 feet away—his friend Caro, her husband Chris, and some guy I'd never seen before. "You see the guy in the backwards hat?"

"Yeah?"

"That's Chris's brother, Hunter. He's like, the bro-iest of bros. Even more than you," he said, grinning at Luke. "So I need to get Bea hooked on the gay agenda before he can do too much damage to her."

"I'm trying to decide if I'm offended by that, or flattered," Luke said with a puzzled look on his face.

"Oh please, like you don't die from happiness every time someone checks out your quads," Tyler said, rolling his eyes. "Weren't you voted most likely to open a Bally's Total Fitness back in high-school?"

"Most athletic," Luke corrected him.

"What's the difference?" Micah asked, a saccharinely sweet smile on his face.

"Lucky for you, your reunion's coming up," Tyler said, his eyes glinting. "Mom told me. Maybe you should just go in your rowing uni. The better to show off your pecs."

"I hate all of you," Luke said. "And I'm not going to that reunion, so if Mom wants you to pressure me into it, it's not going to work."

"Why aren't you going?" I asked, genuinely curious. "Compared to all of us, you definitely have your life the most together. And don't have anything too embarrassing in your past, I think."

"Yeah, why not?" Tyler pressed. "Are you really worried about impressing people? Or maybe just impressing a particular someone."

"No," Luke said, way too quickly.

"Right," Tyler said with a dry smile. "Because that's believable. I'm the actor in the family, big brother, not you."

"Not anymore though, right?" Micah said. "Gray tells me you're taking a step back?"

"Sorta," Tyler said, grinning nervously. "I mean, it's not official or anything, but I've been working with Danny on getting their scripts sold and we just got a bite on one yesterday."

"He's being modest," I said, putting my arm around his shoulders without thinking.

I froze for a second, wondering if I should pull it back, before Tyler leaned into me and put his arm around my waist. God, it was nice to be able to do that and not care who saw. Tyler smiled up at me and I could tell he was thinking the same thing. I kissed him on his brow.

"Um, hi," Micah said, shifting Bea to his other hip and waving his hand in front of our faces. "Hate to interrupt the lovefest but you are still in the room with the rest of us and last I checked, we were mid conversation."

"Sorry," I said, laughing. "What was I saying?"

"You were talking about how modest I am," Tyler said, arching an eyebrow. He looked back at Micah and Luke. "Besides we can't have two actors in a relationship or our egos will explode. It's like trying to double up on condoms. And since Gray's turning into the next Cary Grant—"

"Hardly," I interrupted.

"No, Tyler says you're doing really well, though," Luke said.

"I'm doing *okay*."

"You landed two roles already and you're up for a third in a huge movie," Tyler said. "I think that qualifies as a little better than '*okay*.'"

"Holy shit," Luke said. "Congrats, that's amazing."

Micah laughed and turned to Luke. "Gray's allergic to actually being proud of himself, you have to understand."

"Well, that's why he has me," Tyler said, pressing close.

"Who has who?"

Ben's voice floated up from behind me as he, Adam, and Nick walked over to join the group.

"Me," I said with a laugh. "Is had. By Tyler. Or, I think. I'm not really clear on the syntax of that."

"Yeah, we sorta saw that," Ben said. "Congrats."

"Welcome to the club of outing yourself in front of a room full of people," Adam grinned.

"How're you guys doing?" I asked. "I saw you got caught up with some reporters. Hope that wasn't too annoying."

"Oh, nah, it was fine. I mean this one had to actually, you know, talk about himself, which is basically a fate worse than death—" Ben said as he put an arm around Adam and kissed him on the cheek, "but otherwise, it was great."

"Ben's just being dramatic," Adam said. "I only wanted to die like… 10, maybe 20% of the time."

"Hey, that's an improvement for you," Nick said. Adam stuck his tongue out at him.

I snorted. "Well I'm glad you're getting recognized for it. The work you did was amazing."

"Hold on a second," Adam said suddenly, his voice suspicious. He was looking over at Nick—or more specifically, at the phone in Nick's hand. "Did that text message just say it was from Eli?"

"Holy shit, really?" Ben's head swivelled in Nick's direction. "I thought you said that was done."

"It *is*," Nick said insistently.

"Okay, honestly, who is this Eli guy?" I asked, "and why do we care so much about him?"

"No one knows," Adam said. "And that's *why* we care. Because Nick made this huge deal about meeting him—"

"You mean *you* made this huge deal about me meeting him," Nick interjected.

"Potato, potahto," Adam said with a grin. "But then suddenly it's all, *'Oh, no, nothing happened, nothing to see here, absolutely no reason for why this guy I was totally into is suddenly a non-entity, move along.'* With no explanation whatsoever. It's highly suspicious behavior."

"Clearly a cover-up," Ben added.

"Yeah," Adam continued. "And now, he's texting with the guy, so the plot thickens. *J'accuse!*" he said, pointing a finger at Nick, who was clearly doing his best not to look uncomfortable, and just as clearly failing.

"This is fascinating," Micah said, looking first at Nick, then at Luke. "I love all these weird secrets no one wants to talk about. I don't even feel the lack of my own love life. I can just live vicariously through yours."

We talked some more as the party wound down, but after a bit, Micah left to give Bea back to her parents, then drifted away to talk to some other people he knew. Luke bowed out soon after, citing an early morning run the next day. Eventually, it was just Tyler and me again. I looked down as he slipped his hand into mine.

"Why *did* you decide to say something tonight?" I asked after a moment. "Not that I'm complaining. Just—you know you didn't have to, for me, right?"

"I know," Tyler said, smiling broadly. "But I wanted to. I just... I don't know, I was sick of feeling like I had to hide it. And fuck it, I *want* everyone to know I'm with you."

"Well," I said, pulling him in for a quick kiss, "ditto."

"Plus," Tyler said, "if I'm lucky, this could be the last time I have to do a press tour like this. Figured I might as well go out on a high note."

I grinned, then looked around the room at the crush of people laughing and talking. "You sure you're not going to miss this?"

"Yeah. I really am." Tyler paused for a moment. "For the first time, I get to live my life in private. Just for me. And sure, I could be sad about everything I've been through, everything that happened before I got to this place. But at the same time—all of that bad stuff? It brought me to you. And I couldn't be happier."

I smiled. My whole life, I'd wanted to belong. Wanted someone to love me. Wanted to be part of a family. And in Tyler, I'd found just that. My family. And he thought he couldn't be happier?

I wrapped my arms around him and kissed him deeply, then smiled as we pulled apart.

"You know something? Neither could I."

THANKS FOR READING!

Check out some of my other books no the next page! But before you do... want to know what's next for Gray and Tyler?

MR. RIGHT

Free Bonus Chapter

You can read *Mr. Right*, a free, explicit bonus epilogue for *Gray For You*, just by joining my mailing list. *Mr. Right* is an explicit follow-up, taking place after the end of *Gray For You*. Sweet and sexy, it's the perfect happy ending for Gray and Tyler! You know you want that, right?

Oh, and also, you'll be notified of my new releases and when I have more free stuff, you'll be the first to know.

Sign up at: http://eepurl.com/deH83X

www.spencerspears.com

ALSO BY SPENCER SPEARS

Have you read *Adam's Song*, Book I of my *8 Million Hearts* series? Check it out below!

Adam's Song

Stay tuned for the next *8 Million Hearts* book. In the meantime, check out my *Maple Springs* series!

Billion Dollar Bet

Beneath Orion

Sugar Season

Strawberry Moon

Adam's Song

They say it's a bad idea to fall for your best friend. But since when do I say no to bad ideas?

Adam: It's not like I wanted to fall in love with Ben. When we first met in college, I thought he'd be like every other hot jock who'd made my life hell in high school. It's not my fault he turned out to be sweet, funny, and insanely talented. We moved to New York after college to break into the music business and of course Ben got signed by a major label—they'd be stupid not to want him. But even though he's a famous popstar now, he still wants to be friends with a nobody like me. Honestly, if he didn't want me falling for him, he should have been less goddamn perfect.

Well, except for the part where he's straight. Did I forget to mention that?

In my defense, responsible decision-making has never been my strong suit. Case in point—collapsing on stage, guitar in hand, after discovering my then-boyfriend, now-ex was cheating on me, and downing a bottle of bourbon in response. But I'm cleaning up my act—no more hiding in the closet and no more bad life choices. But that also means no more waiting around for the day Ben magically decides he likes di...sgustingly sappy guys with secret crushes on him (aka me).

So why did Ben have to pick now to make me question everything I thought I knew about us?

Ben: It's not like I planned this. I was on tour when Adam collapsed back in New York and he wouldn't even let me come home early to visit him. But that's Adam for you—brilliant, breathtaking, and pathologically afraid of vulnerability. All I wanted was to be there for him—and him coming out didn't change that in the slightest. Yeah, I couldn't help seeing him a little differently. And no, I couldn't quite explain why I was suddenly noticing the curve of his back, the freckles on his cheeks, or wondering what his lips tasted like. But whatever weird awakening I was having, Adam needed support, not more confusion.

And then I kissed him. Whoops.

And I know it's fast. I know it's unexpected. I know my label would be livid if they found out I was dating a guy. But I also know—deeply and inexplicably—that this could be something real. I just have to convince Adam of the same thing. Beautiful, broken Adam who looks at the world through 14 layers of irony. Adam, who'd rather get an appendectomy than admit that he needs someone. Adam, who still doesn't know all of my secrets.

So do I convince him to risk everything—on me?

Adam's Song is **Book 1** in the **8 Million Hearts** series. While each book can be read on its own, they've even more fun to read together. Adam's Song is a 120,000 word m/m romance full of snark, sweetness, and a healthy serving of steam. Friends-to-lovers and hurt/comfort themes. No cheating, no cliffhangers, and a guaranteed HEA.

Billion Dollar Bet
What would you bet for a chance at true love?

Hopeless romantic Kian Bellevue can't help falling for the
wrong guys. Maybe it's because he lost his parents so young,
maybe it's just his caring nature, but he can't stop diving in
when he should be heading for the hills. And just when he
decides to swear off guys for the summer, he meets drop-
dead gorgeous Jack Thorsen, who might just be the man of
his dreams.

It's not fair, because Kian doesn't even have time for guys
right now. His hometown of Maple Springs, Minnesota is
considering selling miles of pristine wilderness to a Wall
Street billionaire who wants to open a resort and play at
being a hotelier. But Kian's spent his whole life fighting
against big businesses and he's ready to go toe-to-toe with
the mystery mogul - until he realizes that the billionaire is
Jack himself.

Billionaire Jack Thorsen is married to his work and likes it that way. Growing up in foster care taught him to look out for himself and since the day he left for college, he's never stopped striving. Despite his best friend's urging, he's not looking for a guy. Even after he meets sweet and sexy Kian Bellevue, he's still determined to keep his guard up. People can't hurt you if you never let them close.

But it's not like Jack doesn't have a heart. When he finds out that Maple Springs, the home he left behind, is on the brink of bankruptcy, he proposes to buy their unused public lands and create an eco-resort. It's an obvious win-win - who could oppose it? That is, who, other than Kian, the guy he can't get out of his head.

Jack needs Kian on his side if he wants the town to vote in favor of his resort and he's not afraid to play dirty. His proposition: Kian spends the summer with him. If Jack convinces Kian to support him, Kian will get the town on Jack's side. But if he fails, Jack will withdraw the proposal completely. It's a crazy bet, but Kian would be crazy to turn it down - right?

There's only one problem. Jack - tall, handsome, and emotionally unavailable - is exactly Kian's type. And Kian is surprisingly good at breaking down the barriers Jack spent years putting up. With their hearts on the line as well as a hotel, will both men risk it all for a chance at love?

Billion Dollar Bet is Book 1 in the Maple Springs series. While each book focuses on different characters and can be read on its own, they're even more fun to read together.

Billion Dollar Bet is a 55,000 word m/m romance novel with sizzling summer heat. No cheating, no cliffhangers, and a guaranteed HEA.

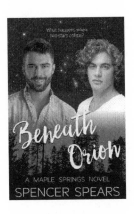

Beneath Orion
What happens when two stars collide?

The first lesson Colin Gardner ever learned was not to trust. The second was that love hurts. Growing up in an abusive family, he turned to the night sky for comfort and buried himself in science. It wasn't easy being the only gay guy in school and Colin made peace with the fact that he'd never fall in love. He won't risk that pain. Especially not for a guy who's never dated men before. No matter how much he's tempted.

Charlie Keller doesn't date. How could he risk his kid growing attached to someone when it might not last? The divorced dad's life revolves around his daughter, his dog, and his job as Maple Springs' resident handy-man. But when Charlie helps Colin out in a pinch, his world changes forever. Charlie can't ignore his attraction to Colin, but he can't act on it either - can he?

As winter deepens, Charlie and Colin are drawn into each other's orbit. But when Charlie's ex-wife threatens to move his daughter across the country, he realizes his worst fears might come true. And when Colin's past comes calling, it raises demons he's not sure he's strong enough to fight. Will Colin and Charlie's love flame out, or can they find a way to make a new constellation - just for the two them?

Beneath Orion is Book 2 in the Maple Springs series. While each book focuses on different characters and can be read on its own, they're even more fun to read together.

Beneath Orion is a 55,000 word steamy, contemporary, gay-for-you M/M romance. No cliffhangers, no cheating, and a guaranteed HEA.

<u>Sugar Season</u>

They say it's better to have loved and lost. They have no idea what they're talking about...

Police officer Graham Andersen already had his happy ending. A whirlwind romance, a young marriage, more happiness than he knew what to do with. And then it was over, almost as soon as it began.

After his husband Joey died, Graham knew he'd never find that kind of love again. But what he'd had with Joey was more than some people ever got in life. He'd had his chance at happiness. He couldn't ask for more.

When chef Ryan Gallagher is swindled out of his savings right before he can open his restaurant, it almost seems right. One more failure for his long list, one more way he'll never measure up to his older brother. Joey might be gone, but he still finds a way to overshadow Ryan.

With no money and no prospects, Ryan has no choice but to move home to the family that rejected him and his sexuality.

But when he goes out to the local bar one winter night, he never dreams the hot guy he's hitting on used to be his brother's husband.

Both men insist that they're not interested. And yet neither can resist the desire they feel. But relationships require love. Love requires risk. And both Graham and Ryan know this life offers no guarantees. After a long winter in both their hearts, are they finally ready for spring?

Sugar Season is Book 3 in the Maple Springs series. While each book focuses on different characters and can be read on its own, they've even more fun to read together.

Sugar Season is a 75,000 word steamy, contemporary, second chance m/m romance. No cheating, no cliffhangers, and a guaranteed HEA.